ADVANCE PRAISE FOR
MY TIMESWEPT HEART
A 1992 GOLDEN HEART FINALIST

"MY TIMESWEPT HEART is a compelling story filled with adventure and charm. Escapism at its very best! But I ask that the reader beware, the virile Captain Dane Blackwell is set to steal your heart from the moment he walks on that page."

ROSALYN ALSOBROOK,
bestselling author of TIMESTORM

* * *

"Amy J. Fetzer weaves an enjoyable tale that draws readers effortlessly from the present to the past and leaves them satisfied at the end."

CONNIE MASON,
bestselling author of ICE AND RAPTURE

* * *

"A fast-paced, thrilling romance! MY TIME-SWEPT HEART takes you on a swashbuckling adventure filled with drama and passion! Time-travel fans — enjoy!"

SAMANTHA JAMES,
bestselling author of MY REBELLIOUS HEART

ONLY BY HIS TOUCH

Tess reached out, her fingertips trailing across Dane's cheek. "It's really sweet of you to want to defend my honor."

His face was still creased in a deep frown. "Can you forgive me for putting you through this, Tess?"

"Sure." She shrugged, her eyes dancing with mischief. "But will you now demand satisfaction for *me* seducing *you?*"

Dane blinked, shocked, then his chiseled lips slowly stretched into a wide grin. "God's teeth, but you're a bold wench."

"Yeah, and you love it," she quipped, struggling in the heavy skirts to rise. Instantly he gathered her in his arms, pulling her across his lap and kissing her slowly, erotically, a lesson in pure torture to her senses.

"Aye," he breathed against her lips. "I admit I do enjoy your saucy ways, witch."

She pressed her mouth to his, her tongue snaking out to slowly lick his lips, and his deep shudder steamed all around her like warm velvet. She met his ice-mint gaze, and Dane was jolted to his boots with what he saw there. "Last night, Dane," she smoothed the lines of his face, "I discovered what I've been missing out on for five very long years."

Her fingers tunneled into his hair, and she captured his mouth once more, letting her emotions spill over onto him. God, she loved kissing him. He was so damn good at it! Dane Blackwell was a man she couldn't resist, lie to, or walk on, and Tess was suddenly thankful she'd been tossed into his world.

Amy J. Fetzer

My Timeswept Heart

ZEBRA BOOKS
KENSINGTON PUBLISHING CORP.

ZEBRA BOOKS are published by

Kensington Publishing Corp.
475 Park Avenue South
New York, NY 10016

First Printing: October, 1993

Printed in the United States of America

To Robert,
my breath,
my life,
my forever rogue.

and

To the men and women of the United States Marine
Corps, who have kept the words *honor, pride,* and
valor alive for over 218 years.
Semper Fi

Acknowledgments

To Sherry S. Brune — "sisters" doesn't come close to saying what you mean to me. This one is yours, too, Sherry-san.

To Sara E. Baker — who told me when I stunk, yet laced it with love. Pals for life, Capt'n.

To the Queen Mum, Bernice Dicks — who said it was okay to have a one-word sentence, and to the Black Blade, Jeannette Barnes Thomin — who said cut it anyway.

To Jetta J. Cook — enthusiasm and encouragement are your middle names, girl.

To Jackie Harper — when they all left us, Ten Don, imported coffee, juicy plots, and brownies-from-hell kept us going. And we did.

To Joyce A. Flaherty — my agent. In the Corps we'd call you a "hard charger." Thanks for believing in me and my work.

And to the members of the Okinawa Writers Guild — See guys, all that coffee paid off.

Chapter One

Tess Renfrew turned off the motor of her '65 Mustang and stared at the steering wheel.

She was scared.

This was really stupid.

If she got caught, she'd be arrested. Even if Penny backed her up, even if Sloane came off her mighty horse and admitted to her blackmail threat, she'd have a record. No mother in her right mind would allow her to coach a child again. Her career would be over.

"Simple," she told the charging horse emblem. "Don't get caught."

She looked up the tree-lined block to the Rothmere Building, the white fortress reminiscent of the Citadel. It was old, an architect's dream in eighteenth-century design: cracking Spanish stucco, scrolling iron rails, slightly Gothic in flavor with the wide

7

ledges and decorative crenelation around the windows and along the roof.

Good for footholds.

It would be easy except for the fact that it had an alarm system. She could tell that by the little silver shield on the stone column near the iron gate. Nothing like advertising to a thief what to expect.

Shoving a stick of Juicy Fruit in her mouth, she checked her pinned-up hair and slipped a wool cap over the ebony mass. Locking her oversized bag in the glove box, she taped the key to her leg along with a pick set. She smiled. Dad had actually given her the set. She'd been called on more than once to open cars or homes with the keys locked inside. Her adoptive father was famous for that. She picked locks as a hobby, for the challenge, not to steal. That part of her life was long over.

But tonight it *was* stealing. It didn't matter that it was damaging evidence that could destroy a friend's career, didn't matter that Sloane, in her gloating glory over her revenge, let valuable information slip, and Tess knew in which room, which drawer to search. Penny was right. It wasn't a college prank. Not this time, she gnashed, furious at what Sloane Rothmere's games would cost her and Penny if she failed.

In college Tess had lifted a crystal-ball paperweight from the dean's desk. Dean Whingate was noted for caressing the clear-glass globe just before he condemned you to a life on the cafeteria staff, or expelled your butt. She'd scaled the admin building, stolen the globe, then waited until the entire campus discovered its absence, for the Dean to turn the loveliest shade of purple, before she returned it. Only the sisters of

Delta Pi knew who'd actually taken it, and they were sworn to secrecy. That was over six years ago.

Let's see if I still got it, she challenged, climbing out of the vintage car. She secured the convertible top, locked it, then slipped into the shadows. For half an hour she watched for movement around the old building. Silent. Dark. God, it was unnerving. Not even a cat, dog, bug. Nothing. She could feel her body perspire beneath the snug cotton Lycra. Finally gathering her nerve, she rosined her hands, approached the fence, and grasped the iron poles. Pulling with the strength of her arms, she raised her body until the top spikes were at her waist. Slowly she spread her legs, hovering lengthwise over the points, then twisted, swept up into a handstand, and released. Dropping silently to the ground, she quickly crouched. Ten points for difficulty, ten for execution and landing, Renfrew. She ran across the Astroturf lawn to the structure, flattening herself against the cool stone. Calmly she located the room and planned her route. Porch, window, flagpole, window.

Piece of Danish. Drawing her arms back past her sides, knees bent, she leapt, strong fingers catching the edge of the porch roof. Curling around the edge, she climbed. Just like when I was eight, she thought, and Dad caught me. Standing atop the porch, she turned, faced the wall, and balanced along the decorative ledge toward the window above. Four inches, how convenient. Using her fingers and bare toes in the crenelation design, she worked her way up and caught the lip. Seconds later she was above the window on the scalloped overhang.

Concentrate. Deep breaths. Smoke gray eyes

trained on the flagpole a few feet out and above her, perpendicular to the wall. The only sound was her body whispering through the air as she dove out, caught the pole, and swung around it full circle into a handstand. Inch by inch her hands moved toward the wall. Spine straight, she eased her legs down until they touched the bolts and brackets securing the pole. God, it was dark. If not for the silver sheen of the pole, Tess wouldn't know where her feet were touching. Ten points. No. Eight and a half. One more level, she thought as she carefully straightened and looked above her head. The room was about five feet away and just as far up. No ledge. Now what? Her face plastered against the stone wall, Tess stretched her muscles to the max, feeling for gouges large enough for her hands to grasp securely. She smiled, finding the little niches.

"Spiderman, Spiderman. Does whatever a spider can," she mumbled the tune as she chewed and climbed. "Can he spin? Yes, he does." Fingers and toes caught in the ancient cracks.

Tess was agile, very strong, yet graceful. It's what made her a champion gymnast. Her specialty was the balance beam and unevens. She wasn't afraid of heights; the street urchin in her thrived on a little adventure in her otherwise dull life. But the adopted daughter of a Marine Sergeant-Major, who'd raised her with a strict code of honor, rebelled at what she was doing. Dad wouldn't like this a bit. Mom either. A silent jab of guilt pierced her heart. They're gone and Penny needs me. Adapt and overcome, Tess, she told herself, shoving the thought aside as she faced the window. Perched on her knees, she ripped off four strips of metallic tape she'd wrapped around her wrists, and taped them to the pane below the window locks. Alarm conductors and she hoped they worked. If not, she'd find her butt in jail within the hour.

Removing the glass cutter tucked in the pick set, she cut a small circle in the pane, the sound grating like nails on a chalkboard. Then she stuck her chewed gum to the glass, tapped the cut line, and pulled. It popped out easily. She set it on the sill to her right. Cautiously she slipped her hand in the hole with what looked like a long, thin, metal toothpick and began to work the keylock. Sweat formed on her upper lip; she licked it. Almost there. She wriggled the pick. *My knees hurt. Don't think about it.*

Hearing a noise, Tess froze. Footsteps. Heavy ones. Her heart pounded so hard she thought whoever it was would hear it. Terror blended cruelly with adrenaline, her blood coursing through her veins like arctic seawater.

Balancing on her knees, one hand grasping the brick window frame, the other about to be sliced to ribbons, she waited, breath trapped, muscles clenched, until the sound faded, then worked the lock with record speed. *Enough is enough! Nothing was worth this fear.* Two twists and three grunts later, it sprang. She eased the window up, slipped into the room, and James Bond would have been proud as she cracked the desk lock and opened the bottom right-hand drawer. It was there. A bulky plain Manila envelope. She started to stuff the packet down the back of her leotard but halted, her conscience prodding her to open it to see if what Sloane claimed was true. *I'm risking everything for this,* she mused, hefting the evi-

11

dence. The hairs on the back of her neck suddenly stood at attention when her gaze caught on a portrait hung high on the wall behind the desk, a viewing lamp perched beneath. The seconds wasted were her biggest mistake. The thud of footsteps jolted her. She jammed the package down the back of her top, jerked her sleeve down over her hand, swiped at the fingerprints, then raced to the window and climbed out. She was just sealing the window when the door burst open. Light flooded the room and, no doubt, her shocked face. A figure pointed at her.

"There she is!" she heard, and two stocky shadows ran toward her.

"Ohh, shit!" She straightened and without a thought, twisted and dove the ten feet downward to the flagpole. She caught it, thank God, the momentum sending her around it twice.

"Hey! You! Stop, or I'll shoot!"

Shoot? Holy Christ! This only happens in movies. Ian Fleming, write me out of this one, she thought as her supine body spun around the pole. She released. Her body was like a slim black dart as she sailed through the air and caught the porch roof. Her unusual speed propelled her further, and she lost her grip, crashing painfully into clay pots of fake rhododendrons and ferns, sprawling like a ragdoll in the far corner. It seemed all Rothmeres are fakes, she decided as she spat artificial moss and scrambled to her feet. She sped toward the fence, odd noises penetrating her panic. It sounded like thumps, soft and airy, with a faint whine. Her eyes widened, and her bare feet chewed Astroturf. A damn silencer! Her body slammed into the sharp spiked fence but she couldn't

12

wait for the pain to subside. Pulling up, she clumsily swung both legs over and pushed off just as a pack of Dobermans was unleashed. Two and a half execution. Ten points difficulty.

She ran. Her lungs burned. Her knees bled. Her cap fell off, sending shiny black hair spilling down her back. Bare feet slapped the concrete. Oh, Tess. Big guns. Big trouble! Her hands shook as she ripped the car key from her leg and jammed it into the lock. Dogs barked, metal screeched, engines revved.

Don't look. Don't look.

She opened the door and literally became the driver's seat. She breathed deeply so she wouldn't do something stupid like flood the engine, and the twenty-four-year-old cherry red classic started on the first try. Tess burned rubber for a block. Encroaching headlights reflected in her rear-view mirror, retreated, then grew larger, brighter, so close she could see the chrome around the lights. They rammed her classic Mustang, her face nearly colliding with the steering wheel before she swerved. The dark car started to move alongside her, and she gunned the engine, but not before she heard a sharp pop. Instinctively she ducked, and in the same instant the seat beside her jolted, followed by a sound like weak ice fracturing on a pond. Her gaze darted to the mirror and her heart jumped to her throat. There was a clean hole in her rear window, the glass a crackling maze of spidery veins about to shatter.

Jesus! Who was I fooling, trying this? she thought, terrified.

She didn't chance a look at the car seat, knowing it would have a bullet buried in the old leather. Her foot squashed down on the pedal as another silent torpedo plunked somewhere in the car's metal shell. Tires squealed.

Recklessly Tess drove down every side street she could remember from her college days, and some she didn't, until she was certain she'd lost them. Pulling behind a Seven-Eleven, she shut the motor off, her heart pounding in every pore of her body. Reaching down her back for the packet, she tossed the sweat-stained evidence on the seat. She glared at it for a few moments, then snatched it up, shakily broke the wax seal, and dumped the contents in her lap.

"That little bitch!" Tess Renfrew knew, without a doubt, she'd been set up tonight. To die.

Chapter Two

Tess slammed the door, frantically flipped and closed a series of locks, then plastered herself against the wood as another barrier. She squeezed her eyes shut. This can't be happening, she thought wildly.

"Did you get it?"

She gasped, eyes snapping open. "God, Pen, you scared the hell out of me! I forgot you were here!" Penny stood in the middle of her tiny living room, committing murder on a hanky, her face bearing the marks of a good cry. "Get back from that window," Tess commanded, moving around the love seat that separated them.

"Why?" Penny briefly glanced behind her. "You did get it, didn't you?"

"I did." And more, she thought, unzipping the bag and taking out the envelope.

"Oh, thank you!" Immediately Penny went for it, but Tess held it out of her reach. "You going to black-mail me, too?" Instantly she regretted that. "God,

Tess. I'm sorry. It's just that—"

"I know, bud." Tess opened the packet and withdrew the negatives and photos. "Burn them. Now." When Penny simply stared at the scandalous photos, Tess picked up the crystal lighter from the coffee table, lit the flame beneath the corners, and waited for them to catch. She dropped them into a pewter ashtray and went to the window, brushing back the curtain. The streets were empty. Waves crashed, the calming sound reaching out to her from the beach beyond the avenue. I'm safe, she thought, glancing back over her shoulder.

Her former college roomie continued to watch the flames consume what was left of her past. Penelope Hamilton was an extraordinary actress, copper-haired and slim and sexy. And Liz Claiborne would have been proud of the justice Penny did to her white linen design. To her growing public she was worldly, sophisticated, and in control. Tess knew better. Though aggressive when it came to her craft, Penny was basically a vulnerable, gentle spirit. And those burning photos could have ruined her unblemished career because of something stupid she'd done when she was hungry and homeless. Tess understood what that was like.

She turned back to the window and sucked in her breath, gaining Penny's attention.

"What is it?"

"Leave, Pen." Her Lycra-covered legs were already moving across the studio apartment, her slim hands snatching up the oversized bag and the envelope as she went. She was never far from her survival kit filled with an assortment of clothing, cosmetics, ace

16

bandages, ointments, medicines, toothbrush—everything. It was habit left over from her days as a competing gymnast traveling to meets. Ready for anything and always on the move. As she was now, in her closet, jamming garments into the duffle.

"Christ, Tess, will you talk to me?"

"Penelope," she warned without looking up.

Penny raced to the window, drawing back the curtain to see two average-looking men with above-average muscles climb out of a dark Mercedes.

"Jesus, you were followed!"

"Get back!" Tess shouted and Penny did, green eyes demanding an explanation. "I was nearly caught, Pen. They saw my face and—" She waved at the obvious.

"And?" No answer. *"And?"*

Tess didn't look up from filling her duffle. "They took a couple shots at me."

"Oh, God!" Penny dropped into a chair, stunned, then her eyes narrowed on her friend. "What else is in that envelope, Renfrew?"

"Let's just say I've a feeling the IRS doesn't know exactly how rich Daddy Rothmere really is or they'd have called the police by now."

"Let me see it." Penny's manicured fingers wiggled beneath her nose.

"You don't want to know." She flipped black hair over her shoulder and continued to stuff. "So don't ask."

Penny recognized that determined tone and tried another tactic. "Change clothes with me." She unbuttoned her cuffs.

"No!" Tess straightened abruptly. "It's over for you!"

"Don't argue! We have to do something," she said, wiggling out of the dress. "My car's out back. I'll take yours and lead them away."

Tess shook her head. "It's too dangerous, bigger than we imagined." Penny lifted the dress. "Damn it, they—have—guns," Tess enunciated, grabbing Penny's arms and making her listen. "And they *like* using them."

"I know, bud," Penny whispered. "I have to do this."

Tess briefly closed her eyes, her arms falling loosely at her sides. "Why does Sloane hate us so much? What did we ever do to her?"

"We worked hard and got famous, Renfrew. You know how us no-background types succeeding always rubbed her raw."

Sloane was vindictive, Tess knew, doubting her father was aware of the vengeance his princess engineered.

"Come on, dress. I've booked myself on a cruise." At Tess's raised brows, Penny said, "If you couldn't help, I was going to take a trip. Then come back after the news hit the papers. *After* it had cooled down."

"Oh, real smart move, Pen." She grabbed the dress. "Nothing like running and making yourself look guilty." She stepped into it anyway.

Penny ignored that, riffling through Tess's dresser, then shimmied into a pair of holier-than-thou jeans and an overwashed sorority tee-shirt.

"The ship leaves at midnight." The redhead opened her clutch and withdrew the ticket. "Pier Four." She stuffed the Jaguar keys and ticket in Tess's hand as she passed. "There's an overnight bag in the trunk. Use my credit."

"No!" Tess barked over her shoulder before checking the front of the house. They were there, waiting, watching.

"Use it, damn you. You're in this mess because of me. And cover your hair; there's a hat on the car seat."

"Yippee. I get to play movie star," she remarked in a flat tone, heading toward the back door. On impulse she grabbed up a silver frame and stuffed it in her bag. Her hand on the knob, she turned back to the actress. "The keys are by the phone. Stay here a while if you can, then run the creeps to Miami and back." A tapered black brow shot up. "Maybe even into Sloane's house?"

Penny grinned. "Enjoy the cruise. Bahamas, first class, port out."

"My, aren't we the snot."

They laughed for a brief second, then sobered.

"In the desk, bottom left drawer, is—" Tess swallowed—"my will."

The other woman's eyes filled with panic. "Won't need it." Then she peeked around the faded gingham curtain. "We'll bop till we drop when this is over." As Tess turned the knob, Penny gave her a quick fierce hug. "I owe you, bud," she whispered, tears flowing.

"Never owe the ones you love, Hamilton. Don't you know that by now?"

Tess was gone.

"Capt'n?"

"Has she shown her colors?" Captain Blackwell asked without looking up from his charts.

The boatswain dragged his cap from his head, crunching it nervously. "Ah, nay, sir."

"Then do not disturb me until she does." Only his eyes lifted, and the boatswain couldn't keep from flinching. "Unless, of course, she sends a volley our way." The captain's lips twisted wryly. The sarcasm was lost on the man. "Dismissed, Mr. Potts."

"Aye-aye, sir." The young boatswain made a hasty retreat.

His shirtsleeves rolled up past his elbows, fists braced on the desk, Captain Blackwell examined the charts and maps for another moment, then, with a curse, straightened and turned away. He snatched up his spyglass and, through the broad window in the aft of his cabin, sighted in the approaching ship. Who have you sent this time, Phillip? Am I that near to discovering your lair? God's teeth, but she was closing fast! Likely naught in her hold, he mused, his powerful legs shifting unconsciously with the roll of the vessel. Dark clouds tumbled overhead, graying the sea. The storm would reach them by nightfall. They'd have to sail further out, clear of the reefs and rocks to remain safely in these waters. He lifted the glass again for another judgment. Suddenly he grabbed his weapons, strapping on his sword and shoving the flintlock through the belt of his breeches as he strode from the large cabin, jackboots thumping on slick wood.

Duncan McPete suppressed a smile when the captain climbed up onto the quarter deck. Knew he couldn't stay below, Duncan chuckled to himself. He could see the eagerness in the man, the hope that this would be the time he would send the bastard to Davy Jones.

"What ails you, sir?" Duncan asked when a dark scowl creased his captain's tanned features. The man kept blinking, then sighting down the scope.

Captain Blackwell held the glass out to the man beside him. "Take a look, Mr. Thorpe," he ordered.

The first mate scanned the horizon for the ship, then repeated the measure. He lowered the scope, flushing red.

"What see you, Mister?" the captain demanded.

"I-I can't seem to locate her, sir."

Blackwell dropped a hand to the man's shoulder, giving it a squeeze. "Neither could I, mate. I thought perhaps I'd suddenly gone mad."

Gaelan Thorpe sighed with relief as the captain called up to the crow for a report and was relayed the same readings with equal amounts of embarrassment.

"There she is, sir!"

All turned starboard aft to see the vessel even farther away than before. Captain Blackwell knew his crew, his ship, and the courses set. They couldn't have veered off and never so quickly.

" 'Tis a damned ghost ship!" someone shouted.

"Aye," another said, several voices rumbling in agreement.

"The keeper of the treasures be angry, Capt'n. Turn

21

about!"

His boot braced against a crate lashed to the rail, Captain Blackwell twisted slowly, eyes pale as seawater sweeping over his crew. "Not — another — word." He spoke softly, yet the warning carried to each and every man. Men scurried to their duties before catching the cat.

Blackwell didn't believe in the myths that prevailed in these waters. Yet as he turned back and saw a shroud of black fog magically engulf the other vessel, for an instant he doubted. His God and himself.

Tropic of Cancer
Bahamas
1989

She blended easily with the vacationers in her French-cut, black maillot swimsuit. Relaxing for the first time in a week, Tess adjusted the canvas chaise, stuffed her bag beneath her head, then donned her mirrored sunglasses. She'd spent several sleepless nights until she was certain those meat chunks hadn't followed her to the Bahamas, then finally began to enjoy Penny's generosity. The *Nassau Queen* was on its return trip to Florida. She still didn't know what to do with her little acquisition, but hadn't been without it once. Tess couldn't go to the captain or the police; that would force her to explain how she happened to possess the packet and why. And then there was the possibility of her juvenile record surfacing. She didn't think she could stand the shame of her past coming back. Not now.

She flinched, startled when a waiter bent close, warning her about the sun and asking if she'd like something cool to drink. Iced tea, she decided, then sat upright, unzipping her bag to obediently apply some sunscreen. She was coating her leg when she saw them. The bottle dropped to the deck. She didn't retrieve it. Panicked, she stood, automatically zipping closed the bag and slipping the strap over her head and beneath an arm. How did I miss them? Then she realized that they must have flown to the Bahamas and chartered a boat to one of the outer islands to have caught up with her. Oh, God! What did that matter now?

They'd found her.

The two men were dressed like the waiters, blue flowered shirts, white trousers; one balanced a tray, a glass and a folded linen cloth resting in the center. It was the waiter who'd taken her order. Tess glanced fearfully around her. Calypso music blared, vacationers danced dirty, played shuffleboard and water polo, flirted, and baked in the sun, happy, relaxed. Oblivious. No one noticed their approach. Maybe if I call attention to myself, they'll leave me alone, she thought desperately, unwilling to chance a bystander getting hurt. The man with the tray slipped his hand inside the cloth. Her gaze caught on the nose of a silencer two seconds before he lifted the linen — and the weapon.

I'm a dead woman.

In one fluid movement Tess backflipped over the rail and plunged feet first into the Caribbean waters. The impact sent her glasses scraping against her face, her sandals tearing from her feet. The bag clubbed her in the head. She swam for the surface as soon as she could bring her arms down. Muscled legs scissored, arms dug through the liquid, air passed her lips, churning with the bubbles of the propellers. She went deeper than she anticipated and was gasping for air when her head surged above the cool water. She managed to suck in a lungful seconds before she was dragged into the ship's backwash. Terrified, she fought, the undertow quickly pulling her toward the propellers. Her strength was depleting. For God's sake, she begged wildly, stop the engines! Then through her blurred vision beneath the tropical waters, Tess saw the distinct shape of a fin.

Chapter Three

Propellers, like blades of a massive Cuisinart, churned, drawing their tender meal closer. The engine hummed, its sound vibrating the water sealed over her helpless body. Bubbles, her own and those of the ships, swirled, grazed her skin like delicate fingers, teasing her with their valuable contents. Tess desperately fought the scream grinding in her constricted throat when the daggerlike fin passed again. Her lungs begged for mercy as she swam frantically against the current. The shark bumped her. And the scream erupted, silenced by a gush of water. She was drowning, arms flailing in a wild frenzy.

It nudged her again, her back, then again under her arm, and just as black spots cloaked her vision, she was catapulted to the surface. She choked and sputtered, struggling to tread water while vomiting up food and half the Atlantic. Exhausted, her eyes stinging, Tess inhaled a waterless breath and realized the ship was moving rapidly.

Away.

Panic shot through her like hot lead.

"Come back! Oh God! COME BACK!" she screamed, but her throat was raw, and nothing emerged above the thump of the engines. Frantically she waved her arms, coughing on the backwash bubbling at her throat. No one had noticed her unusual departure. Except the two men looking down at her from the rail, grinning. And waving back.

Then she realized she was moving also.

She twisted sharply, her eyes rounding in horror at the sight of a fin slicing through the water beside her shoulder. The shark, she thought hopelessly, strangling on a new wave of terror. She fought, yet couldn't take her eyes off the fin as it suddenly dipped below the surface, instantly replaced with the slick, rounded snout of a dolphin. Treading, she blinked back salt water, gaping in disbelief. A dolphin! Her muscles relaxed and Tess laughed out loud, her incredulous relief blending quickly into hysterical sobs. It was useless, she knew, no one to hear, no one to care.

The dolphin chittered, its nose nudging her. She focused on her . . . it? . . . him?

"Well, I'll be damned," she said, her voice sandy-rough. The duffle, her cheap, yellow-plastic K-Mart special was buoyant, filled with air, and the strap still entwined around her was trapped in the dolphin's mouth. "Thank you, you beautiful creature," she sobbed, patting and hugging hard, wet skin. "Thanks."

Clinging to the mammal, Tess dunked her head back, smoothed the hair from her face, then scanned the open seas for land. She waited for her fear to subside into something more rational. It didn't.

26

No land, she thought matter-of-factly, adjusting her grip. She froze.

"No land!" she whispered, her head snapping in all directions. She went berserk, twisting and turning, her eyes wild as she searched the horizon. "Oh God, oh God, oh God! NO LAND!" She gripped the dolphin, wrapping her arms around its torso enough to crush it. It squeaked, shooting a mist out the hole on top of its head, then dipped beneath the surface. Tess came up sputtering. "Calm down, Renfrew," she told herself, gaining only marginal control after she'd located the cruise liner sailing away under clear skies. No help there, she thought, dismally watching any possible rescue within the hour rapidly fade. Those goons would never alert anyone to her predicament. She twisted a look in the direction the swells were taking her and sucked in her breath, choking on a mouthful of water. Tess stared in horror, alarming dread sapping what was left of her composure.

"Jesus H. Christ!" Where the hell did that come from?

The blue horizon had vanished behind a jet black wall, not like a storm but nearly opaque swirls of dense fog climbing upward from the ocean into infinity. The surface wobbled eerily, a velvet drape scarcely catching the breeze, smoky mist curling and convulsing like a living thing. The rumbling echo of thunder reached her above the din of the sea. She recoiled.

"Take me that way!" she commanded the animal, wrapping an arm around its fin and trying to urge it back toward the cruiser. It squealed, its powerful flippers dragging her through the water—toward the ebony curtain.

This is a hallucination, she reasoned wildly, a near death kind of vision, and she briefly considered releasing the dolphin. But it was her only lifeline. The current would take her in the same direction regardless.

The elements gave her no choice.

Closer. Closer. Her stomach rolled with burning nausea. Closer. Her head suddenly felt light, as if just waking from a dream. Lightning crackled violently across the murky blanket. A sickening, heavy sensation melted through her limbs, numbing them, and Tess strained to keep hold of the dolphin. Closer. Her heart drummed so hard she could feel it in her throat, hear its frantic thump in her ears. Never a religious person before now, she prayed for strength, for anything that would keep her alive.

The dolphin carried her — closer.

Sinking into unconsciousness, Tess never saw the undulating fingers of mist reach out, never felt the icy tentacles wrap around her and suck her past the barrier, swallowing her. Instantly the black wall vanished behind her, leaving no trace of woman or dolphin on calm seas beneath blue Bahama skies.

1789
Tropic of Cancer
West Indies

The last of the seasoned deck hands raced to secure crates and barrels as the storm raged, bearing down upon them with a swiftness none had ever seen. They fled belowdecks to safety and to wait out the storm as the frigate pitched and rocked, towering walls of water crashing over its starboard side, washing anything poorly roped into its blackened depths.

The captain manned the helm, his tall form lashed to the wheel, relentlessly guiding his ship further beyond the scattered barrier islands. The *Sea Witch* was an armed vessel, heavily loaded with fresh stores and merchandise; therefore, her water line was already low. She plowed into the storm and like an angry parent, it slapped her back, her figure-headed bow dipping, taking on more water.

"Get below!" Blackwell shouted, his words carried away on the wind.

The few remaining above deck were only too pleased with the command, yet Mr. Thorpe shook his head. "You can't do this alone, with only one lookout!"

"That's an order, blast you!" Blackwell's eyes pierced the younger man and, even in the torrential downpour, Gaelan Thorpe recognized his fury. The first mate nodded sharply and using a hand spike, knifed a path to the passageway. He allowed himself a last look at his captain. He was without an oil cloth, barefoot and barechested, his powerful arms struggling with the wheel. Normally they would have simply ridden out the storm, but the treacherous waters forbade such a luxury. Gaelan's eyes widened as a mountain of water welled up beyond the port side. His gaze shot to the captain. He was fearlessly waiting for the crush. It hit, and Gaelan Thorpe was washed below by the force.

* * *

The woman clung to the dolphin, her head resting on top of the smooth slope just beyond the fin. She could hear his breath through the hole near her face. It was a comforting sound. He'd saved her life, kept her afloat, and she rewarded him the only way she could—with a name. Richmond—Mighty Protector. One arm was slung limply around his fin, the other dangled in the water. It was useless, the arm, having been wrenched badly during the storm; the pain of it throbbed up to her neck. Her left leg burned near the ankle. Her shoulders were scorched, and blisters had formed, burst, only to be replaced by more. The cycle was continuous since the storm had subsided and the sun had shown its angry face. Her skin felt tight, itchy, her lips dry and cracked. Her stomach roared at its emptiness, and she heaved. But there was nothing left to vomit. Her thirst was insatiable.

Tess was oblivious to her surroundings, to the clear azure waters, the schools of brightly colored fish skittering playfully around her legs, or the twenty-four-gun frigate sailing within a hundred yards of her.

Anchored in calm waters, repairs to the frigate were underway when the shout, "Man off port!" came down from the crow, the seaman pointing out the area.

Captain Blackwell frowned, scanning the crystal surface. "All are accounted for, Mr. Thorpe?" he asked, putting the spyglass to his eye.

"Aye, sir. We lost no one," the first mate answered, his gaze dropping to the blistering rope burns about the captain's forearms. He had yet to see to his own wounds, more concerned with how his men and ship had fared.

The captain perused the waters. "I see I must take the boy to task," he mused aloud, "for 'tis but a dolphin." Captain Blackwell lowered the glass, watching the animal draw closer.

Duncan McPete suddenly appeared with a tray bearing peculiar-colored drinks.

Blackwell arched a brow, his gaze shooting between the man and his tray. "Another one of your mysterious concoctions, Mr. McPete?"

Duncan lifted his chin—and the offerings. "I assure you, sir, 'tis naught but the juice of fruits from our stores."

Blackwell sighed, snatching up the glass, unwilling to insult the man with a reminder of how ill Duncan's last formula had made him. He examined the contents in the sunlight. "Pink, Duncan?" he questioned skeptically, then took a sip. Both brows shot up, and the captain drained the glass without stopping, eliciting a huge grin from his manservant as he plunked the glass back on the tray. "Write that one down," he said softly, patting his stomach. His rare smile faded when he saw nearly half his crew scurry toward the rail.

"Captain! Come quick, sir!"

Blackwell was already striding across the deck, muscled legs easily adjusting to the dip of the vessel. He could hear the ear-piercing squeak of the dolphin as the crew stepped back to allow him passage. His chiseled features spoke his annoyance as he folded his arms and addressed his crew, refusing to take the three paces to the rail.

"This ship will not sail itself, gentlemen, and I believe she suffered enough damage last eve to warrant

31

that all of you have not a single moment to spare."

Gazes dropped under his penetrating regard, and men dispersed, glancing almost fearfully over their shoulders toward the port side.

"Captain," Duncan called from the rail, gesturing wildly. It was the horrified look on the old man's face that alerted him. Blackwell leaned over the salted wood.

"Mother of God!" Immediately he shucked his boots and climbed to the rail. He dove, surfacing beside the dolphin.

The animal released the strap caught in its jaws and the survivor slithered into Blackwell's arms. Instantly he knew he held a woman. The soft curve of her breast molded to his palm as he flipped her face up and checked her breathing.

"Praise be!" he mumbled and, bracing her lolling head against his chest, swam back to the ship. A rope ladder tumbled down, and with the experience and strength of long months at sea, he ascended, the woman hanging limply over his shoulder. Blackwell slung a leg over the rail and braced himself before he lifted her more comfortably in his arms and stepped fully onto the deck.

"God save us! It's a woman!"

"Astute observation, Mr. Potts," the captain quipped dryly, gently laying his catch on a blanket Duncan had ready, then kneeling beside her.

"Throw her back, Captain," the boatswain pleaded.

"Aye, 'Tis a sign. A bloody curse to have *that* aboard!"

The captain ignored the superstitious pleas and

pulled back the clumps of hair from her face and bare shoulders. The grumbling gradually quieted as he revealed more and more of the woman to their eager eyes.

"Lord in heaven! She's naked!"

"It be a bloody mermaid!" A deck hand gawked. "Look at that skin!" He pointed a shaking finger at her shiny black covering.

Captain Blackwell tossed the blanket over her bare limbs and slipped an arm beneath her back, lifting her upright. She coughed and water spilled from cracked lips.

"Oohh," she moaned, lids fluttering upward for a breathless moment.

Tess Renfrew stared into eyes of the palest green, thinly rimmed in dark jade. Her stinging gaze sketched the owner's face. What a hunk, she thought, before she slipped deep into unconsciousness.

Capt. Dane Blackwell quickly gathered the woman in his arms and came to his feet, then strode to the passageway. Kicking open the door to his cabin, he carried her to his bed and gently laid her in the soft center, then settled down beside her. Cautiously he removed the satchel strap wrapped around her sunburned shoulder and tossed the brightly colored case on a nearby chair. Smoothing the hair from her face, he tenderly pulled the ebony mass from beneath her, noticing that the area where her shoulder and arm met was swollen. How long had she been in the sea?

"Sir?"

Dane nodded acknowledgment, unable to release his gaze from the woman as Duncan set a tray laden with cloths, pitcher, and bowl on the commode beside him.

"I am at a loss, Duncan." He spoke softly as if the admission shamed him. "If this were a man I would not think twice about stripping garments from such wounds, but a woman . . . Lord, look at this thing!" He plucked at the garment, feeling the fabric give beneath his touch.

Duncan smiled indulgently. Fierce and cold-natured as he appeared, Captain Blackwell was truly a gentleman.

"Allow me, sir," Duncan said, solicitously unfolding a sheet and draping it over the woman. Gingerly he reached beneath the coverlet and with instructions to the captain, they carefully removed her clothing.

Duncan stared in amazement at what remained in his hand. "It appears to have shrunk, sir." The shiny black garment was half the length it had been on the woman.

Dane took it, pulling it this way and that. "Keep this to yourself," he said, tossing it with the satchel.

Duncan nodded, coming around to his side of the bed and pouring water into the bowl, soaking a cloth, then wringing it out. He held it out to the captain.

Dane shook his head. "You were the married man, McPete."

"I believe 'twould be best, sir, if the lady suffered only one humiliation when she awoke. Both of us seeing her unclothed would be too much of a shame for her to endure."

Dane cast him a side glance. "You've deduced she's a lady, have you?"

"Oh aye, Capt'n." He grinned. "Bones like that do not belong to some tavern wench."

Silently Dane agreed, accepting the cloth and gingerly cleansing her face and throat. "Lady or not, considering the horrible state she's in, I've no doubt she'll be most grateful."

Duncan's lips twitched. "No doubt, sir." The young man had no idea he was holding the lass's hand, Duncan decided, moving to a cabinet and collecting creams and bandages. He glanced up when he heard the captain curse. "A problem, sir?"

Dane tossed the sheet back to her knee, revealing a shapely calf with a swollen ankle. "The lady appears to have crossed an angry jellyfish. Have Higa-san prepare one of his compresses to ease the sting and swelling, and fill my bath, Duncan, with cool waters. Her body is too parched for this sponging nonsense."

Duncan obeyed quickly, and within moments Dane lifted the woman, sheet and all, and entered his private bathing room, gently lowering her into a large hip bath. He forced cool water between her chapped lips, stroking her throat to make her swallow.

"That will be all, Duncan. I can manage." Dane pulled a small stool beneath him as he drizzled water over her head.

"Aye-aye, sir. Shall I see that the cook prepares a clear broth, perhaps, for the lady?"

"Aye, but tell him not to rush," Dane murmured softly, if a bit sadly. "I fear this battered creature will not survive."

"Let us pray you are incorrect in your judgment, sir." Duncan moved away from the bath's threshold, taking the few steps to the door.

"Duncan?"

"Sir?" he replied, his hand on the brass latch.

"How do you suppose she came to be floating in the sea?"

Duncan blinked owlishly. "I cannot imagine, sir." The manservant knew the captain wasn't really asking him for a solution, he was simply thinking aloud; Captain Blackwell detested being ignorant of any situation.

"And what of that dolphin, holding her above the surface like that?"

"Peculiar, sir. I'll have fresh water warmed if you need, sir."

Dane didn't acknowledge the offer; he was wincing over her blistered and burned skin. "God's teeth, but she's a damned mess!" Dane muttered, lifting her arm and gently rinsing away the sheen of salt.

"Aye, Capt'n." There was laughter in his voice. "And as we're both quite aware, sir, she's a beauty as well."

Dane jerked around to comment on the man's brash assumptions, but the servant was gone, leaving Capt. Dane Alexander Blackwell alone with his mysterious charge.

Chapter Four

Duncan McPete hovered over the woman lying in the captain's bed, applying cool compresses to her face and throat. The door burst open, and he looked back over his shoulder to see Captain Blackwell's tall form filling the portal.

"The fever's come, sir."

Dane's gaze shot to the woman. "Why did you not send word?" he barked, storming across the room, unbuckling his sword and laying the sextant and charts aside as he moved.

Duncan stepped back. "She showed no sign until now, sir."

Dane froze at the side of the bed. Her loveliness seemed cast in rose porcelain, so still she lay. Her shoulders and arms exposed above the pristine sheet were bare, the blistered skin showing the signs of healing. A thin mist of perspiration glistened on her complexion like a dusting of crystal powder, and yet with the aid of Higa-san's mysterious potions, the fiery redness was fading. Her lips were pasty white. Dane gingerly sat down on the bed, his fingers unwillingly sifting the river of black that spilled over his pillow. It was lustrous, nearly blue but for the few coppery wisps that haloed her forehead and temples.

Who are you, my lovely? he silently asked. Are you the witch my men claim you to be? What forces put you in the sea? And what of your big gray friend keeping vigil at my bow?

Dane shook himself, drawing back his hand as if burned, suddenly aware he was being watched.

"If you desire, Capt'n, you may return to the quarter deck. I will tend her." Duncan soaked a cloth, then moved to place it on the woman's forehead.

"Nay!" An arm shot out to block his way. "Nay," he added in a softer tone. "I am not needed." He paused. "And I'm famished, Duncan."

The servant took the hint, suppressing a smile. "Aye-aye, Capt'n."

Dane snapped a look at the old man, yet saw nothing in his expression that spoke of the humor in his voice. Duncan, with his head bowed in an uncharacteristic show of obedience, closed the door as Dane turned back to the woman, gently bathing her face and arms. His gaze traveled across her shrouded form, and he suddenly throbbed to know what sweet treasures lay beneath the cloth. Dane remembered all too well how the damp sheet clung to her when he'd removed her from the bath in the days before, yet the tantalizing memory only served to stir his mind into a lustful frenzy.

She was long and sleek like a cat, tall for a woman, he assumed, not having the opportunity to come face-to-face with her on sure-footed ground. Her arm, shoulders, and calves were unusually sculptured, hard muscles well-defined, yet she was light of form, less than nine stone, he deduced, resoaking the cloth and continuing with his task. Nay, 'twas not a task, but a pleasure. This lass would not allow him such liberties were she capable of speech, Dane considered, longing to hear the sound of her voice, to see any expression on her face but the still blankness he'd witnessed for the past days.

"What name goes with your beauty, little mermaid?" he asked in hardly a whisper. She began to shake violently, and when his fingers grazed her skin, it was as if a blaze raged within her.

Duncan spun away from the cabin door and strode jauntily toward the companionway, his bearings set on the galley. He wasn't fooled. For over a week now, the captain had come into his cabin thrice during the day, claiming he wished to dine in private. The food was always left untouched, and the woman seemed to be constantly between the bath and his bed, the stone-faced captain soothing her skin with creams. Hungry, my arse! 'Tis not food you be wanting, sir!

Duncan was still grinning when he stuck his head into the galley and addressed the cook. Higa-san's head bobbed, the only indication that he'd heard, as he continued to wield a massive knife over a carrot, shredding it into slices as thin as hair. Duncan shook his head and waited for the little man to gesture that he could enter. No one ventured into the galley without Higa-san's permission. One crew member had disobeyed the order, and his index finger had been the price.

"Captain's hungry." Higa-san spared him a questioning glance. "Aye, fever's got her."

The small man stopped chopping, laid down the knife, and, with an efficiency of movement that amazed Duncan, prepared a tray, then added a handleless cup to the meal. He gestured once to the delicate cup filled with brewed herbs, then picked up the knife and went back to work. Duncan lifted the tray and cautiously backed out of the galley, then headed toward the cabin.

Shouldering his way inside, Duncan saw the captain lift the woman and stride toward the bath.

"Never mind that. Cold water, Duncan! Now!"

Duncan didn't remark that the captain was using up his personal rations on the woman and did as bade.

For three days Dane labored continuously over the lady, bathing her, forcing a clear broth or a smelly tea down her throat.

"You must eat, sir." Duncan stood off to the side, indicating the meal gone cold.

"Take it away." Dane waved, his attention riveted to the woman.

Duncan sighed resolutely, shaking his head. "You need rest also, sir. May I take over while you—?"

"Nay! No one touches her!" he roared, jumping to his feet and glowering down at the servant. "Is that clear?"

"Aye-aye, Capt'n!"

The old man's offended expression quickly brought Dane to his senses. His broad shoulders drooped before he said, "I ask your indulgence, my friend. That was uncalled for." He laid a hand on Duncan's shoulder and squeezed, not understanding his own outburst. "But I can manage." Wearily Dane sank into the stuffed chair.

"My services are here if you should feel the need, Capt'n." Duncan spoke softly as the captain fought the heaviness of his lids and unwillingly closed his eyes. Duncan wasn't offended by the chastising; the crew's harsh talk was enough to warrant a bit of caution. But somehow the lady had struck a tender chord in the sleeping man, and with Duncan's knowledge of Dane Blackwell, he knew it to be an extremely rare occurrence. Only Desiree had been able to bring out this degree of tenderness. God's bones, but the captain had scarcely left the cabin at all, deeming his first mate capable of sailing the new courses. The servant hadn't finished setting the lavish cabin to rights and replacing the water when Captain Blackwell woke with a start, bolting upright, looking childishly panicked before his gaze fell on the woman. He checked her breathing, her temperature, then with a disheartened sigh, continued his vigil.

The tray of untouched food in his hand, Duncan was just closing the door when he heard him softly beg her to live.

"You must try, little one. You've come too far."

It was late one Thursday evening when the raging fever broke, and she fell into a safe, exhausted sleep. Duncan knew that only two people aboard the *Sea Witch* cared whether she lived, for most of the crew

41

were cursing her, wishing she'd perished in the storm. He quickly amended the count, for though he never voiced it, Higa-san had expressed to her more kindness than he'd bestowed on anyone, except the captain.

The stirring of life melted down her body like warm honey as Tess began to waken. She was safe. Sighing deeply with the pleasure of being alive, she nudged away the heaviness of a drug-induced sleep and cautiously tested her limbs, stretching slowly like a gently roused cat.

This mattress is as soft as goose down, she thought sleepily, surprised to find her skin so supple. She expected her arms and shoulders to feel like a freeze-dried apple. It took a considerable amount of time for her to open her eyes and even longer to adjust to her shadowed surroundings. She glanced around, startled fully awake.

She'd expected a hospital.

My God, what is this place? Suspended on a hook from the ceiling was a thin, white netting draping seductively to the four posts of the huge bed, the portion beside her drawn back with a silk cord. Very sexy, she thought, attempting to sit up. The effort cost her what little strength she had, and with a tired sigh, Tess fell back onto the billowy linens. Her gaze drifted around the room, the view hazy through the webbing. Off to her left, a worn oxblood leather chair rested behind a desk cluttered with papers, and beyond that a massive pane window stretched the width of the room, heavily draped with burgundy velvet.

Beneath the thick glass was a cushioned bench of matching fabric, dusky light spilling over its faded richness. A polished Chippendale dresser was built into the opposite wall, tucked in a corner; next to that stood an old-fashioned wardrobe. A door, ornately carved and hinged in brass, was closed, a small potbellied stove a few feet to its right. She counted eight chairs surrounding a long glossy table adjacent to her and against the same polished wall as the bed was a tall, broad cabinet with beautifully etched glass doors in the top of the hutch. She frowned. She could spot an antique when she saw one, but these, they were in excellent condition. And why was everything bolted to the floor and walls? There were other things that made her uneasy, besides the spicy scent of cologne clinging to the pillows or the boots neatly placed beside a trunk.

The room was moving. Not moving, but rocking?

Incredible. How can this be? she wondered, propping herself up on one elbow, then stuffing the mountain of pillows comfortably around her. She adjusted the sheet and suddenly realized she was completely naked beneath it.

It was this alluring picture that greeted the captain of the *Sea Witch* when he entered his cabin. He stood frozen, his hand on the latch, half in, half out, his gaze drifting over her sculptured body draped in white linen. The image of a feline came to mind again, seeing her reclining on her side, ribbons of black silk streaming over bare shoulders and pooling on the bed. She had a confused look about her, the sheet grasped tightly to her chest with one hand.

Dane stepped inside and sealed them in.

43

Her head jerked up at the soft sound, and Tess absorbed the sight of a man coming toward the bed. Broad-shouldered and tall, he moved across the room with a grace and sensuality Tess had never witnessed in a man. Lord, what a piratical getup! Long legs encased in tight-fitting black pants covered the space that separated them in seconds, cuffed boots that reached his knees clicked twice before they touched on the carpet. Sharply he brushed back the drape.

Tess stared. He wasn't just a dream, she thought, reacquainting herself with that face. He's beautiful; black hair, shiny and curling beyond his collar, a square jaw, great nose, and all the skin she could see was bronzed like a rich wood. He was looking her over as well, and her gaze met the most dangerous pair of eyes she'd ever seen. They made her heart stop, then beat like a drum roll. He said a hundred things with those mint-frost eyes, yet revealed nothing.

"You are well?" Dane demanded impatiently, securing the drape without looking away.

She blinked, startled by his harsh tone. "Ah, yes. Thank you." She paused to swallow dryly. "Where am I?"

"You are aboard my ship, the *Sea Witch*."

"Ship?" He nodded sharply.

So, that's why we're moving, she thought, examining the richly appointed room once more. The *Nassau Queen* was a very stable floating four-star hotel, each cabin complete with small refrigerator and a wet bar, but this place, though filled with expensive antiques, was spared any convenience. It didn't even have a T.V. or intercom system that she could see. In

44

fact, it lacked outlets or switches of any kind, not to mention electric lamps, only sconces and small oil lamps anchored to the wall. Dangerous. Certainly doesn't look like any ship I've ever seen before, she added thoughtfully, returning her gaze to him.

"What happened?"

His eyes glazed over her bare shoulders. "I had hoped you could enlighten me to your circumstances."

Tess pulled the sheet up to her throat, but it didn't seem to do much good. He was looking at her as though he could see beneath it. "Do you have a robe or a shirt I can borrow?"

Rebuked for his gawking, Dane nodded once, then went to the wardrobe. After sliding back three evenly spaced bolts, he withdrew a black velvet robe. He hoped it cloaked her to her throat. Recovering in his bed was one matter, awake and tempting him to madness was quite another. He breathed deeply, excitement spinning through him. How long had he waited for this moment?

He has a ponytail, she thought with a bit of shock as he tossed the garment over his arm and returned to her side of the bed.

"Do you need assistance?"

"Ah, no, I can manage. Thank you." Tess accepted the robe, frowning at his manner, stiff and aloof like some highclass maitre d', and hadn't expected him to turn his back while she shrugged into the robe. A soft groan escaped her lips as she tried to tug it beneath her.

He turned sharply at the sound, treated with the sight of a pale, bare thigh.

"I guess that'll have to do," she muttered, annoyed at her lack of strength and falling back onto the pillows.

He cleared his throat uneasily. "May I?"

Tess's brow wrinkled, not knowing what he wanted. "By all means."

Dane bent over her, slipping an arm behind her back and lifting, while the other arm swiped the robe beneath her legs before he set her down. Solicitously he plumped pillows, then eased her back onto the mound.

"Th-thank you." She'd never been treated like this before and found she enjoyed it, especially from a babe like him.

"Are you feeling well enough for a little conversation?" Please say aye, he hoped, pouring her a glass of water from the pitcher perched on the commode beside the bed.

"Sure. Fire away," she said, accepting the glass, eager to know about where she was and with whom.

His brows shot up; then he shook his head, lifting a chair and positioning it beside the bed. "I believe introductions are the first order."

"Tess. Tess Renfrew," she said, holding out her hand before he could speak.

The name befitted her, he thought, grasping her hand and bending slightly as he drew it to his lips.

"A pleasure, Mistress Renfrew," he murmured huskily, his gaze never wavering as he placed a soft kiss to the back. "I am Captain Dane Alexander Blackwell, at your service." His heels clicked once before he straightened and gestured to the chair, asking permission to join her.

Tess nodded mutely, clamping her gaping mouth shut and slowly drawing her hand back. Good gravy, what an oddball, she thought, feeling like a queen granting an audience as he took his seat.

"Now, how did you come to be floating in the sea?"

Those eyes demanded the truth. "I jumped off the *Nassau Queen*."

He relaxed back into the chair, frowning, stroking the stubble on his chin. "I've never heard of such a vessel, but—no matter." He shrugged, and Tess couldn't help but notice the play of muscle beneath the billowy white shirt opened at the throat. And laced? "Might I ask what possessed you to do such a thing?"

His deep voice intrigued her, and she settled more comfortably in the bed. "Two men were trying to kill me."

His eyes narrowed a fraction, his only response. So much for shocking him.

"Would you care to start from the beginning?"

"No."

So, she has secrets. "Are you aware a dolphin kept you afloat?"

Her smile was blinding, and Dane felt he'd just taken a blow to his middle.

"Yes, I am. And that's Richmond." A black brow arched questioningly. "I felt I had to call him something after he'd saved my life. The ship's propeller backwash was pulling me into the blades, and before I was chopped into shark bait, Richmond caught the strap of my bag and dragged me to the surface." When she glanced around, he gestured absently to the bright yellow sack in the corner. "How come you just

47

didn't look inside it? My identification is in there. You'd have known who I was then."

"Madame." He sat up straighter. "Be assured I would never rifle through a lady's belongings unless given leave to do so." Did that mean not without my permission, she wondered as he added, "And as you were unable to disembark on your own power, I saw no urgency in the matter."

Good Lord! What's with this guy? He actually looks insulted!

"And if I may ask —" his voice tightened a fraction — "*what* is a propeller?"

She blinked owlishly. "A propeller." She made little circles in the air with her finger. "You know, the thing at the back of a boat that makes it go in the water."

He braced his hands on his knees. "Mistress Renfrew." Dane drew on his patience. "Wind," he enunciated, "fills a sail to move a ship."

"Sure, clippers, Hobe Cats, Catamarans, sailboats, but not a four hundred-something-foot steel cruise liner. Why am I telling you this? *You're* the captain."

His expression went suddenly blank, unreadable. "That I am," he said, standing abruptly. "I suggest you rest now, mistress. I shall have a dinner tray sent in, post haste. Good evening."

He bowed curtly, then spun away, and Tess noticed for the first time that suspended from a belt around his waist was a gleaming silver cutlass.

Chapter Five

Dane stared at the closed door for a moment before his posture slackened, and he rubbed the back of his neck. Peculiar woman. He'd expected a weeping, frightened little flower, not that seductive bundle of spirit. What an odd clipped manner of speech she possessed. And he wondered further about this propeller thing she seemed convinced would sail a ship. Shaking his head, he turned away and found his path blocked.

"The lady has awakened, sir?"

"She has."

"What is she like? Her name? Was she frightened? Did she—"

Dane put a hand up, irritated at Duncan's eagerness. "Our guest is Mistress Tess Renfrew, and no, she was not frightened." Dane decided to keep her strange statements to himself, especially the notion of a four-hundred-foot steel ship. Any *sane* person would know such a vessel would sink.

"Renfrew, you say?" Duncan mused aloud, scratching his chin.

"Aye, and have a light repast prepared for the lady."

Duncan responded absently to the request, engrossed in his thoughts.

"What troubles you, McPete?"

The use of his last name told him the captain was out of patience. " 'Tis her surname, Capt'n, Renfrew. It be familiar somehow, but—" He shrugged. " 'Twill come to me in time, sir." Duncan moved away.

"Keep her recovery to yourself, man," Dane called when the servant reached the companionway. "I don't need a mutiny on my hands." He paused. "And Duncan—"

"Aye, sir?"

"I suggest you knock next time."

Duncan grinned, descending the ladder. "Aye-aye, Capt'n."

Tess thought of herself as a sensible person, a realist, and after living by her wits until she was eight, then all over the world because of her father's military career, sampling different cultures, she'd learned not to give the odd too much consideration. All it took was someone to shove a plate of raw squid in front of you, assume you were delighted to eat the spongy stuff, insulted if you didn't, and you had the sudden tendency not to expect anything else to ever be quite so peculiar. But this stateroom was incredible. Strange and quaint, she allowed, yet the absence of electricity, cellular phones, and engine noise made her wonder what it looked like above deck. But then, what did she know about pleasure yachts. She'd never actually been *on* any ship, other than the *Queen,* and that was designed for a week-long celebration of fun, flirting, and vacation sex.

Tess propped herself on both elbows when a knock sounded. After calling for whomever to come in, she watched as a robust little old man carrying a tray nudged his way inside. Interesting-looking character, Tess thought as she sat up, the delicious aroma of fresh-baked bread teasing her taste buds.

"Good evenin', miss." His shaggy gray head bobbed. "I be Duncan McPete, the capt'n's manservant," he introduced, and with one beefy hand lit an old-fashioned oil lamp.

Manservant, huh? She studied his every move, amazed one so bulky was that dexterous. "Hello, Mr. McPete. I'm Tess."

He glanced over his shoulder. "Aye, that you are, lassie." His smile was warm and friendly as he replaced the glass globe and faced her. " 'Twould please an old salt if you be callin' me Duncan, miss."

Her gaze slipped over his baggy brown knee pants, dark shirt, and worn silk vest. "Sure. If you call me Tess."

He froze. "Oh, nay, miss! I cannot!" Duncan's face clearly displayed his shock. "The capt'n would have me head for takin' such a liberty!"

"Calm down, Duncan, okay." Criminey, what's with these men? "Call me whatever you want," she told him, and his stout body sagged with relief.

Bandy legs shuffled to the side of the bed, and he placed the tray on the mattress, then drew back a cloth. "Hungry, miss?"

Tess's mouth watered at the appetizing meal. "Oh

51

yes, Duncan, starved."

His wrinkled leathery face lit up, and his smile broadened, making his single gold earring wink in the lamplight. "Enjoy the fare."

Tess folded her legs Indian style beneath the sheet, popping a berry in her mouth. "There's plenty. Join me, Duncan?"

"Oh, no, miss! 'Tis not proper!"

Her head jerked back. "Proper? Good grief. It's only dinner."

Fearing he'd insulted her somehow, he explained, "I've duties to tend before the next watch."

Marines had the duty; Navy had the—"Watch?" Tess heard herself say. No, they couldn't be *U.S.* Navy. They didn't live this good. And with that accent and those clothes? British yachters, maybe?

"Aye, the crew takes turns keepin' watch for the enemy, miss."

"Enemy?" She swallowed the banana slice, her eyes narrowing. "You're joking, right?"

" 'Tis no jest, but do not worry yourself, lass. Yer safe now."

Tess munched on a crust of bread, staring but not seeing. "Where are we?"

"Atlantic waters, miss. South of the Tropic of Cancer."

That wasn't any help. "Is that near Cuba?"

"Nearly three hundred miles to the east," he said carefully. "In the West Indies, miss." To Duncan she appeared ready to bolt.

Besides Castro, what enemies are there around here? she wondered. The British and American authorities took care of that, so who were they watching for? "This ship, Duncan. What kind is it? Exactly." Tess was afraid of the answer.

The old fellow's pale blue gaze examined her confused face, and for a moment he debated whether or not to tell the poor lass. "The *Sea Witch* is a twenty-four-gun frigate, miss."

"Oh." Flat, stunned. So much for her yacht theory. And twenty-four guns? Weren't frigates made of steel with giant howitzers or something? The mullion-paned window and roomful of antiques contradicted any *outside* image she could conjure.

Duncan felt a gentle stir in his chest at the sight of her bowed head and wringing hands. "Enjoy the meal, lass. Dine slowly. If you be needin' anything, I'll see to it."

She nodded. "Thanks, Duncan."

He departed quickly, at a loss as how to ease whatever troubled her.

The minute the door shut, Tess scooted to the edge of the bed, her appetite gone. Her feet tingled as they touched the rough carpet, and she had to grasp the post to stand. She hated being this weak, but she had to investigate this room. Clamping a hand onto the nightstand, Tess worked her way around the room to the desk. She plopped into the chair, her head reeling. God, it's hot in here, she thought.

Taking a moment to rest, she swiped the back of her hand across her forehead, then began sifting through a stack of papers. She paused, fingers rasping over the thick quality paper of a hand-drawn map. Parchment? She continued looking through the desk drawers, not at all ashamed of snooping; this place was too bizarre not to.

No ballpoint pens or pencils, only sticks of graphite, a quill, inkstand, and a box of sand? She shook her head and sighed back into the chair. Not even a paper clip. This was getting weirder by the moment. Forced to hold on to the desk ledge to make her way to the wardrobe, Tess moved cautiously, drawing the line at looking in the dresser. Have to do it somewhere, she mused. Opening the closet, she discovered men's clothes in rich fabrics: velvet and brocade jackets, fine lawn and silk shirts, suede and satin knee pants, along with coarse-feeling trousers. She blinked. No zippers, no snaps, just wood or ceramic buttons and crude hooks. She closed the door, relaxing back against it, then moved to the door she assumed was the bathroom. Her hand on the brass latch, Tess tried to open the door, but her equilibrium shifted abruptly, her brain spinning, and she felt queasy and weak. I'm not going to make it back to the bed, she thought, her arm reaching across the expanse. The door opened and when she snapped a look, her ears rang, her legs buckling beneath her.

"Ohh-noo," she whispered, and strong hands caught her before she hit the floor.

Dane swept Tess up in his arms, holding her high against his chest. "You should not have tried to walk, Mistress Renfrew," he scolded gently.

"Gee, woulda never guessed," she slurred, dropping her head to his shoulder.

He smiled, enjoying the solid feel of her in his arms for the few steps to his bed. Reluctantly he laid her on the mattress, then stood back, hands on his hips. "Madame. Have you eaten?"

"Some." Why do I feel like a little kid about to be

grounded? she wondered.

"Then I suggest you finish that." He nodded to the meal, then turned away.

"That sounds like an 'or else,' Captain Blackwell."

He spun back around, frowning. "I beg your pardon?"

"Or else you'll stuff it down my throat if I don't?" He smiled, and if she thought he was handsome before, nothing prepared her for the impact of those dimples.

"If I must."

"Not unless you join me." When he looked surprised at the offer, she added, "Please. I'm bored to tears," telling herself that was the *only* reason she wanted him to stay.

Dane felt weak in the knees at her soft plea and nodded agreement, knowing 'twas unwise to be so close to her. She did something to him no other woman had. Tess Renfrew fascinated him. He pulled a chair to the side of the bed as she scooted back, moving the tray between them.

"Dig in." She tasted a chunk of mango, then drained the cup of herbal tea.

"You have not sampled the beef as yet, mistress?"

Mistress? Madame? Awful formal for a man dining on a bed. "I don't eat red meat," she told him, popping a slice of melon in her mouth. She hated to think what chemicals were in that underdone carcass.

"Fresh beef is rare on a ship, Mistress Renfrew." Dane tore off a chunk of bread and stuffed it with the juicy slices.

Her brows wrinkled. "How is that possible?"

His gaze flew up. Was she that sheltered? "Live

stock of that size take up valuable cargo space and, when butchered, it spoils quickly," he said, then took a bite.

"So freeze it."

His chewing slowed. "In this heat?" He gestured to the room as he swallowed. "Mistress Renfrew," he said patiently. "It is impossible to keep anything even slightly cool in the tropics, let alone blocks of ice."

Tess eyed him. Was he dense? "Why do you need blocks of ice? There is such a thing as refrigeration, you know."

His gaze sharpened. "Nay, I do not know."

"Rapid cooling, electric? Freon moving through coils?" She waited for him to nod agreement. He didn't. "A box that keeps things cold constantly, any-where?" He looked at her as if she'd blown a gasket. "Skip it," she mumbled.

Tess kept her gaze on the plates of food. Who was he fooling? How could he not admit to knowing about refrigeration? And live animals on ship? The possibility was unnecessary and, if anything, revolt-ing. They'd have to kill them on—she shook her head. This place was like a trip to the twilight zone, she thought, bracing herself on one locked arm and leaning over the tray just as he did, unaware that the velvet robe sagged open.

Dane's gaze dropped to the skin exposed, and his pulse quickened. The soft swells were pale, round, and he gnashed his teeth against the urge to brush the velvet aside and sample the creamy flesh.

Tess looked up. He was inches from her, and those eyes, they'd changed. Black pearls on pale jade. God, he was sexy. She sketched his features, her gaze ending on his lips. Her head reeled—from lack of food or from him?

"Mistress Renfrew," he warned softly. God's teeth, did she have to say so much with that look!

Raven lashes swept up. "It's Tess."

"Tess," he murmured, his gaze drifting over her face. Something drew him closer, against his will, he insisted as his knuckles grazed her cheek. She was so lovely, her beauty vivid. He knew this was wrong but couldn't seem to help it. Like the delicate flutter of a butterfly wing, his lips brushed hers, and he heard her sigh.

He stole it.

He was stealing her breath, her soul, she thought, as his lips rolled warmly over hers. Tess's head was spinning again, wilder this time, her insides tumbling. His tongue slid across her lower lip, slowly, then pushed inside, his warm fingers slipping into her hair to cup the back of her head. He cherished her mouth, coaxing her pleasure to a lush peak, and in one moment showed her he was caring and loving and wanting. Tongues battled languidly, a blaze spiraled through her already-weakened limbs, and she pressed a hand to his chest to steady herself.

Assuming she was pushing him away, he drew back.

"Wow," she whispered, sagging down on one elbow, breathless. *I've never been kissed like that!* she thought.

"I apologize for my boldness, Tess." He stood abruptly, shoving his hands in his pockets to disguise her effect on him. "I shouldn't have—you're ill."

She smiled up at him. He didn't look *that* apologetic. "Now I wished you'd looked in my bag."

He frowned, puzzled. "Whyever for?"

"Because I searched your desk."

"Is that so?" His lips twitched. God's teeth, she was priceless.

"And your closet."

"Anything else?"

"You caught me first."

He nodded thoughtfully. "What is it that you wish to know, Mistress Renfrew?"

So, they were back to that again. "Why I am on a — a — ?"

"Frigate," he supplied when she yawned. "Forgive me, but I am still at a loss."

"Why didn't you just put me ashore, send me to a hospital?"

He could see the tea was taking affect. "We are still days from land and I doubt there are adequate hospitals on those islands, if any."

"Oh, be serious!"

"I have no cause to deal you half-truths, Mistress Renfrew. Believe me when I say I *am* quite serious."

He was. Tess knew it from the look on his face. She mentally examined all she'd discovered — no modern conveniences. None. And the way he acted dumb when she spoke of anything remotely technical. His eloquent speech and formal manners, his clothes, this room, hell, this ship!

"What year do you believe this is, Captain Blackwell?"

He scowled at the peculiar question and her superior look, as if she was indulging a child she knew couldn't answer correctly.

58

"I do not believe, Mistress Renfrew," he fairly snapped. "I *know* it is the twenty-third day of June in the year of our Lord, seventeen hundred eighty-nine."

Tess wanted to cry.

He was an eccentric! That had to be it. He was rich and bored, and this was his "Fantasy Island," playing pirate on an eighteenth-century warship. And he was into it deep, God, real deep. She cradled her head in her hands. Oh, why did he have to be a space cadet?

"And might I ask the same question of you?" Her head jerked up. "What do you believe is today's date?"

She dropped her hands and sighed. "I'm not sure of the day, but it's June," she paused, gauging his expression, *"nineteen* eighty-nine."

His eyes sparked, and his lips thinned. "At least we agree on the month," he said, then walked over to the hutch.

Disheartened, Tess fell back onto the mound of pillows, her eyes following his movements as he withdrew a key from his pocket and unlocked the cabinet. He removed a beautiful crystal decanter and poured a drink.

"Would you care for a brandy?"

Tess yawned, shaking her head. "That stuff's poison to your liver."

He spared her a glance. "Since in your eyes, Mistress Renfrew, my liver is already two hundred years old, I do not see the harm."

Tess smiled sleepily. "Touché, Captain Blackwell," she mumbled through another yawn. I'll indulge him, she decided. Why not? It could be fun. He was certainly a change from any man she'd met before.

When Dane turned back to the bed, he found her asleep, curled on her side, hands folded primly beneath her cheek. He remained there for a moment, absorbing her serene beauty, then strolled across the room to his desk, sinking into the soft leather chair, and propping his booted feet on the cluttered surface.

Nineteen hundred and — he didn't want to think on her words. It confirmed his suspicions. He wanted only to recall the delicious feel of her firm body pressed against him when she'd nearly fainted, the long sleek legs draped over his arm. And God, the maddening taste of her. Like sweet energy. She was inexperienced, he deduced, perhaps even a virgin. Tess Renfrew was candid and strong and aye, desirable, and he admitted enjoying her company. She was like no other lady he'd encountered in his thirty-three years. Dane tossed back the brandy and stood. He wanted her, but he knew she was insane.

Chapter Six

Dane muttered a curse, raking his fingers through his midnight black hair. "You must be wrong, Duncan."

"Nay, sir."

"How can this be?" he hissed, keeping his voice low. "To commit such a cruelty against one so lively and beautiful." Dane spun away from the man, staring at the moon-danced ocean.

"I'm sorry, sir, but it must be the reason." Duncan felt his own kind of rage at the injustice. "Renfrew, 'tis a noble name. There's even a shire of the same name."

Dane sighed deeply, looking to the stars. "But to set her adrift in a storm?"

"Them nobles an' richies would do it." He scuffed a bare foot on the smooth planks, darting a look at the sleeping men sprawled around the deck. "See, sir, ah, sometimes if a relative, ah, be touched in the head they—" His words were sliced off when the captain's head snapped to the side, cold rage contorting his shadowed features.

"Damn you, McPete!" he snarled softly. "Damn you to hell!"

Duncan lifted his chin a notch, his pale eyes narrowing. "I'm rather fond of the lass, *Captain Blackwell*. An' I'd not besmirch her nor cause her a moment's distress."

They stared at each other; a black cloak, thick with the current of resentment, hung between them. Then like a slow ripple across cool waters, the tension melted out of Dane.

"I know." He nodded, then braced his hands on the rail, dropping his head between outstretched arms. "Forgive my rashness, Duncan," he muttered to the deck. When he didn't accept the apology, Dane lifted his head, glancing to the side.

Duncan was grinning.

"Unusual creature, isn't she, sir?"

Dane's lips quirked, remembering the effect of her kiss. "Aye, that she is."

"Miss Cabrea doesn't—"

"Nay," Dane cut in sharply, straightening. "She does *not* compare. Lady Renfrew is neither weak, nor prone to tears—" His lips twisted in disgust. "Nor to dramatic swooning simply for attention."

"Nay, the lady stirs your blood, lad."

Dane leveled a look at the amused servant. "Get you to bed, old man. I'm tired of your endless prattle."

Grinning hugely, Duncan saluted smartly and spun about, trotting off to his bunk, a hearty chuckle following in his wake.

* * *

Tess climbed from the bed, testing her muscles. She had to work out. Her legs were stiff and it was driving her nuts. She shrugged out of the heavy robe and slipped into an extremely large shirt that had been discarded over the back of a chair. A scent filled her nostrils as she buttoned it. His scent, of wind and sun and—man. She smiled, remembering how he'd kissed her, how she'd felt: warm, sexy—hungry for more. Nice, she decided. *Very* nice.

Tess had never been close to many men. Except her father. Her sport had taken up too much time in her life until the accident, and then she'd become a coach. Her one and only affair had been a humiliating disaster. Before she got depressed, she clasped her hands over her head and stretched, then swung down, resting her palms on the floor. God, this feels great. She straightened, propped a heel on the edge of the desk and began her ballet workout.

Dane entered the cabin, freezing in his tracks, his eyes greedily traveling up and down the shapely calves revealed beneath his shirt. She resembled a swan, one arm up and curved, back straight, her bending descent, slow and graceful. God's teeth, but that garment never looked so enticing! He heard voices in the passageway and stepped inside, closing the door behind him.

Tess jerked at the sound, glaring back over her shoulder. "Don't you ever knock?"

He brushed aside his rudeness with, "I hardly think 'tis necessary, considering this is my cabin," then moved across the room to the chiffonnier, soaking up the delicious sight of those gorgeous limbs.

"Your cabin?" she squeaked, dropping her leg.

"Wh-why didn't you tell me that?" She darted behind the desk chair, suddenly aware she was naked beneath the thin shirt. "I thought this was a stateroom."

He glanced up from perusing his wardrobe; the dusky outline of her nipples briefly drew his gaze. "This isn't one of your four-hundred-foot vessels," he quipped, then selected a fresh shirt.

"Very funny, Blackwell." She scooted out of his way and grabbed the robe, slipping it on and belting it tightly. "I'll move to another room."

"Cabin," he corrected. "And there are no others." Tossing the fresh clothing over his arm, he faced her. She was nearly at the door. "And if you so much as step one foot outside this cabin, Lady Renfrew, I shall bodily carry you back."

Tess whirled about. "*Lady* Renfrew! Aren't you spreading it on a bit thick, Captain?"

"You are Scottish, are you not?" He held his breath.

Smoke gray eyes narrowed. "Yes." Somewhere, she thought. "How did you know that?"

He ignored the question, his gaze claiming her. "Come here, Lady Renfrew."

Tess stiffened. "No way, Blackwell." Who did he think he was anyway?

Feisty little wench, he thought, keeping his features impassive. "Then by all means—"he waved—"depart." She turned to the door. "One hundred eighty hearty souls who haven't been near a woman in months will undoubtedly consider your alluring attire their good fortune."

Her shoulders drooped. "Anyone ever tell you you can be a real creep?"

"Pardon?" Then he chuckled softly, guessing at her meaning.

She faced him, hands on her hips. "If this is your cabin, where have you been sleeping?"

Dane folded his arms over his chest, crushing the clothes. "That needn't concern you."

But it did. "Where?"

"Lady Renfrew," he warned.

Something snapped in her. "It's Tess, damn you! Plain, ordinary, Tess. No Mistress, no Madame, no Lady anything! Don't make me someone important when I'm not!" She turned sharply, pressing her forehead to the door, angry at the sensation of losing control—of everything and so quickly. *Improvise* with what's available to survive; *adapt* to the customs, the environment; *overcome* each obstacle, one at a time. Tall order. Tess straightened, willing back the wetness stinging her eyes.

Dane eyed her dejected appearance. Why would she deny her heritage? he wondered, coming up behind her. His hands rose to grasp her shoulders, suddenly aching to hold her close and offer a haven from her secret troubles. But he let them drop to his sides when he saw her spine stiffen, his fists clenching against the urge to touch.

"Are you unwell?" His voice was near her ear, the husky tone soothing her.

"No, I'm fine. Or I will be when I find something to wear."

"Duncan will provide you with adequate clothing, post haste."

"Thank you. I'm going stir crazy in here. I need fresh air and—freedom."

"Promise you will not leave this cabin without me."
He still had her safety to consider.

"Am I a prisoner?"

"Of course not."

She turned. "Then why?" He was standing close.
So close she could see the tiny creases at the corners
of his eyes, each incredibly thick lash, his five o'clock
shadow. A bead of sweat made a lazy trickle from the
base of his throat down his chest to vanish beneath
the deep vee of his laced shirt. She suddenly wanted
to follow the path of the droplet. Ridiculous.

"What I said was true, Lady Renfrew." He smiled
at her sour face. "My crew has been at sea for
months. Our last port forbade them leave ashore—"

"Okay, okay." She put up a hand. "I get the picture." A hundred and eighty confirmed horny devils.

"Duncan will bring water for you to bathe if you
wish?"

"Why, do I smell?"

He blinked, taken back. "I beg your pardon,
m'lady. 'Twas not my intention to insinuate—"

She rolled her eyes. "Good gravy, do you *ever* relax,
Blackwell? Do anything just for yourself?"

Something flashed in his frosty eyes, turning them
nearly white. It was a scary thing to see.

"Nay, not anymore."

He bodily moved her aside, opened the door, and
walked out. Tess closed it softly behind him. That
man was hurting and angry—and hiding it.

"Just like joining the cast of a play," she said, staring at the incredible array of clothing laid carefully

66

on the bed. "Improvising and adapting made easy."

An old-fashioned gown, corset, stockings, yards of petticoats, and Tess hadn't the vaguest idea how to get inside them and stay there without female help. Well, it had to be easier than rinsing that harsh soap out of her hair in a narrow hip bath with one pitcher of lukewarm water. But she was still the only woman aboard with over a hundred and eighty men. And it was the ship — a reproduction, she'd deduced earlier, sort of like the Naval Academy used for midshipman training — she wanted to see. And Richmond. Duncan said the dolphin hadn't been far from the bow since she'd been rescued.

Trial and error, she supposed, studying the assortment of silk, lace, and ruffles, then slipping on the chemise. Certainly was an awful lot of clothing for this kind of weather, she mused, skipping the corset and pulling on the transparent old-fashioned panties, then tying on the lace petticoats. She felt strange in the garments, delicate and feminine, and that was new to her, having spent a considerable portion of her life in leotards and sweat suits. Plopping onto the bed, she slipped a stocking over her foot. They were heavy compared to pantyhose, seamed, and scarcely reaching beyond her thighs. The garters were nothing but ribbons with lace and bows. Sexy. She stepped into the gown and pushed her arms into the sleeves. It was heavy and belled out for yards in the back. Tess glanced over at the contraption lying on the trunk and assumed it was a hoop to support the fabric, like Scarlet O'Hara's. No way was she going to be harnessed into that thing. Not even for Act One. Besides, she thought, stepping into soft kid slippers, the gown barely hit the floor as it was.

Tess was out of breath and perspiring with the effort to fasten the first few hooks in the back. Sighing, she blew a wisp of hair out of her mouth. *What I wouldn't give for a tee-shirt and cut-offs right now.* Then she caught her reflection in the mirror and stilled. *This gown looks like it belongs to Glinda, the Good Witch of North,* she thought with a grin, her gaze absorbing the crisp muslin in deep rose trimmed with pale, silver gray lace. The full skirt draped open in the front to show the pink-ribboned petticoats beneath, its waistline coming to a point in the front and back. Stiff ruffled lace circled behind her throat to slope into the neckline, and she tugged at the plunging fabric, trying to cover the cleavage it exposed. *I look like I'm offering myself on a doilied platter,* she judged wryly, sighing at all the skin revealed. *It's either this or nothing,* she realized, plucking at the sleeve caught snug at her elbow, the soft lace cuff fluttering downward in a long, wide funnel.

Twisting and turning before the mirror, Tess suddenly itched to play out Captain Blackwell's little farce. Looking down at the extra ribbons and pearl pins, she shrugged. *Why not?* Then picked up the brush and comb laid out for her. She wove a rose pink ribbon into her hair as her fingers swiftly created a French braid down the back of her head. Years of managing long hair for meets made it quick work. Tess let the braid drape over her shoulder to her waist and secured the end with thin silver ribbon. The pearl hair pins were unnecessary, she decided, and a bit much. The gown still gaped open in the back, and she wondered how a woman managed to get dressed in a rush if she had to do this every time.

Dane opened the door and smiled as she wrestled with the dress. "Having a little difficulty, m'lady?"

Tess yelped, holding up the material as she whirled about.

The hot anger in her eyes told him what he suddenly realized. He hadn't bothered to knock. "Please, forgive my old habits. But I didn't mean to startle you." A ghost of a smile played on his lips.

"Oh, yes, you did," she replied, attempting to fasten the dress.

Dane came up behind her, brushing away her hands. "May I?"

"Please do," she gritted over her shoulder, sensing he was laughing at her. Dane unfastened a few hooks.

"What are you doing?" she asked, jerking away. "I want to stay in it, Blackwell, not fall out!"

He grabbed her arm, turned her so her back was to the mirror, then with his hands twisted her head for a look. "Oh, sorry about that," she muttered, her cheeks staining pink upon seeing the cockeyed job she'd done. Obediently she faced the mirror.

Dane's gaze caught briefly on the canvas corset and panniers lying across the sea chest, and he marveled at the tiny waist concealed in thin batiste, finding no need to tug the fabric to fasten it. Most women wore the constricting garment to disguise an overindulged figure, but this woman, though slim, was shapely, her skin a tight sheath over muscles. Muscles! The notion was as strange as the lady herself. He glanced at her reflection. Utterly breathtaking. Pale creamy skin and those dark eyes and hair. The contrast was enchanting, and he had the sudden urge to drape her in jewels and silks—and himself. Erotic images flooded his mind; hot damp skin, delicate fingers moving over his body, those shapely legs entwined around his hips, pulling him deeper inside. . . . His hands began to shake as he secured the hooks, his fingertips grazing her smooth skin.

Tess's eyes shot to the mirror, meeting his in the silver glass. The innocent touch sent a burning ripple of goose bumps up over her shoulders and neck. She could smell the spicy scent of his cologne, feel his warm breath on her bare shoulder. Her heart slowed to a heavy thud, each pound vibrating up to her throat. She swallowed it down. God, he was handsome. There was something unusual about Captain Blackwell, not just the fact he was an eccentric, but as a man—he was like a caged panther standing behind her. Dark, predatory, anxious to be set free. To do what? she wondered.

A thought suddenly occurred to her. "Are you married, Captain Blackwell?"

"Nay." The reply was curt, not inviting any questions.

Tess ignored it. "How come?"

"I could ask the same of you."

"I suppose you could."

A black brow shot up, and Tess's insides tumbled at the seductive look. "Are you wed, Lady Renfrew?" Dane felt his entire body clench.

"No."

"I find it difficult to believe there is no betrothed anxiously awaiting your return."

Her gaze clung to the floor. Why did she open up this subject? "No, Captain Blackwell." Her voice dropped to a whisper. "There is no one."

At the pain in her tone, Dane wished his words back. Duncan was right. No one had wanted her around to tarnish the family's reputation with her disturbed mind, and the captain found it all rather hard to stomach.

"Are you through yet?" she muttered tightly.

He stepped back. "Aye."

"Good." Without looking at him, she gathered up the heavy skirts. "Let's see this ship you're so damn proud of." She didn't wait for him and headed for the door.

He was there in an instant, reaching around her to grasp the latch.

"The *Sea Witch* awaits your presence, m'lady." He opened the door a crack.

Tess forced her eyes to meet his. His smile was faint, somehow sympathetic, and the sudden tension weighing her mood vanished.

"I'll have you know I want the grand tour." She finally smiled.

"You, Lady Renfrew, may have anything you desire."

Her gaze dropped to his chiseled mouth, and she unconsciously licked her lips. "Careful, Blackwell. You may regret those words."

Winter mint eyes drifted slowly over her bare shoulders, healed and smooth and golden, then to the blossoming fullness of her bosom before he forced himself to meet those haunting smoke-soft eyes.

"Nay, Lady Witch," he murmured huskily, "I truly doubt that."

Tess was trying to grab on to what was left of her

71

composure when he thrust open the door and cautioned her as she stepped over the high threshold. I'm playing with fire, she thought crazily, *way*, way out of my league. The corridor was damp, narrow, her skirts taking up most of the space. The closeness of his warm body seemed to intoxicate her further, and she grasped his arm as the ship lurched.

He stared, his palm spanning the small of her back, her body pressed lightly to the length of his own, scented and yielding. Dane didn't think there was another time in his life when a woman affected him like this.

"This way." He gestured down the passageway, and Tess preceded him, her legs easily adjusting to the sway of the vessel. He reached around her, warned her to shield her eyes, then opened the wide oval door and helped her onto the deck.

Bright sunlight drenched over her, and Tess closed her eyes against its brilliance, tilting her face to the sky and soaking in the warm rays. She breathed deeply of the clean salty air, filling her lungs over and over, unaware of the thoroughly feminine sight she portrayed to Dane.

A soft wind teased the short, deep copper wisps surrounding her face, and a delicate hand floated up to brush them back, golden beams shimmering over her complexion. Her gown rustled enticingly, and Dane dragged his gaze from the gentle rise and fall of her lush bosom, up the slender column of her throat to her serene features. Bewitching. The transformation from the spirited ragamuffin in his robe to this alluring creature hit him all at once. An odd sensation swept over him, and he fought the selfish desire to escort her back to his cabin and lock her inside. With him.

"It feels wonderful to be outside. Thank you," she whispered happily, then before she opened her eyes, Tess prepared herself for her first look at his eighteenth-century warship. She was awed.

It was massive.

The scene was a flurry of activity. Nearly a hundred bare-chested men of varying colors and sizes were scattered around the deck, twining rope, stitching sails, polishing, adjusting rigging, some even pulling up nets, their burly muscled torsos gleaming with sweat. Not a man she could see wore shoes. Most had long hair pulled back in a ponytail like Blackwell's, yet regardless of its color, the crews' little tails appeared to be black and slick. Tarred? Talk about an eye for detail. The wind shifted, and her nose twitched as the pungent odor of unwashed bodies assaulted her nostrils. Aw, come on! This was too much. Ever heard of soap, guys? she wondered, turning her face from the smell. They seemed oblivious to her and their captain. Until he spoke.

"The grand tour, m'lady?"

Heads snapped around, and Tess didn't mistake the hatred directed solely at her. Several dozen pairs of eyes narrowed, and some men turned abruptly away from the sight of her. Others stared, mouths open, looking her up and down, making her feel like some sort of freak. One man dropped his mop and moved back, obviously terrified.

Did they resent her intrusion on their little game that much? But to be afraid of her?

Tess never saw the maiming glare the captain shot

73

his crew.

"Lady Renfrew?"

Tess jolted, looking down to see that he was holding out his arm. She was about to tell him she was quite capable, then decided against it. When in Rome, she decided, slipping her hand into the curve of his elbow.

They strolled slowly, Dane naming each towering mast and snapping sail, its purpose, pointing out the quarterdeck, capstan, helm, where a very attractive blond man was manning the huge wheel. The ship was majestic, wood and brass gleaming in the bright sun, proof of hard work and diligence to keep the reproduction in perfect condition. Good Lord, she marveled, he must have sunk a fortune to play out his whims with such realism. Nevertheless, she absorbed it all, including the pride in his tone.

"It's beautiful, Captain, magnificent. I never imagined it to be this large."

"It must seem rather puny compared to your mysterious four-hundred-foot vessel," he whispered with a crooked smile.

"There really is no mystery, Captain," she began until she saw the look on his face. "Honestly, why do I even bother?" she muttered under her breath and for an instant thought he'd pat her on the head and say, "Yes dear, I understand, dear," so condescending was his expression.

"A word of warning, Lady Renfrew." She nodded, waiting. "You are forbidden to venture belowdecks."

She cast him a side glance. "And why is that?"

His lips quirked at her sudden rebelliousness. "There is no need."

"So you say."

"Duncan will see to anything you desire."

"So, I'm to be dumped on the poor unsuspecting McPete, is that it?" Laughter danced in her eyes.

"A job he would relish, I assure you." He sounded annoyed.

"I'm really a nuisance here, aren't I?" she said after a few steps.

"I apologize if I've given you that impression."

"You didn't, but I realize it now." She nodded to the men working, wondering how long they trained to be so good at their *jobs*. "You certainly have no need of inexperienced workers on your ship."

"I did not pull you out of the sea to put you to work, Lady Renfrew."

"I've never accepted charity."

Dane felt her stiffen beside him, saw indignation leap into her eyes. Proud wench. "You are a guest." He put up a hand to halt her protest. "Please, m'lady," he said tiredly, a teasing light sprinkling his tanned features. "Indulge the captain in his whims. He has so very few these days."

Tess tilted her head, smiling. "Well, if you're going to be a pest about it, sure."

"I am truly honored," he quipped dryly, pausing to give her a mocking bow.

She couldn't suppress a short laugh at his dramatics. "Duncan said this ship had twenty-four guns. So where are they?"

"Second deck." He gestured toward the fat quartz prisms set flush with the wood deck to catch sunlight and cast it below. "When I commissioned William Hacket with her construction, I made a few adjust-

75

ments. Cannons, rods, balls, and powder take up valuable space when a battle is being waged."

That brought her up short. She stared into his eyes, failing to decipher the joke hidden within. He honestly believed he'd do battle with a cutlass and flintlock pistols and his twenty-four cannons! Impossible. There had to be a law against actually arming a vessel like this. There had to be.

Frightened? he wondered, for she was looking at him as if he'd magically lost his ears.

"Wha-what other changes did you make?" she asked, trying to forget he was nuts. A confrontation? Nah, never happen.

Unconsciously Dane gave the small hand tucked at his elbow a reassuring pat. "My cabin for one. The ceiling on a ship is usually so low one must constantly stoop."

That statement answered itself, Tess decided, looking him up and down and enjoying every second of it. He had to be well over six feet, splendidly packed with enough tanned muscle to keep a girl occupied for days, eccentric or not.

Sweet Neptune save me from those blatant eyes, Dane thought, his body suddenly challenging his control. It was refreshing to discover a female who hid nothing of her emotions and, ah God, her desires. "I also had some other personal items added," he said, slighty strained.

"Duncan mentioned that it was unusual to have a bathroom, tub, and—"

"My bed," he finished in an intimate tone, a devilish smile playing on his lips, and Tess felt her knees instantly liquify. "Usually there's a bunk built into the wall, but I find little comfort in being squeezed into a drawer when I need rest."

She frowned thoughtfully up at him. "You've been sleeping out here, haven't you?" His expression remained impassive. "You have!" She twisted away. "Oh, now I really feel like an intruder." She'd been shoved out into the cold once too often as a child and didn't care to do it to anyone else.

He caught her shoulders and spun her back around, mint eyes demanding her full attention. "In this weather I usually sleep on deck, Lady Renfrew. To be honest, I wonder if you are not suffocating in that airless room."

"Cabin," she corrected.

He grinned crookedly, and those dimples made her insides jingle. "Do not fret over something so insignificant. And I shan't —"

His words stopped when her eyes suddenly went round as saucers. He heard her breath catch in her throat an instant before her head whipped to one side. As if some force willed it, she tore from his grasp and ran to the bow, lacy skirts hiked up to her calves. Her mind has snapped, he thought with horror, momentarily stunned. Then his heart slammed against the wall of his chest as she agilely climbed out on the bowsprit. Dane raced after her, unaware that all activity on the vessel had ceased.

Chapter Seven

Dane grabbed Tess around the waist and yanked her back onto the deck, then roughly spun her about to face him.

"God's teeth, woman!" His fingers dug into her shoulders. "What the ruddy hell were you trying to do?" he shouted, his expression sharp and harsh.

Breathless, Tess blinked at the rage directed at her. "I-I—why on earth did you do that?" His eyes bored into hers, and she was touched, suddenly remembering that all he knew of her was that she'd jumped off the *Nassau Queen*. "No one is trying to kill me now, Captain. I wasn't going to jump. I only wanted to see the dolphin."

Dane searched her upturned face, the openness clear on her delicate features. She was telling the truth. Or was she? With a demented mind one could never be certain. Damn! It was bloody unfair.

"Captain? You're hurting me." She spoke softly, laying a hand on his arm. Her touch burned through the fabric of his sleeve, jarring him, his expression softening slightly while callused hands gently rubbed her shoulders.

"I fear you shall have bruises because of my—my—" He sighed, dropping his arms. Christ, his heart was still pounding like a thoroughbred's at full speed.

"Your what, Captain?" Her smile was impish. "Concern? Rage? What is it?"

That this slip of a woman could twist his carefully controlled emotions so profoundly tore at his vitals. His crew had witnessed this, he realized at the ominous silence. When had he become so lax, so easily maneuvered by her smiles and frankness? He'd always preferred quieter women, certainly ones with a bit more flesh to their bones. Blast it! He'd lost sight of his purpose the instant he'd dragged the woman aboard. Foes were going unvanquished while he chased after a female with half a brain in her skull.

Tess saw the change in him, like the dawning of a new idea.

"As captain of this ship, Lady Renfrew," his tone was brisk, cold, "I demand that in the future you refrain from being quite so exuberant in public."

She planted her hands on her hips. "Demand all you want, Blackwell. And see how far that gets you," she said, matching his sudden change of mood. "And I might suggest you do the same. You were the one making a spectacle of yourself."

"And what, pray tell, do you call exposing your—your—" he waved at her skirts, "person to my crew, *running* across the deck and—God save us—climbing onto the bowsprit like a God-rotten street urchin?"

It was the way he'd said "street urchin" with such disgust that Tess felt it like the burn of a slap. It was

79

what she was. A survivor. And the look on his face was painfully familiar, like the people who saw her digging through garbage cans for scraps of food and discarded clothing or shoved her away because she stank for lack of washing; she would have, had she known even the essentials of decent hygiene. She was only four years old then. Tess was proud she'd survived long enough for the Sergeant Major to rescue her from that ugly world. And in Captain Blackwell's eccentric brain, he chose to believe she was someone worthy of his attention, calling her lady and madame, because if he didn't, he'd feel uncomfortable around her. Like those faceless strangers. Whether it was just his attempt to make the game more real or not, she could never be certain. Damn him! Oh, he made her body and heart do all sorts of nice, warm things, but his snotty lord-of-the-manor attitude just trashed it. Probably regretted ever pulling her out of the ocean, she thought, hurt beyond reason.

"Just because I'm dressed in this," she plucked at her skirt, "doesn't change who I am, Captain Blackwell. I'm quite comfortable with that, but if you aren't, then put me ashore, a.s.a.p."

He scowled. "A.S.A.P.?"

"As soon as possible."

"Be assured I will."

"Good!"

"Fine!"

"Pardon the intrusion, Captain."

Dane's head snapped to the side. "What now, Mr. Thorpe?"

Gaelan pointed. "There, sir."

They all turned to see the gray beast skimming the

80

water on his flukes. Tess ran to the rail, waving at the dolphin's antics.

"Hello, sweet baby," she called out. "I'm fine, see?" The dolphin leapt, plunged into the sea, then broke the surface in a smooth arch and dove again beneath the waves. Over and over he popped up and down, chittering wildly, moving closer. "Did you miss me?" Richmond squeaked, his entire body nodding in agreement. "I missed you, too. It was nice of you to stick around."

Dane stared, shocked that the lass seemed to have command of the grampus, and it appeared they could actually communicate. Dear God! What kind of woman was this?

Then the air was suddenly punctured with sharp demands and fearful cries.

"God save us, she ken talk to the grampus! I tol' you she be a bloody witch!"

"Aye! A sorceress! Send her over, Capt'n. Be rid of her now!"

"We're doomed if she stays. Cursed, I tell you!"

"Aye. Damned pretty clothes ain't changin' what she is!"

Tess turned slowly, struck numb with what she heard, then saw. Captain Blackwell stood a few feet from her, silent, hands braced on his hips, his expression more than leery. Not so for the rest of his crew, their faces depicting a bizarre mix of terror and anger, swords and vicious-looking knives, spikes, and hooks drawn and primed for attack. On her.

This was definitely not the Welcome Wagon.

No one moved. Her heart ricocheted in her chest. And in a split second, she remembered a visit to Fort

Wayne where everyone in the wood structure spoke and acted as if they were living back hundreds of years. They'd labored at chores, making everything by hand, even cooking over an open hearth, and the people refused to be swayed into speaking of the twentieth century. Was this truly the same? Like those men who reenacted the battles of the Civil War? Were they all so engulfed in the fantasy they'd forgotten it was fake? Tess examined each face, the fingers flexing weapons, and could find no hint of reality in anyone. This is ludicrous, she thought wildly, her gaze locking with Blackwell's. She took a step, lifting a hand to the captain.

"Come on now. A witch? Be serious, Blackwell. Tell me you—" A movement beyond him caught her attention.

Tess froze, her arm outstretched, eyes rounding, unable to move as a huge hook winch dangling at the end of a taut rope came singing through the air toward her head.

Dane whirled about and without a moment's hesitation flung himself into the path of the razor-sharp sickle, grabbing Tess around the waist, shielding her as he dropped to the deck just as the brass hook imbedded itself in the bowsprit.

The breath knocked out of her at the impact, she gasped, sucking deeply to refill her lungs, wincing as stinging pain shot up her body from her knees. Pressing her forehead to the deck, she waited for everything to come back into focus.

"Are you injured?"

"No," she muttered to the wood. "How about you?"

"Nay, nay, I am well," he said impatiently. "Are you certain you're unharmed?"

"Yes," she gasped. "Although breathing easily is an entirely different matter. Good gravy, you weigh a ton, Blackwell."

His lips quirked briefly as he eased himself off her and sat upright.

Tess inhaled slowly before pushing herself off the deck, brushing the braid out of her face. She didn't do more than that when she heard him curse and was swept up into his arms. He straightened and headed for the passageway.

"Put me down, Blackwell."

"You're bleeding."

She looked at the source of her pain. "Scraped elbows, big deal. I've hit the ground with more speed than that before." His brow arched, puzzled, but he didn't stop moving. "I can walk by myself."

" 'Tis likely so, Lady Renfrew, but I shall not chance it."

Just a moment ago he wouldn't even open his mouth in her defense before his crew's ridiculous accusations, and now he was playing Sir Galahad! "Listen up, Captain Blackwell," she said lowly. "If you don't put me down this instant, you'll see exactly how much of a *God-rotten street urchin* I am!"

Her wounded tone gave him pause, and he stopped, gently setting her on her feet. Her lips thinned, and she seemed about to say something, then decided against it and turned away, spine rigid as she walked toward the passageway.

After a few paces she stopped. "Thank you for saving me, Captain Blackwell," she murmured tightly without looking at him, then continued on her way.

Dane scowled at the hatch long after she'd closed it behind her. Somehow he'd hurt her feelings, deeply. He knew his temper had bested him when she'd climbed the bowsprit and he'd lashed out, but when he'd seen that winch coming toward her heart, all his misgivings had vanished. Blast the troublesome wench, he thought as his first mate came up beside him.

"Well, Mr. Thorpe?" His gaze never left the door.

" 'Twas Mr. Potts's station, sir. He insists 'twas an accident."

"Not bloody likely," Dane muttered, storming up to the quarter deck.

Tess was fuming. Hurt, angry, and shaken by what happened, she paced the cabin, deep in her own torment. Every member of this ship seems unwilling to bend from the fantasy, including its captain. No one would allow a twentieth-century thought to even enter his stupid head. What about that hook thing? Surely *that* was an accident. And were they so caught up they couldn't discern fantasy from reality? And where did that leave her? The only guest to this bizarre scenario? Days, possibly weeks, from civilization on a boatload of loonies? She'd have to wait this out, wait to be put ashore or for a rescue party, which meant she had to first be discovered missing. And only Penny could do that. Tess stopped pacing. God. She must be going crazy by now. A week on the cruise ship, forty-eight hours maybe, in the water, Tess calculated, not to mention however long to recover.

Yeah, Pen would be in a fine panic, feeling guilty about it, too. Tess prayed the actress didn't catch any backlash over the theft; the whole plan was to keep her name out of it. Jesus, what a mess!

Conceding that now was not the time to ask the captain if he had a HAM radio aboard so she could contact Penny, Tess tried to remember her history lessons and the beliefs of the eighteenth century. Information was power, she decided, mentally reciting what she knew from the American Revolution onward. 1782, England recognizes the independence of the U.S. Massachusetts Supreme Court outlaws slavery. Let's see, 1788, Continental Convention held in Philadelphia; 1789; Washington elected president.

"What else, what else?" She thumped the heel of her hand against her forehead as if it would make the information surface. "Oh, crap! What's the use?" she mumbled. "Nothing I can remember will be any help. To them I'm a damn witch!"

They once hanged suspected witches, she suddenly recalled, locked them in stocks or burned them at the stake. Would they take it that far, to actually physically harm someone for simply answering the playful antics of a dolphin?

It wasn't that Tess couldn't believe they thought her a witch—true witches existed, she herself knew of one *white* witch, a healer actually—but it was the manner the crew went about *voicing* their strong opinions. She shook her head, recognizing Dane's crew sincerely believed in the existence of the opposite, the black witch or warlock, fostered by legend, brewed in the frightened imagination. Black magic had nothing to do with true witchcraft, but everything to do with

Satanism. Obeah worship, Nazis, and demented creatures like Charles Manson were continuous testimony of the people who practiced such garbage. Truly offended they considered her to be of the latter quality, she plopped on the bed, deciding she knew nothing useful to ease their twisted fears.

A howling cry brought her to her feet. Tess waited, breathlessly counting the passing seconds, certain it had been the wind. Then it came again, louder, and before it faded to a low wail, she gathered up her skirts and fled the cabin. Tess ran down the corridor with surprising speed. Racing onto the deck, what she saw was like a kick in the teeth. Bare from the waist up with his arms stretched above his head and lashed to the mast pole, a man was being whipped.

Crewmen shielded her from a better look, but she could see the man's skin was already bleeding from the two previous strikes. Out of breath, she pushed her way between the smelly bodies, then froze, horrified as a sailor's arm drew back, then descended sharply, nine knotted tails slapping bare skin, curling around its victim's chest. The man screamed, his body going rigid, back arching, and Tess's knees wobbled. Her gaze shot to where the captain stood, motionless, fists clenched at his side, his expression impassive, carved in stone.

Dane cringed inwardly as the whip cracked but forced himself to watch, no matter how much it appalled him. The boatswain had been careless. Whether it was intentional or not, he could never be certain, but the inexcusable neglect nearly caused the lady's demise. In that, Dane was unforgiving. The whip raised again.

"Nooooo!" Tess screamed as she lunged forward, putting herself between the prisoner and the whip. Her breath hissed out as the thin tarred hemp bit into her tender skin and she recognized the captain's curse above the surprised shouts floating around her.

"Mother of God!" the second mate uttered, dropping the whip as if burned. He snapped a frightened look to his captain. "Beggin' the captain's forgiveness, sir, I didn't see her! I swear — !"

Dane lashed a hand through the air for silence, his gaze on the ugly welt rising on her shoulder. God curse this day, he thought.

Gritting her teeth against the searing pain, Tess turned abruptly, arms thrown back to protect the victim. "Blackwell, you bastard! What the hell are you doing?"

"It is not your concern, woman. Get below." His voice was even.

"The hell I will! This is barbaric!"

Dane didn't take his gaze from hers. "Mr. Thorpe, escort Lady Renfrew to my cabin." The words rang as icy as the look in his eyes. Pale, furious, white frost.

The first mate made a move toward her. "Touch me and you're dead meat, buster," she sneered at the blond, still shielding the young man.

Duncan stepped forward, his gaze shifting between the lady and his captain. "Please, m'lady, do not interfere."

"Put a sock in it, McPete," she barked, her eyes still on the captain. "I'm not budging until someone explains!"

Duncan looked to the captain, and Dane nodded curtly, his temper barely held in check. " 'Twas Mr.

87

Potts that allowed the winch to come unhitched," he said uneasily from her side. "He is the cause of your near death."

"So you're beating the pulp out of him? Good God, Blackwell! It was an accident toward me, and I should be the one to bring charges, if—I—wish!"

"Lady Renfrew," Dane began in a tone that formed icicles. "This is my ship—"

"And of course, you're lord and master. How foolish of me to forget," she said, contemptuously looking him up and down. "You disgust me, Blackwell. I thought you well beyond anything this—"she lashed a hand to the whip lying at his feet—"revolting."

Her words sliced him to the bone. She couldn't know how much the punishment sickened him. Yet to be lenient would mean chaos, a crew who lacked respect for him, his decisions. And by God, it was not her place to question the matter! Couldn't she see they wanted her gone anyway they could!

"Missy! Don't. I beg of you. 'Twill go worse for me." The plea came from behind her, and Tess twisted slightly, nose to nose with the seaman.

"Did you really try to hurt me, Potts?"

He turned his face away, ashamed.

"My God, why?" Her voice cracked.

"You be a witc—I thought you was goin' to hurt me captain," he finished lamely.

Such mindless loyalty, Tess thought, shooting a disfiguring glare toward Dane. "You're all sick, and you deserve whatever your warped imaginations can come up with," she sneered over her shoulder, trying to release the man's bonds.

She didn't see Dane tiredly plow his fingers through

88

his hair, then nod to Mr. Thorpe before the man came to her aid. Ignoring the first mate's wary looks, Tess stormed purposefully down the deck to the bow, the captain hot on her heels as she withdrew a handled peg from the rail. She spun about and held it out to Dane.

"Hit it against the side of the hull."

He scowled. "Get below, Tess."

"Now you call me Tess! Well, you lost that right, *Captain*. I dare you. Hit the rail, the deck, anything."

"Is there a purpose to this insanity?" he ground out, hands on his hips.

"I'm distraught. Humor me."

"So help me, woman—"

"Scared, Blackwell?"

His nerves singing, Dane knew he was being goaded as he yanked the marlin spike from her grasp, then knelt, pounding the deck, then the inner hull, taking out his rage on the frigate.

"What in God's name is this supposed to accomplish?" he gnashed up at her.

"I know you lack intelligence, Blackwell, but try. I'm proving a point." A taut wire was strung between them, and she knew if something didn't happen to change it, it would snap and any friendship they'd formed would be destroyed.

"Keep tapping," she told him as he straightened before her.

"You're mad," he growled, thumping the rail.

Her laugh was ugly, tight. "Me? What do you call beating a man as if he were nothing more than an rug?"

He ran his fingers through his already mussed hair,

hating the disgust he saw in her eyes. "You do not understand—"

"You're right, I don't understand," she cut in, her outrage overriding what his nearness did to her. Her gaze encompassed the entire ship in one sweep, irrational reasons for this fiasco struggling to congeal in her brain. "And I never will, Blackwell." She met his gaze. "Not in a hundred years."

A piercing sound spiked the air, and she leaned over the rail, the crew gravitating with her. The white-bellied dolphin chittered happily on the port side, diving beneath the surface and coming up in one graceful arch.

"By the saints, lass," Duncan asked from her side. "How did you call him?"

"I didn't. Dolphins respond to sound vibration." She looked pointedly at Dane, lifting a gently tapered brow. "Now who's the witch, Blackwell?" she said softly, then turned away from him, pushing through the throng of men.

Chapter Eight

Dane stood outside the door to his cabin, his fist raised to knock. Why was he hesitating? Perchance he knew he wouldn't be greeted kindly when he entered. His mind's eye mirrored the rage on her face, the ugly words she'd spat at him over Mr. Potts's punishment. Disgust, sick, barbarian—bastard. They were like knives to his heart.

It was *she* he was trying to protect, *her* honor he strove to regain in the eyes of his crew. And it was only the Lady Renfrew, it seemed, who possessed the ability to wound him with naught but those smoky eyes. Damnation, what was it about the wench that stripped him of all logical thought? He lowered his arm and turned away, deciding he needed to think on the matter a while.

Duncan rapped softly; then, with no answer forthcoming, he opened the door a crack and peered inside. His shoulders drooped as he spied the lady sitting on the window bench, gazing out onto the ocean. She hadn't moved since this morn. Poor lass, he thought, stepping inside and quietly setting the dinner tray on the table.

"You best be eatin' something, m'lady." He spoke softly so as not to disturb her more than was necessary. Her response was an almost imperceptible nod. "Aw, lassie," he said sympathetically, moving closer. "You shouldn't take it all so hard."

"You don't understand, Duncan. What I saw goes against everything I believe in. And that the captain condoned such an act—"

"He doesn't."

Tess jerked around. "What do you mean?" she demanded sharply. "He ordered it, didn't he?"

Duncan's chest tightened at the tearstained cheeks, the disenchantment in her eyes. "The capt'n, miss, well, it troubles him sorely to order such harsh punishment, but—" He held up a hand to stop her question. "He must. Whether you were harmed is not the soul of the matter."

He gestured to the space beside her, and she nodded, pulling her skirts close as he seated himself. He sighed deeply before he spoke. "You see, miss, had Mr. Potts allowed the winch to be released, regardless if you had been in its path, he would have been punished. If not, the crew would be believin' the capt'n didn't have pride in his vessel, nor in them. And when he issued an order 'twould be done lazily or perhaps not at all."

Like being reprimanded for failing in your job, she reasoned. "But Mr. Potts said he did it because he thought *I* would harm the captain. How much more loyalty does Blackwell want?"

He shook his head. " 'Tis been loyalty well earned, that I can tell you truly. I'd give me life for the capt'n, as would any man aboard, and I can count one occasion more than I care to of when the boy's—eh, the capt'n's risked all to save just one of us." His eyes sparked with pride. "Aye. He's a fair man, lass. Fairer than any capt'n most of these men have served afore. Such a careless act as Mr. Potts is guilty of could possibly be the cause of all our deaths. Harken to me." He shook a finger for emphasis, then caught himself, reddening. "The *Sea Witch* needs every able hand mannin' his station and doin' his job or 'tis no doubt she'd perish."

Tess stared blankly at Duncan. Beam me up, Scotty, she thought dismally. "Duncan, this isn't real. It's a game, a play, and you're all—actors. It's supposed to be *fun*."

The old man blinked, his brows raised high into his scalp. "I beg your pardon?"

"Blackwell is simply a bored little rich boy with money to burn and time to waste, and you're all participants in his little fantasy." Her tone was flat, tired.

He stood abruptly. "I don't know where you've gained such ridiculous information, but though Capt'n Blackwell be a wealthy sort, he's in these waters for a purpose! And I assure you, Lady Renfrew, he is neither bored or wasteful."

She latched onto that, for it was clear she wasn't going to get a confession to the masquerade. "And what *is* that purpose?"

Duncan turned his face away. " 'Tis not me place to speak of it," he muttered, then moved across the room to the cabinet and withdrew two small jars and a bottle. Without a word he went back to her, and whether she requested it or not, he tended the welt on her shoulder.

"I want to see Mr. Potts."

"The capt'n will not allow it."

"I don't care what he'll *allow*."

"The capt'n saw to the lad's wounds himself."

Tess looked back over her shoulder. "Did he really?"

"I told you, miss. It sickened him as much as it did you." He paused, then added, " 'Twas the capt'n himself that tended *you,* lass, neglecting all else to see you through a dangerous fever."

For a full minute Tess allowed the thrill of those words wash over her. She rubbed her forehead. "I'm so confused, Duncan. He's been so kind to me and then to witness that behavior—I think you're all taking this too far. Blackwell could go to prison for that."

"Not likely. And be assured no one aboard believes 'twould come about." It was a quiet moment before he said softly, "It was your reputation he sought to clear."

She looked up, eyes round. With a beating?

"And whether it pleases you or nay, Lady Renfrew, here the capt'n is the law."

The law. Obviously there were rules to this game she wasn't aware of but they were eager to adhere to. Tess recalled the boatswain's confession. He knew the punishment before he let the hook loose, admitting his guilt. Christ, what else were they prepared to do for this adventure?

"How is Potts?" She couldn't help but be sympathetic to such a demented soul.

"At his duties."

"What? You can't be serious! He was so hurt." She started to rise, but he gently held her down.

"He considers himself fortunate to have received only two lashes to the ten ordered." He paused. "You're to be admired for your conviction, lass."

"Fat lot of good it did," she hissed when he applied a stinging lotion to her wound. "Why do they all think I'm a witch, Duncan?" She had to grasp their reasons, if anything, to get a handle on this.

He shrugged. "Tales are told, Davy Jones, sirens of the deep luring sailors to their death, and all they know of you is that you came from the sea."

So, she thought with a touch of surprise, Blackwell kept what he knew to himself. "And because they thought I could talk to the dolphin?"

"Aye." He finished the treatment and stepped back.

Tess turned fully, hands folded on her lap. "I can't, you know. It was merely his response to me. He *can* communicate, in his own way —" Why am I explaining all this? He had to know *that* much about the animals. God, she was starting to think like them!

Duncan saw her rising agitation and said, "A dolphin is good luck if it follows a ship."

"And a woman aboard is a curse!" came from the doorway and they both looked up to see the captain enter and toss several charts on the table. His expression said he was angry with her.

"Then put me ashore."

"Would that 'twere possible," Dane remarked a tad wistfully, then gestured sharply to Duncan. The old man gave her a sympathetic look, then went to the

95

captain. They spoke briefly, then Duncan turned toward the door, glancing uncertainly between the couple before he left them alone.

Tess was feeling a little guilty. Very little. She'd interfered in the workings of his ship, called him names before his crew, oh, jeez—and it was clear now her presence was no longer wanted. Not that it ever was, she thought, rising slowly from her seat. Why does that hurt so much? Because this is their party and you're the uninvited guest, or rather witch. But that didn't change how she felt about the whipping. Her gaze crept across the floor and up from his boots to meet those dangerous eyes. His body was rigid, a muscle working furiously in his jaw.

"Your shoulder?" It sounded like a demand.

"It's fine."

"Good. 'Twas extremely idiotic of you to put yourself into that situation."

Her dander rose. "Look, Blackwell, I'm sorry I've interfered in your fun, but—"

"Fun! You think I am here for bloody holiday!" His sharp bark of laughter made her flinch. "Woman, you are definitely the most confusing creature I have ever encountered. A man tries to kill you and you defend him, take a lash for him! Any other female would demand he be drawn and quartered!"

"That's disgusting!"

"Ahh well, at least your views of me have remained evergreen." Caustic, mocking.

"Why are you sailing in the West Indies?"

Something flickered in his pale eyes. "That—madame—is none of your business."

That stung. Tess walked across the room, her intention to go above deck, but she hadn't made it as far as the door when he grabbed her arm.

"Where, pray tell, do you think you're going?"

"For some fresh air. It's become noticeably colder in here."

"I forbid it."

"Guess again, Blackwell." She tried prying his fingers from her arm.

"You would risk your life for a few breaths of air?"

"Call me reckless."

"Damn it, woman!" He jerked on her arm. "Did this morn prove naught to you?"

She went still. "Yes, Blackwell, it certainly did."

Dane searched her face. She distrusted him. Perhaps loathed him, he feared. He'd worked himself into a splendid rage upon deck and had every intention of ignoring the woman and the power she wielded over him. He simply could not allow her to so undermine him, no matter how she felt. But with her alluring presence, his emotions were in a fine mess. He thought he'd had them sufficiently focused before he'd entered the cabin, but one look at her crestfallen expression and he felt ashamed. He shouldn't be, but he was. To have sunk so low in her eyes was a sensation he neither liked nor cared to admit.

She was a sadly twisted flower, he reminded himself. After all, she believed it to be the twentieth century? And did she not talk to the grampus? Was that why her family had set her adrift? For the lady's imagination was not to be believed. And her actions? Climbing the bowsprit!

"What are you thinking, Blackwell?" she whispered

softly, penetrating his thoughts. His expression had revealed so much in those few seconds.

"I was curious as to why you were so offended at the words 'street urchin'?"

Her gaze narrowed to mere slits. "That, Captain Blackwell, is none of *your* damn business."

"You curse like a fishwife."

"So do you."

"I'm a man."

A brow lifted. "Double standards, how unique."

"Nay, I dare say yours are much higher than mine."

"Let go of me, Blackwell."

Suddenly he pulled her into his arms, his gaze briefly slipping over her face before his lips crashed down onto hers. She fought him, pushing at his chest, her head thrashing from side to side. His response was to bury a hand in her hair, imprisoning her as he deepened his kiss to mind-boggling proportions, prying open her mouth and pushing his tongue inside. She moaned, small fists pounding his biceps and shoulders, trying to battle the gush of heat spilling over her body. He took her breath inside himself, pulling her flush against him, and even through the heavy layers of cloth Tess felt his arousal, bold and hard with his sudden need for her. Her! He was unrelenting, large hands moving urgently over her slimness, mastering her until she ceased her fight. Then, abruptly, he gentled his assault, caressing the curve of her back, lightly licking her bruised lips, then tasting her again with exquisite tenderness as if apologizing for his brutality.

"Let go."

"Nay, not yet," he murmured against her lips, his

strong arms swallowing her in his embrace as he captured her mouth again.

"Damn you, Blackwell," she whispered breathlessly when his lips drifted across her cheek to the sensitive flesh below her ear.

"Aye, damn me, but I cannot," he murmured huskily. "I cannot." He nibbled, pressing her tightly, her firm breasts mashing deliciously against the hard wall of his chest. She tilted her head back, and his lips moved to the soft swell above her breast, his tongue liquid over the pale softness. He heard the breath sigh out of her as her fingers slid into the hair at his nape, and Dane thought he'd die with the wondrous pleasure of her touch.

Tess gently rubbed the knotted muscles in his neck, wondering how her anger could dissolve so quickly as she allowed herself to be swept up into the storm of emotions raging within her. Surely Duncan was right, she questioned herself, and the captain had been forced to do what he did. That she could have been killed *was* accurate, but what of the harshness of the punishment? Was it all fake? No, the sting in her shoulder denied that. Yet now, with him touching her like this, she couldn't imagine him a cruel man. How could he run so hot and cold, worrying over her scraped elbows one second, ordering a whipping in the next? Could she forgive that possessed Captain Bligh side of him and draw the tender man back to reality—the man who'd saved her life twice? And why couldn't she count one mistake, not one slip up in the script of this voyage? Nothing was right about this place, this man, and what he did to her, and yet somehow, Tess felt Dane Blackwell had won more than just this battle.

He straightened, willing her to look him in the eye. Sooty dark lashes swept up, and Dane saw the turmoil written there. A callused finger brushed across her cheek, tucking a stray wisp behind her ear. "Do not worry yourself, little one." He saw moisture bloom in dove gray eyes.

Her hand moved into the soft raven curls at the back of his head, urging him closer. "Kiss me again, Blackwell." Her voice shook, the soft plea sounding desperate.

Unable to deny his own need of her, his warm lips brushed hers, a whispery breath across velvet petals, and Tess leaned into him, allowing his sensuality to drape over her misery. *Forgive him,* a voice urged. A lump formed in her throat as he worshiped her lips, and she lost herself in a hunger she never knew she possessed.

Neither heard the door open.

Gaelan Thorpe stood in the doorway, watching the passionate embrace, envious of his captain and the beauty he held in his arms. He smiled to himself. The man had been furious enough to chew nails but minutes before. This must be a new way to express one's pique, he thought cheekily, then cleared his throat when the second mate came up behind him.

Tess's head jerked back, her gaze darting over Dane's shoulder to the men converging in the doorway.

"Do not be ashamed, fair sweet," he whispered, instantly feeling her desire to hide.

"I'm not," she lied softly, trying to move away. "Please, let me go, Captain." He did, and she felt

100

small, embarrassed, an unaccustomed blush, and couldn't comprehend any of it. It was only a kiss, well, more than a simple kiss, but — good gravy, what's the matter with me, she agonized.

"Come inside, gentlemen," Dane ordered, frowning at her strained expression. Only his eyes shifted. "And since you have chosen to be rude enough not to make yourself known, Mr. Thorpe, I will deny you proper introductions — for the time."

Tess's head snapped up at the icy tone, and she saw the first mate flush, then look at his boots.

Dane knew she was going to run. He reached for her, but she was already out the door, pink skirts fluttering around the door jamb.

"I apologize, sir."

Dane's gaze honed in on Thorpe. "You will, to the lady. But later." With a dismissing glance at the door, he unrolled a chart onto the long table, spreading his palms over the corners. His cool green eyes measured each of his officers. "Now, gentlemen, in a few hours she should be close enough to show us her colors."

"Aye, sir," they said in unison, eager for the conflict.

Chapter Nine

Deep in her own confusion, Tess didn't notice the activity surrounding her as she grasped the railing and filled her lungs again and again with crisp, salty air. Why did she run? Was she going crazy? God, she felt like she was being sucked into a whirlpool, caught in their game. And having a tough time separating their reality from hers. She fought back the rush of tears, her mind spinning with thoughts and reasons. Adapt, overcome, she commanded herself, shoving her emotions aside and attempting to discover a logical excuse for what was happening to her. No, not to her, but these men.

A "Fantasy Island" was how she'd explained it away before, but even in a good play someone makes a slip, blows a line. And of course her arrival hadn't been expected. Yet that curve thrown hadn't fazed them much. But she still couldn't dismiss the fact that they'd beaten a man. What else could she do about it that she hadn't already? Not a damn thing. Each man knew the consequences and accepted them. She'd already absolved the whole mess knowing Captain

Blackwell patched up the young man himself. Going soft, Renfrew.

Regardless, there were other confusing factors; Tess couldn't find even the slightest discrepancy in the authenticity of the ship, its furniture, the clothing. She looked down at her gown, examining the seams, and was surprised to find the stitching small, erratically even, yet not very tight as a sewing machine would have made. Aw, jeez, hand sewn!

Her hand shook as she covered her mouth. It was as if she was misplaced in a different time, and until they let her go, took her to shore, she was a prisoner in this bizarre production. If what Duncan had told her was to be believed, they were all here for a reason, some mysterious quest, and ready to pay any price to play it out. With their captain. Dane Alexander Blackwell. Fire and ice. Half animal, half gentleman.

The man was gorgeous, sexy, too damn masculine for his own good and, and—and when he touches me I melt into a puddle, she confessed silently. Even when he's angry, he excites the heck out of me. No man had made her feel so much in such a short time. The power and sensuality he exuded set off danger signals in her head, but a moment in those strong arms, with him kissing her—God, it was worth the risk! She felt like a real woman when he was near, feminine, delicate, seductive. Just thinking about him made her uncertainly warm. Whoa, Tess, she scolded herself. Keep your head together. You can't get involved. It can't go any further than a kiss, and that was already more than she'd done with any man after so short an acquaintance. This will be over soon, and—she braced her elbows on the wood, dropping

103

her chin into her palms with a sigh, deciding she'd never had a more interesting time in her life. Chaos or not.

She'd calmed down considerably when a shout brought her around. Men climbed high into the rigging, checked sails, pulled ropes, lines, secured hooks, and cleared the deck for an unobstructed path. Moving faster, more efficiently than before, she thought, walking toward the bow to see if the dolphin was still near. She couldn't help but notice how the crew sent her cautious glances, hoping not to be caught staring. Several made a big show of moving far out of her way until she passed, as if she had some contagious disease, and if she happened to meet with a crew member's gaze, a sudden fear made him look quickly away, his attention instantly engrossed in his duties. If they wanted to keep their emotions secret, they were lousy at it. Feeling like an intruder in the biggest way made Tess turn back toward the passageway.

"I say we do away with her ourselves," a deck hand muttered to his comrades after casting a suspicious glance at the woman's retreating form.

"Yer a damned fool, Sikes, if you think the capt'n would allow us to see morn."

"Aye," several agreed with quick nods.

"I'll not be party to murder," another added, shaking his head as he twined a keel of rope.

"She ain't a witch, and yer all daft."

Heads jerked up to see the boatswain moving into the small circle.

"How ken you be sayin' that, Mr. Potts?" Sikes demanded. " 'Twas you that—"

104

"I know that! But the lady took a lash for me. 'Tis not something I ken forget. She stood up to the capt'n, din she? Anyone a' you ever dare do that?"

" 'Tis proof then!"

"Nay," a burly man said, bending to the small group. "But we'll be needin' proof she's a true witch."

"Or proof she ain't," Potts said, his ire pricked.

"You'd risk yer job fer her?" someone asked.

Evan Potts stared at his bare toe for a moment. He didn't know what she was, but she couldn't be evil. Not and care about a nobody like him, enough to court the capt'n's wrath on his behalf. Potts lifted his gaze to his mates.

"Aye. I would."

Standing outside the cabin, Tess could hear the murmurs of conversation. What could they be discussing? She hated to interrupt, but since she wasn't allowed to go anywhere else on the ship, she knocked. The door opened.

A young man, dark haired and very tanned, smiled, his brown eyes briefly glazing over her before he stepped back.

"M'lady," Aaron Finch said, making an elaborate sweeping bow and hoping it was his finest.

All conversation suddenly halted, several pairs of eyes going to the woman on the threshold.

"I'm sorry. I seem to be in the way no matter where I go today."

Several looked away at her bold reminder, and there was a pregnant silence before Duncan took the initiative.

"Nay, lass," he said gently as he grasped her hand, pulling her inside.

Her gaze drifted to the captain, and he smiled softly. It was like a magical spell, those mint eyes, those dimples. Tess felt a bizarre shift of emotions as he moved around the table toward her. He stopped very close, and she couldn't help but recall his brutal kiss and how intimately it ended. She flushed at his rascally expression. Christ, he knows what I'm thinking. Fleetingly she wished they were alone.

Dane absorbed the sensual look in her eyes and prayed it meant more than he was forgiven for any pain he'd caused her. He ached to kiss her. Sweet Neptune, but he'd been unable to concentrate with her out of his sight, fearing for her safety on deck alone with no protector. But he'd had plans to make and knew there wasn't a man aboard who would dare test him further this day.

Gaelan Thorpe's gaze bounced between the captain and Lady Renfrew. They were in each other's pockets without ever touching, he mused, jealous at Dane's good fortune.

"You promised introductions, Capt'n," Gaelan encouraged.

Dane dragged his gaze from Tess. Eager puppies, he thought, irritated at their roving eyes. He sighed, facing them, and with a great deal of formality, introduced his first officers to Tess. He was thankful the men showed their best behavior, keeping their language pure, the remarks wittier than the next. Which put a strain on their manners, he mused, considering the last time they'd been in the company of one so fair. The bows were so elaborate Dane fought the urge

106

to laugh, then glared the drooling sots back when the kisses to the back of her hand lingered a bit longer than was truly proper. When, in a soft whisper, Gaelan apologized for intruding before, Dane felt a peculiar, and definitely unwanted, emotion when she brushed the whole event aside as if it were naught.

"May I get you some refreshment, Lady Renfrew?" Gaelan asked.

"No, thank you," she replied, not caring to be the center of their attention just now.

"A chair perhaps?" Aaron asked, offering his own. "You must be fatigued?"

She shook her head. "I'm fine, gentlemen, please don't let me disturb your meeting," she said, then started to move away. She glanced down at the maps, then did a double take. "This map is wrong," she told them, bending over for a better look. She scanned the markings on crude parchment. "There's an island or two somewhere around here." Her finger vaguely circled the area. "I'm sure of it." When she straightened, it was to see several indulgent smiles. They didn't believe her! She shrugged. "Suit yourselves." It was one thing to play as if in the eighteenth century, but an island was an island, she thought peevishly, and it couldn't be placed elsewhere for the thrill of the game.

"You can read a map?" Gaelan asked.

"Of course I can!" Her ire rose with those surprised looks. "I know you guys don't want me here, and I can't begin to imagine what you think of me, but it clearly isn't as though I don't have a brain in my head! That map is incorrect, but if you all insist on—"she snapped her mouth shut. "Never mind," Tess muttered, feeling waspish. What was the use? Accept it, believe as they did. Her mind would certainly be more stable if she could. "Why don't you just break your silence and radio the Coast Guard to come pick me up?" she said to the captain. His frown deepened to a scowl, and her gaze moved to his men, pleading for a crumb of confirmation.

A couple of men cleared their throats and looked away; others glanced at each other in utter confusion.

"Ra-di-o, m'lady?" Aaron questioned, a wide-eyed puzzled look on his young face.

"What is a 'Coast Guard'?" Gaelen asked carefully.

"You're a seaman, Mr. Thorpe, figure it out." When he continued to stare at her, she practically shouted, "They *guard* the *coast!*" then spun away, moving to the large window and wrapping her arms around her middle.

"Sir, forgive me. If we've upset the lady, I shall—" Aaron Finch cut his words off when his captain inclined his head sharply for them to vacate his cabin.

"No one meant to insult you, m'lady," he said after they'd departed.

She laughed short and without humor. "Yeah, right. They just think I'm playing with half a deck." And I know *they* are. If she played along better she'd certainly look less of a fool. "When do we get to shore, Captain?"

Dane took one last look at the map before he rolled it up and tied the hide lacing. Phillip was on one of those uncharted islands. He was sure of it. Yet without any coordinates he'd been unable to locate the exact one. How could she know of its existence? He'd

108

only gleaned that much from crude translations with a few natives and an old Dutch missionary.

When he didn't answer, Tess glanced over her shoulder. "Blackwell," she persisted. "When do we get to dry land?"

"We don't."

He removed his sword and belt from a series of hooks on the wall, strapping them on as he strode to the hutch. Opening a drawer, he removed a large wood box, then lifted the lid. Tess was mesmerized as he swiftly loaded two antique flintlock pistols, then shoved them in the band of his trousers. He slipped a knife into each boot, then removed a third from the drawer and walked over to her, holding it out.

Tess frowned between the vicious-looking blade and the man. "What are you up to now, Blackwell?"

"Take it, protect yourself."

"From what?"

"Stay below and lock the door behind me."

Tess shook her head. "Quit ignoring the question and tell me what's going on."

He grasped her hand, his eyes turning paler as he forced her to accept the sheathed knife. "Do not come on deck *for any reason*. Is that understood?"

Tess shrugged, then twisted slightly and tossed the knife on the velvet bench. When she turned back, he was already stepping out the door, a hand on the latch.

"How did you know the existence of the islands?" he asked softly, his back to her.

"I've seen it on a tourist map. Or have you forgotten that *I* still live in the twentieth century?"

His broad shoulders sagged a bit. "Nay, Lady Renfrew, I have not forgotten." Then he closed the door behind him.

Over the stern of his ship, Dane sighted down the scope, his lips pulling into a thin line. The vessel was weaving, shifting ballast, trimming sail, testing her speed. Showing her muscle. A sure sign she intended to do battle.

"Wind speed, Mr. Finch?"

"Twenty knots, sir."

"Ours?" Dane lowered the scope.

"Nearly twelve, sir."

The captain muttered a curse, squinting against the setting sun. The brig was sleeker, mayhaps a touch faster, for her hull was empty, above her water line; she'd covered too much distance not to be.

"Mr. Thorpe, full sail. Let's not give her a gander at what she's challenged." The boatswain's whistle shrilled and men scurried up the rigging. "Mr. Potts?"

"Aye, sir?"

"Is your station fit?"

Potts flushed, then straightened his shoulders and met the captain's ice green eyes. His duties included the charge of the forward hull, its equipment. "Aye-aye, Capt'n. Fo'c'sle cannons ready an' armed."

The captain nodded sharply, calling for reports from the gun deck. Men bellowed into funnels, deep voices carrying down through narrow pipes running between decks, alleviating the confusion in the companionway.

His legs braced wide apart, the stiff breeze plastering his dark shirt to his chest, the formidable Captain

Blackwell on the quarter deck instilled confidence in the men preparing for battle. He watched the brig approach. The *Sea Witch* was swift, strong, heavily gunned, and Dane knew how to maneuver her as instinctively as he breathed. Though the sun was rapidly descending, the frigate had one more advantage; she was painted pitch black and now sported solid black sails.

His gaze darted to each station checking the area, then he nodded to a crew man. Lifting the scope to his eye, he could count her guns, fewer than eighteen topside, and could make out her numbers to be half his own. Silently he said a prayer that she would not engage, for their sake. Another champion, Phillip? Bloody coward, he thought, hoping the worm was aboard, itching to run the bastard through himself.

For a brief instance his mind conjured his father, thin, pale, broken; his fortune gone; his home stolen, destroyed. And Desiree. His chest tightened, every muscle in his body clenching with reined anger as he remembered her unspeakable disgrace. The situation forced Dane to reassess his priorities, and somehow Lady Renfrew had slipped into that category, though he was loath to admit it. He lowered the spyglass and mashed a hand over his face, trying to clear his thoughts for what lay ahead.

"What's going on?"

His hand dropped sharply. Tess stood before him.

"Have you no sense at all! Get below!" The brig was swiftly approaching.

"I will not!" she blasted, hands on her hips. "And you don't have to bite my head off!"

A low growl rumbled in his chest as he advanced,

111

and she took a step back, bumping into the rail. He caught her shoulders. "Must you always fight me?"

She twisted out of his grasp. "I don't *always* fight, Blackwell. Not until I met you. And you can't just give me a knife, tell me to protect myself, then order me to stay put! It doesn't work that way."

"It does on my ship! Now get below!"

"Hell, no!"

Heads came around at that. "Don't you understand?" he said, his gaze darting to the brig. "The sight of you aboard will be cause enough for attack!"

"That's ridiculous!" she scoffed.

He grabbed her by the arms, hoisting her off the deck and up in his face. "For the love of God, woman, get to safety! I cannot be worried for your life and my men and ship, too!"

She blinked. He looked so desperate she almost relented. "Don't you think you're overreacting just a bi—?" She was cut off in mid-sentence when he unceremoniously tossed her over his shoulder, then stormed to the passageway.

Her humiliation was nothing compared to the air being punched out of her lungs with each step he took, her pounding on his back of no consequence against his determination. He's enjoying this, she thought, his hands clasping her bottom and thighs with a bit too much familiarity. She felt a painful jolt as he kicked open the cabin door, and her ears were ringing when he pitched her on the bed. She started to get up, but he shoved her down, pointing a finger in her face.

"Stay there! Do not move or I swear, by all that is holy, I will tie you to this bed!"

She bristled at that. "Just try it, you ape, and—"

In a heartbeat he was in her face, hands braced at her hips, and he continued to bear down on her, forcing her to dig her head into the pillows.

"I cannot spare a man to post guard, but if forced, be assured I will. Is—that—clear!" A thin frost hung on the edge of his words, and Tess nodded mutely, fear stinging down her spine. He seemed to always be angry at her, but never like this. Black hair tumbled low on his forehead like a raven's wing, his expression dark, chiseled in amber, and those eyes belonged to a panther, the pupils mere slits of black. God, it was awesome.

He straightened abruptly, glowered down at her for a second, then turned away. She lay there frozen until her fear swiftly burst into indignation, and she leapt from the bed, racing after him. He was already closing the door, and she caught a sardonic smile as he shut it in her face. Her eyes widened when she heard the click of the lock. Tess paled with anger, so furious she could hardly speak. Not that it would do her any good to yell; she could already hear his boots thumping down the hall.

"Chauvinistic, sexist pig!" she muttered to the room. "He may as well have bashed me over the head with a club and dragged me down here by the hair!"

Tess tried the door anyway, then sighed back against it. Let them have their fun. She'd make that man's life a living hell until she got off this tub.

Chapter Ten

The sun and moon battled for supremacy for a breathless moment, the silver crescent claiming the victory high in the sky, waiting for the vanquished to slink in retreat. And like a gypsy's red coin slipping into an indigo silk bag, the sun disappeared beneath the horizon. Darkness quickly fell, blackening the sea, pearly moonlight streaming across the eerie calm like the gleam on polished onyx.

The *Sea Witch* plunged across the waters, allowing its pursuer to give chase for several miles, letting them believe she thought herself outmatched and wished to escape the conflict. As the captain anticipated, the brig lowered more sail and shifted ballast to increase her speed.

Dane's smile was thin. I'll give the bastard every advantage, he decided, refusing to fire the first shot. He spoke softly to the second mate.

"Trim a might off the fore, main, and mizzen sails, Mr. Finch. Discreetly. Let us give the lady something to be cocksure about."

Aaron smiled, and without benefit of whistle command, he quietly relayed the order, knowing this would slow them down a little, giving the brig a chance to keep them in her sights. The frigate's crew were well-sailed, and her captain knew how to get the best speed out of her. When the time was right.

The hour seemed to stretch in endless agony while the crew nervously waited, hearts pounding and cannons loaded for the attack. Not one man aboard doubted it would ensue. Three had come before her, and thrice they'd sent the vessels to haunt with Davy Jones. When the brig was close enough, the command came to extinguish all lanterns, and as if by the graceful stroke of an artist's brush, the *Sea Witch* melted into the night.

The brig was easily seen in the meager light, for she bore a white stripe above her water line, a foggy splash on the canvas of black. In the ordered silence, the men aboard the frigate heard confused voices carrying across the ocean. So close. Eyes shifted between the brig and their captain, each mate anticipating his signal. It was nearly relief when it finally came.

Rope creaked against wood as men strained to tack mizzen yard, position fore and aft booms. Black sails unfurled, whipping and cracking as they billowed, catching the wind and harnessing its invisible power. Swift and sharp the *Sea Witch* came about. The powerful frigate dipped windward, whispering across the inky velvet like a rapier through humid air. The brig had long since lost sight of her in the darkness and never realized she'd turned back and was now adjacent, sailing behind the dual-masted craft. Then the pitch black frigate maneuvered into fighting distance with all the noise of hungry shark.

* * *

Sprawled across the bed reading *Common Sense*, by Thomas Paine, Tess had already discarded her slippers, stockings, and the first three under petticoats because of the heat in the cabin. For the moment she'd given up the need to see Blackwell squirm with some sadistic revenge. Wasted energy, she decided, worrying over something she could not change, and gave up the attempt to understand the political theorist's writings. She closed the book and picked up another. *Gulliver's Travels*. Blackwell certainly had a wide variety: Chaucer, Shakespeare, Defoe. Some books were even written in French and Latin. Bet he can't read them, she thought maliciously, flopping over on her back and wishing she had a copy of S.E. Baker's latest spy thriller to lose herself in.

Thirsty, she rolled to the edge of the bed and reached for the pitcher. Suddenly the ship listed to one side, and the ceramic urn crashed to the floor. Tess caught the edge of the mattress, straining not to fall on the broken pottery until the vessel righted itself. She scooted to the center of the fluffy down, watching loose items roll off the desk.

"What in God's name are you up to now, Blackwell?" she muttered at the ceiling. When she deemed it safe, she climbed off the bed, cleaned up the porcelain shards, then moved to the desk, bending to pick up the charts and ledgers. A loud crack burst into the silence, and her yelp of surprise was immediately drowned by a thundering boom. Stunned, she dropped the ledgers. The frigate pitched furiously, and her arms waved in a useless attempt to grasp something stable. An instant later she found herself dumped on her rear. She stayed there for a second, cursing the handsome lunatic, working herself into a state of madness, then struggled in the limp skirts to stand.

She could hear rapid footsteps above her. Shouts from all directions but starboard. She whipped around toward the window, and her eyes widened. Bright flashes of light reflected off the ocean with every vibrating crash. Water sprayed in towering fountains as Tess groped her way to the velvet bench. She swallowed convulsively, plopping onto the seat, shocked beyond any further movement. She couldn't see much, but Lord, could she hear it. Screams of pain, of sheer agony echoed down to her, making her skin crawl up her neck. It was all so realistic! Then the frigate shuddered as it repaid cannon fire three times over. She heard water splash, wood crack, metal scrape against metal, and sails rip. Please don't let it be ours, she thought, not sure this ship could stand such an authentic reenactment. The odor of gunpowder drifted to her, and she watched in horror as a cannonball plopped into the ocean only a few yards from the open window, close enough to send water spraying in her face.

That's it, she thought, swiping at the dampness and latching the window. Tess left her seat and ran to the door, slapping the wood, desperate to get top side. She heard the thump of footsteps in a dead run outside and yelled to be let out. The steps slowed, paused, then raced away, their owner ignoring her call. This was insane! What if this tub actually sank? Frantically she jiggled the latch, but it wouldn't budge. Then she smiled, stepped back and lifted her skirts above her thighs. She concentrated and took aim, kicking the wood just before the latch. It gave the tiniest bit and with the sounds from above drowning any noise she made, Tess continued to kick with the ball of her foot until she heard the wood crack. She jerked and pulled at the latch, straining until it burst open, and for the second time she went flying across the room. No time to muster dignity, she thought, barely catching the table ledge, then racing out the door.

The passageway was clear, and she headed down the corridor. Yanking up her skirts in one hand, she paused before the hatch, bracing herself for what she might find. She could hear Blackwell shouting commands and curses. The roll of cannons moving back to be reloaded rumbled beneath her feet; then the ship lurched with another boom and she was thrown viciously against the door. It burst open at the impact, and she sailed out, sprawling onto the wet deck. Quickly Tess rolled into a sitting position, spellbound at what filled her vision.

Two sweaty men dueled with swords scarcely a yard from her, and she quickly scooted back out of their way. She heard one call the other a "scurvy rat" and saw him raise his sword. Light flickered off the steel as a man she recognized brought the blade down. The other man screamed horribly, and Tess gaped as a hand thunked to the deck before her knees, the quivering fingers still curled around the hilt of his own cutlass.

Her stomach lurched, her gaze snapping to the injured man in time to see his opponent send the blade into his chest. He howled before it poked out the other side, then crumpled to the deck in a twisted heap, blood still gushing from his stump. She scrambled to her feet and ran to the rail, vomiting over the side until she had nothing left. Tearing off a piece of her petticoat, she wiped her mouth, then tossed the scrap into the sea. When she turned back, the opponent and sword were gone, his kill bleeding on the wet planks. It isn't real, she reminded herself, trying to control her rapid breathing, forcing herself to move toward the man.

It's fake! Studio special effects.

She knelt, her arm shaking violently as it reached out, then jerked back before meeting the man's flesh. He's alive, she silently prayed and reached again. Her fingers trembled as she touched the warm skin at his throat. Tess searched for a pulse. Nothing. Her gaze shifted to the dark stain spreading across his chest. She touched it, rubbing the sticky wetness between her fingertips, then inhaling the coppery scent. Oh, God! OH, GOD! Tess laid a hand on his chest. Nothing. She hardly noticed when someone bumped into her as she made a last-ditch effort and placed her fingers beneath his nose. A strangled cry escaped her as she abruptly stood, backing away, a shaking hand covering her mouth. Dead. She could smell it; burning gunpowder, flesh, and wood melting together, assaulting her nostrils. Her head whipped back and forth, a fiercely gruesome battle playing out around her as if she were a ghost. This can't be happening!

She choked back a shriek when another man fell at her feet, his eyes glassy, his arm reaching up to her for a split second, then dropping as blood gurgled out between still lips, pooling on the deck. Dead eyes stared up at her. Panicked, Tess lunged for the companionway hatch. The ship heeled, and she lost her footing, tripping over the threshold and slamming into the far wall; she bit her lip to hold in the scream of pain. Swaying dizzily, and not waiting for the sting to subside, she grasped the wall rails and staggered back to the cabin. She leaned heavily against the doorframe for an instant, then rolled inside and shut the door. Her legs crumbled, and she slithered to the floor in a pink pile.

It *was* real, she thought, swallowing repeatedly. She stared at nothing, then squeezed her burning eyes shut and dropped her head back against the wood. Dear God in heaven, it wasn't a game! They were actually killing each other up there! Her stomach rebelled at the memory of that hand, still alive, ready to keep on killing. Oh, what did she do now? How could she stop this? She couldn't, she realized, wiping her bloody hands on her skirts. They won't give in, and she couldn't begin to fathom a logical reason for a real battle. The crack of splintering wood penetrated her chaotic thoughts with a jolt, and one image flashed in her mind.

Blackwell! Where was he? Good God, was he sprawled on the deck somewhere bleeding to death? And Duncan and Thorpe and—they could be dying while she sat here, she thought realistically, shoving her hair out of her face and jumping to her feet. Bizarre as it was, Tess knew one thing for certain. Her situation had suddenly become a matter of pure survival!

She fought with the dress, tearing it off her shoulders and wiggling it past her hips, then kicking it aside. Tossing the petticoats atop the soiled gown, she strode to the captain's chest of drawers, riffling through his clothes, then searched a trunk, finding a worn pair of trousers and a shirt. Stripping down to the chemise, she donned the shirt, tying its tails at her waist. Shoving a leg in the pants, she looked around for something to hold them up. Seeing nothing available, she tore a strip of petticoat and fashioned a belt. The pant legs pooled for more than a foot around her ankles, so she took up the knife and cut slits in the hem, then ripped the seams to her knees and tied them off. At least I can walk, she thought, slipping the braid down the back of her shirt as she moved toward the door. Halfway there she halted and made a beeline for the hutch, splashing brandy into a glass and draining it. She instantly regretted it when her eyes watered as she choked violently on the amber liquid.

Artificially braced, she left the cabin and made her way down the companionway. I'm a fool, she thought, gripping the wall rail. An idiot not to stay safely tucked below and wait this out. But, she couldn't. I improvise with what's available, she could hear her father say; adapt quickly to the situation, and you can overcome any obstacle.

Tess pushed on the latch.

Bursting out onto the deck, she surveyed the chaos around her. Swords clashed and rang, pistols cracked, their blasts flashing white fire in the dark. The air was thick with smoke, and men screamed, dropping into the water as their opponents continued on relentlessly from over the side of the *Sea Witch* and onto the other vessel. Criminy, Blackwell, your own ship isn't enough! She was caught off guard for an instant when a snarling man lunged for her. Her foot connected with his solar plexus, and he doubled over, giving her time to run onto the poop deck and climb several feet up the rigging. Thank God for those Karate classes, she thought, nerves stretched taut, her position offering a view of the other ship.

Its main mast was ablaze, but no sign of Blackwell. She climbed higher, easily adjusting to the swing of the lattice ropes. Had Blackwell attacked the ship? Could he be that ruthless? A free rope threaded around her thigh and wrapped around her ankle for stability, Tess dangled from the main mast, waving a hand before her face to clear the smoke. She squinted, her gaze careening off anything that moved. Her heart drummed in her throat as she searched. Where are you, you archaic squid? Muscles worked furiously in her arms, and her entire body clenched as Tess fought the urge to scream out. Oh God! Was he already dead? Had he gone overboard? Tears pricked her vision. Please God, no!

His fine Toledo sword clashed, and Dane strained, hilt to hilt, his greater power sending the man over the rail as he boarded the brig. Another came and his blade sliced across the man's bare chest, laying it open. The seaman shrieked, staggering back and falling across a cannon barrel, his flesh searing on the hot metal. His wail was deafening, but Dane pushed on, thoughts of Phillip grinding him to seek a measure of revenge this night.

On the deck of the brig, Dane Blackwell wielded the silver cutlass, hacking his way toward her captain. The sniveling coward stood on the quarter deck, surrounded by men, his sword drawn, ready for the moment when he must defend himself. Dane's lips twisted in disgust. The wigged dandy pushed his men before him, doing naught but shouting frantic orders and waving his weapon. Dane saw no reason to kill uselessly and shoved men out of his path until forced to run them through. He'd given the vessel the chance to surrender, even after they'd fired the first shot; the returning volley had destroyed her main mast.

Dane grabbed a rope and swung onto the rail, advancing without interruption. He leapt to the deck.

"Do you ask for quarter, Bennett?" he shouted and watched Captain Bennett's eyes widened. "Aye, I know you. Only a coward would champion a sot like Rothmere!"

Thus dared before his crew, Bennett lunged forward, shoving men from his path in an effort to get to the legendary captain.

Tess's eyes widened as she watched Dane fight, his sword chopping through flesh as if he were cutting weeds. Clad in black from head to foot, he was awesome, like something out of *Captain Blood*. He must have said something to further enrage the man ridiculously dressed in a white wig and yellow silk coat because the fellow no longer stayed hidden behind his men. He leapt forward, drew the hilt of his sword before his face, then touched it to the deck.

Timber crackled and burned, debris fell to the

123

deck, yet the ash-filled air seem to suddenly grow quieter as the captains squared off, crewmen clearing a path for the duel. Bennett lashed the air, the sound a shrill whine, and Dane caught the blade against his own, flicking his wrist and sending the man back. Bennett parried, lunged, and met Blackwell's strikes head on. He'd underestimated the infamous captain and his ability to maneuver his ship. The *Sea Witch* was like a phantom, vanishing into the night only to reappear where her master chose. Bennett felt a measure of panic, staring into those accursed eyes. The man wanted blood—Phillip's, but his, it seemed, would suffice for now. Frantically he swung the blade, crisscrossing a hairs breadth before Blackwell's chest.

Dane blocked the stab to his heart, yet the tip caught him, slicing open his shirt, blazing a red streak up across his shoulder. Tess gasped, expecting Dane to fall, but he didn't even flinch, his stance remaining relaxed, pale mint eyes narrow and keen. Metal sang again and, like an artist painting a scene, Captain Blackwell wielded his sword with cool expertise, as if the heavy steel were merely a feather.

Dane pressed on, forcing Bennett to back up toward the stern. Though only slightly smaller, the man was losing strength, his heavy clothing constricting his movements, making him work harder, and with each parry, Dane maneuvered closer. The backs of Bennett's legs touched the stern rail, and with all his remaining strength, he lunged at Dane.

But the dark captain was lightning quick, snaring the thin blade against his Toledo steel. "You were part of it, admit it?" Dane demanded into the man's face, hilt caught to hilt.

Bennett's smile was sadistic. "Aye. Desiree was quite the wildcat, Blackwell, screaming for your aid."

A low growl rumbled in Dane's chest, his lips twisting cruelly. Bennett's muscles strained to keep the man back. Phillip was wrong, Bennett thought, Blackwell's ship could not be taken down, yet the man was a different story, he decided, confident in his expertise with a sword.

"Phillip has guaranteed me sanctuary to spend your money," he grunted, throwing his weight forward in an attempt to take Dane off balance. It didn't work.

A black brow lifted. "Rather difficult, I promise," he snarled. "For you shall be quite dead."

Something flickered in Bennett's eyes. "Care to make a wager, Blackwell?"

Tess nearly swallowed her tongue as she caught sight of a turban-clad man advancing on Dane from behind, a wicked machete brandished high above his wrapped head.

"Dane! Behind you!" she screamed, but it was lost in the din of the battle. No one intervened, and Dane didn't hear the frantic shouts from his own men. Her pulse staggered, her fingers clenching the ropes. Oh, God, help him! Please! He'll be killed! Tess did the only thing she could. She became the wind.

Chapter Eleven

Tess didn't stop to think, but drew her arms back and dove out, her petite body like a shooting star as she flew to the mizzen mast. She prayed, for it was a greater distance than she had ever dared, and thanked God when she caught the wood, spinning around it into a supine position. Ten points for execution, Renfrew.

The broad pole braced at her abdomen, her movements were swift, urgent, yet confident as she spread her legs, her torso twisting until she straddled the pole, then curled her legs back, hooking her ankles on the wood behind her and pushing to a stand. The wind's too hard for the easy way, she thought, handstand to round off. She grasped a rope, tugging it once to be certain it was secure, then threaded the thick hemp between her thighs and around one leg. Leaning back slightly for a better stance, Tess saw the machete near Dane's back and again called on her championship abilities.

With the cry of "Oohh-Rahhh!" Tess pushed off, sailing through the darkness, feet first. Her heels connected with the turbaned head, and she heard a sickening crack, yet the momentum forced her high into the air and she smacked into a charred sail like a fly against a swatter. Holding onto the rope for dear life as she dangled uncontrollably, Tess shook her head, then slithered down to the deck. Then wished she'd stayed up there. Turban lay beside the capstan, his neck twisted at an impossible angle.

Dane caught a glimpse of the machete and its dead owner. "You fight with no honor, Bennett," he snarled. "And tonight you die with none." Driven by revenge, Dane's muscled arm shot forward, his fist cracking against jawbone, sending Bennett against the rail and nearly dumping him in the water. It isn't over yet, Dane thought, I haven't tasted enough blood.

Bennett stared into those determined eyes and saw his death plainly etched. The man was possessed, in league with the devil, he thought, and he's been playing with me since the first. Damn you, Phillip, and your arrogance!

Growing tired of this squabble, Dane set upon the man with a vengeance, thrust, parry, thrust, the first laying open the man's cheek, the second cut slitting his coat crossways from shoulder to hip. Blood burst across the yellow fabric. Bennett went mad, his powdered wig slipping over his forehead until he discarded it into the sea, the bald pate amusing Dane and enraging the Englishman. Bennett swiped the air in a wild frenzy, overextending his thrust.

Dane allowed the man to advance several steps and in the process found himself backed up against someone.

"Hate to interrupt this splendid sword fight, Blackwell, but this tub is on fire." Her words were rapid, frightened.

Dane's eyes widened a fraction at the familiar voice, his heart skipping a beat. How the bloody hell did she get here? he wondered, then pulled her close behind him, his sword swiping so close to Bennett's face the man jerked back.

"You haven't the sense God gave a pea, woman," he growled, then with the blade point plucked several buttons from Bennett's shirt.

"I'm impressed, Blackwell, but—" She gulped, her eyes darting to the flames quickly engulfing the ship. The vessel rocked and the foremast toppled, its top gallant crumbling into the sea. "Oh, God! See what I mean!" she choked, gripping the back of his shirt.

"Strike your colors, Bennett," he demanded in a cold voice.

"Nay, Blackwell, never." Bennett lunged, aiming for Dane's heart.

It was a flash of a moment. Dane caught the thrust, twisted his wrist in a spiral motion, and Tess watched as he made three sharp revolutions, the fourth flinging Bennett's sword straight up into the air. As if in slow motion, it tumbled end over end, plummeting to the sea. An instant later Dane's blade point was tucked beneath Bennett's chin, bringing the man up short.

"Do you beg quarter?" Dane asked, and Tess's soft gasp made him step back. His free hand caught the knife heading for his stomach, and before Bennett could reply, Dane sent the cutlass deep into his heart. Bennett slithered to the deck noiselessly.

Tess's stomach lurched as Dane callously yanked the blade from Bennett's chest, swiped it across the man's yellow coat, then returned it to its loop. He grabbed her arm, tugging her from the gruesome sight as she continued to gape at the dead man.

"Where the hell are you going?" she cried, jerking free when he started down the burning ship's companionway. "It's going to sink!" Men jumped overboard, and Tess felt the almost uncontrollable urge to join them.

"There are maps and pilot rudders aboard I must possess," he said, descending the ladder.

Not knowing what else to do, Tess followed and under less terrifying circumstances she would have smiled when he repeatedly banged his head on the ceiling. The cabin was a cracker box.

Dane rifled through the desk, ignoring her frightened expression and gathering up all he could. After stuffing the items down his shirt, he dragged her out of the cabin, his long strides forcing her to run. He didn't give her a chance to mount the steps and slung her over his shoulder.

"I got over here on my own, Blackwell. I can certainly get back!"

He didn't respond. The second they were topside he called across to his first mate, ordering speed as he stepped over bodies and debris.

"Your Neanderthal qualities are showing, Conan."

He grasped a rope, checked its stability, then wrapped an arm beneath her bottom, slipping a hand between her legs and gripping his own shirt for security.

"Blackwell?" she squeaked at the intimate position

129

of his hand. No answer. "Blackwell?" She twisted, her eyes widening. "Oooh, no, you don't!"

He looped the rope around his boot, then took a few steps back.

Tess let out a piercing shriek as they left the deck and flew through the air, her hands buried in his shirt so tightly she heard it rip. The wind jolted out of her lungs when his feet hit solid ground, and through blurry eyes she saw the remaining masts and poop deck of the brig collapse. Close call. Instantly hands steadied them. She heard Dane bark a few orders, but could understand none of it; her ears were buzzing much too loudly. In the next heart beat, she was dumped on her rear.

"You, madame, are the most brainless twit I've had the misfortune to know!" Dane growled down at her, hands on his hips, eyes ablaze with fury.

She rolled her eyes. "Says the man who should be living in a padded cell." Let him rant, she thought, still shaking from what she'd witnessed and experienced in the last hour. "What happened to those fine gentlemanly attributes, Blackwell? Lose them too when you hacked those men to pieces?" Tess shoved the loose strands from her face and struggled to stand on rubbery legs.

"Lady Renfrew? Is that truly you?" Gaelan asked, assisting her to her feet, his sooty face a mask of disbelief.

"Yeah, it's me." Her gaze never left Dane's. "How could you be so ruthless, so cold? Christ, I saw you kill over twenty men!"

"I plead guilty," he said without a trace of remorse. "And as you can see," he made an impatient gesture

130

to his vessel, "we have been *hacked to pieces* as well."

"It was *you* who saved the captain, m'lady?" Gaelan put in incredulously.

"Unfortunately, yes," she muttered, then turned to view the ship.

Dane frowned at his first officer. "What say you, man?"

"It was she, sir, that—" Gaelan pointed to the mast, made a swinging motion, then shrugged.

Dane snapped a look to the mast, then to the burning brig. The turbaned man, he thought, some peculiar emotion assailing him. He glanced down, expecting to find the lady before him. She wasn't. Then he heard her voice, sharp, clear, giving commands, and his gaze followed the sound to where Tess knelt beside a crewman..

Tess examined the sailor's leg wound. It wasn't too deep and as she pressed a less-than-clean cloth to it, decided it could wait.

"You'll be fine, but others are worse. I'll be back." She ordered the sailor to maintain pressure, then moved to the next man. He'd lost a finger and had a large gash in his side. She wanted to vomit but couldn't spare the time and bound his hand and ribs, ordering an uninjured sailor to hold pressure. She went to another victim and knelt beside him.

"Aren't you Sikes?" she said, ripping open the bloody shirt and examining him.

He seemed shocked she would know. "Aye, miss," he gasped. "A ball caught me."

"I can see that." Tess glanced up. He looked more frightened of her than anything. "You'll be first, Mr. Sikes. Mr. Potts!" she shouted, knowing no other

131

name to call.

"Aye, m'lady?"

"I need any medicines you have aboard, *clean* cloths torn into strips, water—fresh water," she stressed, brushing back her braid as she moved to the next man. "Have every able hand rinse the decks immediately," she ordered. "Then move all the wounded you can to one dry area." She glanced around her, then added, "If you can find one."

Everything was either wet or bloody. Deck hands were already clearing away the dead and Tess shut the thought of who they were out of her mind. She was running on pure adrenaline, her nerves taut, her mind blocking the truths she could plainly see.

"Beggin' yer pardon, m'lady, but the cook and Mr. McPete usually tend to the wounds."

"Then I suggest you get them up here, Mr. Potts, because I need help!"

Satisfied she had the bleeding under some measure of control, Tess straightened. So many hurt, she thought, squeezing her eyes shut and massaging the bridge of her nose. How many would live? Three times she'd come across wounds wrapped in dirty bandages smeared with some foreign crap that stunk. In a modern hospital the wounds would have needed minor treatment, but here infection could run rampant. My bag, she thought, breaking into a run. She must have something in it that would help. She was almost to the companionway when a noise like nothing she'd ever heard made her stop.

The brig was like a Viking funeral ship, an orange fireball on the sea for an excruciating moment before it exploded, fiery debris shooting into the black sky, the luminescent banners of defeat fluttering to the ocean to hiss and sizzle. More death. Tears burning in her tired eyes, Tess ducked through the passageway.

The *Sea Witch* had sustained minor damage — splintered wood and several torn sails — yet compared to the brig, she had come through unscathed. Blackwell stood at the helm, maneuvering his ship swiftly away from floating debris. At his command, men tossed out ropes to those of the brig that had survived. Leaving the helm in the care of the coxswain, Blackwell strode to the rail. They would be given the chance to swear an oath to the captain of the *Witch* and join her crew. If not, they would be shackled until they could be put ashore at the next port. A merciful act, for any other captain would have made sport of the prisoners. With that consideration, the frigate gained twelve new crew members. Dealing a sharp nod and orders to see wounds cared for, the captain turned away to begin repairs on his ship, to roll back the black sails of war and begin anew.

Muscles strained as Dane yanked the rope, holding it taut as a seaman secured the winch. Hearing the feminine voice, he glanced up from his work. Lady Renfrew had recently come on deck with an armful of supplies; where she'd found the containers and bottles he'd no idea, but now she worked furiously to remove the ball from Mr. Sikes. God's teeth, she was an astonishing female, unflappable, it seemed. And Dane wasn't certain he liked knowing she was more capable than any man. Ahh, but she was pure woman, he thought, his greedy gaze drifting down over the gentle swells of her plump breasts concealed in his oldest shirt. A tender emotion he couldn't name stirred in his chest at the mere sight of her, and he realized it mattered not whether she was clad in silks and lace or as she was now, her compact figure disguised in men's garments.

Suddenly the entire ship seemed to go deathly silent when she asked Mr. Potts for a sharp knife.

"Potts?" Tess wiggled her fingers, then glanced up when the asked-for knife wasn't placed in her hand. Her gaze slipped across the men surrounding her, to Sikes, then back to Potts. Jeez! What was the matter with these guys now? "Come on, Potts, up the blade. Now!"

Almost smugly Potts handed it over. A witch could not touch cold steel. The second her fingers closed around it everyone within the sight of her collectively sighed. Tess never saw Dane's soft smile as she drew the blade briefly over a lantern flame before she went back to work, absently noting that Sikes seemed a bit more relaxed.

"Talk to me, Mr. Potts." She needed something to distract her mind as she dug out the bullet. "How about telling me where you were headed before I was rescued?" Sikes's breath hissed through his teeth as she wiggled the knife. "Sorry," she muttered, then nodded to Potts to give the seaman more rum.

"We was fightin' a fierce storm, miss," Sikes mumbled, watching her work.

"Quit flapping your jibs, buster. You're wounded, remember."

Sikes grinned weakly. Cheeky wench, he thought, admiring her spunk.

Tess felt the blade tip scrape metal. With the tweezers from her manicure kit, she plucked the soft metal ball from his shoulder, dropping it into Potts's outstretched hand. Her stomach rolled at the gush of blood, and she swiftly covered the wound.

"Aye, 'twas the worst I've seen," Potts said. "Not like a hurricane, mind you. But mean, tossin' the *Witch* like a twig, m'lady, near a wall of black thunder clouds."

Her movements stilled, but she didn't take her eyes from her work as she held pressure to the wound. She swallowed thickly. "Say again?" The muscles in her shoulders tightened.

"I spotted it first," a young man said smugly, hunkering down opposite her.

Potts lips twisted with condescension. "You're the crow, Tuffy! Yer *supposed* to sight anythin' first."

"You was ascared as the rest!" Tuffy shot back.

"Mind your tongue, boy!" Potts snarled, and the crow was instantly contrite.

"Gentlemen, please!" Tess interrupted sharply, every nerve singing as she braced herself to stitch human flesh. Her head throbbed with questions she couldn't ask. The wall. The wall. The image kept flashing in her head. Tess blinked rapidly, biting her lip as she took the last stitch, then snipped the thread and spread the wound with clear bacitracin. Nodding slowly when Potts offered to bind the wound, she twisted to tend the next sailor.

"Keep going, Mr. Potts," she said shakily.

"I'll be speakin' the truth, m'lady," he began in a conspiratorial whisper, unaware of her torment. "A mighty ship, white as an angel's wing and as swift as

135

any afore her, stern one moment, port the next. Give me the willies, it did. Never seen anythin' so grand!"

The *Nassau Queen,* Tess thought, and felt the hackles rise on the back of her neck. "What—ah," she swallowed. "What did you mean by a wall of thunderclouds?"

Finished, Potts leaned closer, his stomach tightening at the frightening memory. "This great ship was far off our stern, heading right at us. Then suddenly," he waved dramatically, "she appears at port, moving away!"

"She asked about the wall, Mr. Potts," someone said.

"I know, I'm gettin' tah that!" he snapped, then turned a gentle smile to Lady Renfrew, in his glory to be the center of her attention. "The captain called for reports from Tuff here." He tossed a thumb at the boy. "And when we looked again the ship had vanished behind this movin' curtain of mist."

"We've all seen fog on the sea, Potts," Sikes added weakly. "An' that 'tweren't it!"

Several men had come up close, nodding agreement. "Aye, a fog don' move like snakes!"

Despite the heat Tess felt goose bumps prick the skin of her arms and neck as she rose unsteadily to her feet. In a trance she remembered the clear skies when she jumped ship. And how frightened she'd been to be heading toward the blanket of swirling mist. Vaguely she recalled hearing the clap of thunder, seeing the jagged spark of lightning. Had the storm these men experienced been on the other side of the dark partition? Her heart clenched painfully. Did I pass through it or under it? And into what? Her body trembled hard, her hands shaking as wild thoughts collided in her brain.

Tess staggered to the rail, her knuckles going white with her fierce grip. Everything rushed at her in a tidal wave of facts. Yes, they were facts now. The clothes, the furniture. The archaic beliefs, the crude weapons, and dear God, the death. In the lantern-lit darkness Richmond chittered happily in the waters below, and Tess cried out in despair.

"Why have you taken me here, Richmond? Why?" she demanded, unaware she'd spoken aloud. "Whose time have you dumped me in?" She slapped a hand over her mouth, biting the heel in an effort to hold back the boiling scream. Say it, her mind begged. Face the truth. Squeezing her eyes shut, Tess allowed the thought to take form. There was no other explanation than the one she'd avoided. The black wall had been a doorway.

Into the past.

"Lady Renfrew?"

She spun about, her gaze meeting those startling green eyes.

"You," she accused, stumbling backwards. "You're a pirate! A damned pirate, of all things."

He stiffened, eyes paling to white frost. "I beg your pardon?"

"Don't look so insulted, Blackwell. You know what you are," she spat, gunmetal gray eyes raking him in disgust.

She was exhausted, Dane thought sympathetically, on the verge of collapse. He could almost see the restless energy surging through her. Nearly explosive, as if waiting for something to spark the fuse.

137

I can't handle this, she thought, her gaze careening nervously over the ship. I can't! Tess raced to the companionway, passing Duncan, his arms laden with bandages and ointments. She never saw him, stumbling over the raised threshold. She skidded into the cabin, tearing clothes from her body as she moved toward the bathroom. The hip bath was filled with warm water, and somewhere beyond her turmoil she knew this was Duncan's thoughtfulness. She bent over and dunked her head into the water, staying that way until she had no more breath to hold. She straightened, flinging her head back and letting the warm water splash the walls and cascade down her body. The odor of death clung to her. Trembling violently, she stepped into the tub, making record time with soaping her hair. She scrubbed vigorously, then scrubbed some more. Her skin burned when she stepped from the bath and wrapped in a towel.

It changed nothing.

"I've got to get back," she mumbled, shoulders hunched as she anxiously paced the cabin. Two hundred years backwards. No longer did she deny the possibility. Everything made too much sense now. Tess suddenly had the overwhelming need to connect with something from her time and went to her yellow duffle. With jerky movements she pulled on a soft black satin chemise and short kimono robe.

She stared at the yellow bag.

My past, she thought, then she flung the satchel across the room. It smacked the wall, dropping to the floor with a solid *chunk*. Tess stood in the center of the lavish cabin, motionless, staring at nothing. Then with a strangled moan, she sank to the floor to

138

her knees.

"I don't belong here," she cried, wrapping her arms across her middle. Tears streamed down her cheeks, splashing on her bare knees. "I don't."

Chapter Twelve

Dane stared after her. The agony he'd seen in those eyes made his heart drop to his gullet. Sweet Christ, had the day's events snapped her deranged mind? Her screaming at the dolphin was certainly testimony to her unbalanced state. Please, God, he silently begged, don't let that be the case. He didn't want her to be insane. He wanted her whole, logical.

And that was what was so confusing, for the courage and ingenuity she'd displayed today were unmatched in any female he'd met before her. He looked up at the mast — still unable to comprehend exactly how she'd managed to get aboard the brig — then glanced around at the men lying on the deck, treated wounds cleanly bandaged, some even sedated. The lady's compassion was unbounding, especially to men who had treated her so poorly.

"Captain?" Dane's eyes shifted to the boatswain. "Is the lady unwell?"

Unwell? Dane nearly laughed at the suggestion. The lady's emotional stability was definitely under question.

"She is simply tired," the captain excused, deciding he'd give her a moment to compose herself. He rubbed the back of his neck. "What did you discuss, Mr. Potts?" Dane needed to know.

Potts hesitantly relayed the conversation, wondering also what he'd said to cause her to flee.

Dane rapped softly on his cabin door. No response. Leaning closer to the wood, he could hear no sounds coming from within, and a sudden panic swept through him. Was she even in there? Was she perhaps wandering belowdecks? Or had she—jumped overboard? He thrust open the door, his gaze searching the dimly lit cabin. He started to step back outside when a faint sound caught his attention. His brows furrowed as he tried to determine the source.

"I don't belong! I don't belong!" The whispered words knifed him the instant before he saw her, sitting back on her heels, clenched fists thumping her thighs. He could scarcely make out her huddled form in the darkened cabin and could see nothing of her face. Black hair draped over her shoulders, grazing the floor.

She didn't notice his cautious approach.

Her shoulders shook, and he heard her sniffle. God's teeth, she was crying! The thought jolted him to his boots. She hadn't spent a single tear since she'd been rescued. Ahh, lass, I wish I could help you, he thought, and was startled when she threw back her head and sobbed helplessly.

"I want to go home! I must!"

"Nay!" he said instinctively.

Her head jerked around at the denial, and Tess leapt to her feet. "Leave me alone, please!" she begged, swiping her cheeks with the back of her hand.

Dane's gaze was immediately riveted to the display of unusually muscled legs, bare beyond the short black satin—whatever that was. He swallowed. God, the limbs were magnificent!

"Please, Blackwell! Go away!" she cried brokenly.

He forced himself to lift his gaze. "Lady Renfrew—"

"Don't call me that!" she shouted, suddenly up in his face. "I'm Tess. Do you hear me? Tess! For God's sake, at least let me be what I am!"

She swayed weakly, and he grasped her shoulders. "Calm yourself, lass. You're merely exhausted."

Tess froze for a moment, staring at him. A peculiar giggle bubbled in her throat and came out in choked spurts. Then it burst, and she laughed hard, the merry sound twisting into hysterical cackles.

"Exhausted?" she shrieked, gasping for breath and despite her laughing the tears came in a gush. "Christ, I wish it were that simple!" Her trembling fingers curled in the folds of his shirt. "I don't belong here, Blackwell," she cried desperately, jerking him down in her face as if it would make him understand. "This isn't my time." His frown deepened. "Don't you see? Richmond brought me through the wall. To *your* time. I must go home. I belong in the future!"

"Nay!" He shook her, the thought of her going anywhere driving him to tighten his grip. "Please, m'lady. Do not speak this nonsense!" It tore at his vitals to see her this distraught. "This is the eighteenth century! You are Lady Tess Renfrew, daughter of a noble Scotsman!"

"No! I'm a nobody! A nobody!" She thrashed, fists striking out and connecting with his ribs. "Oh, God! I've traveled back in time, Blackwell! No one knows I'm here! No one cares!"

Abruptly Dane slammed her against him, pale eyes demanding she hear his words. "Listen to me, woman! *We* know you're here, and there are over a hundred men on this ship whose admiration and respect you've gained this night! *They* care what happens to you!" Tears rolled down her flushed cheeks, and the sight sliced him in two.

"You bastard!" she snarled. "Don't start lying to me now!" then kicked him in the shin and managed to sock him in the chest.

" 'Tis not lie!" Dane felt he'd ensnared a hurricane.

"I don't believe you!" She twisted wildly, and Dane wrapped his arms around her, burying a hand in her hair when she tried to get free.

"Cease, Tess! For God's sake. Cease! This fight will do no good!" He feared she had finally gone over the edge. " 'Twill be fine soon, lass. I swear it!"

"No! It's not fine! It will never be fine again!" Her fists thumped his back. "You don't understand! How can—oh, let me go!" She pushed at him and he tightened his hold. "Please, God. I can't handle this. I don't want to!"

She pressed her forehead to his chest, her battered emotions dissolving in the sea of tears, hopeless sobs raking her slender body. Tess cried for herself, something she hadn't indulged in since she was a small child, abandoned in a dingy hotel room at the age of four. The sensation wasn't much different now.

Her tears soaked his shirt, never ceasing, and Dane's

chest constricted at the agonized sound. The heat of her lithe body scorched through his damp clothing, and he fought the nearly ungodly hunger merely touching her evoked in him. He squeezed his eyes shut, blocking the sudden image of those gorgeous bare legs from his mind.

"Oh, I just want to die," she sobbed.

He yanked on a handful of hair, jerking her head back. "Do — not — even — think — it!" he growled in a dangerous voice, eyes bright. "Promise me now, woman! Promise me you'll not harm yourself!"

His gaze searched her face, waiting for her answer, and Dane felt a fear he'd never experienced before. The passing seconds thumped with the beat of his heart. Then suddenly he crushed her mouth beneath his, his lips demanding her promise of life, drinking in her sorrow. She was still crying.

This man is all I know, Tess thought. I've nothing left. Alone and defeated, she felt the uncontrollable need to cling to him. His musky scent filled her being, intoxicating her. A primal craving she'd never known rocked her to her bare feet when his warm tongue pushed between her lips. She snared it, answering the blaze, yanking the shirt from his trousers and slipping her hands beneath.

"Nay, lass," Dane murmured against her lips. He strove for control, attempting to extract himself, yet his mouth still hovered close.

"Yes," she whispered shakily, holding tight. Her hands molded up his back, stroking damp, ropey muscles, driving him mad with desire. She caressed the tight skin of his ribs, small hands moving urgently up over his broad chest, then fumbling with the wooden buttons of his shirt.

Dane ground his teeth, painfully aware of how much he wanted this woman. He sensed her agony as if it were a piece of his soul, a deep unwelcome ache that spilled over into her jerky movements. He gazed longingly into those storm-cloud eyes, dark, turbulent — lonely. She was a lady much too vulnerable for this, he tried to reason as her ripe curves pressed so intimately to his long body. Dane made a valiant effort to resist.

"Ahh, lass. Do not do this," he rasped deeply when her lips ground down the length of his throat. "I beg you. I cannot —"

Buttons sprang, shooting across the cabin in rapid succession as she ripped open his shirt, her lips and tongue hurriedly devouring every inch of flesh she exposed. Between her thighs grew warm and damp, tingling with excitement as she peeled the fabric off his shoulders, catching it roughly on his forearms. She could feel his arousal stiffening against her. The power thrilled her. He was ready. A typhoon unleashed itself inside her, her body on fire with the ecstasy only his touch could bring. Tess swiftly shrugged out of her robe, the satin pooling on the floor around her feet before her hands raked over thick biceps, across the wide expanse of his chest, satisfying her need to feel the hard bronzed skin. Warm, solid. Dangerous.

His breath quickened.

Dane sagged heavily against the edge of the desk, claiming her mouth as he pulled her tightly between his thighs, shaking with the force of her touch. He was about to shatter with the effort to restrain his body's need. It wasn't working. He was burning, rock hard, and throbbing — for her. Ahh, God, but the woman was a blessed wildcat, he thought, her lips clinging to his skin, the pressure demanding, her tongue licking erotic circles around his nipples. His knees suddenly turned to water when her fingertips trickled over the solid ridge straining against his breeches, squeezing down the length of his thigh. Her hand moved between his legs.

He tore his mouth away. "Tess, Tess," he moaned. "We — I — God's teeth, woman!" he uttered when she cupped him, squeezing firmly. His powerful arms instantly swallowed her. His will vanished as he crushed her lips beneath his with a ravenous need. Fool! Fool! I should never have let it go this far, Dane agonized, shoving the satin strap off her shoulder, his lips tracing a swift steamy path down her chest. I've been a bloody idiot to believe I could resist her spell, he silently admitted. But the woman robs me of all coherent thought with naught but those eyes. I've wanted her from the beginning. And now, Christ, I'm bloody starving to be inside her. A warm callused hand covered her firm breast. Her nipple tautened beneath his touch, boring into his palm. Dane lowered his head.

Tess gasped with pleasure as he captured her nipple, his tongue flicking the tender peak. Then he drew it fully into his mouth, tugging, suckling almost painfully at the rosy tip. Heat splashed down her body in a quick surge. Her hands gripped the lean flesh of his ribs as he bent her back over his arm, her bosom plumping under his moist attentions.

Her lids fluttered, her gaze briefly skimming the cut on his shoulder. The memory of the day's events rapidly flooded her mind. Tears pricked her eyes as she pulled at his belt. He caught her fingertips, straightening. Eyes locked and held.

A crystal drop fell, splashing on her bared breast. She swallowed, aching to feel anything but the turmoil churning inside her.

"I want you, Blackwell," she panted against his lips, jerking open the buckle. She freed a button. "Now!"

Two buttons. Three. His heart slammed against the wall of his chest. Each bold release was like a gunshot. His legs threatened to crumble. Four. Five. His manhood sprang free, pushing against her satin-cloaked stomach. Without taking her eyes from his, her hand slid inside his trousers.

"For the love of God!" he choked.

"No. For me," she whispered intensely as her hand closed around him.

Dane's breath charged in his lungs; blood rushed through his body, burning his loins as she stroked him. Her fingertip made an agonizing circle over the moist tip of him, and he fought to fill his lungs. The ship creaked.

Never had he wanted a woman more.

His mouth slashed hard against hers as he shoved up the satin. A large hand slid between her thighs. She whimpered, pushing against his fingers, and Dane thought he'd die with the sheer pleasure of it. It was excruciating, almost painful to touch her. She was a sorceress, a lady witch, he thought, his head reeling with the musky scent of her. His tongue slickly outlined the curve of her lips, brushed back and forth across her teeth, then thrust inside as his finger slipped into the damp nest of black curls.

He found her. Hot and wet. The sudden knowledge nearly wrenched free the rigging on his restraint, challenging his need to take her quickly. A finger probed the soft dewy folds, searching for the bud of her desire. He touched it, and she exploded in his arms, grinding against his hand.

"Please! Now!" she cried breathlessly, grasping his trousers and pulling him with her as she sank to her knees.

Immediately she straddled him, muscled limbs wrapping deliciously around his hips. His mouth and hands were everywhere, tasting, fondling, stroking. Her fingers dug into his shoulders as she inched upward.

"Hurry, hurry," she begged.

The head of him entered her slim body. Dane shuddered violently. Grasping her hips, he watched her face as he pulled her downward. Her lids fluttered, a guttural moan of satisfaction escaping her lips as she sank onto the length of him. She lifted, then slammed down. Eager and hungry and breathless. Strong legs pulled him deeper inside her. The pleasure built to torturous proportions. Christ, she was so tight. Her arms wound around his neck, soft shudders tumbling into his mouth. She rode him. It was sizzling, vigorous— powerful. Her womanhood throbbed, blood coursing around his hard staff, pulsing, squeezing. He moved with her.

"Blackwell!" she screamed.

Suddenly he trapped her against him, stilling her frantic ride. "Say it!" She met his piercing green eyes, brilliant with desire. "Say my name, Tess!"

"Dane," she breathed.

His smile was animal-wicked as he lowered her to the carpet.

148

"Dane," she whispered again, cupping his jaw and possessing his lips before her back met the floor. Her fingers plowed into his hair, dragging away the black ribbon tied at his nape. Onyx curls spilled over his broad shoulders. He pushed. She arched, claiming his buttocks, pulling him farther inside her.

"Look at me," he demanded. She did. He withdrew, then entered her again with exquisite tenderness. Tears bloomed in her eyes. She was strung tight, every nerve singing with a wondrous ache. Her body screamed for a fulfillment she'd never known.

He grasped her hands, placing them on either side of her head and lacing his fingers through hers. Locking his elbows, he moved, rhythmically, watching her sculptured body quiver and tremble beneath him. Sleek, untamed—damn bewitching. Her silken hair spread across the floor, undulating like black mist as each buffet drew her closer to ecstasy. His mouth brushed her lips as he surged forth, long and smooth. Their breaths mingled, sharp and sweet.

His body quaked. Dane withdrew fully, then plunged forth, again and again. Her cries of delight filled his head, making him dizzy, her low purrs and husky entreaties pushing him to the brink. He quickened his pace, the pumping cadence vibrating to treasured agony.

Her head thrashed on the carpet. She wouldn't survive this. It was too much. She knotted tighter with every stroke. "Dane. Do something! Ple-e-ease!"

His arms slid around her, clutching her close as he deepened his thrusts.

Tears dripped across her temples, melting into her hair.

149

Close, so close.

Every nerve in her body suddenly wrenched tight, and she stiffened beneath him, gasping for the breath that would not come. Her eyes flew open and she stared up at him. For one earth-shattering moment Dane stopped, letting her hover on the passionate rim, teeter on the summit of blinding ecstasy. Then he plunged once more, hard and solid, flinging back his head and crying out her name. Tess toppled over the edge, her feminine muscles clenching the life from him. Searing waves crashed over her, shooting sparks to her weakened limbs, and he absorbed the low keening sigh of rapture with his mouth as his powerful body sang for several glorious seconds. He closed his eyes, tremors suffusing his being, then shuddered raggedly with the unbelievable release, burying his face in the cool drape of her hair.

"Sweet witch," he groaned on a shallow breath, then a moment later heard her watery reply.

"Damned pirate."

Chapter Thirteen

For one idiotic moment Dane wondered if he'd dreamt all that had transpired. Transpired? He smiled wryly at his mediocre choice of words. It was magnificent, a passionate eruption. I've passed into a new realm, Dane thought, his heart still thumping a wild tattoo as he lifted his head. It was a monumental effort. His breathing had yet to return to normal as he gazed tenderly down into her flushed face. Neither had hers. He brushed a lock from her cheek and felt the dampness.

"Tess?"

"Shhh," she hushed, pulling his head down and kissing him languidly. His breathing quickened, and he firmed inside her. One eye opened. "Are you always that easy to take advantage of?" she teased. His grin was slow, a rascally smile that made her breath catch.

Saucy wench, Dane thought, lifting his weight from her chest. She stretched slowly, catlike. He started to withdraw, and she quickly grasped him. "No, not yet."

"The bed offers a sight more comfort, love."

Tess melted into a puddle. Love. His tone was husky

soft, intimate, and when she opened her eyes, she wanted to freeze the expression on his face forever. She reached up, tracing the line of his lips with her thumb, fingertips rasping over the stubble on his chin. Was it simply the look of a satisfied lover? He caught her hand, nibbling her fingertips, then kissing her palm. Her heart tripped at the lingering gesture. Was he for real?

"Yes, I suppose it would," she finally managed, suddenly breathless. He left her, the emptiness sending a sharp pain through her chest. She wouldn't think about that. Not yet, not tonight. She closed her eyes, damming back the burn of tears. No more, she scolded herself. Adapt, overcome. Suddenly she was swept off the floor and into his arms.

"As fetching as you look on my carpet, Tess, you shall not sleep there." He carried her to his bed, placing her in the soft center.

"And if I really want to?"

How she managed to look so defiant while she yawned, Dane didn't know, nor care. God, she was enchanting, he thought, stepping back, hands on his hips. He flashed her a grin. "Are you always in such a fighting snit after having your pleasures?"

Dane chuckled lowly when she stuck out her tongue as she sank deeper into the down.

Tess felt the heat burn her face but didn't care. Her eyes were glued to the sexiest sight she'd ever seen. Her heart thrashed in her chest, and she knew a hundred women who would kill to trade places with her at this moment. Shaggy locks tumbled in a thick black wave, dipping low over his brow, and all she could see beyond the hair was one frosty green eye making a leisurely journey up the length of her body. Long raven curls brushed his shoulders, and she was entranced as he stripped off what was left of his shirt. A light dusting of dark crisp hair tapered down his chest, disappearing into his trousers where the buttons of his pants were left unfastened. The belt hung open. A dangerously rumpled panther, she decided drowsily.

Silence was broken with the soft splash of waves, the gentle sway of the ship, and Tess fought against her heavy lids, then gave up, exhaustion quickly sapping what was left of her strength. Several moments later she felt a damp warmth between her thighs and it took a second to realize the soothing heat was a wet cloth. There isn't another like him, she thought.

Dane cleansed his seed from her body, listening to her soft sighs. He soaked the cloth again, wrung it out, then cleansed himself before he tucked her beneath the sheets. She snuggled into the mattress, kicking her legs free.

Dane told himself he must leave and started to rise. She reached blindly, grasping his arm.

"Don't go. Please."

He cleared his throat. Her voice was like liquid smoke. "I cannot stay, Tess. 'Tis nearly morning."

"Just for a little while?" She tugged.

Dane hesitated. God's teeth, she could demolish a man's sense of duty, he thought, his gaze sweeping over her satin-clad form, the sweet curve of her buttocks teasing him from twisted sheets. Her reputation would be ruined if he were discovered here in the morning.

Tess opened one eye. He'd taken off his shirt and boots. She suggested he keep going. He groaned as if in pain. "I want to feel *you*."

153

"Nay. I will not compromise you, Tess."

"I believe it was the other way around, Captain." She jerked hard on his arm, and he fell down beside her.

"Demanding little witch, aren't you?" he muttered, unable to resist the tantalizing offer.

"Yeah, and you love it," she yawned hugely, smiling when he punched a pillow. "Dane?" She twisted a look at him. "The pants."

"I beg you, Tess, not another word." Dane pressed a finger to her lips when she continued to protest. "Blast it, woman," he muttered tightly, battling the urge to pull her beneath him. "I'm not a damned saint!" Then he slung an arm over her waist and cupped a plump breast.

Tess sighed contentedly, wiggling into the curve of his body and instantly falling asleep, unaware of how tense Dane was tucked behind her.

Just for a moment, Dane decided. She needed him. And loath to admit it, even to himself, Dane Blackwell needed her.

A breakfast tray in his hand, Duncan knocked softly, and when he heard no sound from within, he slowly opened the cabin door. He froze, the sight that greeted him leaving the old salt stunned. And bloody furious. Damn you to hell, Capt'n. Duncan backed up, shaking his head and closing the door with a sharp snap.

Dane's eyes opened abruptly, and he was suddenly aware of nothing but the womanly curves pressed intimately to his body. Tess. Sweet witch. The past hours flooded back with a heated rush, and Dane smiled softly, shifting to view the sleeping woman whose dark head was pillowed on his chest. Her beauty was flawless, the light browning of her skin somehow becoming. Her lips were slightly bruised from his kisses, and the thin strap of her chemise had slipped off her shoulder, availing him an enticing view of the lush bounty displayed. His hand rode up the soft curve of her hip to her waist, and in her dreams she flung an arm possessively across his chest. Her body was chiseled perfection, and Dane wondered how a woman could gain such a splendid physique. Aye, strong and graceful — his smiled widened — and extraordinarily passionate. He was tempted to wake her and feel that glorious explosion again. Though he'd had his choice of females, Dane never knew a lass to be so erotically brazen in her lovemaking, aye, nor to enjoy it quite so much. And he silently admitted he'd never felt more vulnerable in his entire life as when she'd held him snugly inside her body.

His manhood responded with amazing swiftness to the steamy images his mind conjured, and Dane knew that one taste of this woman would never be enough. His desire was a hunger that had begun when he'd first held her in his arms, and he was helpless to control it with the knowledge that she desired him so freely. Brushing back a raven lock, he placed a soft kiss to her forehead. Her slender leg entwined itself tighter around his own. He bent his head to taste her ripe mouth when he heard footsteps outside the cabin door. His body instantly tensed, his gaze snapping to the window. Damn and blast! Daylight. Carefully he disentangled himself from her. She moaned yet didn't waken, simply snuggling around his pillow. Climbing from the bed, he withdrew his pocket watch, flipped the spring catch, and checked the time. It was early, just past dawn.

Guilt suddenly weighed heavy in his chest. He hadn't

meant to fall asleep. He'd planned to leave the cabin early in order for them not to be discovered like this. He couldn't bear it if she were openly compromised before his crew because he couldn't control his rutting nature. Dane was honest with himself. Tess had been severely distraught, ranting incoherently, and even though she'd been more than wanting, he knew he could have halted their lovemaking at any time. A little voice mocked him. Who was he trying to fool? He'd desired her so fiercely his body ached with it. He rubbed the back of his neck, absently curious as to what had wakened him in the first place.

He strode to the chiffonier and removed a fresh shirt and breeches, quickly changing. Searching the cabin for his boots, he spied them beside the bed. He was shoving a foot in when his gaze bounced off, then returned to the bowl of water from last evening. His eyes widened. Water tinged pink with blood. Sweet Jesus! He looked at Tess. How can this be? He'd felt no obstruction when he entered her. And she seemed, well, experienced. She was twenty-five, for mercy sake's! Then he recalled something else. She may have known how to stir a man to incredible heights, but Dane was certain she knew next to nothing about her own body's response, just now remembering the startled look on her face when she'd reached fulfillment. Was it possible she was a virgin in that sense?

A strange emotion warring within him, Dane yanked on the bootstrap, then straightened and went about discarding the water and collecting the strewn clothing. He stilled when he lifted the short robe from the floor, rubbing the fabric between his fingertips. It was crisper than silk or satin, yet thinner than the latter. He started to toss it on the foot of the bed

He frowned as he read the scrolled writing.
Kimonos. Made in Japan. Japan? He read the
side. *Washing instructions. Machine wash, delicate
cle, cool. No bleach. Tumble dry.*

Brows knitted tightly, Dane dropped the robe
chair and moved toward the door. He hated not
able to understand the meaning of the words. Wash
garments by a machine? Surely they would be shredded
in the process? And tumble dry? In what, and how
wasn't about to make himself look the imbecile by asking Tess.

He paused, his hand on the door latch, listening before he opened it. Cautiously he peered out, then
stepped into the corridor and made his way topside.
Dane answered to no one, was questioned by even fewer,
yet for Tess, he realized, he would go to any lengths to
see her spared any more ridicule.

He needn't have worried, for the crew of the *Sea
Witch* adored her. Without realizing it, she'd won over
their barnacled hearts, and there wasn't a soul aboard
that would not lie down and die for her. She'd saved
their lives, the captain's, and most important, she'd forgiven their malicious behavior.

Tess woke slowly, a dreamy smile curving her lips as
her hand reached out to the pile of covers, searching.
When she found the space beside her cool and empty,
she opened her eyes, propping herself up on one elbow.
Despite her disappointment at being alone, Tess smiled,
smoothing the sheet. Last night was wild and exciting.
Nothing like she'd ever imagined it could be. She

aggressive behavior, flopping back
ows. That's what I get for being celibate for
ve years, she thought. All that stored up sexual
ty.

lity crashed into her sensual memories with the
of a slap.

ptain Blackwell was no longer the eccentric, but
th. I'm living in 1789, she admitted again. The previous day skittered through her brain with amazing
arity. The winch, Mr. Potts, the battle, and the blood.
A shiver passed over her when she remembered how
close Dane had come to death. What would I have
done? What do I do now, she agonized, her emotions
swelling, eyes burning. Tess sat up, swinging her legs
over the side of the bed and rubbing her face. Get a hold
of yourself, Renfrew. Lamenting doesn't help, tears accomplish nothing. You're stuck here. Adjust your
thinking. Jesus. Two hundred years, she thought, standing and reaching for her robe. She paused, her hand
outstretched. Carefully placed across a chair was a crisp
burgundy taffeta skirt, a black sash, and a beautifully
embroidered burgundy silk blouse, delicately trimmed
in matching lace. Corset, chemise, stockings, petticoats, the works—again. And all in a deep wine pink.
Tess frowned. There certainly is an abundance of wom-
en's clothing on this vessel, she thought, annoyed.
Damn pirate, plundering women's shops, no doubt.

Washed and dressed, Tess decided she'd rather go
barefoot and nudged the slippers under the bed. She
pulled up the bedcovers, tucked and fluffed, realizing
she wasn't ready to go above. After plumping the same
pillow a third time, she grabbed up a hair brush and
went to the window bench, sinking onto the velvet.

I'm here to stay, she thoug[...] wall shows up. Get real, Renfrew. T[...] happened in the first place were one in a t[...] what if another black wall did show up? she debat[...] dragging the brush through her hair. Who was to [...] she would pass back into her own time or into ano[...] Would she go forward? And how far? The 60s? 70s? The nineteenth or twentieth century? What if [...] did find the wall and was transported further back? Maybe to another location? Should she take the chance of finding herself in a worse situation?

No, for now, she was here in 1789, the Caribbean. She'd make the best of it. A smile curved her lips when her gaze settled on the carpet. It seemed she'd already managed that.

Tess still hadn't gathered her courage to go topside when a knock sounded.

"Come in," she called, searching for something in her bag to pin up her hair.

Duncan peered his head around the door, and she smiled brightly.

"Good morning, Duncan."

His hands occupied with a tray, he shouldered his way inside. "Be near half past four bells, m'lady, but good mornin' to ye just the same."

Tess spared a quick look at the sky as she twisted the braid into a bun. I must have slept over twelve hours, she thought, then looked back at the old man. "I guess it won't do me any good to insist that you call me Tess?"

He set a tray on the table with a firm clink. "It certainly would not."

uttered as he drew back the
... Duncan, you don't have to wait on
...s." She waved at the tray, a lace cuff flutter-
... "I've been taking care of myself for a very long
..."

...en 'tis about time you're to be pampered," he said
...o-nonsense tone, snapping open the linen napkin
... gesturing for her to sit.

She did, and when he went to place the napkin on her
...ap, she snatched it. "I'm not a child," she reminded,
then ordered him into a chair.

He grinned, dutifully taking the seat across from her,
thinking what a lovely sight she was for his tired eyes.
Fresh and energetic. It was no wonder the captain—he
frowned, suddenly lost in thought. The young buck had
taken advantage of her, Duncan concluded, knowing
the captain's way with a pretty wench. And Duncan
would make certain it would not happen again, duly ap-
pointing himself her guardian. At least till vows were
spoken, he added silently. His brows crunched tighter.
Duncan admitted that the lass didn't seem to be upset
by anything that had happened the day before. Not like
he'd witnessed in females of the past. One ripple in their
delicate world, and it was a bloody week's worth of vapors and swooning and whining—

"Did you hear me, Duncan? Hello? Hello?" She
waved a hand in front of his face. "Earth to McPete?"

He blinked, flushing. "Beggin' yer pardon, miss. I—"

She laid a hand over his. "You okay?" He looked puzzled. "Forget it," she waved, offering an apple slice. "I
asked about the men, the wounded."

Duncan sighed, his features smoothing out as he allowed her to coax him into sharing her meal. " 'Tis fine

they are, lass. Don't you be fashin' yerself none. Most are mannin' their stations now."

"Not Mr. Sikes?" she questioned, amazed at the fortitude of Dane's crew.

Duncan grinned. "Restin' in the sun, as ordered, miss." The burly sailor was likely telling the tale of her heroics for nigh on the tenth time this day.

"Good. I want to see him later."

Duncan was nibbling on a biscuit when Dane stepped onto the threshold, his gaze settling immediately on Tess. She stared. He offered her a lopsided grin, and her heart skipped a beat as she drank in the masculine sight of him, her imagination running amok with sizzling memories of fiery kisses, slick skin, and—pleasure.

She licked her suddenly dry lips and in that instant knew where her priorities lay. She had to convince him that she wasn't insane, that she really was from the future. In a heartbeat she could prove her story, with what was in her bag and the bag itself, but for reasons Tess didn't want to examine too deeply, she needed Dane to take her at her word. To believe in *her*.

And it wasn't going to be easy, she decided, recalling how angry he'd become at the mention of the subject before. Dane Blackwell would not accept the truth as gospel, and Tess knew she couldn't convince him in one sitting that she'd actually traveled from the future. Hell, she hardly believed it herself. What she had to do was put doubts in his mind, questions he would be forced to ask her. Only then could she tell him everything.

"Good day, m'lady," broke the extended silence, his voice deep and rough.

"Hello, Captain." For one ridiculous moment Tess wondered if she'd forgotten her shirt with the way he

161

was looking at her.

"Evening, Duncan," Dane added, stepping inside and moving toward his desk.

The chair scraped back as Duncan abruptly came to his feet. "Evenin', Captain Blackwell," he stressed, the sharp tone drawing Tess's attention.

Dane paused in flipping the pages of a ledger. A brow arched. The servant looked like an armed guard, eyes hard, jaw set.

"If yer finished, lass, I'll escort you topside," Duncan said while glaring at his captain.

Dane scowled at the pilot rudder. "I wish to speak to Lady Renfrew, Duncan. You may leave," he said, then turned a page.

Duncan didn't budge an inch.

What the hell is going on? Tess wondered, rising slowly, her gaze shifting from one man to the other.

"You are dismissed, Duncan," Dane repeated, seating himself at the desk and dipping a quill into the inkstand. He began making entries in his log.

Tess could see it was an effort for Duncan to comply and not to speak whatever was on his mind. He picked up the tray, his knuckles turning white with their fierce grip.

Tess laid a hand on his sleeve. "I've never seen you like this, Duncan. Can you talk to me?"

He sighed, his features softening. " 'Tis fond of you I am, lass. An' I'd never forgive meself if I be doin' poorly by you."

Tess frowned, even more confused as he reached out and touched her cheek, then quietly left them alone.

She looked at Dane. "Any idea what all that was about?"

He set the quill in its holder, sprinkled his writing with sand, then relaxed back into the leather chair. His gaze made a lazy parade over her body as he spoke. "Aye. Duncan appears to be upset with me. For reasons I've yet to fathom."

Her heart skidded at the sultry look. "But you don't even care, do you?"

"He has a tendency to mother," he explained, leaving his chair and coming around the side of the desk.

I can't let him touch me, she thought, yet couldn't move a muscle as he neared. Before she could draw back, he grasped her arm, pulling her sharply into his embrace and kissing her hungrily. He plundered her mouth, pushing his tongue past the ivory barrier and sampling her sweet energy. He licked, nipped, then swallowed her low moans. God, I'm drowning, he thought, wild for the feel of her.

Tess sagged against him, looping her arms around his neck and answering the demand of his lips. Why fight it now? She was melting, turning all butter soft inside as his hands molded over her curves, mashing her to his hard length. She was breathless and dizzy when he drew back.

He pressed his forehead to hers. "God's teeth, I've been aching to do that since I left you this morn."

"Gee. Could have fooled me," she panted.

"I apologize if I've caused you any undue discomfort."

"Not really, but you certainly say a lot with those dimp — hey, what's the matter?" He was looking at her so strangely.

He brushed a fingertip across her lips, his voice dropping to a whisper. "Did I hurt you, lass?"

163

She frowned, leaning back, totally confused. "What do you mean?"

Briefly he closed his eyes and sighed. The questions that had destroyed his concentration today must be answered. "Last night—there was a bit of blood, yet I felt no maidenhead when—"

"Whoa, wait a minute, Blackwell." She pushed at his chest, not hard, but enough so he got the message and let her go.

Tess turned away, gathering her composure, discovering it was difficult to locate when he was near. Why did he have to open this subject? Why? Damn it, her past was her secret to keep buried.

"Christ, you've got your nerve, buster," she said in a tight voice, her back to him as she stared out the window.

Dane felt her anger even from across the room, yet couldn't seem to stop the words. "Tess, I do not mean to pry—"

"But you will," she cut in. "And I damn well resent it!"

A muscle worked in his jaw. "I have the right to know the whole of it, woman."

"Oho, no you don't, Blackwell." The words dared him to push her. "That's just your male ego talking." She paused. "I suppose you were expecting a virgin?"

"Nay, and it did not matter."

She scoffed. "At the time—"

"And even now, Tess. I swear it!"

"Then why are you doing this to me?" She rubbed her forehead. "Listen, Blackwell, you've had other women in your bed and I don't question you, so don't force the issue, okay?"

164

Dane reached for her, pulling at her arm until she turned toward him. She kept her head turned in the opposite direction, refusing to look him in the eye. Tenderly he cupped the curve of her jaw and forced her to meet his gaze. It was then that he saw the glistening of tears in her pewter eyes, the utter humiliation written on her face.

"Ah, Tess," he murmured softly, pulling her into his arms. "What in God's name did he do to you?"

Chapter Fourteen

"He used me," she whispered, so softly he almost didn't hear. "Used me like I had no feelings to hurt." She buried her face in the crook of his neck and cried, a quiet sound of shame and regret. His hands, warm and soothing, rubbed up and down her spine. His touch was hesitant, but gentle. So gentle.

Tess wanted to be angry at this invasion of her privacy, but she couldn't. The honest sympathy marking his features had dissolved her resentment. He hadn't asked to be mean so he could watch her suffer; Dane had tried to spare her much of that lately. He'd been confused, and this eighteenth-century man needed answers, and for reasons she couldn't define, she needed to tell him.

Dane pressed his lips to her scented hair. Sweet Christ, what vile thing had the man done to cause her this grief? He squeezed his eyes shut, disgusted that he'd opened such a wound, and worse, with no more tact than a schoolyard bully.

"Shhh, my sweet," he murmured, sweeping her up in his arms and carrying her to the window bench.

166

He sat down, cradling her on his lap, her quiet tears cutting him in half.

"It was my fault, really, for being so stupid. You see." She sniffled. "In college I was an athlete—" she gulped—"with a reputation of being a loner and, well, men thought of me as an odd sort of challenge."

"Nay, Tess. Say no more. 'Tis your secret. Forgive me for intruding where I had no right."

Tess lifted her head, swiping at the dampness trickling down her cheeks, continuing as if she hadn't heard. "Emile was handsome, seductive, and I let myself be seduced. I was in his bed, and he was inside me and—" Dane watched as the shame spread across her features—"he laughed at me, said he couldn't wait to tell his pals that I wasn't a cold bitch after all, just a scared little virgin." Her breath shuddered raggedly with her effort to keep it together. "It was all a joke, Dane, a game. Taking me to bed was a bet between fraternity brothers; my virginity was the prize." She cringed at the memory, her voice turning colder than he'd ever heard. "I shoved him off me, grabbed my clothes, and was out in the street before I stopped to dress." Her gaze narrowed on some distant spot. "He never stopped laughing, and I never let a man get close enough to try that again." She closed her eyes tightly, calmer now; the telling had somehow lessened the humiliation of the whole disgusting mess. She was silent for a long moment before she whispered, "That was five years ago."

Rage swept through Dane like a hurricane. "The bloody bastards," he growled, and her eyes snapped open. "I shall demand satisfaction for this!"

Tess fought back a smile. Her finding humor in his archaic reaction wouldn't do his ego any good just now. "You can't do that, Dane." She slid from his lap to the space beside him.

He gave her a side glance, a muscle working in his jaw. "Be assured, woman, I will."

"Blackwell," she said patiently. "Emile won't be born for another hundred and seventy-five years."

"Tess," he warned, not liking the conviction he saw in her eyes.

She wouldn't push. "Never mind." She waved. "Let's just say he's not anywhere you can find him."

"I will find him. And I'll—"

"You'll what? Kill him?" The look on his face said he'd take pleasure in doing just that. "Why? It's over. I don't care, Dane. Not anymore." She reached out, her fingertips trailing across his cheek. "But it's really sweet of you to want to defend my honor."

His face was still creased in a deep frown. "Can you forgive me for putting you through this, Tess?"

"Sure." She shrugged, her eyes dancing with mischief. "But will you now demand satisfaction for *me* seducing *you?*"

Dane blinked, shocked, then his chiseled lips slowly stretched into a wide grin. "God's teeth, but you're a bold wench."

"Yeah, and you love it," she quipped, struggling in the heavy skirts to rise. Instantly he gathered her in his arms, pulling her across his lap and kissing her, slowly, erotically, a lesson in pure torture to her senses.

"Aye," he breathed against her lips. "I admit I do

enjoy your saucy ways, witch."

She pressed her mouth to his, her tongue snaking out to slowly lick his lips, and his deep shudder steamed all around her like warm velvet. She met his ice mint gaze, and Dane was jolted to his boots with what he saw there. "Last night, Dane—" she smoothed the lines of his face, "I discovered what I've been missing out on for five very long years."

Her fingers tunneled into his hair and she captured his mouth once more, letting her emotions spill over onto him. God, she loved kissing him. He was so damn good at it. Dane Blackwell was a man she couldn't resist, lie to, or walk on and Tess was suddenly thankful she'd been tossed into his world. A groan rumbled deep in his chest when her tongue darted between his lips, and he squeezed her tighter, a hand moving down her burgundy-covered hip. Then to his disappointment, she abruptly pushed out of his arms and stood.

"We'll be missed, Captain," she said shakily, urging him to his feet, reminding him they were not the only people on board, as much as he wished it to be so. Tess smiled softly when he mumbled a curse at the floor and rubbed the back of his neck. He was in a bit of pain, she could see, and it pleased her. She wasn't in such great shape either.

She moved away before she was tempted and was almost to the door when a thought occurred to him. "Tess? You went to a university? A college?"

"Yup. Graduated with honors." She opened the door.

"How is this possible?"

She paused, looking back over her shoulder. "You

169

know, Blackwell, you sure ask a lot of personal questions for a man who hasn't shared one speck of *his* past." She held his gaze for a moment longer, her expression telling him he had to give to get and that this one-sided relationship was beginning to bug the hell out of her. Then she stepped out, leaving him alone in the cabin.

Dane stiffened, insulted by his own curiosity. College — bah, she was lying, he reasoned. No university allowed women to enter its halls. Damn and blast! He rubbed his nape, already second-guessing his initial conclusions. He strode after her, not about to let the little witch give *him* such a set-down. Not when she was telling lies.

The smell of food and the happy sound of a flute filtered to Tess as she made her way down the narrow corridor. She checked her appearance just before she opened the hatch that led topside and stepped out.

"Evenin', miss." Duncan grinned at her captivated look, latching the door so it stayed open.

Tess didn't take her eyes off the sight before her. The ship glowed, as if sprinkled with thousands of fireflies, yellow light radiating from the lanterns swaying with the dip of the vessel. Bare feet tapped while their owners listened to the cheery music, sipping drink from wooden cups and dining from meat-heavy platters that rested on crates and barrels. Two men danced a jig, one obviously playing the role of a female with a kerchief tied beneath his chin.

"What's all this for, Duncan?"

" 'Tis a celebration, Tess," Dane said, stepping

170

onto the deck behind her. His eyes were narrow and wary as they met hers.

"What have you got to celebrate?"

"Why, a victory, of course," Duncan put in, lightly grasping her elbow and leading her toward the rail.

She jerked her arm free, rounding on the old man. "You mean you're celebrating the sinking of that ship! That's disgusting," she hissed, glaring at Dane. "Dancing on the graves of all those poor men!"

Tess was outraged for about two more seconds, then she remembered where she was. She took a deep breath, mollified when she saw the captured sailors, clean and adequately dressed and eating like starved animals. God, they looked so thin.

"I'm sorry for that," she said, lifting her gaze to meet Dane's, then offering Duncan her best smile. "I realize it could have been that idiot in yellow satin who could be celebrating tonight." And likely doing it on me, she thought with a blast of reality. This was going to take some getting used to, and a bit more thinking before she opened her mouth again. "Ah, did you lose any men, Dane?"

"Nay." He saw relief sweep her features.

"Well. That's reason enough to have a party."

"I'm delighted you approve," he shot back sarcastically.

Tess frowned, unreasonably hurt by his attitude and was glad when he left them alone. What's gotten into him now? she wondered, watching his retreating back as he strode to the helm. Her gaze shifted to her surroundings again and she saw that every man aboard was smiling at her. What's changed their attitudes toward me? Don't ask, Renfrew. You'll never

171

get a straight answer.

"Good evenin', Lady Renfrew." She turned toward the voice. Gaelan Thorpe, blond and handsome and dressed in much finer clothes than she'd seen on him yet, was holding out a wooden mug.

She accepted it, thanking him as she took a sip. She coughed and sputtered for a moment, leading Gaelan to think he'd somehow poisoned her.

"Are you ill, mistress?"

"No," she managed in a squeak, waving away the hand that was about to slap her back. "I don't drink, Mr. Thorpe, at least not straight rum."

"Forgive me, m'lady." He flushed, looking down at his hand. "It seems I've given you my cup."

Her gaze shot between the containers, and Tess burst out laughing. He looked too upset over such a little thing. "How's mine, Mr. Thorpe?"

"Oh, I haven't tasted it, m'lady, I swear."

"Calm down," she told him, switching the cups and sipping the sweet fruit drink. "You should have, it's great. Maybe we ought to mix them?" she said, making a move to pour some juice into his.

"Mix?" He covered the mouth of the cup, appalled at the suggestion.

"Sure. I had this drink once when I was about seventeen, a Bahama Mama. If we blend the two I bet it will come close." She didn't mention that it crept up on her that night, beaning her like a sledgehammer, and she'd found herself in the back of a vegetable truck on the way to Miami with no notion as to how she got there. She did remember it took a week to recover. That was her last drink.

"Not game?" She grinned; he was still protecting

his drink. "Suit yourself." She lifted the cup to her lips but stopped before it touched. Her eyes grew wide, and Gaelen saw stark terror blanch across her face. Trancelike, she set down the cup and, not taking her eyes off some distant spot, moved with a rapid step to the passageway. A hand covered her mouth before she dragged her eyes from the horizon and ducked through the portal. Tess grasped the wall rail, then sagged back against it. Oh, God, oh God, not again! She didn't think she could take it. Another ship, another battle, the blood, the death — flooding her mind was the image of the machete coming toward Dane's head. Her hands trembled. A tightness formed in her throat.

"Tess?" She looked up. Dane was scowling at her. "What is the matter?"

"Th-that ship — ?"

"Aye," he said slowly, watching her.

"Well!" she demanded. "Whose is it? Is it friendly? Will there be a battle?"

Dane relaxed. He'd been ready to cut Gaelan to shreds, having thought he'd offended her. He offered his arm. She stared at it for a moment, then looked up at him. "Come see for yourself what flag she flies," he challenged, a ghost of a smile tugging at his lips.

Relief swept through her. Dane wouldn't take her back up if there were any danger. Lifting her chin, she accepted his arm and stepped through the doorway with him. They walked toward the starboard rail, and Tess saw a small boat coming toward the *Sea Witch*. The other ship was as large as the frigate, glowing like a sparkling topaz on the black velvet waters. Her skin chilled at the mystical vision, sails flapping gently, the hum of flutes drifting on the breeze. The four men in the small dinghy disappeared from her view as they neared. Unable to douse her curiosity, she stepped away from Dane and peered over the rail as one man, darkly dressed, climbed up the side of the ship, his booted feet catching the wood rungs embedded in the hull, powerful legs eating up the distance with a strength and agility even Tess could admire. She moved quickly back behind Dane and Duncan and the first officers. She still wasn't sure about all this. The visitor climbed onto the rail, standing straight and tall, his hands on his hips, legs adjusting to the dip of the vessel.

"Blackwell, you bloody clank-napper," he bellowed. "What sort of captain are you to leave a rum doxy's trail of debris halfway across the Indies!" Then he leapt to the deck with a thud, landing a few feet before Dane.

"I'm your superior, that's the captain I am. Show some respect, you horse's arse, 'afore I run you through," Tess inhaled sharply as Dane went for his sword.

"Forgive this young pup, m'lord," the visitor spoke in a mocking tone, sweeping into a low bow. "Your humble servant, sir. I've forgotten that I stand in the presence of a scholar of the sea."

"More like the scourge," someone behind him said. Dane and the visitor locked gazes, then the pair burst into laughter. Both men stepped forward, grasping hands, then finished with a firm embrace, slapping each other on the back.

"God's teeth, Ram, it's good to see you," Dane said, moving back, his pale gaze looking over the man.

"Aye, and you also, my friend." His brows drew together. "How goes your quest?"

Dane frowned. "Bennett's pilot rudders were not of much use. The man's writing is abominable, and not one of us can decipher the mess."

"Mayhaps you'll give this lowly servant the opportunity to have a look," Ram tossed cheekily. "I daresay I managed to read your scratching for years."

Dane chuckled. "Only if that arrogant attitude improves."

"As I recall, 'tis what moved you to contract me, Dane," Ramsey said as he glanced over the ship, remembering a time long past, yet as he was about to bring his gaze back to Dane, it halted on the figure standing between Duncan and the first mate.

"What tasty piece is this, Dane? Since when have you taken to allowing cats—"

"Have you suddenly gone blind, man?" Dane hissed, his eyes filled with quick anger.

Ram glanced at Blackwell, arching a brow at the muscle working in the man's jaw. His eyes shifted back to the woman. If she was not a whore, then . . . Ignoring all, he moved toward her, his stride purposeful, his smile rakishly charming. Dane groaned audibly, matching his steps. Ram stopped before Tess.

"Such a rare beauty," he murmured as if to himself; his eyes, dark as chocolate, skimmed her from head to toe.

What a line, Tess thought, then said, "Thanks,"

offering her hand with the intention of shaking his.

The man grasped her fingertips, bringing her hand to his lips. His eyes never left hers. "Don't tell me you've taken a wife, Blackwell?" he questioned before placing a soft kiss to the back.

"No, he hasn't," Tess corrected quickly. Jeez, what a hunk!

A chestnut brow lifted, and his lips pulled into a pleased smile. "How fortunate," he whispered. Slowly he eased her hand down, his gaze never wavering. "I beg an introduction, Captain Blackwell."

Dane gnashed his teeth, unsure what he was feeling after her quick denial of their relationship. "Gentlemen, may I present the Lady Tess Renfrew of Scotland."

Tess shot Dane a sour look. I suppose that "lady" stuff will never change, she thought, deciding to let it go. She drew back her hand.

"Lady Renfrew, this drooling sot is Ramsey O'Keefe, Captain of *Triton's Will,* sister ship to the *Sea Witch.*"

Sister ship, huh? Remembering where she was, Tess curtsied, looking up as she straightened. "Pleased to meet you, Captain O'Keefe." She smiled, her gaze shifting beyond him. "And the other men?" Ramsey gestured sharply for the men to come forward and introduced his first and second officers, shocked when she heartily shook each man's hand. Aye, there was something different about this woman, and he made it his first priority to discover exactly what it was.

"Where did you find her, Dane?" Ramsey asked, glancing to his friend.

176

"Blackwell fished me out of the sea, Captain O'Keefe, and I can answer for myself."

Dane fought a grin at the surprised expression on Ramsey's face. Ahh, but Tess will set the rake on his rear, he thought, and wasn't certain he wanted her within yards of O'Keefe, master of debauchery that he was.

"You must be the reason we've been asked to dine aboard."

"I doubt it." Tess folded her arms beneath her breasts. "Captain Blackwell doesn't inform me of his plans." Her tone implied she didn't care for this little surprise.

"God, Dane, she's priceless!" Ram looked at Blackwell. "Is she wed? Betrothed?"

Tess glanced around herself. "Did I suddenly disappear or something? If you talk to me, Captain O'Keefe, then talk to *me!*"

He grinned. "It will be a pleasure, m'lady."

"Sure you can manage that?"

Ramsey chuckled deeply. "Aye. I believe I can."

Captain O'Keefe was a handsome man, Tess thought, and he damn well knew it. On a scale of one to ten, Dane being her idea of a ten, O'Keefe was pushing a strong eight. O'Keefe was ruggedly handsome, well-built, confident, almost too confident for those tight britches of his, but that's where the similarities between the men ended. Dane wasn't aware of his good looks, and when he looked in a mirror it was to check for food on his face or something like that. O'Keefe had a winning smile, oodles of charm, and used them to his advantage, mostly with women, she gathered. He was interested in the

177

image he projected, which wasn't bad because it certainly was a fine, *fine* image.

Dane watched as Tess let her gaze wander over Ramsey. He could recognize admiration when he saw it. And worse yet was that Ram returned the perusal. I should have gone to the *Triton,* Dane thought, then chided himself for this sudden spurt of jealousy. Tess wasn't his, at least not in her eyes. And in yours? he silently asked. Do you want this woman? A woman who insists she's from the future?

"Dinner will be served in less than an hour," Duncan spoke up in the hard silence.

"Come look over those pilot rudders, Ram, whilst I change for dinner," Dane said, drawing Ram's attention from Tess.

"Nay, I believe I'll stroll the deck with the lady, Captain. Get to know the lass before you shove me overboard."

"Gee, sure was nice of you to ask, O'Keefe," Tess bit out sarcastically, then turned her back on the man and spoke to Gaelan. "How about a turn around the deck, Mr. Thorpe?"

Gaelan cleared his throat, his gaze shooting between his captain, who was desperately attempting to hold back his laughter, to Captain O'Keefe, whose mouth was hanging on its hinges.

"An honor, m'lady." Gaelan offered his arm, trying to hide a smug smile as she accepted it.

"Call me when chow's on," she tossed over her shoulder as she moved in a sedate pace with the first officer.

"Chow?" Ramsey asked curiously. Dane shrugged.

Ramsey folded his arms over his chest, admiring

her slender curves, the gentle sway of her hips. He shook his head in self-recrimination. Any man could see she was not a bawd, and as his eyes touched on Dane's crew, Ram noted he wasn't the only one who'd come to that conclusion. Men admired her as one would a Rembrandt, from a distance, daring not to touch lest they destroy the masterpiece. Ram loved art, the kind you could fondle a bit.

Dane chuckled close at his side. "Your charms are sadly waning, old man. I dare say 'tis a first, Ramsey O'Keefe, denied the company of a lady and at her own choice." Dane's laughter was quiet and hearty.

Ram didn't take his eyes off her. "Is she yours, Dane? Have you bedded—?"

"Don't be crude," Dane growled softly. "And after that royal set-down, 'tis clear even to you, the lady belongs to no one."

Ramsey's lips split into a wide smile. "Then she's fair prey?"

"The woman's not a pheasant, Ram."

When she glanced back over her shoulder, Ram nodded ever so slightly. "What is it about her, Dane?" Ramsey asked quietly, then looked at his friend. "Do not tell me you have not noticed this? Her clipped speech, that frosty independence? I don't believe I've ever encountered a woman quite like her."

Blackwell inclined his head to the passageway, and Ram followed. "And in you entire life, O'Keefe, I doubt you ever will," Dane heard himself say.

Chapter Fifteen

"She has arrived, sir."

The blond man tensed, yet no one would know it, for his slender body remained draped across the delicate chair, a leg flung over the arm.

"Send her in," he ordered with a lazy wave, as if he really couldn't be bothered. He brought the crystal goblet to his lips and sipped, staring out the open veranda doors, the soft trade wind gently ruffling the sheer drapes.

A moment later the liveried servant reappeared in the doorway, eyes downcast.

"Mistress Cabrea, sir."

The man in the chair inspected the ocean view for another moment before he lifted his gaze to the woman.

"Yellow doesn't become you, Lizzie. You look as if you've been painted all one hideous shade."

She flushed at the insult. "A gentleman usually stands when a lady enters the room, Phillip."

"When a lady does, perhaps I might consider the absurd notion."

The corner of his mouth lifted, and Elizabeth's

lips pressed tightly together in her effort not to snap at him. She busied herself with methodically removing her gloves, finger by finger, then slipped the small feathered hat from her head. She carelessly tossed the dusty articles on the polished table and moved into the room, the wide panniers swaying as she strolled to the sideboard. Elizabeth lived for the moment when she could relay her news the instant she'd confirmed it. She allowed herself a small private smile as she filled a miniature goblet with the sweet orange liqueur.

"Lizzie."

His voice sliced the quiet, a note of warning in the tone. She jolted, spilling a tiny drop on the wood table. With a finger, she swiped at the spot, sucking the liqueur from her fingertip as she faced him.

"Must I force the information from you, my pet?" His tone implied he would enjoy the task. Her fingers tightened on the goblet, her perfect features marked with quick fear. She swallowed. Phillip Rothmere was not a man one should aggravate, she reminded herself.

"Oh, honestly, Phillip," she said, lifting her chin and nervously tucking in a stray blond curl. She adjusted her gown, tugged at her sleeve, then focused her attention on the lush scenery beyond the terrace, uncertain what he would actually do when he heard.

Out of the corner of her eye she could see him rise from his chair and move toward her. Then he was near, a long thin finger pushing beneath her chin, forcing her to meet those Nordic blue eyes.

181

"The *Chatam*. What's become of her and her captain?"

Elizabeth briefly considered why she associated herself with a man who would send an unguarded woman to the most dangerous section of this island to do his bidding. It was the money, she finally decided, bringing the glass to her lips.

" 'Twas destroyed." He tensed beside her. "All but one are dead, and your precious brig is naught but a pile of kindling floating on the sea," she finished with some satisfaction.

His nostrils flared, his eyes narrowing to mere slits as his heavily jeweled fingers tightened on the delicate goblet. It shattered, spraying them both with the blood red wine. Elizabeth didn't dare comment.

"How?" he breathed. He hadn't moved.

A pale, tapered brow arched. "Need you ask?"

He grabbed her by the hair. "Tell me!" he said softly, yanking her head back. His liquored breath was hot on her cheek, and Elizabeth lost her nerve, fearing he would strike her.

" 'Twas Blackwell—" She didn't get any more than that out when he shoved her to the floor, then strode to the bar. He sloshed wine into a fresh glass, tossed back the liquid, then refilled the crystal, lifting it to his lips. Suddenly he hurled it across the parlor. The fine glass crashed against the stucco wall, wine dripping like blood, the outburst sending inquisitive servants scurrying for cover.

He whirled about, his ice blue gaze skewering the woman. "You lie!"

"Nay. 'Twas he!" Elizabeth recoiled against the

curtains as he stormed toward her. "A man was found yestereve on the shore. 'Twas Bennett's quartermaster." Her words rushed out as she came to her knees, her expression pleading for him to believe.

He loomed over her, his broad hands closing painfully over her arms. "Where is this sailor?" he said carefully.

"At the church. He is dying, Phillip. I tested his strength last eve with your questions until the friar bade me go."

His grip tightened, and she cried out. "What else, Lizzie?"

Tears wet her eyes; Elizabeth swallowed repeatedly, not daring to climb to her feet to ease his hold. "Blackwell has the pilot rudders." His glare sharpened and a muscle ticked beneath his eye. "The sailor saw him and a young boy go into the captain's cabin, Phillip. Blackwell has them! He will come for you!"

Phillips face suddenly cleared and he chuckled lowly, shoving her away as he straightened. "I so dislike the hope I am hearing in your voice, Liz. Rid yourself of it," he commanded with a wave of his hand.

Elizabeth tried with a little dignity to right herself amongst the cumbersome layers of fabric and whalebone of her gown as he casually strolled to the open doors and rocked back on his heels.

"Nay. The honorable Captain Blackwell is driven by revenge. Such a useless emotion, that. So many mistakes can be made." He sighed tiredly, his gaze moving between the palm fronds to the young brown-skinned girl picking flowers in his garden.

" 'Twill take the pompous braggart years to find me among these islands. 'Twas the sole reason I chose this bug-infested paradise." He turned his head. "Yet you can be most assured I will enjoy the confrontation, should it arise, Lizzie. Be most assured." His smile was thin, confident, and it made Elizabeth shiver. Phillip was pleasant to look upon, slim, fair-skinned, thick light hair neatly tied, yet it was those eyes that gave a person pause—shark-cold, merciless. And Elizabeth wanted naught to do with the secrets kept there.

Phillip held her gaze, enjoying the ripple of fright on her carefully painted face, the trembling of her hands. It made his body grow warm and hard. The little chit was far too transparent for her own good.

"No doubt Blackwell is aware of your duplicity," he reminded needlessly.

Elizabeth's gaze dropped to the spot before her skirts. Nay, Dane was unaware, she prayed. She was there when he'd discovered what had happened to Desiree. She'd witnessed his ungodly fury, the way he tore through the city searching for Phillip. It was she who had brought Phillip to Desiree and her father, she who'd given her blessing of his worth. A delicate shiver passed down her spine. Dane would not harm me, she insisted silently. If perchance she did meet with the dark captain, Elizabeth was positive she could convince him she'd been duped by Phillip, too. She absently fingered the string of topaz glittering against the milky skin above her breasts. Truly, she couldn't give a care to what Phillip had actually done to the gullible child; her conscience would not allow such thoughts. Elizabeth would get her coin as soon as she was able, find a ship, and depart this wretched little scrap of land. Before Dane found them.

"I must leave, Phillip," she said while looking at her ruined gown. "I need to change." When he didn't respond, she looked up. The air rushed into her lungs at his expression. "Nay!" she wailed, struggling to rise.

Phillip's lips twisted in a cruel smile as he slipped the ascot free from around his throat, then slowly unbuttoned his shirt. Lace fluttered at his cuffs as he moved. Gemstones flashed, catching the light as he quickly stripped the fabric from his torso. He watched as she nervously licked her lips, and he was there when she managed to climb to her feet.

"Nay, Phillip, please. Not again." Regardless of her pleas, she stood frozen beneath his empty gaze. His palms roughly covered her breasts, his fingertips catching in the neck of her gown. She gasped as he rent the fabric to her waist. He shoved her to the floor, then freed the buttons of his breeches. Her eyes widened, and she choked on a sob, trying to move away.

He backhanded her, his ring slicing open her cheek. Then he grabbed her jaw, the vicious grip whitening the flesh around his fingers as he turned her face to him. "Never deny me, Lizzie. 'Tis a day you will regret."

Terrified, she nodded meekly, tears spilling from round, dark eyes. He chuckled at her dread, bending over her, his tongue snaking out to lick the trickle of blood moving toward his fingertips, delighting when his half sister cringed.

Chapter Sixteen

As Tess stepped into the cabin, several elegantly dressed men turned toward her. Heat warmed her cheeks, and she self-consciously brushed the stray hairs from her face, offering a small smile. The cabin, once seeming spacious, was now cramped with officers.

She stepped back against the wall as aproned sailors filed in before her with garnished trays of poached fish and chicken, baked apples and sugared beets, pots of sauce-covered noodles and silver platters of hard crusty bread and churned butter. Real butter, Tess marveled, as a deckhand poured red wine into crystal goblets.

Her gaze danced around the dining area, softly lit with lanterns and candles. The long scarred table was covered with a pristine cloth and set with fine polished pewter, silver, and crystal, the aroma of food making her mouth water. Her eyes came to rest on Dane where he was standing before a mirror, tying a tie, of sorts. Dark green velvet stretched tight across his broad shoulders as he fiddled with the neckcloth, and Tess's heart jumped when he caught her gaze in the silver glass. Damn, he looked good.

His coat was long, the hem sweeping back almost like tails, the fabric unadorned, its standing collar stiff and high. Frothy cream silk spilled from his throat and cuffs, and Tess thought that any other man, in her time, would have looked ridiculous in that outfit, but Dane made her hot. His trousers were buff-colored, showing every contour of his powerful thighs, and, like O'Keefe, he wore knee boots instead of stockings and buckled shoes. His long hair was pulled back in his customary black ribbon, and unruly still damp curls framed his throat. He turned to face her, giving his green brocade vest a tug.

She took a slow breath to calm her pulse. "You look very nice this evening, Dane." Her eyes danced with mischief. "Who would have thought you'd clean up so well for a pirate?"

There was a soft chuckle from somewhere to her right, and Tess looked over to see O'Keefe reclined casually on the bed, his torso supported on a bent arm. "Ahh, Blackwell, she's enchanting. Such wit and left-handed compliments are succor to a man's self-esteem."

"I think you'll survive, O'Keefe. You have enough self-esteem for all of us." Several men choked on their drinks, but Ramsey merely grinned.

"You don't care for me very much, do you, lass?" he said, agilely climbing off the high bed scented with her perfume.

"I don't know you well enough not to like you,"

she replied as he moved toward her.

"Mayhaps this evening we shall change your poor opinion of my debauched soul?" He grasped her hand, giving her knuckles a quick kiss.

Tess craned her neck to look up at him. Oh boy, was he smooth. "We'll see, Captain O'Keefe. I reserve the right to withhold judgment until I'm ready. Now, if you're through with this." She pulled her hand free. "Excuse me, while I freshen up." Tess slipped into the bathroom, sighing against the closed door. Freshen up! God, she never thought she'd hear herself say that!

She looked down at the chamber pot and shivered with revulsion. Never in her life did she appreciate modern plumbing more than at that moment. Managing this is an art, she thought, making use of the crude facilities. She washed the thin sheen of salt from her face and hands, pulled the pins from her hair, and brushed the jet black mass until it shone, then swept the tresses into a soft chignon, leaving a few wisps to frame her face. Tess was glad her gown wasn't like the first one. This was more sedate with a higher neckline. She hated to think what O'Keefe would do if he had a look at some skin. Jeez, the man was a walking di — now, Renfrew, she scolded herself, that isn't very nice.

Tess had to remind herself where she was and the double standard that existed. The gentler sex, they'd called her. Wonder what Amelia Earhart, Rachel McLeish, and Sally Ride would have to say about that. She'd never been in the company of so many men as she had in the past two weeks and still wasn't used to all the attention. This was going to be a challenge, and she knew she had to watch what she said or, rather, how it was delivered. Ramsey was Dane's good friend, probably his best friend, as well as the captain of one of his ships, and she didn't want to be the cause of a rift between them, no matter how far-fetched the idea sounded. Checking to be certain nothing embarrassing was showing, Tess braced herself for the evening ahead. Show no mercy, Renfrew. Cut no slack.

Dane kept a casual eye on the bathing-room door. When she finally appeared, he fought the urge to climb over the furniture to get to her. How in God's name was he supposed to function as a leader if all he could think about was this woman and what it was like to hold her, kiss her, make love to her? He set aside his drink and shifted around Ramsey, unaware that he'd ceased talking in mid-sentence. She was moving toward him. The burning memory of only last night, her muscled body, slick-hot and writhing beneath him, begging him to show her what she'd never known, filled his mind. All he could think of was this woman and how she'd given him the most passionate night of his life!

They were moderately alone in the center of the room.

"Good God, Blackwell. What on earth are you thinking?" she asked softly. "That look on your face is positively obscene!"

He grinned a bit lopsidedly, making her pulse stagger as he grasped her hand and tucked it in the crook of his arm. He leaned close to whisper, "My thoughts are far too bold to be spoken aloud, love."

Tess nearly choked at the endearment, her senses

reeling back to the first time he'd called her that, when he was buried inside her on the very spot they stood. Unable to help it, she glanced down at her feet, then lifted her gaze to his.

"Great minds think alike, eh, Blackwell," she murmured throatily.

He tossed his head back and laughed, the sound rich and hearty, bringing several heads around.

Ramsey's head jerked up, his features pulling taut. It had been a while since he'd seen Dane laugh, and he couldn't help but smile. The man was so filled with revenge of late that he hadn't made time to enjoy anything. Were I he, Ram thought, envious of the secrets the pair were sharing at that moment. The intimate look Tess sent Dane brimmed with heat and sensuality, and Ramsey felt a sharp jealous ache that she'd bestow such a glance on his friend. He calmed himself. They had yet begun the evening, he decided confidently.

A chime sounded, and Duncan announced that dinner was served.

Tess turned to see the officers standing behind their chairs as Dane maneuvered her to the far end. She adjusted the heavy skirts and sat down, glancing back over her shoulder at Dane as he scooted the chair beneath her. There was a silent message in that soft look, she thought, and wondered what it was. Chair legs scraped against the floor as the men seated themselves only after she was firmly planted. A girl could get used to all this chivalry, Tess decided as Dane took his place directly opposite her. To her left was Captain O'Keefe, smiling that sexy heart-stopping smile; to her right was Gaelan

Thorpe. She couldn't help but notice that every man appeared interested in how she placed her napkin.

Dane watched her, unaware of what he was putting on his plate. Though hers was full, she waited patiently until all had been served, then finally tasted the meal. Unused to the female company, men devoured the fare before them with a vengeance, but Tess dined slowly, savoring each bite. Her manners were impeccable, oddly meticulous, and he observed as she set the knife aside after each cut, then switched hands. So elegant. Every other soul kept fork and knife in his grip constantly, himself included.

"I see you still employ the same cook, eh, Blackwell?" Ramsey commented, enjoying the delicate flavor of the poached fish. "The odd little man certainly does put on a splendid fare."

"Aye, with meager stores he does do rather well," Dane replied.

"Have you met the cook, Lady Renfrew?" Ramsey asked.

" 'Fraid not." She sipped her wine, wishing it were a Diet Coke. "Captain Blackwell forbade me to go belowdecks, and I assume that's where the chef is."

"A wise command, Dane," Ramsey said, glancing at the captain, then shoving a generous portion of chicken into his mouth.

"I still don't understand what's so bad about going below?" Her remark caused several men to chuckle.

" 'Tis not a fit place for a lady," Gaelan told her. "And our cook has a reputation. One does *not* enter his domain."

Tess's eyes widened a fraction. "No one?" She looked at Dane. "Not even you?"

"He has some peculiar possessiveness about the galley." Dane shrugged, sawing into his meat.

"He lopped off a sailor's finger once for sneaking a taste of his cakes."

Tess set her fork down with a sharp clink. "That's barbaric!"

Dane dealt Aaron a harsh glance, then looked to Tess. "Do not worry yourself, Lady Renfrew. He rarely shows himself above decks and does not speak at all." His cool tone implied the matter was not up for discussion as he addressed the man beside him.

Tess fumed at his attitude and ground out, "What type of ship is *Triton's Will,* Captain O'Keefe?" before turning to look at the man.

"A frigate, m'lady, a duplicate of the *Sea Witch.*" Ram hid a smile as he slavered butter on a small crust of bread, then popped it into his mouth.

Hard arteries by forty, she thought. "Exact? The ceilings raised, I mean." He nodded. "I guess it's necessary with you being so tall."

His grin was devilish. "Ahh, so there is something the lady has noticed of this poor, lonely seaman."

"You mean besides your conceit?"

He covered his heart with his hand, dark eyes twinkling. "Ouch, you wound me dearly, fair lady, with the venomous arrows you thrust deep into my tender heart."

"Your skin is too thick, O'Keefe," she murmured, her eyes laughing.

"Yet you have pierced its many layers, m'lady."

A tapered brow rose. "Cowhide that soft, huh?"

Gaelan tried to disguise his chuckle, but Ramsey threw his head back and laughed aloud.

"Ahh, such a sharp tongue you wield, lass. Pray, what cause have I given for you to be so harsh with me?"

"I'm not being harsh, Captain O'Keefe. Truthful I think is a better word. You're an outrageous flirt, and I know it."

Ramsey enjoyed her frankness. "Sweet lass," he grasped her hand. "Is there any way to win your cold heart?"

She pulled free. "I didn't know it was up for grabs."

Ramsey frowned, taking a moment to understand what she meant. "Do not all ladies of age seek to find their heartmate and wed?"

"You're of age, are you?"

The comment brought soft laughter from the men sitting close. Ramsey sighed heavily. "I fear I shan't marry in the near future."

Her eyes sparkled. "You mean, not unless there's a gun aimed at your head." Ramsey actually flushed at that. "Why do men think all women have on their minds is marriage, children, cooking, cleaning, and laundry. Have you ever done laundry, Captain?"

He shook his head, then asked, "Have you, lass?"

"Sure."

Ram was shocked that she had. "Ladies usually leave such chores to servants," he told her. They were all looking at her rather oddly now.

She lifted her chin defiantly. "Hard work is good for the soul, or haven't you heard?" She was glad to see them look a bit shamefaced. "I've always taken care of myself, Captain O'Keefe, and laundry's a real pain. Not what I'd call a great way to spend the day." Tess knew doing laundry in 1789 bordered on beating it against a rock. "And it's certainly not my prime goal in life."

"Dare I ask what is your," his brows scrunched, "prime goal?"

Tess glanced at Dane and noticed that he'd been listening. "A couple of weeks ago I could have told you, but now, I'm not so sure," she answered softly.

"Will you return to your home, then?" Ramsey asked, then watched her expression cloud. She looked down at her plate.

"I can't, O'Keefe. I can never go home." Because it doesn't exist, she thought, and for a second wondered about Penny, hoping her career was still intact. Then it hit her that Penny wouldn't be born for another hundred and seventy-five years!

"Surely there are people looking for you? Relatives? Your parents, perchance?" Ramsey's tone was one of honest concern.

"Hardly." Her gaze met Dane's. "They're dead. A car—carriage accident," she corrected quickly. A drunk driver, Tess raged silently. How could she explain she'd been thrown to the floor of the parked car, and the only injury she'd received was a wrenched kneecap, her foster parents killed, and her Olympic career trashed for good.

"I'm sorry for your loss, m'lady," Dane heard Ram say and felt a moment of confusion. If her family had not set her adrift, then who? Had she truly jumped ship in fear for her life? He'd once

194

considered that statement simply to be the ravings of a madwoman. But now—

"Thanks, O'Keefe. Where are you from?" she said, changing the subject.

"I hail from Lexington, m'lady."

"How come you don't have an accent?"

"Mayhaps because I have not set foot on dry land for any length of time in nearly fifteen years."

"Good God! You mean you've been on ship that long?"

"Aye, a seaman is a seaman, lass." He focused his attention on his meal.

"You too, Mr. Thorpe?"

Gaelan swallowed, delighted she finally noticed his presence. "Aye, I fear I'm not as worldly as the captain here, m'lady. 'Tis been a mere ten years since I've stepped onto my family's plantation in North Carolina."

Tess relaxed in her chair, glancing between the two. "I bet the pair of you left a trail of broken hearts up and down the East Coast."

"I hold no such honor, m'lady," Gaelan put in with a chuckle. "I've not the reputation with the ladies as does Captains Blackwell and O'Kee—" He cut himself off when her smile drooped. "Forgive me, Lady Renfrew. I did not mean to insult you."

"You haven't." Her gaze shifted. "So—you and Blackwell have a reputation, huh?"

Ramsey leaned closer. "Is it possible 'tis jealousy I hear in your voice, m'lady?" She chuckled throatily, the husky sound warming Ramsey to the core.

"Nope, the God's truth, I think." She sampled the fish. "What sort of reputation, Mr. Thorpe?"

He looked uncomfortable. "Not one I would discuss with a lady," he mumbled, glancing away.

"Oho. *That* kind." Her eyes twinkled at his distress. "Relax, Mr. Thorpe. Men and women are a fact of life."

"So delighted to hear you speak so, Lady Renfrew," Ramsey murmured silkily.

Tess glanced to her side. "Down, boy, down." She was close enough to catch the woodsy scent of his cologne, see the unbelievable length of his lashes. One of these days, she thought, he was going to get his comeuppance. He'll fall madly in love with a woman who is unaffected by his good looks and charm, and Tess silently hoped she was around to see the man suffer.

"Nay, I believe if we strengthen our military it will only give the notion that we wish to fight," someone said loudly enough for her to hear. Her curiosity piqued.

"You wish the United States to be left vulnerable to the British?" Dane remarked.

"They would not dare to attack!"

They do, Tess thought, in 1812.

Dane smiled indulgently at the young officer, wiping his lips, then tossing the napkin on his plate. "We are a young country, Mr. Fleming, with a government that is but a babe, hardly knowing how to crawl."

"Yet on the subject of the militia, Captain, you wish us to run with the likes of England and France and—"

"We can," Ram put in. "Have we all not proven 'tis so?" Murmurs of agreement sounded around the table.

"I agree." All heads turned toward Tess, expressions of pure astonishment marking their faces.

"I beg your pardon, m'lady?" Fleming said, obviously annoyed at her intrusion.

Tess looked around at the poorly hidden lack of respect for her opinion. She leaned forward, ready to give them a small lesson in equal rights. "I agreed with Da—Captain Blackwell. If other world powers see us as easy to conquer, our ports unprotected, then we are vulnerable to attack. But if we strengthen our Navy and Marines to match or better them, then countries will understand that we mean business and will think again before they decide to invade."

There was a sudden silence, and at the far end of the table Dane looked at her through lowered lashes, admiring her tenacity to join in such a conversation she had no business entering. He leaned forward, bracing his elbows on the table and resting his chin on folded hands.

"And what, pray tell, do you propose we do about the situation, Lady Renfrew?"

Tess ignored his condescending tone and took a deep breath, gearing her thinking back two hundred years. "Exactly as the Constitution states."

A raven black brow rose. "You've read the document?"

"Yeah, want me to recite the Preamble?" she shot back and Dane's lips twitched, realizing 'twas likely she could. "It says the government will provide and maintain a Navy." But they don't, she recalled suddenly, not for a few more years.

"The Constitution allows Congress to raise and support armies, yet those monies shall be approved for no longer than two years," Dane countered, rising from his seat and moving to the hutch.

"I'm aware of that," she said, watching as he poured several brandies, then shaking her head when he offered her one. "But what happens if we need them for longer than that? I think we should finance an army and a fleet of ships on a full-time basis."

Dane whispered something to a sailor about to leave with a tray.

"Why not simply call for volunteers when the need arises?" someone interjected. "Our freedom from the Crown is proof that it works."

"True, Mr. Cambert, but if every able man leaves, then who is left to work the farms, produce food, clothing, gunpowder, and mine metals needed to outfit the men on the front lines?" There was a silent pause as the obvious sunk in. "We are not self-sufficient. Can we afford another Valley Forge?"

Men shook their heads gravely.

Dane dropped lazily into his chair, absently toying with the delicate stem of crystal, and said, "You cannot expect businessmen to give their goods freely. Where will the monies to pay for the forces come from?"

Heads shifted to see how she'd answer.

"A small tax on the sale of goods in the United States and taxing goods entering our ports should boost the treasury."

" 'Tis exactly as the British had done!" Cambert

sneered.

"No." Tess leaned forward, unaware of the little man entering the cabin. "They tried to tax and starve us to death, to control us, and our *troops* proved they couldn't. Not flowery speeches and dumping some tea. We owe it to ourselves not let lack of funds destroy what all those guys died for." She shook her head, thinking of how many wars would still come. "A government can't run on promises you know. Supporting our Congress and the President isn't enough. Taxing ourselves is the answer."

"You truly believe in a salaried militia?" Dane asked, thinking of the same discussion he'd had several months past.

"Sure. You wouldn't use say—a—a blacksmith's services without paying him, would you?" She didn't wait for a response. "Paying for the protection of that freedom means a professionally trained, well-outfitted military. Not to mention the advantage that readiness allows." That brought grudging nods. "I know I'd sleep better knowing the seas were patrolled, the shores protected." There was a strange look in Dane's eyes that Tess couldn't fathom just then.

"A point well made, Lady Renfrew," Ramsey commended, casting a quick conspiratorial glance at Dane.

Gaelen shook his head, properly stunned. "I admit 'tis the first occasion I've heard of a woman expressing such views, m'lady, especially such an interest in her country's defense."

"Have you ever bothered to ask a woman her

opinion, Mr. Thorpe?"

He flushed. "Nay, m'lady."

"Try it sometime. You might be surprised."

"May I inquire, Lady Renfrew," Aaron Finch spoke, "how is it that you are so informed?"

Because it's history to me, she thought, but said, "My father was a military man, Mr. Finch, my mother a schoolteacher, and I've seen a lot of our country from a very different viewpoint." Jeez, what an understatement!

Dane couldn't deny the conviction of her words yet still didn't know what to think as he sat back and listened. She held the roomful of men in the palm of her hand, utterly captivated, as she described the land west of the Colonies. The details of mountains, plains, and timberlands she offered could not be fabrication, he decided when she first noticed the handleless cup steaming with green liquid.

"You say farmland is richer in the west, Lady Renfrew?" someone asked.

"Yes, east and south of Ohio—Territory," she added, lifting her gaze to the small silver-haired man garbed in a short black kimono jacket and baggy pants. She immediately noticed his distinctive features as he placed an airy confection on a tiny plate, then set it beside the cup. *"Domo arigato,"* she said, taking a wild stab he was Japanese. His gaze shot to hers and Tess gasped, so intense was the look.

"EE-ehh. Doh-ee tah shee-mahsh-teh," he replied softly, bowing from the waist.

All sound ceased.

Dane abruptly straightened, his eyes widening as Higa-san spoke rapidly to Tess in a language he'd never heard. She laughed softly, spoke to him again in the same choppy tongue, and he slowed his speech. Words, Dane reminded himself, he was not aware the man capable of until now.

"Tess?"

She looked up.

"What has he said to you, lass?" Dane asked softly, lowly.

Tess looked around her. It was as if she'd told them she'd traveled through time. Well, well, well. She addressed Higa-san, asking if he understood English.

He shook his head, then sighed and nodded, measuring the air between his fingers. They spoke a moment longer before she turned her attention to Dane.

"He speaks too fast, and I told him my handle on Japanese was rotten. He said it was sweet music to his ears."

"You understood that?" Gaelan said, astonished.

"A little. It's been a while. What's the big deal?" There was a community frown. "Why so shocked?" she clarified.

"This man is our cook, Lady Renfrew," Dane said. "And he has uttered but five words in the ten years he has served us."

It was her turn to be surprised. This kind-faced man was the finger stealer? "Do you even know his name?"

"That much we have managed to ascertain," Dane muttered tightly.

Tess turned to Higa-san and spoke, thumping her forehead when a phrase wouldn't come quickly enough. He replied slowly, and she grinned, her reply leaving the man beaming as she looked down the table. "He is from Okinawa, the Ryukyu Islands south of Japan, in the East China Sea. I had the pleasure of living there for three years."

"I have heard of these islands." Dane looked to Ramsey. "Captain John Green spoke of them," he reminded.

Ramsey leaned back. "Aye, China, 'tis where the silks come from and the porcelain." He straightened. "Pardon the insinuation, Lady Renfrew, but I understood that these people allowed no one to enter their country, except the Dutch."

"Not China, Okinawa, big difference, guys. And that's very likely—" Tess looked directly at Dane— "In 1789."

She downed the tea and stood, bowing to Higa-san and thanking him again. He bowed, then collected the tray, placing the sweet cake on a napkin. He headed toward the door, his step jaunty as she snatched up the cake and followed.

"Tess!" Dane barked. "Where in God's name are you off to, woman?"

She smiled. "Higa-san offered to show me his galley." She bit into the delicate pastry, her smile cheek-bulging smug.

Chapter Seventeen

Every living soul around Tess, except the coxswain and crew, was asleep, passed out from a drunken night of partying. She smiled when someone snored and another called out a woman's name in his dreams as she braced her forearms on the rail, letting the salty breeze cool her skin. The heat had been oppressive below in the galley, and she needed relief. She and Higa-san had managed to communicate with two-word sentences and hand gestures for the past hour, and twice Dane had come below to check on her, a confused look on his face as he'd stood in the doorway; then, without so much as a hello, he'd turned away.

The moments with the quiet Okinawan man were a sharp tug from home, her century, and a lump slowly formed in her throat. Well, there is something to be said about being thrown back in time, she decided. No pollution, ozone layers, nuclear wars, plane crashes, car accidents—AIDS. America was untamed and mostly uncharted. Indians roamed free with the buffalo. The list was endless, just as were its faults. Poor medical aid—she'd already experienced that—preventive medicine was practically nonexistent, children worked in factories, women were considered second-class citizens and denied the right to vote. In Tess's heart the worst abomination of all would exist for another seventy-three years. Slavery.

What would she do for a living? There certainly wasn't any need for a gymnastic coach in the eighteenth century. Her degree in physical education might come in handy. With what? she asked herself. A mean spike in volleyball was totally useless. It wasn't like exercise was a top priority in the education system in 1789. Tess tried not to feel sorry for herself, but a subtle depression shrouded her mood as she thought of her time and the wonders of the twentieth century. What had she actually left behind? Clothes and a '65 Mustang? No family, few friends. Was anyone looking for her? Did anyone, other than Penny, care enough to even bother? Tears blurred her vision and she squeezed her eyes shut. I'm just tired. I have the advantage here, she reminded herself. I know the future. And I have plenty of time to convince Dane that I do.

"Tess?"

Somehow she knew he was alone.

"This summer, Dane, French artisans storm the Bastille, and it will mark the revolution against the ruling class," she said softly, then turned, leaning back against the rail. Over Dane's shoulder she could see *Triton's Will,* her lanterns lit, the ship dipping with the swells of the ocean. It was quiet, too. "In 1812 we will go to war—again." His eyes widened a fraction. "With England."

"They have no reason to attack, Tess." His tone was snide.

"Jeez. Weren't you listening in there? They burn Washington. English ships fill Lake Erie." He looked briefly away, then back to her. "Don't worry, Oliver Perry and his fleet become famous for his tactics in defeating the English."

"Your imagination is remarkable," he sneered. That there was a chance her words were truth angered him.

She shrugged. "Well. The French revolt is a couple of weeks away. We'll see, won't we?" Then she frowned thoughtfully. "How long does it take for word to come from Europe?"

"Three months, at the least."

She groaned, disappointed. "Well, if I'm still around, that'll be proof, won't it?"

Dane refused to acknowledge the ache the words "if I'm still around" gave him and folded his arms over his chest. "Where do you plan on going, Tess? You have no coin, no home, no protector." He paused, his eyes mocking. "Other than myself."

She was suddenly up in his face. "Listen up, Blackwell, you aren't responsible for my welfare, and I managed alone in my century; I can certainly manage in yours." She brushed past him, heading for the passageway. He grabbed her arm. "Let go," she hissed, jerking against his hold.

"You must cease this talk, woman. What if another were to hear of it?"

Her lips thinned. "Stop calling me a liar, Blackwell."

205

"Nothing you have spoken since we've met has been the truth."

Her eyes were silver fire, challenging the insult. "Just because you don't know everything, just because it's not simple and clear, doesn't mean it isn't true. I can hardly believe what's happened myself, and I'm not sure I want to spend so much time convincing you. Can't you be willing to give me the benefit of the doubt?"

She held his gaze for a moment longer, and when she received nothing but that frosty glare, she looked away, fighting her emotions. I'll never convince him without material proof, she thought, and I'll never be happy here.

Her expression fell, hard, to a portrait of hopelessness that made his anger wane. "Woman," he growled, trying to ignore the impact of those sad liquid eyes. "You are too ruddy different from anyone I've ever met."

"Doesn't that tell you something?"

"Aye. 'Tis telling me you are mad," he said as if the words left a foul taste in his mouth.

Anger shot through her. "Then why don't you make me walk the plank—"

"Tess."

"—Or feed me to the sharks—"

"Tess—"

"Or better yet, Captain Blackwell, dump me on a deserted island? There are plenty—"

"Tess?"

"What!"

He relaxed a little. "Can you not see what I am viewing, a woman who claims to be from—"his voice lowered—"the twentieth century. You make such outlandish claims, Tess, a steel vessel over four-hundred feet, a system that pulls a ship through water without benefit of wind, a way to cool food in the tropics, islands that are not charted, and now, predicting a damned revolution! What am I to believe?"

"In me, Dane."

"I cannot."

She stiffened and started to pull away. "Well, then, I guess we've come to an impasse."

"Nay."

"Yes." She yanked, her eyes sharp. "What we shared the other night, Dane, isn't enough to justify all these accusations and questions." Her expression brimmed with pain. "I'm beginning to regret ever mak—"

He swiftly gathered her into his arms, cutting her off. "Nay, my witch, 'twas not the act of an insane female." His expression was suddenly softer, full of hot memories and the promise of more.

"Then what was it?" Did he have to look at her like that—right now?

" 'Twas wild." His eyes sparkled in the moonlight, and he pulled her more firmly to him. "Aye, and you cannot deny 'twas so."

She toyed with his silk ascot. "No," she almost pouted. "I told you I don't lie." She lifted her gaze. "How can you do this to me, make me forget my anger? Nobody likes being called a liar."

"I know, lass," he said regretfully. "I shall make the effort to refrain in the future." The future. Dane tried desperately not to believe her; he didn't want to admit aloud the doubts assailing him now.

"Why are you here?"

"I came out for some fresh air. Bennett's scribble—"

"No, I mean in the Caribbean?"

" 'Tis not your concern, Tess."

She stiffened in his arms. "Thanks a heap for trusting me, Blackwell." She shoved at his chest, startling him enough to gain her freedom. "You've got to be the most arrogant man I've ever met," she said, then quickly moved out of his reach and to the passageway. "Besides Ramsey, that is."

"Come here, Tess."

She stepped over the threshold. "Doubt me, will you? Hah! This game is over, finished—"

"Tess!"

"—Finito! You expect me to *prove* who I am, where I come from, when you don't offer a single bit of yourself. You're a bloody pirate, for Chrissake!" She stepped into the cabin, her words and presence bringing quick silence and startled looks. She didn't notice any of it. "The mighty Captain Blackwell," she raged on, "plundering on the high seas in the name of adventure and greed."

" 'Tis a lie!"

She whirled about, her gaze shifting rapidly to Dane, Ramsey, and the officers. They all looked stunned out of their knee pants. Duncan was cleaning up around them, failing miserably to hide his grin.

"Then what's the truth, Blackwell?" She strolled across the cabin, stopping a few inches in front of him. "Why are you here? What's so important about

208

those pilot rudders?" She nodded to the ledgers lying on the table, surrounded by men and scratches of paper. "And don't tell me it's none of my concern because it is. I'm stuck on this tub, too, you know."

His eyes narrowed and his lips thinned. "The *Witch* is not a tub."

"Don't change the subject. Cut to the chase."

"If I may interrupt —"

"No," she said, glancing sharply to the side to glare at Ramsey.

"You have not told the lass, Dane?" he said anyway.

"Nay."

"He doesn't trust me, among other things," she gritted.

Dane and Tess waged a battle with their eyes as Ramsey gestured for the men to leave.

As the last man departed, Ramsey said, "She wears Desiree's clothing, Dane. I thought surely you would have explained this much."

Her expression went bleak. "No, Captain O'Keefe, he hasn't," she muttered, and before she looked away, Dane could have sworn he saw the gloss of tears. "Thanks, Dane, she whispered. "You've made me feel like a complete ass — again."

Dane realized she was referring to her first lover's humiliation, and the thought made his chest tighten painfully. "Ah God, Tess, nay. I did not mean —"

She shot him a glare and a single tear spilled. "I'm tired. Go away, please." Discreetly she brushed at her cheek, then moved to Ramsey, extending her hand. "Good night, Captain O'Keefe. It was nice meeting you," she managed over the rock in her throat. "Maybe we'll see each other again?"

His smile was rakish and crooked. "You have my word on it, Lady Renfrew." He accepted her hand, raising it to his lips and giving it a soft kiss. "I, for one, will not let so rare a find slip from my grasp."

She offered a weak smile, pulling her hand free. He was certainly great for a girl's ego. "Have a safe voyage, Ramsey."

He frowned, his gaze shifting between Dane and the woman moving toward the window bench. Did she not know the *Triton* would be but a cannon's fire away? He strode to Dane. The man was examining the carpet's quality.

" 'Tis a bloody shame 'twas you who pulled her from the sea, man, instead of me."

Dane's head jerked up and his eyes narrowed dangerously. "You want naught with her as with every wench, Ram."

O'Keefe looked back over his shoulder at Tess. "Nay, not this one, Blackwell." He returned his gaze to Dane. "And I will confess I shall be most pleased if you fall from the lady's good graces."

"Get out, Ram," Dane growled softly. "And do not believe you have a chance with my lady."

O'Keefe arched a brow at the blatant claim. "Time will tell, my friend." The two captains fought a silent challenge; then Ramsey bowed shortly, spun on his heels, and left the room, his boot heels clicking in the heavy silence.

Tess picked at the loose threads of her hem, realizing her going barefoot did damage to the delicate fabric. Desiree's gown. Her throat swelled until it ached to breathe, to swallow. Damn! It shouldn't

210

hurt this much.

After closing the door, Dane moved to stand behind her. "The clothing is yours, Tess."

"Now who's the liar, Blackwell?" She unpinned her hair. "I would have liked to think it was stolen than to know it actually belonged to one of your women." The last word came out bitter and hard.

"Desiree is — was my sister."

Her head came up. "Say again?"

His shoulders drooped, and he settled his hip against the desk, talking to her back. "Desiree was but five and ten when I last saw her."

Tess could hear the pain in his voice. "When was that?"

"Two years past."

"Then she's only — "

"Dead, Tess, she is dead."

She dropped her forehead into the window frame. "Oh, God, I'm sorry, Dane. I didn't know."

"I did not see her before she died, Tess. Nay, I was off seeking my fortune, having adventures on the high seas." His chuckle was condemning, mocking himself. "I wasn't even aware of her death until a few months ago." Tess turned to face him. He was staring at the floor. "Events have occurred that you couldn't possibly understand, and I see no need to involve you in my personal affairs."

"That's hitting below the belt, Dane." He looked up, scowling. "Don't you think I care?" She stood and moved toward him. "I saved your sorry butt on that burning ship, Blackwell." She thumped his chest. "I nursed your crew, put up with your arrogance and your horny friend. I've tried to be accom-

211

modating, Captain, told you stuff no one knows." She stared at him for a long moment, her eyes begging him to let her in. "I could have sworn we had something good going here, Dane. Or was last night really just a roll in th—?"

Abruptly he gathered her close, his mouth claiming hers in a silencing kiss. His fingers dug into her hips as he pressed her more firmly to him. She could feel his urgency as his tongue pushed between her lips. She moaned, greedily accepting the hot energy. A tingling raced down her spine, settling hotly between her thighs, and Tess slipped her hands inside his coat, feeling his silk-covered ribs. It's the same every time, she thought dizzily, burning, breathless, out of control.

"Do not belittle yourself, nor what has passed 'atween us, Tess," he murmured into her mouth. "Please. I cannot bear to hear the words again." She melted at his softly spoken plea as his lips slid to the warm flesh at her throat.

"What or who are you looking for?" she panted, tilting her head so he had better access.

He stilled, leaning back, his frosty gaze drilling her. "A murderer."

Her brows furrowed, pewter eyes sketching his features. "You're going to kill this person, aren't you?"

"Aye."

She gripped him close. "Dane, no, capture him maybe, take him back to America to stand trial, but don't kill him. You'll be as bad as he is."

"He deserves no less than a painfully slow death." She gasped at the coldness of his voice, the pale gleam in his eyes. Her arms dropped to her sides, and he moved away. "He courted Desiree like a fine gentleman, promising love and vows. He managed to fool my father and lure my sister into his lair, then after he'd embezzled her dowry, he brutally raped her!" Dane lifted his gaze to Tess, his expression a mask of torment. "When the beast was spent, he allowed his friends to have her." He smacked his hand into his fist and squeezed his eyes shut. "She attempted to take her own life, but he would not allow her even that small dignity and killed her himself." Dane shook his head and looked up at her. "Nay, Tess. The bastard must pay. He has shamed us, stolen our coin and our fairest life. He will die by my hand."

There was no convincing him otherwise, Tess thought. His face was closed, hard, and there was a cruel twist to his lips she'd seen once before—when he was fighting with Bennett. Tess wanted to shake him. But she couldn't stop thinking of the seventeen-year-old girl, and what she had gone through and how she'd died. Her stomach churned as her imagination formed the gruesome picture. This slime ball deserved the electric chair.

"Dane," Tess said softly. "You don't have to do this yourself."

He glared at her. "Aye, I do. 'Twas my fault."

"No! It wasn't." She came to him and grabbed his arm. "How could it? You weren't there!"

"Do you not see, woman?" He shrugged off her touch. "If I had been there, this would not have occurred! Sweet Christ, she was but a babe, an innocent woman-child, coddled and kept safe all her

213

life! Aye," he lashed a hand in the air, "while the grand Captain Blackwell was off a-pirating—"his lips twisted in disgust—"his sister found naught but disgrace and death."

He stared at Tess for a moment, his body rigid, white-knuckled fists clenching as he fought with the agonizing memories. Then he spun about and strode to the door. He paused, his hand on the latch, then glanced over his shoulder to see a single tear roll down her cheeks, her expression sympathetic.

"Don't leave like this, Dane. Let me help you." The words filtered to him over the creak of the ship, the splash of waves.

"Nay, lass. 'Tis my battle this time."

Chapter Eighteen

Dane stood outside the door like a stone wall, body rigid, jaw set, and teeth gnashing. He closed his eyes and dropped his head back. A hurricane raged inside him, a gale force blowing out of control. He turned toward the door, about to re-enter the cabin, but his hand fell away. He rested his forehead against the polished frame. 'Twas not the time to be near her. He wanted her, always wanted her. But he feared he'd abuse her kindness, release his anger on the innocent. His mind saw her tears, the silent plea to allow her to share his burdens.

Tess would be willing to fight alongside him. Nay, he corrected with a weak smile, she would *demand* the opportunity. He rolled around and let his breath out with a deep sigh, rubbing the back of his neck. He desired nothing more at this moment than to gather her in his arms and hold her softness close, inhale the scent of her hair, feel her feminine warmth surrounding him. Ah, God, he thought, what a temptation you lay at my feet. Dane admitted he had never been more confused over a woman.

He battled over her outrageous behavior, her acid mouth, and her absurd claims, yet an instant in her arms, a brush of her skin, her lips, and it was easily cast aside to the stirring brought by her touch. He rubbed the bridge of his nose with a thumb and forefinger.

"Sir?"

Dane's head jerked up.

"Will the lass be needin' anythin' this evenin'?" Duncan asked, a frown creasing his already-wrinkled face.

Dane glanced briefly at the buckets of steaming water the man held. "You may ask her yourself, Duncan. I have learned not to assume a thing about the lady."

Duncan grinned. "Aye, sir. 'Tis an amazing female."

"Aye," Dane answered without hesitation.

"Captain Ramsey seemed quite taken with the lass, too," he commented needlessly.

Dane's expression turned menacing. " 'Twas obvious, McPete," he ground out, straightening.

"Will the captain be dining with us tomorrow evenin', sir?" Duncan needled.

"Nay, he will not," Dane muttered tightly as he pushed away from the door. The *Triton's* master had sorely strained their friendship as it was this night.

Duncan grinned, watching Blackwell step through the passageway, then turned and rapped on the door. He heard her voice call from within and pushed the wood aside, placing the heavy buckets on the floor. She was sitting on the window bench, her back to him.

"Lass," he called softly.

"Hey, Duncan. What's up?" Tess swiped at her cheeks before she turned to face him. "Oh, don't look at me like that. He didn't do anything to hurt me." Duncan sagged with relief. "Jeez, McPete, you're like a damned watchdog."

He smiled warmly. "I've grown rather fond of you, lass."

"Oh, yeah, then where were you when O'Keefe was around?"

"I wasn't aware you needed my aid then." His lips twitched as he straightened the chairs, then moved to the bed.

"A woman needs a suit of armor near that man."

He looked up from turning back the bedcovers. "Liked him, did you?"

She smiled back. "He's a . . . a . . . he's hard to describe."

"Has he captured your heart?" Duncan was still.

"Good God, no!" she said and the old man chuckled deeply.

"I knew you would see the rake for what he is, m'lady."

His reference to farm implements confused Tess, and it took a second to match it with the twentieth-century equivalent of a playboy.

"He is a bit transparent."

"Aye. Capt'n Ram does love the ladies."

She rolled her eyes. "Tell me something I don't know, McPete."

Duncan gathered up the pilot rudders and maps and put them away in the desk, then retrieved the buckets and disappeared into the bathroom. A second later she heard the slosh of water, and he appeared with the empty pails and asked if there was anything else she needed.

"No, thanks, Duncan. I appreciate your thoughtfulness."

He smiled tenderly. "I know you do, lass."

He moved to the door, his hand reaching for the latch when she said, "He told me about Desiree and why he's here."

Duncan whirled about, his eyes wide. "Truly?"

She nodded. "Did you know her?"

His pale eyes grew sad. "Aye, since she was a babe."

"Then you have my sympathy, too."

Duncan nodded gravely, still unable to believe Dane had spoken of his mission to anyone. He looked at her. "She would have liked you, m'lady."

"Think so?" Tess glanced down at her skirt. "Maybe not after I ruined her clothes, though," Tess said for lack of anything better.

"The garments were not meant for Mistress Blackwell, lass." Tess's eyes widened. "I recall the purchase. 'Twas like an obsession. The captain spent a great deal of coin and, I daresay, pleased the seamstress, for he departed with half her shop. Aye. 'Twas strange, m'lady, for he knew as well as I that they would have been too large for his sister. She was not a woman, as you are, but a child in more ways than her slight form." He adjusted the buckets, his brows drawn deep. At the time, Duncan had thought the captain was easing his conscience for not tending to Desiree for so long, but now, he was inclined to believe that the man had somehow felt

Lady Renfrew's coming.

"Then why did O'Keefe say that?"

"To stir the seas, lass. He loves a good row."

"That's mean."

"Mayhaps." Duncan shrugged. "Yet because of this, has not the captain revealed what you wished to know?"

"Yeah, but he won't let me help, Duncan."

"Be patient, m'lady. If you've a mind to." He held his breath.

Tess sighed and stood. "Don't have any place else to be," she mumbled, plucking at her skirts.

He grinned, bidding her good night. 'Twas an admittance of caring, he thought happily, even if it was lacking a bit in heart.

Tess awoke and knew the minute her eyes opened, she wouldn't be able to go back to sleep. It was still dark out. Naked, she slid from the bed, pulling the sheet with her as she lit a lamp, turning the fire low. She settled on the window bench, watching the moon glittering across the rolling ocean. Catching her lip between her teeth, she glanced over her shoulder at the desk. No, I can't, she thought, looking back to the sea. It was several moments later when she stood, discarded the sheet, and slid into a gold satin nightgown. She laughed to herself, realizing the clothes she'd frantically stuffed in her bag were nothing more than a bathing suit, a leotard, a couple of tee-shirts, one pair of cut-offs, and lacy lingerie of the wildest variety. A lousy packer under pressure, she thought, then stretched, pulling up the gown and lifting her leg until it was parallel with her body. I need to work out in the morning, she decided, then dropped into the chair behind the desk. She stared at the drawer, trying to justify snooping—again. It was the ledgers, those damn pilot rudders that nagged at her. How come all those intelligent men couldn't make any sense of them? She took a breath and opened the correct drawer. She'd seen Duncan put them there. The lump wrapped in oilcloth stared back at her as if daring her to remove it. With a shrug, she lifted it out, untied the laces, and carefully opened the leather-covered logbook. She turned the pages one by one, reading each entry. Dane was right, it was a mess.

A half-hour later she still hadn't made sense of it. The letters were unevenly scrawled, and spatters of black ink littered the heavy parchment, making it harder to decipher the scribbling. Tess rubbed her forehead, then stood and walked to her bag, digging through the assorted junk for a Tylenol and a pen. She poured a glass of water and took the tablet, the pen poking her in the eye as she washed it down. She rubbed, then grabbed up the bag, searching for a notepad when a thought suddenly occurred to her. Code. It had to be a code.

With all of her father's military crap scattered around the house, she'd had a chance to look at one or two code books—outdated ones, that is. Hell, Marine kids used to send messages using simple forms of code. Every kid did it once in his or her life. She carried the glass, the pen, and pad to the desk, then settled cross-legged in the chair, ready to begin. She tried several versions she remembered from the books. None of them worked, but she kept at it, knowing she was on the right track.

"Pay dirt!" she said aloud, nearly an hour later, not really shocked that it was one of the simplest. The alphabet was split in half, then the letters reversed; the same was done with the remaining letters, which meant that the seventh and twentieth letters didn't change. Child's play. The numbers were coded in a nearly identical manner. They were longitudes and latitudes, and Tess didn't know that from beans, but she wrote it down just the same. There were symbols substituted for something that she didn't understand. So she skipped it, with just a small notation.

She stilled for a moment, thinking of Dane and what he'd do to her when he found out she'd snooped so deeply into his desk. Well, the worst he could do was throw her overboard, she decided, and kept on.

What bothered her most was what else she discovered in the process. There were bits of Bennett's memoirs in the pilot rudders, which wasn't the norm, she knew. And Tess passed on writing down what she read. Dane didn't need to know the sickeningly graphic details of his sister's death or exactly how his father had been duped out of half his fortune. She slipped the decoded sheet between the parchment and moved to the next page. A stack of crumpled papers rose around her as she wrote. She took a break to use the facilities and refill her glass. Her eyes hurt and her back ached, but she shoved the pain and the paper mountain aside and continued, never noticing dawn breaking behind her.

* * *

Gently Dane opened the door and peered around the slab of polished wood. He frowned, stepping inside and closing it behind him. Tess was sound asleep, slumped over his desk top, paper littering the surface around her head. He walked toward her, his frown deepening when he saw the pilot rudders pillowed beneath her cheek. He stood over her, his hands on his hips, ready to chastise the lass for intruding in his private affairs. Until he noticed her hand. His tight muscles relaxed, and he reached for the instrument lying between her lax fingers. He stared at the slim cylinder, turning it over in his hand, then depressed the silver top. It clicked and from the bottom appeared a sharp point. What the bloody hell? he wondered, glancing to her, then back to the cylinder. He leaned over and scraped the tip and wasn't so shocked to see that it delivered ink onto the paper. He wrote his name, perplexed that the ink gave off no odor and, as he rubbed his finger over it, that it was already dry! He clicked the pen over and over, watching the tip disappear into the black tube. *Property of the U.S. Government* was inscribed in white on the side. His eyes snapped to Tess, and for one ridiculous second thought she was a spy. Nay, there is a logical explanation for this, he decided. His gaze drifted over the papers, and he unfolded a few, examining her writing, neat, small, precise. Like her.

She moaned softly, her spine shifting at the discomfort. It was unfair to leave her sleeping like that, he thought, and gently roused her. She fell back into

222

the leather chair, curling her legs to the side, but didn't waken. He smiled softly and scooped her up, carrying her to his bed, his eyes greedily soaking in the soft swell of her breast as the thin strap dropped from her shoulder. He deposited her in the center of the mattress, the slim column of satin hugging her sculptured body, teasing him with what lay beneath.

Her eyes fluttered opens briefly. And she looked scared.

"Don't be mad, Dane," she whispered. "I was only trying to help."

He sat down on the bed beside her, pulling the sheet over her bare shoulders. "I am not angry, love." She smiled then, and he brushed the web of hair from her face, tucking it behind her ear. "You have aided me greatly, and I am thankful. But how did you know 'twas a code?"

"Daddy taught me," she mumbled with a yawn, snuggling deeper into the feather mattress.

Oddly wishing he'd known her father, Dane leaned down and placed a soft kiss to her forehead, and she sighed, drifting off with a pleased smile curving her lips. Dane watched her for several moments, wondering what he'd done to deserve a woman like her in his life. When his life was such a bloody mess. She'd been opposed to his seeking out Phillip yet had solved the largest portion of the puzzle for him. All through the night, he realized, glancing at the cluttered desk. He rose and was moving toward the desk when his foot caught on something. It was that gaudy yellow satchel. It was open or torn, he couldn't be certain, and some of its contents were in clear view. Enticing bits of lace and silk spilled from the bag, and he recognized the scrap of black satin and the print of her robe. It jolted his memory, of how it looked draped across her muscled body.

An opaque bottle, the handle of a brush, and some frayed pale blue fabric seemed to beckon him. He bent slightly, reaching, then immediately straightened, forcing himself not to pry into the lady's things. She had assumed he'd done as much before, he reasoned to himself, itching to look. Nay, he decided, then settled behind his desk. She would show him when she wished. Dane opened the rudder, reading her decoded words. He frowned, pausing to finger the evenly tattered paper. The quality was magnificent, no graininess, no dots of pulp wood, and it was ruled with pale pink stripes. He saw the slab of paper with a wire coiled through the top. He lifted it, flipping the sheets. So this was how it was torn so evenly. Ingenious, he thought, closing the tablet. His gaze immediately fell on the scroll printed beneath a coat of arms on the thick board backing. *Stuart Hall, Kansas City, MO 64108*. Where was this place? And who was this Stuart person? A Scot? A friend of Tess's, perhaps, that had gifted her with the fine paper? The thought annoyed him, and he tossed it and the tablet aside, more important matters calling him as he examined the rudders. Yet his gaze kept straying between the bulky satchel, the writing instrument, and the man's name, the bold print taunting him.

TO GET YOUR
4 FREE BOOKS
MAIL THE COUPON BELOW.

Heartfire Romance

FREE BOOK CERTIFICATE

GET 4 FREE BOOKS

Yes! I want to subscribe to Zebra's HEARTFIRE HOME SUBSCRIPTION SERVICE. Please send me my 4 FREE books. Then each month I'll receive the four newest Heartfire Romances as soon as they are published to preview Free for ten days. If I decide to keep them I'll pay the special discounted price of just $3.50 each; a total of $14.00. This is a savings of $3.00 off the regular publishers price. There are no shipping, handling or other hidden charges. There is no minimum number of books to buy and I may cancel this subscription at any time. In any case the 4 FREE Books are mine to keep regardless.

NAME

ADDRESS

CITY _____ STATE _____ ZIP

TELEPHONE

SIGNATURE _____ (If under 18 parent or guardian must sign)

Terms and prices subject to change.
Orders subject to acceptance.

ZH1093

GET 4 FREE BOOKS

HEARTFIRE HOME SUBSCRIPTION
SERVICE
120 BRIGHTON ROAD
P.O. BOX 5214
CLIFTON, NEW JERSEY 07015

Chapter Nineteen

She was hot. His touch was fire. His mouth hovered over hers, teasing her, refusing her the pressure she desired. A perfumed cloak of dampness glistened on her body, and she twisted, a soft moan escaping her lips. No one heard. It was lost in the twilight haze of dreams. He held her close, whispering soft words, his warm hand stroking down her hip, seeking the moist juncture of her thighs. She opened for him, and his fingers pushed inside her, rubbing gently, the sensations created nearly painful in their pleasure. She gasped, arching, welcoming him as he shifted above her—Tess found herself abruptly dumped on the cabin floor. The ship lurched, and she grabbed the bedsheets for stability, but the fabric slipped free, and she rolled over, sprawling on her back.

"What in God's name?" She stood and groped her way to the bed, climbing onto the only stable thing she could find at the moment. She shoved her hair from her face and took a deep breath. God, what a dream! Her body was still locked in that erotic plane, and Tess fought to get control. She plucked at the damp gown, then dropped back onto the pillows, flinging her arm over her face. It was so real. And good. Damn, she wanted him. And if he walked in this cabin in the next two seconds she would be forced to rape the man, she decided. He didn't. So she climbed from the bed and brushed her teeth, splashing cool water on her face and throat.

The ship rolled with the waves, and Tess held on to the commode, glancing out the window. It was gray; gray sea, gray sky, but no rain as yet. The door opened, and Tess twisted as Dane entered the cabin, the wind howling through the corridor. She could only stare at him, licking her lips like a hungry wolf. He wore a billowy white shirt, open at the throat, and tight, buff-colored breeches tucked in black knee boots. His black hair was wind-tossed and wild. And when he saw her, his smile was slow, crooked, as his hand rested on his hip.

"So—my lady has finally awakened." His gaze made a lazy stroll over her body as he closed the door behind him. "And here I thought you fancied lying abed all day."

Maybe with you, she thought, her already sensual thoughts running wild.

"Ahh, lass, do not look at me like that," he murmured huskily, walking toward her.

"And what way is that?" she replied, her face brightening with guilt as she leaned against the bedpost. He stopped before her, his gaze sweeping over her upturned face to the enticing bit of cleavage exposed, then back to meet hers.

"Lovely," he whispered, brushing her hair from her shoulder. "The vision of a man's desire, love."

Tess's knees buckled, and she reached out. That was all it took. Dane gathered her in his arms, pressing her back against the post, and savagely captured her mouth. Her hunger spilled, flowing over him, fanning the ever-present flame that raged inside the pair. His tongue pushed deeply between her lips, and she flowered beneath him, her hand sliding up his chest, squeezing his breast, then slipping around his neck. She held him there, feeling every inch of his long hard body smothering hers. She loved it. Her skin ached for the feel of his hands. Dane's heart thudded against the wall of his chest, the blood rushing in his veins straight to his loins. God's teeth, but he'd thought of little else this morning. And 'twas more difficult, for just to look at the woman constantly tested his restraint. His hands moved to the soft swell of her buttocks, and he ground her against his hardness. She clung tightly, a hand roaming possessively over his ribs, his hip, inviting more.

His mouth tortured hers, his tongue licking the line of her lips, then devouring them again. He was going to explode with his need of her. His palms filled with the firm curve of her buttocks, he lifted her, mashing her against him, his fingertips meeting between her thighs, gently rubbing there in a motion she answered.

She was wild in his arms, stroking the taut muscles of his back, slipping her fingers into the band of his breeches. She ravaged his mouth, nipping his lip, scraping her teeth over the stubble on his chin, working her way to the vee of his shirt.

"I had a dream about you," she confessed in a breathless whisper, loosening the ties of his shirt and spreading the fabric.

"Invaded your sleep now, have I?" His legs trembled.

She looked up, her smile wicked, feline. "Yeah, and I'll give you three guesses what it was about." Her hand slid between their bodies, covering his solid ridge.

A half groan, half chuckle rumbled in his throat. "Sweet Christ, woman, you are a bold one."

"Yeah, and you love it."

His expression instantly softened, different somehow, and Tess was rocked to her feet at what she saw in those pale jade eyes. No man had ever looked at her like he did, as if he'd die without her.

"Aye, lady witch, that I most assuredly do."

"Oh, Dane." Wondrous, heartbreaking joy.

Her lip quivered, and she was having difficulty swallowing over the knot in her throat. His head lowered slowly, the wildness slipping into a moment of incredible tenderness as he kissed her, lazily cherishing her mouth, his arms cradling her gently against his body. It was more erotic than the frenzied minutes just past.

Dane heard the frantic call, but it didn't register until just before the door abruptly opened. He shifted, shielding Tess from the intruder with his body.

"Capt'n! The top mizzen just took to the wind— oh—begging yer pardon, sir."

Dane didn't take his eyes off Tess. "If you value

228

your life, Mr. Finch." The door slammed shut before he finished speaking. He kissed her again, then started to move away. She reached.

"Stay."

He made an agonized sound as he cupped her jaw between his large hands, capturing her mouth in a soft kiss. " 'Tis my duty, love."

He could have anything he wanted when he called her that, like that.

"Is it a hurricane, a typhoon?"

His smile was lopsided. "I daresay not like the one you've created in me, lass, but a storm nonetheless."

She socked him playfully, then glanced to the window. "Is it serious?"

His grin widened. "I'm afraid 'tis fatal."

"Dane!"

He laughed softly. "Nay, 'tis only a squall, but a mean one." He finally mustered the strength to move away from her. He headed toward the door. "Dress, m'lady, and you may come on deck if you believe you can endure the pitching." There was laughter in his voice as he reached for the latch.

"I can endure more than you think, Blackwell, and since when do I need your permission?"

He turned to look at her, his gaze slipping down to her bare feet then back up. The silk shaped her body in a thin veil, clinging to damp muscles, outlining the bend of her leg, the hollow between her breasts, her taut nipples. The strap fell from her shoulder. She didn't move, holding his gaze. Something stirred deep in his chest, something he couldn't name, making him recognize the power she

229

had over his soul.

"I would be most displeased if you were tossed back into the seas, Tess. 'Tis dangerous, these quick bursts." Tess felt there was a double meaning to his words. "I will send an escort for you." She opened her mouth to protest, and he put up a hand. "I beg you to humor me, love. Your safety is all I will think about when I have work to contend with."

She sighed and smiled, giving him a mock salute. "Aye-aye, Capt'n."

He quirked a brow, his lips twitching. "Am I to believe you finally understand who is in command of this vessel?"

"Was there any doubt?"

He threw his head back and laughed, the rich sound coating her warmly as he stepped through the hatch.

The knock sounded at the cabin door just as Tess was finished making the bed. "Come in," she called, and Duncan appeared, his face creased in a frown. He slammed the door. Tess frowned back, immediately noticing his displeasure as she plumped the pillow. "What's up?" His gaze slid to her trousers, then back up. "Oh, come on, the ship is rocking like a cradle. You can't expect me to wear skirts out there."

"Nay," he conceded after a moment. His dark expression didn't change much, brows drawn tight, lips pressed into a thin, white line.

"There's something else bothering you. What is it?"

He didn't answer.

"Spill it, McPete," she demanded, hands on her hips. "What have I done to make you so mad?"

Duncan's stout body relaxed, and he mashed a hand over his face. " 'Tis not you that has angered me, lass." His gaze bounced off the bed. She saw it, her cheeks pinkening at the message she read there. "The capt'n should have moved his things to another cabin! An' the man should not be intrudin' on you whenever he desires!" he blasted.

"It's his cabin, Duncan, his ship, and he's law. Correct me if I'm wrong."

"Aye, but yer not his bride!" He pounded a fist on the table. "He cannot be shamin' you like this!"

"Oh, so that's it. Finch tell you what he saw?"

"Nay, I was standin' behind the dolt."

"Oh." She briefly glanced to the side, checking her temper. "Let's make one thing clear: I'm not ashamed of anything, and my relationship with Dane is nobody's business, Duncan. Not even yours." His expression said she'd hurt his feelings. "I'm sorry, that came out wrong." She went to him. "Look, just because I want to be with him doesn't mean I want to marry him." His eyes widened, and she realized how that must sound to an eighteenth-century man. "What I mean is he isn't making me do anything I don't want." She smiled a little. "It's rather the reverse."

"Lady Renfrew!" he choked, flushing cherry red.

She patted his wrinkled cheek. "I'll clue you in on something, McPete, women think about it as much as men." Then she brushed past him, opened the door, and stepped out. "Besides, he hasn't asked, not that I expect it." The heeling ship forced her to hold on to the rails as she walked the corridor.

"*Would* you marry the man?" Duncan said from behind her. She paused, not turning to look at him.

It never occurred to her. Marry Dane? No. Yes. No! That meant she'd never return to her time. Do you want to? she asked herself, uncertain of her answer. Would she ever have the opportunity to go back? Then be forced to choose? She shook her head. "I plead the Fifth," she said.

"I beg your pardon, miss?"

"Can't answer that, Duncan." She twisted to look at him. "I doubt I ever will." She stepped out, the sharp breeze slapping her face, stinging her eyes till they watered, and she immediately grabbed his arm as the vessel pitched. "And if you try to force him into something he doesn't want, I swear I'll run you through," she muttered behind a sweet smile, aware that all eyes were on her. "Is that clear?"

"Aye-aye, m'lady."

She spared him a glance. Damn if he wasn't grinning.

Satisfied his little tactics had her thinking on the possibility, Duncan patted her hand. Aye, he thought, I'll have the pair wed soon enough.

The wind's force plastered her clothing smoothly to her body. The ship dipped with the huge rolling waves, and she widened her stance in her effort to keep upright. A fine mist sprayed her face as the frigate bucked, and Tess dismissed Duncan's wild notions, scanning the area for Dane. In the past weeks, she'd learned a great deal about the *Sea Witch*. The mizzen, Finch had said, and she looked

232

aft of the vessel. No Dane. She heard his voice issuing commands and lifted her gaze, letting it climb higher and higher. Her breath caught, and her hand covered her mouth.

Nearly a hundred feet above her, Dane was bare-chested, a powerful arm wrapped around one mast pole, the other struggling to secure a fresh sail. A brass ring through which the ropes threaded was caught in a hooked spike he held. The muscles of his arms and chest and back flexed and bunched as he struggled to secure the canvas. Gaelan and a sailor worked with equal vigor on the opposite end, securing their portion. On the deck, several yards from her, two sailors held a rope, its free end swirling like a snake on the wet wood, and her gaze followed the thick hemp line. It was secured at the top of the mast, and a mere ten or so feet farther down it wrapped around Dane's waist, threaded between his legs and hooked beneath the arch of his foot, drawn back up somewhere near his chest. It was his only security, aside from his arm still gripping the large mast boom. The wind taunted his hold, yanking him back and forth from his dangerous perch. But he held tight. And her breathing accelerated as she helplessly watched.

"Duncan! Can't someone else do that?"

"The capt'n would not ask a soul to do something he would not." He shook his head, amused at her unnecessary fears. "All thoughts aside, lass, I think he enjoys the danger."

Even as her heartbeat quickened, Tess could understand that. She walked a four-inch beam for a living, swung from thin poles, defying gravity and hoping her timing was right, that the wood would be just where she anticipated when she sometimes blindly reached behind her. There was no reason to worry, she told herself. He was the captain, experienced, used to doing this stuff in such awful weather. She didn't know her grip was cutting off the circulation in Duncan's arm, her nails digging into his thinly protected skin.

Dane grunted, sweat beading at his temples, his muscles straining to lift the heavy sail. Two more hands would do him a sight more good, but he couldn't risk it. He adjusted his grip on the spar and yanked, cursing the wind that danced him like a puppeteer's toy.

"Go down!" he yelled over the wind to Gaelan. The younger sailor began his climb, but the first mate shook his head. "Damn you, boy, 'twas an order, not a request!"

Reluctantly Gaelan shifted off the spar he straddled and caught the webbed rigging, cautiously working his way down. A sudden fierce gust sent Gaelan to hugging the ropes and Dane high in the air, the sail caught in his spike, the rope twirling him like a top.

"Dane!" Tess shouted, her fear overtaking her common sense not to call for him when he was up there. The wind calmed, and he looked down. Even in the distance she could read his disapproval of her garments.

"Damn breeches!" he muttered, his gaze meeting hers. Alarm, stark and clear, cloaked her upturned features, and Dane knew it was for him alone. A warmth filled him, and he flashed her a broad grin, then turned to his duties, anxious to get below and ease her panic.

Tess watched his every move as he called on raw strength. His back, thick with ropey muscles, rippled and stretched as he hooked the sail and began threading its rigging. Tess admired his physique, tanned, trim, and she wanted to see all of it, touch every square inch of his moist, smooth skin as soon as he got down, and she didn't care who the hell knew.

Her gaze dropped to the waves, gray and angry. Her eyes widened as the ocean swelled and kept growing.

"Jesus H. Christ!" she gasped. "Duncan, look!"

Tess stood helpless as the wall of water seemed to stand still, hovering over the frigate, a liquid devil about to pounce.

"Stand fast!" Duncan shouted, pulling her toward the companionway when she moved to the mast.

"Dane!"

It hit. The unleashed power sent tons of seawater over the frigate. Barrels tore loose from their lashings, live bodies slid across the deck, slamming in the hull, then struggled frantically to get from the path of the rolling kegs. The barrels smashed, spewing their contents over the deck and into the sea. Tess and Duncan held tight to the doorframe, praying it wouldn't give as water rushed over them, snatching their breath and reaching for their lives. Her only thoughts were of Dane. Spars cracked, ropes snapped, men screamed for their comrades, their captain. In an instant it was over, the sea rolling a bit calmer, the wind still flexing its muscles.

Tess choked and sputtered, filling her lungs and swiping the water from her face. Her gaze shot to Dane, and she screamed, a deep, agonized cry.

He dangled in midair, the rope twisted around his legs and chest, the wind beating his body against the booms and sails. The top gallant mast had cracked and he hung out, unable to grasp the wood. Tess ran to the mast, climbing the rigging, ignoring the calls for her to cease. Gaelan chased after her. The end of the rope was tangled in the main's boom and already a sailor tried to free it.

Tess's feet caught the ropes, and she climbed. She bounced, and the breeze took her up with the rise of the ship. It was like trying to climb a rope bridge straight up while someone jumped on it. Then it started to rain. Torrents of water showered the vessel. Tess climbed.

"M'lady, do not try it!" Gaelan bellowed when she sat on the crossjack like a child on a swing. Tess grabbed onto the swaying mast as Gaelan continued to climb.

"No! Don't come up!" she screamed back. "It's cracked and won't hold us both!" She pointed to the splintered wood beside her. "Get below me!" She gestured urgently to exactly where. "Lean out on the rigging and when I give the word, you be ready to catch him!" The rain stung her cheeks, filled her mouth, and she rubbed her sleeve over her eyes so she could see better, but it did little good; her clothes were drenched.

"Get the bloody hell down, woman!" Dane hollered.

Her gaze shot back over her shoulder to where he hovered about three feet below her. Angry

236

red streaks blazed his chest and arms where the rope had scraped.

"Make me!" she shouted and heard a faint chuckle.

Blood flowed from a gash in his forehead and Tess recognized the glaze in his eyes. He was going to lose consciousness any second. The wind kicked in, the ship heeled, and she held on, terrified as the mast lashed the air like a giant whip and Dane was slammed against the sails. She heard his groan of pain and called out.

"Dane! Dane!"

No reply.

She scraped water from her eyes and blinked. "Blackwell, you'd better answer me!"

"That sounds like an 'or else,' love." His speech was slurred.

She managed a smile, hugging the tottering mast. "Damn right it is."

She thought he called her a saucy wench but wasn't sure.

Dane lifted his head, the world spinning around him; the sound of waves crashing and his men calling out vibrated in his brain. Rainwater pelted his face, thinned blood filling his eyes. He squinted through the downpour to see her. Her back was to him as she sat on the boom. His vision blurred. Blood pounded in his skull, and he couldn't muster the strength beyond the hammering to reach out to her as the frigate bucked furiously. Dear God! She was going to fall! Terror lanced through him when she fell back, hanging by her legs, only her knees securing her to the slippery spar. Nay, nay! He tried to reach her. She'll die!

It was his last conscious thought.

Gaelan hung onto the lattice ropes, waiting for her signal. Aaron and Ramsey O'Keefe had joined him, each at a different level. How the *Triton*'s master managed to be here, he didn't know, but they needed his size to grab the captain.

Tess said a brief prayer, tucked her chin to her chest, then began to move. Using her stomach and back muscles, she propelled herself back and forth like a swing. Wood groaned. Droplets pounded the sails, sounding like tacks spilling on wood floors. Her adrenalin pumped. Her breath hissed through her teeth as she tried to keep the water from filling her nose. Arms outstretched, Tess built up momentum, each time coming closer and closer to the rope that held Dane.

"Now!" She caught it, the muscles in her legs screaming at the abrupt stop. She fought the pull, curling forward to bring Dane close. Her palms burned; the wet rope jerked at his weight. Don't let go. Pull, Renfrew, pull! She let out a defeated cry as the wind yanked it from her grasp.

"Got him!" she heard someone shout and looked below to see Ramsey, his arm wrapped around Dane's chest. Gaelan held Dane's legs while Ramsey cut the rope. Men scrambled to the mast base, gently lifting their captain down to the slippery deck. Someone pressed a cloth to the blood seeping from his skull as they laid him on the wet surface and cut away the remaining ropes.

Ramsey stared skyward as she agilely climbed down the lattice rope. Incredible! Her courage and capabilities were unbelievable. He was there when her feet touched the surface. The ship yawed. She stumbled into his arms, and their eyes met briefly, her gratitude clear, grabbing at his heart. Then her gaze jerked to Dane, and she was gone, pushing between the men to get to him.

"Take him to the cabin," she ordered, and men obeyed. Rain poured, the frigate rolled, and she followed alongside, her hand pressed to Dane's head. She fought the sting of tears. He's alive, repeated in her head. "Duncan. Fresh sheets, towels, and water. On the bed," she directed when they entered the cabin. She waited impatiently until he was settled, then pushed people out of her way. She examined the wound. Not deep enough for stitches, she decided. A scrape, really. With her thumbs she opened his lids. Just as she thought: his pupils were unequal in size. She cleaned the area and replaced the pressure cloth with a fresh one.

"Hold this firmly," she instructed Gaelan. "And don't let up until I tell you." She took Dane's pulse. "Dane? Can you hear me?" she called.

No response.

The crew of the *Sea Witch* exchanged concerned looks among themselves. When Gaelan nodded to the door, the men quietly departed, knowing their captain was in the gentlest of care. He and Ramsey remained.

"Get him out of those wet clothes," she said to Ramsey, assuming he would do the honors. Tess didn't think she had the strength to peel off the sodden cloth, and as much as she wanted to see all of that body, she damn well wanted Dane to know she was looking.

She picked her yellow bag off the floor, frantically digging in it for something she might be able to use. Frustrated, she dumped the contents on the desk, feminine debris spilling to the floor. She sorted what she had: bacitracin, Tylenol, heat ointments, bandage tape, scissors, then quickly shoved her junk back into the bag when she heard Ramsey come up behind her.

"Interesting bit of fluff," he murmured, lifting a lacey scrap from the floor. Tess twisted, snatching back the string bikini.

"Now is not the time for your antics, O'Keefe," she muttered. Dane should have at least stirred by now. She moved to him, settling gently on the mattress, pulling the covers over his chest. He was so pale.

"I'll take over. You're needed above," she said to Gaelan. He hesitated, then nodded, leaving quickly, anxious to see to the damage before it worsened.

Ramsey frowned curiously as she unwound a white strip from a metal reel, clipped in precise intervals, then folded the edges. It stuck to her fingers, he marveled, as she made two more like it. She peeked beneath the bloody cloth, then carefully applied an ointment before she pressed the butterfly-shaped bandages to the cut. Her fingers lingered at his brow, brushing back damp curls, and Ramsey stiffened, then silently chastised himself for his jealousy. Duncan entered then, coming quickly to her side and handing her a cloth. Tess cautiously toweled Dane's hair dry, calling his name, then cut small squares of white cloth and taped them to the wound. She sighed and looked up at the two men.

"I think he has a concussion." They frowned together. "It's a hard jarring of the brain." Eyes widened. "There might be damage"—alarm swept their faces—"and there might not."

Ramsey swallowed, his tanned skin measurably lighter. "By damage, m'lady, you mean—"

"Blood clots, swelling of the brain, I don't know. I'm not a doctor, but I've seen a concussion before."

"Then you can treat it?"

She shrugged. "It sort of treats itself. We watch and wait. Wake him every couple hours for the next twenty-four." She looked at Dane, calling him again. "It may not take that long. He could come out of it in a few minutes." Please, God, please, she prayed. The longer he was out, the worse.

"The capt'n'll be fine," Duncan said confidently, giving her a pat on the shoulder. "He's a strong man."

"Aye, lass. I've seen him suffer worse than this."

Tess didn't take her eyes off Dane. In her career she'd witnessed a variety of injuries, even had a concussion when she was twelve. But that was with immediate medical attention. Professionals. All Dane had was her and her first-aid courses. He could actually die!

"M'lady?"

Tess lifted glossy eyes to Duncan. He was holding out Dane's velvet robe. She accepted it, clutching it beneath her chin. Waving at Ramsey, Duncan inclined his head toward the door, and both men slipped quietly out.

Tess stripped out of the wet clothes, donned the

warm robe, then took her place beside him on the bed. She leaned forward and pressed a kiss to his cool brow, squeezing her eyes shut.

"Wake up!" she murmured against his skin, swallowing repeatedly, the pain in her chest telling her just how much of her heart this dark pirate had taken. "Don't leave me here alone, Dane." She leaned back, her gaze riveted to his pale still features. Oh, God! What if he was meant to die today? Could she change his history? And if she couldn't? Her throat tightened, the stone of agony making each breath an effort, and she fought the urge to scream. Covering her face with her hands, Tess gave in, wet fire streaming behind her palms. Her shoulders jerked as she very quietly wept.

Chapter Twenty

"Are those tears for me, love?"

"Course not, I got something in my eye." Tess gasped, dropping her hands when she realized who'd spoken. "Dane! You're awake!"

" 'Tis well, with all that water, I believed we were sinking."

"Why you—you—see if I save your sorry bu—" Tears brimmed again. "Oh, Dane," she cried, laying her head on his chest. Slowly his arms came around her.

"Ahh, God! You are real." There was wonder in his voice, akin to prayer. His embrace tightened. "I thought you had fallen, Tess."

She closed her eyes, listening to the steady beat of his heart beneath her ear. "No such luck," she murmured. His weak chuckle blended with a groan. "Hurt?"

"I believe your prediction has come true."

Her brows furrowed. "I beg your pardon?"

"The revolution of the French, 'tis begun in my head."

She smiled, his words vibrating through her like jello, and she thanked God for the sensation. "It's better than feeling nothing at all."

She leaned back, her gaze sketching his pale face, memorizing every contour and line.

His breath locked in his throat as he drank in the sight of her tear-stained cheeks, the wet hair curling about her slim shoulders, his velvet robe haphazardly wrapped. God's teeth, she was a vision to behold. "You were not hurt?" She shook her head. "You will not risk yourself like that again, Tess." His tone was gently scolding. "Promise me this?"

"Can't. You, Duncan, the crew, you're all I've got left." Her sincerity caught him in the gut. "Besides, it's the only thing I'm good at."

"Nay, I know better."

His hand smoothed up her spine to cup the back of her head and draw her close. His lips touched hers, and he fitted her against his chest, slowly tasting her, his tongue licking the salt from the rosy circle, then slipping inside. She could have died, he thought, and deepened his kiss, her sweet response lessening the sting his pride suffered at being rescued by a woman—again.

His hand moved over her back, slipping forward to cup her breast, and she moaned, a sharp tingling spreading clear to her toes as her body answered the erotic pressure. She allowed herself a few more seconds of pleasure, then drew back, grinning at his childish disappointment.

"You don't need to get excited." Her eyes dropped meaningfully to the bulging sheet. His lips twitched, and he reached for her again. "You need rest,

Dane." Her tone brooked no argument, he realized as she rose from the bed and turned toward the commode, doling out two tablets and pouring a glass of water. "Take these." He looked skeptically from the pills to her. "Trust me. I won't —" Before she could finish, he plucked the white pills from her palm, reading the words etched on them before he shoved them into his mouth, and drained the glass.

"That's a good little pirate," she said, patting his head.

"Tess," he warned, but she grinned widely, arranging pillows, then tucking the quilt beneath his chin. "I am not a babe." He shoved down the coverlet, the abrupt move sending needles of pain into his skull. He grunted, squeezing his eyes shut and gingerly easing back onto the mountain of down.

"Serves you right." She planted her hands on her hips. "Now hear this — you will rest for at least two days. You will not, I repeat, *not* leave that bed. You're not out of danger yet, Blackwell, and you'll obey my orders." She leaned down for emphasis. "Is that clear?"

His gaze dropped to the opening of the robe, her plump bosom teasing his weakened will. He wanted to bury his face in the sweet bounty. Lifting his gaze, he murmured, "Inciting a mutiny, are you, lass?"

"If it will keep you in that bed, hell, yes!"

He reached out, his fingertips grazing down the skin exposed, pushing the robe farther open. Her breath caught. "This could be a very interesting recovery." His palm filled with her breast, his thumb gently circling the rosy peak.

She moaned, briefly closing her eyes, her insides jingling as he tried to pull her down. She forced herself to remove his hand and straighten, then tightly wrap the velvet. She jerked the sash, trying to look stern. "I swear, Blackwell, you scare the life out of me, and all you can think of is—" She waved at the bed.

"Have a heart, love." She fought a smile at his pleading look. "You test a man, draped in naught but that old rag."

"Then I'll count on that to be incentive to be a good patient."

He folded his arms across his chest. "You're going to be a tyrant, aren't you?"

She held his gaze. "Aye, Capt'n, that I am." Never in her life did she want to go through that kind of panic again, and Tess vowed to make certain he was well before he left that bed. No matter how much he complained. Or tried to seduce her.

His lids felt heavy, and Dane battled the sleep that tried to claim the sight of her from his hungry gaze. She was alive. And saucy as ever, he added silently, the pain in his skull ebbing to blissful relief.

Tess frowned. He went out so suddenly. She stepped closer, covering his chest with fluffy down, then checking his pulse. Strong and steady. She brushed the curls from his forehead, absently checking his bandage.

The door opened, and she glanced up.

"Is he—?"

"He woke up," she assured Duncan, and the man's smile was blinding. "And there doesn't seem to be any damage to his faculties." Tess looked away, heat warming her cheeks.

When she looked back, Duncan had vanished, and she could hear his footsteps thumping down the corridor. His voice was muffled, but when he passed like a blur before the open door, she had an idea of what he was up to. The cheers and shouts of his crew thundered down to her, and she smiled.

The squall had been quick, furious, and its damage would take days to repair, but now the ship dipped and swayed with a gentle motion. Amazing. Tess was gathering up wet clothing and discarding the bloody cloths when she spied the maps rolled and stuffed in a canister secured to the wall. She removed the parchment, spreading it on the desk. She examined the markings, then frowned curiously, stepping away to dig in her satchel. Unfolding a rumpled travel brochure, she compared the map to the glossy one printed on the back of the ad. Her smile was slow as she snatched up her pen and tried to mark on the oiled and waxed map. When it wouldn't do, she searched for her eyeliner pencil, then updated Dane's map, charting three small islands where there were none.

She was just putting the chart away when Duncan appeared again, trailed by several sailors. The deck hands filed in quietly, each carrying two buckets of steaming water. Their expressions were of such genuine thanks and admiration, Tess felt her heart clench. She tossed the eyeliner in her bag and went to them.

"Duncan," she whispered, "I can't let them do this. I know how precious fresh water is on a ship."

"Beggin' yer pardon, m'lady," a sailor spoke up,

"but 'tis our way of sayin' thank ye." He nodded toward the bed. "Fer our capt'n."

She turned a pleading look to Duncan, but the old man simply folded his burly arms over his chest, daring her to complain further. "Thanks a heap, McPete," she mumbled, then nodded to the sailors. They grinned at each other, deposited the water in the tub, then moved toward the door, heads bobbing and murmuring their thanks.

The men quickly departed as Higa-san materialized in the cabin doorway. Without a word, he entered the bathing room, setting a tray laden with soaps and little pots on a small stool, then lifted a sack from inside his belt. He sprinkled the glittering contents into the hot water, then turned to her, his hand an elegant wave as he gestured to the bath.

"All right." She sighed. "I give up. Now leave so I can enjoy this gift before it gets cold."

Tess closed and locked the cabin door after them, stripping off the robe as she moved to the bathroom. A giggle bubbled in her as she dropped the velvet and stepped into the scented water, warm liquid quenching her salty skin. She sighed with pleasure, leaning back in the copper tub, watching Dane sleep as she soaked. The fragrance misted around her, the vapors laced with the perfume of spice and wildflowers. She loved it. It was unusual, exotic, and sensual. And for the first time since she'd stepped on deck that day, she relaxed.

Dane stirred, a soft humming filling his head, his lips curving in a smile. He'd recognize her voice anywhere. Cautiously he opened his eyes. He could see her through the open bathing-room door, her arms curved above her, fingers scrubbing her hair. Her breasts, sheened with moisture, swayed above the lip of the tub. His groin tightened at the luxurious vision. She reached for a pitcher and sluiced water over her head, then set aside the urn and wrung her hair, twisting it up in a towel. She relaxed back, her sigh drifting to him on the perfumed air. He tried to sit up, but his wrenched muscles and throbbing skull wouldn't allow the simple task. She was safe and would be there when he woke again. The pleasing thought carried him back into sleep.

Tess rose from the tub, patting herself dry, then investigated the little clay pots Higa-san had left. One contained spice-scented powder, with a tiny quilted puff; the other was brimming with a frothy cream, and she indulged, dusting and smoothing her body into girl heaven. With nothing else to wear, she donned the robe as she left the small room. Tess dropped onto the window bench, toweling her hair dry, realizing every time she took something off it magically disappeared, never to be seen again. Duncan, she decided, picking at the tangles from her hair with a comb, then glanced at the clock perched atop the dresser when it softly chimed. Fifteen more minutes, then I'll have to wake Dane, she decided. There was a timid rap at the door, and she padded softly across the cabin and opened it, pressing a finger to her lips.

Duncan smiled. "Enjoy your bath, m'lady?" he whispered.

She nodded, leaning against the doorjamb. "It was wonderful. Thank the crew for me, will you?" He assured her he would. "I'll wake the captain in a little while. Would it be too much trouble to have a dinner tray brought for him?"

" 'Twill be a pleasure, lass." He started to move away, then paused. "Captain O'Keefe has returned to the *Triton,* but asked that I relay, if you should need anything, to merely send up a shot." There was displeasure in his tone.

Tess looked at Dane. "I have all I need here, Duncan," she murmured. His face creased with satisfaction before he pulled the door closed behind him.

"Dane? Dane? Time to wake up."

"Can a man not find peace in his own bed?" he groused, pulling the coverlet up and turning his back to her. Cannon fire exploded in his head every time he moved. His arms and chest burned, and she wanted him to come out of a painless sleep? For what? To chat? "Go away, woman."

Tess fought a smile. What a grump. Every time she roused him, his disposition grew steadily worse. She couldn't let it affect her. Tess knew the minute her back was turned he'd be topside. She scooted closer, massaging the muscles in his neck. He moaned, and her hands worked down his shoulders. She tugged at his elbow, and he shifted his arm back but didn't face her. Tess manipulated his bicep between her hands, the strength of her fingers soothing the muscles she knew were sore.

"Drink this." Dane twisted to see she held out a glass of water and two of those white pills. He snatched them from her, slapped them into his mouth, then drained the glass. "Again," she said, pouring another glass of water and holding it out.

He waved sharply. "Enough, woman!"

Tess arched a brow, daring him to take it. Dane grabbed the glass, sloshing water over his fingers, but obediently drank while she plumped pillows, her smile sweet and kind. It annoyed him.

"Lie back," she ordered, and when he didn't, she pushed him. Dane gnashed his teeth as she twisted toward the commode, then held out a small towel. He could see the steam rising from the cloth, yet in this foul mood he wanted naught but for her to leave.

"Would you like me to bathe you?" she inquired sweetly.

"Nay. Get you elsewhere, woman. I am capable of—"

"The hell you are," she said with a grin, slapping the towel in his face. Dane dragged it away, glaring at her. She shot him an impish smile, smoothing the cloth over his chest and down one arm. She dipped it in the bowl, wrung it out, about to continue when he snatched it from her and pitched it in the bowl.

"Enough, I say!"

"All right," Tess said calmly. "Hungry yet?" He grunted. "Can I take that to mean yes?" Men, such babies! She stood and went to the table, bringing back a tray, the third one that Duncan had left for him, and setting it on the opposite side of the bed. He wouldn't look at her. She sat down and opened a napkin, placing it on his lap. His gaze shot to her, his expression sharp and mean.

Tess ignored it, slicing some cheese and bread and little bits of warm sausage. She held out a portion.

"Come on, Dane. You need to eat."

"I need naught but for you to cease this endless puttering and be gone!" With his last word he knocked the food from her hand, sending it across the room. Tess stared at the debris, clenching her fists, then turned her confused face to him.

"Now that was real swift. What did that little tantrum accomplish?"

"Leave, Tess."

"For God's sake, why?"

He turned his head slowly from where he had been staring out the window. "If you must know, I need to piss," he lied, "or would you rather do that for me, also?"

She reddened. "My, my, aren't we witty today."

"Tess," he warned. "Go before—"

"Is there a problem, m'lady?" Duncan interrupted from the doorway.

Tess twisted to look at the old man. "No. We're just being a grouch."

"Tess. I swear by all that is holy, I will—"

She looked back at Dane. "Eeek, I tremble. Oh, help Duncan. The nasty old pirate's going to make me walk the plank." Dramatically she pressed the back of her hand to her forehead and sighed.

His brows rose in astonishment, and he blinked, his lips quivering with a smile as he sank onto one elbow, unable to remain sour after that bit of nonsense. "I have struck my colors, woman." He waved. "And beg for quarter."

"Ahh, victory at last," she sighed, quite pleased with herself, then cast him a side glance. "You can be a mean little snot when you want, Blackwell."

"I should be soundly thrashed and hanged from the yard arm for my despicable behavior," he conceded gallantly.

"Sounds good to me," she beamed. "When do we start?"

"Heartless witch." He grinned.

"Yeah, and you love it."

She leaned over to check his temperature, her fragrance filling his senses, and Dane caught her hand, placing a kiss to the palm.

"Forgive me, love?"

"Bringing out the big guns, eh, Captain?" she whispered, suddenly breathless.

Raven curls tumbled over his brow, and a ghost of a smile played across chiseled lips. Tess's heart missed an entire beat. God, he's doing it to me again, she thought.

"I know you don't like being confined, Dane, but wounded pride is no excuse for rudeness."

"I stand thoroughly chastised," he said, his gaze dropping briefly to her lips.

"You've got to stay in bed until tomorrow."

He leaned closer, his breath teasing her mouth. "Understood, Lady Renfrew."

"Your word," she said, and his head jerked back, his brows lifting. "You have a concussion, for God's sake. It's serious stuff!"

He thought for a moment, then murmured, "Aye, I give you my bond."

"Good. You can kiss me now."

He chuckled, tugging at the collar of the robe, his mouth a mere fraction from hers. "Dare I sense that I am forgiven?"

"God, yes." It was a plea for his ears alone. Dane smiled, then kissed her, his lips, warm and soft, slanting over hers. He caught her lower lip between his teeth, sipping there, then pushed his tongue inside, sweeping the dark haven. Tess melted against him, her hand smoothing over his bare chest.

Duncan cleared his throat, and they slowly pulled apart.

"Send me Mr. Thorpe and Finch, Duncan," Dane said without taking his eyes from her. "I want damage reports."

"Aye-aye, Capt'n!"

Dane's pale gaze shifted beyond her to the servant. The old man's expression was cold and damning. Dane returned his attention to Tess. "You have your orders, man."

Tess didn't have to ask what that was about. "Twenty minutes and that's it," she reminded, slipping off the bed, making Dane acutely aware of her clothing, or rather, the lack of it.

She was picking up the tray when a knock sounded and Dane waved, still frowning at her attire.

The first and second mate entered cautiously, and Tess faced them. "Exhaust him and I'll tan your hides—personally." They nodded politely, and she turned once more to Dane. "It's nearly dawn, Blackwell. Give these men a break, huh?"

Dane glanced to the window, then the clock. All three men watched her sweep out of the cabin.

"I cannot believe I'm wishing 'twas me that smashed into the mast, sir." The first mate's eyes were on the empty doorway.

"I'll shoot you in the foot if you believe 'twill help, Gaelan," Aaron suggested cheekily.

"Most amusing, Mr. Finch," Gaelan's tone was dry. "Any man would—"

"Gentlemen!" Dane interrupted, annoyed at the turn of conversation, and they faced him. "I believe *my ship* is the order of discussion?" He gestured curtly for them to be seated, and within minutes they were well into a discussion of the frigate's damage, the length of time it would be to repair, and the new courses to be set.

"How did you know 'twas a code, sir?" Aaron asked a while later as he made notes.

"I did not, 'twas the lady who deciphered this mess." Dane flipped through papers until he found the one he needed.

Gaelan and Aaron exchanged stunned looks. "Truly a fine woman, if I may say so, sir?"

"You have and you may, Mr. Finch." Dane didn't spare the man a glance.

"Sir?" Gaelan said. "The rudders refer to an island three degrees south, but I don't recall one."

"It must be incorrect," Dane waved, ignoring the nudging of his memory. "None that have sailed these waters has ever noted its existence. Get the map." Gaelan rose, searching the brass cans.

"Even with the translation, Bennett's logs are a shambles," Aaron complained as Gaelan returned with the curling parchment and spread it out, the second mate peering over his shoulder, studying them.

"Aye. 'Tis a wonder the man made it this far." Dane rubbed the back of his neck, reading the papers again.

"Ah—sir?" Gaelan began hesitantly. "I beg your pardon, but you have already found it." Dane's head jerked up, his eyes narrowing. " 'Tis charted, sir." Looking confused, the first mate held it out. "And two others."

Frowning, Dane grabbed the map, his features pulling taut as his gaze scanned the black markings. Tess. He recognized her handwriting and a memory surfaced. She'd said the maps were wrong when she'd first seen them. Before she deciphered the rudders! God, nay!

"Lady Renfrew. Lady Renfrew! Blast you, woman! Get in here!"

Tess popped around the doorframe. "You bellowed, sire?"

Dane glared at his snickering officers, then at the woman leaning against the doorframe, a fresh tray in her hands. Gaelan and Aaron hesitantly followed the direction of his gaze.

"Time's up, guys. Out," she said, nodding to the door as she moved to the unoccupied side of the bed and deposited the tray. She poured tea.

Dane folded his arms over his chest, studying her. "You have been scribbling on my maps, lass."

Tess glanced up. "Mad?"

"I have good cause."

"My cartography that lousy, huh?" She leaned against the bedpost, nibbling on a crust of bread.

"How did you know of the islands' location?" Dane wanted to know.

She glanced meaningfully at the officers. "You really want me to answer that?"

"That will be all for now, gentlemen. You may tend to your duties," Dane said in a dismissing tone.

"Aye-aye, sir," the men said in unison, gathering up their ledgers and heading for the door. They both cast an envious glance at their captain, then slipped out.

"You were about to explain?"

"I've actually been on one of them," she said easily.

His brows rose, his disbelief clear. "Pray tell, when?"

"If that's the attitude you're going to take, I'm not going to say another word." They stared, Tess glaring, Dane looking rather unaffected.

But he wasn't. Her calculations were too accurate to be ignored.

"When?"

"A few days before I jumped off the *Nassau Queen*." Tess waited for him to call her a liar. He didn't. He was staring at the map resting on the mattress. Was he ready to believe her? "That scumbag you're after is on one of those islands, isn't he?"

He shifted his gaze to her. "Aye. What were you doing there?"

"Hiding."

"From the men who were trying to hurt you?"

"Not hurt, Dane. Kill. They had a gun pointed at me just before I backflipped off the ship."

"God's teeth!" he uttered, rubbing the back of his neck. "Why?"

"None of your business." He scowled. "At least not until you admit that my story is true." She plopped onto the bed, making little sandwiches, her

257

stomach growling at its emptiness. A thought suddenly occurred to her, her breath jamming in her throat. "You believe me?" she said around a chunk of bread.

"I will consider you may have been on this scrap of land."

Her hopes soared. "How could I not if it hasn't already been charted or inhabited? In my time, Dane, it's populated with hotels and resorts."

When he simply stared at her, she sighed, shaking her head, focusing her attention on the food. Shiny, blue-black hair draped over her arm as she selected a slice of fruit, then popped it in her mouth. She glanced up, grinned sheepishly, then continued to eat. She'd been waiting for him, he realized, picking up a chunk of pork and biting into it.

She shifted, the robe gaping to reveal those gorgeous legs, and he allowed his gaze to travel up the muscled length. She was fit and happy and her mind sound except for the occasions when she—his gaze shot to the desk where he could see the black writing instrument. A cruel warning lanced through his heart, piercing his closed mind. He recalled every instance where she'd voiced her claim of traveling through time, and then there were the dates she'd quoted, the events to come, the amazing items she produced from the gaudy satchel, her knowledge of medicine she insisted was meager, the valuable aid she'd given with her potions. Even his own pain had vanished with the taking of the white pills. Granted, she was an unusual woman, and her tales outlandish, but she was not stupid. And then there was the island. How can I ignore so much? But to travel from the future?

Her words from dinner the previous night haunted him; the commissioning of a permanent naval force. The President had discussed this possibility with him only a few months ago. 'Twas the reason Dane's ships were in Caribbean waters: to protect the Colonies from the British and French that had been attacking American crafts for the past several months. 'Twas an effort to keep a rein on the growing commerce, and Dane's orders were to seize any threatening vessel. He toyed with the fork, watching the lamplight twinkle off the silver. What else can she tell me? he wondered. Will I soon receive orders to halt all French and British ships? And if they reach the Florida coast and should raise an army? Dane conceded the possibility; England still manned forts in the Colonies, and the French owned Louisiana and Florida. Was this the makings of the French revolt? Or the seeds of a war she says will not come for another three and twenty years? How had Tess known of this brewing trouble except if 'twere history to her? he reasoned. His mind floundered until he forced himself to ask her questions.

"Tell me more, Tess?"

No answer. He glanced up to see her leaning back against the far bedpost, sound asleep, a crust of bread lying in relaxed fingers. He smiled tenderly, removing the tray and easing her down onto the mattress. She curled in a ball with a sigh. He tossed the blanket over her, then brushed the hair from her face, touching his lips to her temple. Her scent was glorious. He'd given his word, but the call of nature beckoned relief. Dane went slowly, cautiously shifting his legs over the side of the bed. His feet touched and, grasping the post, he stood. He felt no lightheadedness and took a step.

His foot landed on something small and cold, and he looked down, then bent slowly and picked up the shiny silver object.

He turned it over in his hand. "Sweet Christ!" he whispered, goose flesh racing up his spine, the icy fingers making the hair on his neck stand on end.

Chapter Twenty-one

Dane stared in shock, sweat beading on his upper lip, his body trembling so violently he could scarcely control it. Embossed on the bright metal was the silhouette of his President and beneath that, a date— 1967. 1967! *Nineteen*. His fingers closed tightly over the coin, and he dropped his head forward. Nay. It couldn't be. He looked again, and it seemed to shout at him. Liberty! In God We Trust! United States of America! God's teeth. The future! Currency from the future!

Was he going mad? Nay. 'Twas impossible for her to have minted the coin herself. He turned sharply, staring at the woman sleeping in his bed and the truth he'd just begun to consider hit him like a punch to his gut. Numbly he dropped onto the mattress, knowing in his palm he held positive proof.

Tess Renfrew had traveled back two centuries.

How in God's name had she accomplished such a feat?

He remembered the night of the battle and how upset she had been, her cries of wanting to be returned home—to her time. Had she just realized what had happened to her then? The thought was enough to send a shiver up over his spine and into his scalp. The dolphin brought her, she'd claimed, through the wall. Dane's head turned slowly to the window, his memory of the storm, the curtain of black mist, so clear it was like he was seeing it for the first time. And the eerie vessel, mountainous, white, shifting position so quickly he'd thought himself suddenly losing his senses. 'Twas the *Nassau Queen,* he realized, and prayed to God she'd left her assassins behind.

"For the sake of the lady's reputation, Duncan, leave the door ajar."

"Aye, sir."

"Close it, McPete," Tess mumbled into the pillow. "I'm awake." She lifted her head and turned toward the sound of Dane's voice. Dane was sitting at his desk, bare feet propped on the surface. "And you promised to stay in bed."

He smiled as she sat up and shoved hair out of her face. "I promised only until the morning." Tess glanced to the window, then pushed aside the white netting and climbed from the bed, rewrapping the robe as she walked to him. He poured tea from the service sitting to his left and slid a cup toward her. She ignored it, resting her hip against the desk and checking his bandage, his pupils, and his pulse. The latter was a little fast.

"Does my state of wellness meet with your approval?"

"Hardly. You should be in that bed, resting. Not doing this." She waved at the ledgers, papers, and instruments littering the desk.

"I am fine, Tess, truly."

She snorted. "Then don't come crying to me when your head starts pounding like a Russian racehorse."

He stared at her, wondering what it was like for her to discover herself thrown back into a time that could only be quite primitive.

"Why are you looking at me like that?"

His gaze never wavering, his hand slipped from the arm of the chair and came up with her yellow satchel. Her eyes widened as he dropped it onto the desk.

"Show me the future, Tess."

Her gaze shot between the bag and him as she straightened. "Wh-what? Ah-ah—" She swallowed, and Dane watched as tears bloomed in her eyes, brimmed, then slowly trickled down her cheeks. She trembled, and he saw the pulse at the base of her throat quicken. Slowly he slid his feet from the desk. With a strangled cry of his name, she fell into his arms. Gently he pulled her onto his lap, pressing her head to his chest. She cried, deep, heavy weeping that enveloped him, absorbed into his skin, penetrated into his bones. She struggled to control it, but then it unleashed itself in a fresh wave, and Dane felt the torment she had suffered these past weeks. Because he wouldn't believe.

"Shhh, love, cease, I beg you," he whispered, gently rubbing her spine. " 'Tis killing me, your tears."

Tess lifted her head, swiping at her cheeks.

"When?" she croaked, then swallowed. "What made you change your mind?"

He sighed, dropping his head back. "I suspected the truth of your words when you first made mention of the islands—"

"But that was before the battle!" she interrupted.

"Aye." He looked down at her. " 'Twas your conviction, in every word you spoke, that set me to wondering. I found myself making sense of your logic, and I admit, lass, 'twas unnerving to say the least. Yet with the dates you quoted, 'twas all far too accurate for any man to ignore." He smiled into her smug face, fingering a raven lock, then absently bringing it to his nose and inhaling the scent of spiced flowers. "You've a way about you, lass, openly defiant. Even Ram noticed." The brief darkening of his features said he didn't care for that observation. "Coupled with your extraordinary physical abilities and that political discussion with my men—" He paused. "You know what is to come, that we will tax ourselves." She nodded. "And the Naval Forces?"

"In a few years," she answered.

He was thoughtful for a few seconds, then suddenly grinned. "We would have begun this discussion last eve, but you very rudely nodded off when I was about to question you further."

She snuggled cozily. "I'm sorry I did now."

He held her gaze, his expression regretful. "I confess I thought you insane, Tess. I did not want to believe 'twas possible and tried to find a reason for your peculiar behavior."

"It's okay. I considered all this," she waved absently at the cabin, "and you, an eccentric on a fantasy pleasure cruise. So it took me a while to believe it, too. But why didn't you just write me off as some escapee from the loony bin?"

He chuckled at her choice of words. "Because you, sweet witch—" he tapped her nose "—are not a woman any man with but an ounce of feeling can ignore." Compliments embarrass her, he thought, enjoying her flushing cheeks. She wore her desire like a sensual cloak over her body, and since she'd risen from the bed, he'd tried to ignore it. The woman has naught but to turn those smoke gray eyes on me and I am charred to cinders, he realized, shifting her on his lap and lowering his head. His lips brushed hers, and she moaned his name, leaping up to meet him. To hell with it, he decided, giving up his meager battle. Her hands slid around his neck, and she blossomed beneath him, letting him taste her happiness.

Tongues dueled softly, and Tess leaned back, making him chase her. She laughed, deep and throaty, and he lifted a brow, accepting the challenge. Abruptly he drew her legs over the arms of the chair, imprisoning her in the circle of his embrace as he feasted on her mouth, his fingers loosening the ties to the robe. She curled toward him as his hand prowled beneath the velvet, stroking her bare ribs, then moving forward to smooth over her breast. Her skin was so soft. His thumb brushed her nipple, feeling it plump and harden beneath his touch. Gently he massaged, rotating her breast, and she whimpered against his lips, her fingers plowing into his hair, her body eager and warm for more. He separated the robe and pulled her tighter against him, enjoying the pleasure of her soft bosom pressed to his bare chest.

She purred in his arms, panting his name into his ear as she licked and nibbled his lobe. A blast of fire avalanched down his body. His hand drifted to the deep curve of her waist, over her hip and down the smooth, pale thigh. He heard her breath catch and held her gaze as a callused hand slid between her legs, her look of anticipation making him breathless.

A knock sounded.

"Go away!" they both shouted, the moment frozen, and footsteps rapidly retreated. Tess bubbled with quiet laughter as Dane cursed viciously, shifting uncomfortably beneath her.

Passion cooled by the interruption, she sighed, dropping her legs from the arm of the chair and adjusting the robe. "For once, I'd like to be with you without the entire ship knowing," she muttered as she sat upright.

Her words sent a sharp thrill spearing into his chest. The confession was so matter-of-fact, Dane didn't dare question the depth of it, but 'twas a confession just the same. He suddenly needed to hear more of them.

She glanced meaningfully at the bag sitting on the desk. "Sure you're ready for this?"

Dane closed his eyes briefly and nodded.

Tess left his lap and perched herself on the edge of the desk. Tossing her hair back over her shoulder, she unzipped the bag. The sound made Dane flinch, and he reached out to examine the sack more closely, moving the slide back and forth.

"Ingenious," he whispered, then, satisfied with his perusal, sat back to allow her to continue. An odd sensation swept rapidly down his back as she overturned the bag on his desk. Quickly she started stuffing garments back inside.

"Wait," he said, lifting a small odd-shaped scrap. He held it by the silk ribbons, turning it this way and that, then lifted his puzzled gaze to Tess.

"It's a bra," she explained, snatching it up and placing it against her chest.

His brows rose, then a devilish smile grazed his lips. " 'Tis a garment I would like to see properly worn," he commented, watching her blush.

"In your dreams, pirate," she teased, dropping it into the bag, then handed him her wallet. "My identification," she said, and at his frown, told him that everyone carried something like it in her time. "It gets you in places, proves who you are. That's a driver's license," she added when he slipped the plastic-coated card free, deciding not to go into the subject of cars just yet.

Dane rubbed his fingertip over the likeness of her, marveling at the clarity. 'Twas amazing, he thought, as she explained the way to capture the images on paper through something called a camera. Then to his astonishment, she showed him ones of her parents and friends.

"Who is this?" he said curtly, gesturing to the photo of a blond young man.

"Just an old college friend," she replied, her eyes twinkling at the spark of jealousy. He tossed the photo aside, then fished in his pocket.

"Have you more like this?" he asked, holding out the silver coin. Her eyes widened, then narrowed sharply.

"So—you believed me before—!" She made a wild

grab for the quarter, but his hand jerked back out of her reach, her angry momentum causing her to slip off the desk. He stood, his arm shooting out to catch her and pull her flush against him.

"Aye, Tess." He cupped the curve of her jaw with a warm palm, his eyes intense, penetrating. "I swear by the blood of my sister, lass, I have always known you had come to me by a sweep of God's hand."

Tess was still. "Please don't lie to me about this, Dane."

Silver gray eyes begged for the truth. She looked so vulnerable, so fragile, and Dane understood how much it meant to her that he had believed before he'd seen the proof. "Never, love. She softened against him in a way that drove him wild.

"Thank you," she whispered, closing her eyes, her hand covering the one that held her jaw. The coin must have been the clincher, she thought, then looked up. "That's a fourth of a dollar," she told him, giving him a quick, hard kiss, then hopping back onto the desk.

He shook his head as he took his seat, constantly amazed at her resilience.

Tess opened the change purse to her wallet and dumped the contents on the desk, letting him investigate at his leisure, answering his questions about the coinage, its value. He chuckled secretly to himself when he viewed the face of Thomas Jefferson on a nickel, then tossed it aside, but went still as granite when she slipped a dollar bill out. Dane gaped at the likeness of his president.

"The father of our country," she said, watching him carefully.

He would be most pleased at that, Dane thought, looking over the paper currency embellished with future presidents. Later he would discuss them with her and why they were honored on scrip.

Her wallet in a pile of money, ID's, and old receipts, Tess simply folded her arms and watched. He scrutinized each item, opening travel-sized bottles of shampoo, conditioner, deodorant; sniffing; reading the labels; and she had to stop him when he went to taste the cherry-scented shampoo. He relaxed back into the chair with the travel brochure, his brows furrowed tightly as he studied the miniature map. He opened another fold, then lifted wide eyes to her, straightening.

"This woman is naked!" He shook the pamphlet in her face.

The corner of her mouth quirked. "Not quite. She has on a swimsuit. What one wears to frolic in the water," she defined dryly. God, he looked ready to pop. "A bikini," she added without mercy.

"Ah, Tess, you—ah, you—" He swallowed, unable to ask for fear of the answer.

"Sure. Why not?" She shrugged, enjoying his stumbling.

"Before men?" he exploded. "Like this?" He waved the paper again.

She rummaged in the bag and came out with a hot pink Italian design that would fit in a Band-Aid box. He lifted the scraps and strings, unable to discover the proper angle in which he could imagine—ahh, bloody hell! he thought, tossing it in her lap.

"You may as well discard the thing," he said matter-of-factly. "You will not be wearing it again."

"And what if I want to?" she said defiantly, trying to keep a straight face.

"Sweet Christ, Tess!" He leapt to his feet, grabbing the bikini and holding it under her nose. " 'Tis no more than spinnakers of a child's sail toy!" he raged, then threw it aside and rubbed the back of his neck, looking at the floor. "God's teeth, to think you paraded before a pack of rutting stags in that—that—dressmaker's leavings—!"

"I meant just for you, Dane," she cut into his tirade.

Dane's head jerked up, and he finally noticed the laughter in her eyes. "You did that a'purpose," he accused softly, his shoulders relaxing.

"Guilty as charged," she giggled. Seeing him openly display his jealousy made her feel all warm and buttery inside.

"You're heartless, Tess."

"Hey, you wanted to know. Believe it or not, this will be the height of fashion," she taunted, the bikini dangling from her fingertip, and he groaned miserably. "Cost me sixty dollars."

"Sixty?" he sputtered, dropping into the chair. Dane thought of the cargo equivalent to that exorbitant figure and shuddered at the comparison. His gaze rested on the contents from her satchel and he scowled.

"This is your time, Dane, and I'll play by your rules." She paused, mischief making her cheeks rosy. "Well, most of the time."

Only his eyes shifted. " 'Twill be a first, for you have not as yet."

She tried to look indignant. "Are you accusing me

270

of improper behavior, sir?"

"For my century."

Her face fell. "Have I embarrassed you that much?"

"Nay, the thought never occurred to me!" He seemed surprised she would ask. Then he caught her hand. "But I fear 'tis me that has embarrassed you."

She frowned. "How could you possibly?"

"We've shared this cabin, Tess, yet have spoken no vows."

She jerked free. "Don't do this, Dane."

"I must—"

"Look—in the twentieth century men and women don't marry so they can enjoy each other."

"But you are no longer there, Tess." His voice was tight.

"I know that!" she snapped. "Let's just leave it to my upbringing, okay? Jeez," she rubbed her forehead, "I can't believe we're having this conversation. Any man would be delighted not to be chained just to sleep with a woman!"

His eyes narrowed dangerously, his words cool and measured: "I am not like—!"

"I know, I know," she interrupted, her temper suddenly defused. Her expression went all soft and feline as she looked him over. Yeah, he was different all right. "I was well aware of that when we first slept together, Dane."

He flashed her a cocky grin, lopsided and sexy, and Tess wanted to climb all over him when he looked at her like that. "My memory of that night, love, is definitely not of sleeping."

"Mine either," she murmured huskily, slipping off

the desk. He stared at her, not saying a word as she climbed easily onto his lap. The look on his tanned face was suddenly fierce, agonized, yet so hotly possessive that she frowned, reaching up to touch his cheek. "Dane?"

Abruptly his hand dove into her hair, the other wrapping tightly around her as he claimed her mouth, feasting on her lips as if to draw her inside himself and keep her there. During the past hours a bizarre fear had engulfed the sea captain. Aye, he silently admitted, deepening his kiss. He was deathly afraid of losing Tess—to her own time.

Chapter Twenty-two

Like a black sabre slicing through azure silk, the *Sea Witch* plunged across the sparkling waters. Canvas snapped, filling with power, carrying the frigate to her charted destiny. On the quarterdeck, Dane sighted through the glass, scanned the surface, then called out his orders. The boatswain's whistle shrilled, singing across the wind. Bare-chested men in tattered breeches hustled up the rigging to do as they were bid.

"Have you molasses in your veins?" Gaelan bellowed cheerily to the crew. "Stand fast, mates, we've new lands to discover!"

The spyglass poised, Dane measured his first officer. "You seemed rather pleased this morn, Gaelan?"

Gaelan glanced to his right, looking a bit sheepish. "I admit I thirst for solid ground beneath me this voyage, sir."

A ghost of a smile danced across Dane's lips as he raised the glass to his eye. "I daresay you thirst for more than ground beneath you, man."

"Aye, sir. A soft, sweet-smelling lass would be to my liking," he said dreamily. "Wearing those whatever-they-are that rustle so delicately, enticing a man to imagine the warm treasures that lie beyond—" He cleared his throat and straightened when the captain lowered the spyglass and looked at him with raised brows. " 'Tis difficult not to think of much else, Capt'n," he flushed, "with the Lady Renfrew about—ah—sir."

Dane said nothing, returning his gaze to the sea. Aye, he thought, he had been sorely tested not to keep the woman thoroughly occupied in his bed since they'd met.

Gaelan made a sound of pure misery, then said, "Ahh God. 'Twill never be soon enough, sir."

Tess stood on the lower deck in a soft cloud of royal blue silk, searching for Dane. She spied him on the quarterdeck, did a sedate spin, then curtsied primly. She felt wonderfully pampered. This morning she'd awakened to a woman's fantasy: a roomful of new, expensive clothes. Surrounding the bed were three sea chests brimming with gowns in silk, lace, brocade, rich velvets in hunter green, black, burgundy, subtly trimmed and elegant. The height of eighteenth-century fashion, she knew, still awed by the extravagant collection. Each gown was accompanied by matching corsets, petticoats, stockings, and dainty satin slippers adorned with little bows or beads. But it was the slip of parchment scrolled with dark masculine writing that touched her most: *Welcome to my century, love.* Oh Blackwell, what am I going to do with you? she wondered happily, then walked aft.

A sharp *oof* spilled from Gaelan's lips when the captain, without looking, shoved the spyglass in his stomach and strode toward her.

"No, don't come down. I can manage," she said, gathering her skirts in one hand and ascending the nearly vertical steps up to the quarterdeck, unaware that every man aboard had paused in his work to view the brief display of trim ankles. Over the top of her head, Dane sent them an icy look meant to maim as he leaned down to help her.

His gaze drifted from the silk draped in lush folds like a shawl about her bare shoulders to the swells of her breasts brimming the delicate fabric. The lass was asking to be ravished.

"Sweet Christ, Tess. I'd no idea 'twas so revealing," he whispered close to her ear as she stepped onto the deck.

"I know." She fought the urge to tug at the low cut bodice. "Just compare this to my bikini, and you'll be fine," she replied in a husky tone, and he groaned, winding her arm through his.

"The woman has come two hundred years to prove me naught but a rutting beast in her presence," he murmured lowly, his gaze caught in hers.

"A rutting beast, eh? Care to elaborate?" She stole a quick look down his body, and those tight green pants left nothing to her imagination. "Or maybe demonstrate?"

His breath hissed through clenched teeth. "Woman, do you seek to torture me before my officers and crew?" His breeches tightened across his hips, and he shoved a hand in his pocket. She laughed, quiet and throaty, the sound snapping further at his control.

"You know, you didn't have to leave last night."

"Aye, 'twas necessary," he chided softly, failing to ignore the invitation in those smoky eyes; like last eve,

275

when she was drowsy and playful, purring like a soft kitten, trying to entice him to join her on the coverlet. I should receive a bloody commendation for gallantry, he decided. "And I seem to recall a promise to yield to the ways of this century, Tess."

"Hey, I'm dressed for the part, aren't I?"

His grin was quick with approval. "Change naught but the clothing, love."

A little spark burst in her chest, and the soft squeeze on his arm kept him from taking another step. "I want to thank you, Dane. You've got great taste. The clothes—they're like a fairy tale. I've never worn any-thing so—"she spread the skirts sprinkled with glass beads—"breathtaking."

He turned fully, his smile revealing straight white teeth. " 'Tis time, then."

Tess's heart skipped a beat, then tumbled in her chest. Time. It hit her all over again where she was and with whom.

"A good morning to you, Lady Renfrew," Gaelen said with slight bow.

"Yeah, it is, Mr. Thorpe." Her skirts swished in the breeze and she thought she heard him moan. Dane fought a smile, and out of the corner of her eye she saw sailors removing crates through the forward hatch. "Is that more booty from one of your captured vessels, pi-rate lord?" She nodded toward the bow. Dane chuck-led, catching the shocked look of his first officer. When Gaelan opened his mouth, the first mate felt the captain's silencing glare like a sabre's prick.

Gunfire cracked, and she jolted, bumping into Dane. His hands rested on her waist with a gentle weight, and he could feel her tense fear give release.

Trust. She trusted him. He'd cherish the garnered honor close to his heart.

Shielding her eyes from the sun's glare, Tess watched as the *Triton* came swiftly about the windward side, moving so close alongside the *Witch* she thought they'd collide, but the meeting was smooth, graceful, like lovers sweeping into a gentle dance. Ramsey was perched high on the mainmast rigging, swinging with the dip of the vessel, and Tess felt Dane's grip tighten.

They watched as Ramsey adjusted his footing, then pushed off the spar, sailing across the water at the end of a thick rope. He landed with vibrating thump on the deck a few feet before Tess.

He took in her attire from slippers to bared shoulders as he straightened.

"Morning, m'lady," he murmured with a quick bow, his eyes feasting on the delectable sight as he tugged at his cuff.

She nodded in response, her lips twitching. "You sure got a thing for grand entrances, don't you, O'Keefe?"

"The lady prefers something more subtle?"

"From you? You've got to be kidding." She laughed, and Ramsey was caught again by the stunning beauty of this woman.

Ram turned to Dane.

" 'Tis there," he said excitedly. "By God, man!" He smacked his fist into his palm. "Exactly where you predicted!"

"Whoa, wait a sec," Tess interrupted, wondering if she'd heard right. "What's there?"

Ram's gaze shifted briefly to Tess. "The island we've sought, m'lady," he replied as if she should know, then

277

looked back to Dane. "Her port is small, yet her township is nothing like we imagined. The *Barstow* is moored in her harbor," he added with a touch of rancor. "She's been repainted, but her figurehead is unmistakable."

"You mean you've been there?" she nearly shrieked, her temper boiling.

"Aye, from a distance, of course."

Petulantly she folded her arms over her middle. "When, O'Keefe? Exactly?"

He frowned. "Why, the morn after the squall, m'lady."

"What!" She rounded on Dane, hands on her hips, her body trembling with anger. "You—you sent the *Triton* ahead—!" Before he'd found the coin, flitted through her mind, and she nearly choked on what that meant.

Dane smoothed a thumb and forefinger over an imaginary moustache, trying to hide his smile as the fire suddenly fizzled out of her. Her features softened into a tender smile, and her eyes misted as she stepped closer, lightly resting her hand on his forearm.

Ramsey tensed, unable to tear his gaze from the delicate fingers smoothing over Dane's skin. "That was sneaky," he heard her say. "Just like a pirate."

Ram's head snapped up, his brows raised in astonishment. Surely the woman knew 'twas not the case? Yet Dane seemed to enjoy the insult, making Ramsey wonder what else he was keeping from the lady.

Dane had read her pamphlet that told of the history of the small island. For over one hundred years the small paradise had flourished as a haven for hardened criminals fleeing the law. A true pirate's lair, he thought, looking down at Tess.

But her attention was riveted somewhere beyond him. Dane followed the direction of her gaze.

Sailors reached into wooden crates, removed pistols and muskets, loading the weapons with quick, efficient steps. Tess stared, somewhat awed at what she saw. The crew was acting differently now, no unnecessary chatter, their movements practiced, professional.

She looked questioningly at Dane. "You aren't going to attack this puny island, storm the beaches, that sort of thing, are you?" Reality suddenly crashed in on her. *What kind of future do I have with an outlaw?* Then wondered why she was thinking along those lines to begin with.

Dane seemed to struggle with a decision, then burst with, " 'Tis not your concern."

Flame lit her silver-gray eyes. "Don't give me that crap again, Blackwell! *'Tis* my concern. *I* deciphered those rudders." She poked his chest. "*I* told you where this island was, so don't go spouting that 'I am man, you are mere woman' crud. *Are you going to attack?*" She thumped his chest with every word.

Dane looked down at her. God, she was glorious in her rage. " 'Tis not my intention to—"his lips quivered—"storm the beaches, lass."

"Promise?"

"Aye," he answered without hesitation.

"Good," she harumphed, then moved toward the rail to watch the sailors. Dane turned to Ram, who was looking rather strangely at Tess.

"Make your arrival known, Ram," Dane said in a low tone. "Give the men leave into the town, yet little coin."

He dragged his gaze back to the captain, then nodded agreement. Too many tankards lifted could cost them their lives. "Shall I hoist the Jolly Roger, sir?" Ram quipped dryly.

Dane's gaze shot to where Tess was conversing with Mr. Thorpe, then back to Ram. His lips twisted in a wry smile. "Though it seems to be your forte of late, O'Keefe, 'tis unnecessary to resort to such dramatics."

Ramsey took the barb with an easy grin. "The lass seems to enjoy them," he returned while plucking imaginary lint from his sleeve.

"Unlike the addlepated boobies you are accustomed to—"Dane chuckled quietly—"Lady Renfrew is wise to your ploys."

Only Ram's eyes shifted. "I fail to recognize your purpose in deceiving her, Dane. Methinks you take your oath too far."

Dane stiffened. "The less knowledge of our mission she possesses, the safer she will be."

"You cannot mean to take her there? Sweet heaven, 'tis naught but home for murderers and thieves!"

Dane folded his arms over his chest, resting his weight on one leg. "I am well aware of the danger. What do you propose I do, leave her on the *Witch?*" Dane had no intention of letting her out of his sight.

"I will give you that," Ramsey said after a moment, his shoulders relaxing. He hated to think of her under the guard of mere seamen. "Shall I pay a visit to the governor?"

"If there is one, aye, he is suspect. As well as any authority. We've a duty to discover who is financing these attacks on our ships." Dane rubbed the back of his neck. "Fly no colors, Ram. 'Tis best we not show overmuch. We will weigh anchor on the eastern side with this night's tide."

For the next few moments they discussed their plan, sending the quartermaster ahead for accommodations, where to rendezvous, passwords, who would act as courier. Dane offered a map of the island, points marked in thin black ink. Ramsey frowned as he examined the thin striped paper, then stuffed it in his pocket, said his goodbyes to Tess, and made to depart.

"How will you explain her presence?" The words were laced with a challenge.

Dane's expression hardened. "Again you trod into matters that are none of your affair, O'Keefe." His voice was cool with quiet rage.

"Afraid she'll rebuke a proposal?" Ramsey's brow lifted with the question as he adjusted his grip on the rope, then not waiting for his answer, pushed off the rail.

Dane looked in her direction and knew she would. She'd made that clear. Did Tess value her freedom so dearly, he wondered, or did she not want the ties to this time? Dane realized he wanted her bound so tightly to him that she'd never want to go back. But with the woman's strong independence, he simply did not know how. For one wild instant Dane considered the pleasure of making love to her until she became with child, the joy over creating a life with this woman making his blood sing, before he cast the absurd notion aside. If she were not already from their first and only time, she would never forgive him for such a debase deception. And perhaps question his feelings toward her. Then he recalled she was a bastard or at least had no notion of her parentage, therefore she might not believe being

281

pregnant and unwed a scandal. Not if her painful past was any indication of what the lass could endure. Sweet Neptune, but you sound like a desperate fool! Naught will keep her here if her time wants her back, he realized sadly, his heart sinking to his boot heels. Damn and blast!

A sailor suddenly lost his grip on a crate, and it hit the deck, wood splintering, its contents spilling. He heard her gasp of surprise and hastened his step as she lifted her skirts and descended the ladder.

Tess was already beside the sailor when Dane arrived. Dane's gaze moved to the box, to Tess, then to the seamen. His captain's look was damning. He'd recognized the crate's markings.

She stood motionless, then slowly lifted her gaze to Dane. "You lied to me," she whispered.

Pooled at her feet were the uniforms of the Continental Marines.

Tess pushed between the crewmen, heading for the cabin, Dane hot on her heels. She slammed the door behind her, nearly in his face. His shoulder hit against the oak, sending it banging against the wall.

"Woman!"

"In my father's office there was this print," she said, ignoring his anger. "It was entitled *Changing to the Green*." She whirled on him. "Continental Marines changing from red uniforms to green! What are you, Blackwell, Marine or pirate?"

He stared at her for a tense moment before he said, "Both."

"Boy, do you have some explaining to do." She folded her arms over her middle.

Dane sighed, rubbing the back of his neck. Why was

he hesitating? Didn't he already trust her? Without another word, he moved to his desk and opened the bottom drawer, removing a box. Tess had seen it before, but it had been locked, or she would have snooped there, too. Dane flipped back the lid and lifted out papers sealed with wax. Breaking the imprint, he handed them to her. Tess unrolled the stiff parchment, her eyes widening until they absorbed her face. They were Letters of Marque, giving Dane the right to protect American interests as he saw fit. And it was signed by none other than George Washington. Her body trembled, her hands shaking with the impact of her discovery. The President wrote this himself. Why had she never heard of it?

"Why did you let me believe you were a pirate?" she asked, unable to tear her eyes from the letter.

" 'Twas not my right to tell."

"You're here for two reasons, aren't you?" She looked up, handing him the papers. "This—and to get the guy who killed Desiree."

Dane nodded, replacing the documents. "You must swear not to breathe a word of this."

"Like who am I going to tell?" she snapped, insulted.

Dane couldn't soften. "Your oath, Tess."

"I swear." She moved to him, winding her arms around his waist. "Semper Fi, me hearty, Semper Fi."

The pitch-black frigate rounded the tiny island, blending with the night. Her ebony sails at quarter, Dane quietly maneuvered his ship. No one on this section of the island would question the presence of the dark vessel. There were souls that wished the world would forget they had ever lived. Unable to sail the *Witch* any closer for the reefs, they let down a long boat on the seaward side of the frigate, coming under her bow. Tess sat in the stern of the rowboat as sailors dipped oars into the water with practiced rhythm. No one spoke. Dane sat behind her, steering the small craft. Water lapped at the hull, a small lantern offering the only light. She heard murmurs of wonder, Duncan's soft chuckle, and the boat slowed as they slipped beneath the frigate's carved bow. Her brows furrowed, for each occupant was suddenly studying her with an odd fascination, then the ship. She followed the direction of the crewmen's gaze and gasped, a chill making goose flesh plump on her skin. The figurehead of the *Sea Witch* was visible in the moonlight. And Tess saw a reflection of herself draped in flowing black.

" 'Tis proof, love, you were destined to be here," Dane whispered into her ear. "With me."

Chapter Twenty-three

A bawd in a torn, dirty dress sat on the scarred bar, bare legs dangling over the edge as she munched on a chicken leg. She lifted her ankles when a man slammed into the wood beneath her feet, then slid to the floor in a heap. She bent over, peering between her knees to assess the damage as another man staggered past. She shoved him back into the brawl with a hearty cheer, waving the poultry limb over her head.

A booted foot connected with Ram's stomach, and he buckled over with a loud groan, staggering backward, but not before catching his opponent's heel and toe, twisting it viciously, then planting a solid kick between the man's thighs.

"Now I'm assured of no other imbeciles to litter the earth," Ram gasped, rubbing his stomach as he straightened.

The man writhed in agony on the dirt floor, clutching his groin with both hands, spewing curses on Ram's lineage to several species of swine as men toppled over chairs and benches and bodies. Ram fought to catch his breath, somewhat awed as one of his mates went flying through the smoke-filled air to land on a table laden with food. The impact split the table in half, and young Davey was sandwiched in the middle. Seconds later he sprang to his feet and threw himself into the fray, salad greens hanging from his shirt collar.

Ramsey spit into each of his palms, rubbed them together, then with an eager grin rejoined his comrades.

Dane burst through the tavern door already half off its hinges, then moaned, sagging against the frame.

"He's done it again, Duncan." Dane shook his head.

"Aye, sir."

"I suppose we should come to his aid." Dane winced as Ram took one on the chin. "He doesn't seem to be faring very well this time."

"It does appear to be the case, sir."

Dane sighed, peeled off his coat, and handed it to McPete, then rolled up his sleeves.

"The lady will be most displeased, sir."

"I did not hear that, Duncan," he tossed, grabbing a grimy sot off a *Triton* crewman by the shirt front, then planting his fist in his nose. Dane released the cloth, sucking on his knuckles as the man slithered to the floor in an unconscious lump. 'Tis been a while, he thought, then turned to the next degenerate.

Ram sailed over a broken bench, landing with a splintering crash at Dane's feet. Dane looked down, a hand on his hip.

"When I asked you to make yourself known, Ram, 'twas not in this particular manner."

O'Keefe grinned, accepting the offered hand.

"Bloody hell, man! 'Tis been this way since we set foot on the docks!"

A window shattered with the impact of a body plowing into it. The poor man hung over the sill like dirty laundry as the captains stood back to back, punching anything that came into their path.

"And I'm certain you did not enter this pesthole with your flags out?" Dane remarked sarcastically, then jabbed.

"You do me an injustice, old friend." Dane glared at him out of the corner of his eye. "Well, 'twas this red-headed wench with a magnificent — Ugh! Sweet Christ!" Ram winced when he heard his finger crack with the last blow. The smarting pain was inconsequential when a man the size of a house charged on them. The two captains separated, allowing the bull to speed past its matadors and crash headfirst into the wall. A woman shrieked, skittering out of the way, then hollered at the unconscious heap that he'd spilled her drink. She rifled his pockets for payment due.

"I swear you live by the needs of your prick, Ram. Did you, by chance, discover if there is at least any authority on this island?" Dane dealt with a young pup, retrieving a bottle from the bar and cracking it over his head. 'Twould be unfair to dress his hide, he thought, dusting off his hands, then turning to Ram. Dane waited patiently for his friend to subdue his brawny opponent, then stepped in when it appeared Ram was about to lose a few teeth.

"Your talents are waning, O'Keefe," Dane quipped, his hands on his thighs, trying to catch his breath.

" 'Twas three to one, if you failed to notice!"

A man came from the side, and Dane took a hearty

chop to the gullet with a loud *oof,* folded over, lost his footing, and fell ungallantly to his rear. He was unable to roll out of the way before Ramsey tumbled on top of him.

"I've a meeting with some Englishman tomorrow," he answered with a bloody grin, then quickly rolled off.

"If we should live that long," Dane muttered, leaping to his feet, fists primed.

Clad in a very prim long-sleeved nightgown and robe, Tess worried the already-worn carpet to an early grave with her pacing. *How could he just dump me here, then vanish? Leaving me alone?* Well, I'm not really alone, she thought. Beyond the sitting-room door were three guards; below in the inn's common room were four or five more of the *Sea Witch*'s crew; outside God only knew how many loitered throughout the yard and stables. It was a damned fortress, and Dane was out having some clandestine meeting with Ramsey. But before he'd left, Dane had rented the entire top floor of the inn, apologizing for the accommodations, assuring her a house would be at their disposal in the morning. Tess didn't see anything wrong with the place, other than a few fleas, and it could use a decent decorator. She padded into her bedroom and flopped back onto the mattress, pennyroyal crunching beneath the sheets.

She felt like a prisoner yet knew exactly what would happen to her without Dane's protection. When she'd first entered the common room, nearly every leering scuzzbag started toward her until Dane and his men had stepped inside. Her speech and manners alerted more people to the differences in her, so Tess kept her mouth shut most times. She didn't try to develop speech like Dane's. All those 'tis, 'twas, and 'twere's? Jeez, it made her head hurt to have to think on how to start a sentence. She suddenly longed for the isolation of the frigate. I handled the crew's reservations and suspicions, she thought, but an entire island's?

She stiffened when voices in the hall filtered beneath the locked door: laughter, boots scraping, and a great deal of moaning. Then she heard keys jiggle in the locks and a door bang against a wall. She climbed from the bed and moved to the door leading to Dane's room.

She knocked softly, then heard muffled chuckles, whispers, and shushes coming from beyond. Drunk, she decided, her lips pulling in a thin tight line as she quietly opened the door, folded her arms over her breasts, then leaned against the jamb. Over fifteen members of both crews glanced up, expressions freezing. Bleeding noses, purple eyes, torn clothes, cuts, scrapes, and blackening bruises marked each man in a variety of areas. Two men were in the midst of helping another toward the table, but upon seeing the woman in the doorway, unceremoniously tossed him in a chair. The man groaned, slumping back and hooking his arms over the chair back to keep upright. Mates chuckled and swayed.

"O'Keefe. Well. I might have known. Can't stop making those grand entrances, huh?"

"Evenin' to you, lass." He grinned, devouring the sight of her from behind swollen lids.

"For your sake, I hope the other guy looks worse."

289

That brought a round of laughter, and she eyed the crew into silence. Grown men stared at the floor like regretful little boys. "Jeez, what a mess!" She stepped inside, moving to the nightstand and coming back with a bowl, pitcher, and washcloths.

"We won, m'lady," Gaelan put in, swiping blood from his lip. There was a hearty rumble of agreement.

"Aye, the first mate, here, milled a rascal twice his stone," a sailor admired.

"What would you know of it, Cam, you were the admiral of the narrow seas when I saw you last." The room vibrated with laughter, and the young seaman flushed. Before she got a Marine's version of the bar-room brawl, Tess deduced that meant the poor boy retched in someone's lap.

The door leading to the hall opened, and Duncan and Higa-san shuffled in, bandages and liniments filling their arms. The men stepped aside, and her eyes widened. "Damn!" She set the bowl and pitcher on the table with an angry thump, then pushed bodies from her path. His jacket draped neatly over his arm, Dane stood still as she looked him up and down, then tilted his face to inspect the damage. His jaw was bruised, and his lower lip and knuckles were bleeding.

He glanced at the roomful of men, then frowned down at her. " 'Tis late, Tess, why are you not abed?"

"Look who's talking. Sit," she ordered, pointing to the chair. Several men backed out of her way when she maneuvered Dane toward the table, then pushed him down.

"Get you to bed, woman, or clothe yourself." He made to put his jacket over her shoulders, but she shrugged it off, glaring at the chuckling Ramsey.

290

"You're an unselfish jackass, Ramsey O'Keefe! How could you involve him in this?"

Dane fought a smile. "Tess, please, 'twas not solely his fault."

"Don't give me that!" She shoved his hand off her arm. "He enjoys instigating trouble. Look at him! He can't decide whether to grin or bleed! Jeez!" She soaked the cloth, then wrung it out with a vengeance. "He makes a pass at a married woman and can't understand why her husband wants to punch his lights out!"

"Tess, truly. 'Twas not so bad."

"And you!" She rounded on Dane. "You just *had* to bail him out!" Her gaze shot to Ramsey. "Did you forget he had a concussion?" Despite her anger, she gently blotted Dane's jaw and lips.

Dane jerked his head back from her ministrations. "They are minor, woman, cease."

"I, for one, have several wounds that could use your tender care, m'lady."

Tess sent Ramsey a look meant to grind him into hamburger.

"Careful, Ram," Gaelan said. "In the lady's present state, I daresay you may find your throat cut." The battered group laughed.

"You all really think this is funny, don't you?" She slapped the rag into the bowl, splashing water over the table. "Don't you?"

"Aye," Ram chuckled. "You're radiant when yer peeved, lass."

"Peeved? Peeved is when you get the wrong dinner order! He had a *brain* concussion, for Chrissake!" She measured each man, her misty gaze ending on

291

Dane. "And another blow to your head would have killed you!" She spun away, lacy bedclothes fluttering as she raced out of the room, slamming doors behind her.

The hollow sound echoed throughout the floor.

Ramsey sighed, resting his elbows on the table, his aching head in his hands. The impact of her words had cut him in half. "God forgive me, Dane, I was unaware of the risk." The chair creaked as he sagged back. "Sweet Christ, but I do not envy you this time."

Dane left the chair and walked to the door. Soundlessly he opened it, sealing it behind him.

"She loves him, doesn't she?" Aaron said into the quiet.

Though he was answering the first mate, Duncan looked pointedly at Captain O'Keefe. "And when did you come to that brilliant conclusion, eh, sir?"

Ramsey felt a measure of guilt at the decadent meal he'd just consumed, the memory of his ride from the docks brimming in his head: hovels filled with bony dark-skinned children in ragged clothes, their hopeless expressions, and, worst, their parents' sneers of contempt when he'd alighted from the Englishman's carriage. His host was the ruling official on the island, by his own appointment, Ramsey gathered, not having a chance to verify the man's title. But the Englishman had been waiting on the docks before the *Triton* weighed anchor.

His body aching, he shifted uncomfortably in the small velvet chair and sipped the aged brandy, his eyes on the Englishman's daughter. Monica fanned herself, gold eyes peering at him from over the rim. Ram winked slowly, then winced when she giggled in a high-pitched shrill. 'Twas a duty, he thought, to have spent time with the woman, listening to her complaints about not being at court or the lack of acceptable suitors. Yet between her whining, she'd been a fountain of information during their turn around the elaborate gardens. Her father had been too cautious for Ramsey's allotment of time, though not with his daughter. Ram had already tasted those lips, felt the voluptuous curves, which were merely wads of molded cotton, he'd discovered with a bit of surprise. A spoiled selfish chit, he decided, having seen her order servants with a stinging hand and a superior air that rubbed the American in a most indecent manner. Suddenly his thoughts turned to Tess: her teasing, the truth she spoke so easily, and how the feisty lass could dice this brat to ribbons with her sharp tongue. 'Twas something he would enjoy watching, he thought, then remembered how she hadn't shown herself to anyone since last evening. With a disheartened sigh, he ignored the pain in his bruised jaw and directed his attention to what English was saying.

"I'm certain we can find a suitable buyer for your goods, Captain O'Keefe," Whittingham said in his nasal accent. "I will be delighted to look into it if you'd be so kind as to turn over a list of your cargo."

Ramsey hid a smile. The man was practically sanding his hands together in anticipation. "I'd rather initiate the bargain myself, if you don't mind. 'Tis a half-year's work that I've stored and have many wages to dole. Bothersome chore, that," Ram sighed dramatically, his gaze shifting briefly to the woman, and he flashed her a quick smile, "but then, 'tis why I've seen success of late."

The Englishman bristled. Bloody arrogant Colonist. A rich one, if his attire was anything to measure, yet an ungrateful rebel just the same. Should have shot them all. God, he hated being banished to this island, longing for the dignity and coolness of London. Whittingham stood and adjusted his clothing, a signal the meeting was over, and the captain quickly came to his feet.

"As you wish, Captain. I will send a messenger to your ship on the morrow," the Englishman stated, willing to forgo the man's heritage to see his stores in his personal warehouse.

"Do not bother, sir; you have done enough in my behalf, and I am pressed to see the deed done. I will return with my quartermaster, say around noon?"

Whittingham stiffened. Someone should have finished bashing the Colonist's face! How dare this man question his stipulations? "I'm afraid that will be terribly inconvenient. I've business meetings—"

"Oh, Papa, I've the perfect solution!" Monica gushed. "You have your meetings, and I will entertain the captain until you can join us." She rose with a flourish, then sashayed over to stand between the men. "You will join us for luncheon, won't you, Captain O'Keefe?" She pouted prettily up at the American, allowing her skirts to brush his calves and giving him a splendid view of her bosom.

Lady, my arse, Ram thought. What sot was she trying to make the fool?

"Again you offer your much-needed assistance, daughter," her father said and thought he saw the captain smirk. The girl could finally be of more use than adding bills to his purse. If O'Keefe was occupied here, his men could investigate his ship and cargo, he silently chuckled.

Reminding himself to post extra guards on the *Triton,* Ramsey nodded agreement, catching Monica's pleased smile. He wouldn't dream of denying himself a tumble with a wench that was so willing to give it.

Ramsey bid them good afternoon and departed quickly. When a servant appeared to inform the master that the guest had indeed left, Whittingham turned to his daughter.

"Get you to bed, child, and think naught of the sea captain. The insolent braggart will likely be dead before a sennight."

Monica gasped in horror, and when she started to speak, he bellowed, "To bed, girl!" She fled the room with great haste.

A figure slipped from the alcove near the stairs, startling the elderly man.

"Good God, man!" he choked, a hand covering his heart. "Be chousin' bloody ten years off me friggin' arse!"

Phillip strolled across the room to the bar. "Careful, Nigel, your background is showing." He poured himself a drink, tossed back the expensive liquor, then moved toward the door. "His stores, get them. And the jewels, well, you know, don't you, Nigh?"

"Wait! Was it him?"

"You do go on, Nigel, and—" Phillip looked back over his shoulder, his hand on the latch. "When I decide your pea brain can absorb that much, you'll be a corpse."

* * *

Ramsey leapt from the moving carriage, then slipped into the darkened alley way. He waited for the conveyance to round the corner before his gaze returned to the Englishman's house. The door abruptly opened, and he plastered his tall form back against the cracked wall as a figure stepped out. His eyes narrowed, and his body tensed when the man drew a horse from beneath the shade of a tree and made to mount. Ram moved soundlessly behind crates and rubbish piles to get a better look before the fellow departed. The figure reined around, and Ram caught a glimpse of his profile before he viciously clapped his bleeders to the beast's sides. The sea captain cursed softly, taking off in a run, vowing to discover where the bastard slept.

Chapter Twenty-four

A golden ball of fire hovered above the horizon, its reflecting rays splashing pink, magenta, and cool lavender across the cloudless sky. Out of the open window, Tess watched the tranquil sight for a few moments longer, then let her gaze drift to the streets below. She waved to the guards beneath her window, and they bowed shortly in response. Burros pulled carts filled with goods, their owners prodding them with crooked sticks. Children raced through the alleys, teasing each other. Goats and chickens skittered around the yards, no one paying them any mind. The smell made Tess ill. Women dressed in brightly colored skirts and gauzy blouses converged around the well in the center of the square, filling huge jars, gossiping, then staring occasionally up at her. Tess smiled, waved, and they responded with a look of shock, then bobbed a curtsy. She wondered what they thought of her. The captain's lady or the ship's whore?

She glanced around the room. It was sparsely furnished, yet neat and clean. What she wouldn't give for air conditioning or just an ice-cold Diet Coke or a chance to take a swim in her bikini! Or watch one of Penny's movies, or—what would you give, a little voice asked, to let it all go? She stiffened. That little voice was damned annoying. And Tess wasn't certain she liked the realization that Dane Alexander Blackwell, sea captain, Continental Marine, confidante to the President, had become her entire world. Jeez, he could have easily been killed in that fight! Hell, people in this time died of such minor things she could hardly begin to think of them all. And if she lost Dane?

A sharp pain lanced her chest, threatening her breathing, and she returned her gaze to the street, trying to separate her emotions. What would happen if she got the chance to return to the future? When will it come? Next week? Next year? Never? And what would she go back to? They were the same questions she'd asked since she'd discovered herself in this century. She didn't want to depend on anyone, never had before. She'd managed alone since she was a kid, but in 1789, Tess realized, the opportunities for a woman were slim to none. Men were teachers, politicians, land owners; women were governesses, glorified baby-sitters, maids, and dependent on what men gave them, whether it was their fathers or their husbands. Men ran the show; women paid for it. And the fact that she needed protection from men, by men, rankled the hell out of her. But she could adapt if she wanted. She watched the people below. Living, surviving, loving. What are you going to do, Renfrew, hide for the next hundred years?

"Speak with me, Tess," Dane said from the other side of the oaken door. "This silence will accomplish naught." He received no response to his plea. He'd no doubt she was in there; a maid had deposited two meals and removed her bathwater already this day. He glanced briefly at Duncan, who was setting the table for the evening meal, then shrugged and walked to a chair, dropping into it with a heavy sigh.

Her behavior unnerved him. 'Twas not like Tess to allow things to brew inside her. 'Twas one of the things he enjoyed most about her, that she hid naught of her feelings, said what she wanted, when she desired. Suddenly he sat upright, a horrifying thought occurring to him. Had she received some signal or vision that would send her to her time? He left the chair and strode across the sitting room, pounding hard on the wood.

"She's gone, sir."

Dane spun about to see only Potts's head poking into the room. "Tell me I've heard wrong, mister."

"Nay, sir." Potts stepped inside, scrunching his cap. "The lady said she was needin' some fresh air, sir."

Dane took a couple steps, and Potts flinched. "And you simply allowed her to go!" His voice boomed.

"Lady Renfrew can be very convincin', sir."

Dane bolted out of the room and down the hall, taking the stairs three at a time. "Mr. Sikes has his eye on the lass," he heard Potts holler down the staircase. He met Ramsey at the landing, and the *Triton* captain followed him out of the inn, crew men taking up the rear. Men spread out like a human net, and Dane didn't get but a few yards beyond the street when he saw her.

He sighed with relief, rubbing the back of his neck, trying to calm his racing pulse. Through the palm trees he could see Tess walking on the beach, her slippers dangling from her fingertips, toes kicking at the sand.

Ramsey nearly slammed into him from behind.

"God, what a vision." Her black hair was unbound, wild with the breeze.

"Isn't she, though," Dane replied wistfully, and Ram witnessed the raw emotion his friend kept hidden.

"She is in love with you, you realize that." Regret heavily laced his voice.

"Nay, I do not," he returned softly.

"Then yer an ass, man," Ram scoffed. "And I can admit 'tis a grand bit of jealousy I feel for you."

Dane arched a raven brow, glancing to his side. "You would fight me for her?"

Ram's smile was bittersweet. " 'Twas never a battle, my friend. The woman sees me for what I am. And has made her feelings rather clear that she cares naught for any of it."

Dane returned his gaze to Tess. Dark green became her, he decided. " 'Tis a wish to capture her like that, for I doubt we will see her so serene and quiet again."

Ramsey chuckled softly. "She is a spirited female."

"Aye, and too bold for her own good, sharp-tongued and willful and bloody independent and—" Dane let his breath out in a quick burst and could feel Ramsey's mocking grin. "You were correct, you know. She will not accept a proposal."

Ram frowned, confused. "She cares naught if she is branded?"

Dane shrugged, his expression pure misery. "Tess is most comfortable with the situation as it is."

Ramsey wondered exactly what that meant.

"But you are not content?"

Dane's features hardened. "Never."

"Perhaps 'tis the man and not the offer?" Ramsey

taunted with the last of his hopes. "What if I should ask?"

Dane looked to his side, his eyes sharp as bottle glass. "Only if you desire a leisurely and rather painful death."

Ram chuckled, patting his friend on the back, somewhat relieved 'twas not he that was experiencing that magnitude of torment. "Try again, Dane, and again and yet again. Then if you must, drag the woman bound and gagged to the nearest clergy."

A wry smile twisted at Dane's lips and he knew that would likely be the only way he would make her his wife.

Ramsey took one last look at her, then abruptly turned his back from the sight. "Love her, Dane," he murmured softly, and Dane felt the man's secret heartache. "Love her so fully that I will never live to regret not dueling with you for the lady's hand." He quietly walked away.

Dane's heart pounded heavy and hard in his chest as she strolled the shore. Her expression was forlorn, if not a touch regretful, and Dane wondered what was running through that quick mind. Were her thoughts the same as his? Every moment he was denied the sight of her was slow moving agony. He could not eat, sleep, or concentrate on a bloody thing knowing she was upset, disturbed enough to remain sequestered in her rooms for nearly an entire day.

Was she waiting for the wall to appear, the rip in time, she called it? The thought made his chest tighten till he could scarcely inhale a breath, and he knew he would not survive if she were taken from him now. Because I love her, his mind screamed, and he nearly

301

choked on the realization, sagging back against a palm tree and whispering the words aloud. A warm comfort filled him at finally putting a name to the gloriously confusing sensation. She'd traveled over two hundred years for him to love, and he would never let her go. Even if it meant he would have to follow her into the future to be with her.

He motioned to Sikes, and the burly sailor and several of his comrades strode to their captain.

"Let no one disturb her, and keep out of sight," Dane ordered, giving Tess the privacy she desired, yet with ample protection. He saw her brush at her cheek and could only imagine what caused the tears. With a monumental effort, Dane turned away and headed toward the inn without a backward glance.

"How can you consume yet another meal?" Gaelan asked as Ramsey sawed into his meat.

Ramsey shrugged, his expression not the least bit offended as he savored the roasted pork.

Dane looked at his untouched plate, then pushed it away and lifted the snifter to his lips. Dining around him were his officers and four from the *Triton,* and all Dane desired was to speak with Tess. She'd returned moments after he had, yet she'd gone straight to her rooms without a word to anyone. His gaze strayed to the door yet again, and with a muffled curse, he shifted his chair so his back was to the closed portal.

"How will you get to him?" Ramsey asked, then shoved a knife full of peas into his mouth.

" 'Tis you that has seen the bloody house! Is that not why we are here!" Dane snapped, coming to his feet and storming to the window.

Ramsey swallowed, frowning at the outburst. 'Twas not like Dane to let his emotions rule when a situation demanded his attention. Women—destroyed a man's thinking process, Ram thought with a twisted smile as each mate offered his own plan. The conversation grew animated and loud as Duncan cleared plates and the men positioned themselves around the table. Ramsey swiped at his lips with a napkin, tossed it on his plate, then handed it to Duncan. He drew out a map he'd made earlier, then fished in his coat pocket for a stick of graphite.

" 'Tis on a hill at the far side of the island, a bloody fortress, walls, guards, the bastard even has the place surrounded by water."

Gaelan's brow shot up. "A moat?"

Ram smiled. "I nearly fell into it myself. 'Tis narrow, yet deep and hidden well by vines and bushes. He sleeps here." Ram pointed to the spot, then showed them the galley, parlor, stables, servant quarters, and everything else he'd managed to ascertain. " 'Tis the most strategic spot. He has the sea to his back; any ship as large as a sloop could anchor there." He rubbed his hand over his chin, frowning, thinking. Men waited patiently until he spoke again. "The warehouses are here at the wharf, and Whittingham's is here, just beyond."

"Is this privileged information, or can anybody listen in?"

Dane's heart slammed against the wall of his chest, and he jerked around to see that Tess stood in the doorway. Men leapt to their feet, overturning chairs and nearly the table in the process. Ramsey rose slowly, his gaze darting briefly to Dane.

"Evening, Lady Renfrew." He bowed from the waist, and the crew murmured their greetings.

"Sit down, guys, and call me Tess, Ramsey." Tess walked until she stood before Dane. "Hi," she said huskily, pushing a lock from his brow. "You look like hell."

"A good evening to you, too, Tess." He smiled broadly, his eyes boldly roaming her softer parts as he lifted the brandy to his lips. He tried valiantly not to satisfy the need to smother every inch of her skin with kisses.

"Cut that out," she whispered a bit breathlessly, then gave him her back and peered over Aaron's shoulder at the map. "What's the plan?"

"I fear we have none yet," Aaron said, his gaze drifting over her flushed cheeks and freshly combed hair. So lovely she was.

"You looking to bust your way in or what?"

"Nay," Ramsey said. "We must get a look at the stores in the warehouse without raising suspicion, then find a way into this bloody house. I will do the former in the morning."

"What's so important about the warehouses?"

Ram glanced at Dane, and the man nodded almost imperceptibly. "We must discover how the goods are marked. Our ships sailing in this area have been attacked, yet the culprits have been careful to unload the stores before destroying the vessels. We found a poorly disguised crate with the *Barstow's* markings in a market in South Carolina. The goods are—"

"Being sold to the United States, so—in reality, we're buying back what we already own. You need to see the stuff on their property before it's remarked, right? For proof?"

Ram grinned. God, she was quick.

"And with the information in the pilot rudders, you can tie all that to Desiree's killer?" Ram nodded and saw Dane flinch at her words. "Well, every man or woman—"she added pointedly—"has a soft spot. Does this man have an Achilles heel you're aware of?"

"Women," Dane answered. "Young, wealthy, defenseless women." He leaned against the frame. "And jewels."

"The riches he stole, Tess," Ram cleared his throat, unused to the familiarity—"were solely in precious gems."

"Good Lord," she whispered, then cast a glance at Dane. "Jewels, huh? I take it you don't have any to entice this guy with?"

He shook his head. " 'Twas not only my sister's dowry, but a goodly portion of the wealth my father mined in India, he—"

"Can you buy some?" she interrupted.

Dane shrugged. "There are none to be had here, at least not enough of a fine quality or that I can afford to purchase."

"Not to mention the man would catch wind of it before we could act," Aaron added.

"Before *I* can act," Dane clarified, and his mates grumbled.

Tess's eyes widened. "You're going after him by yourself?"

"Of course! Without question. 'Twas my family he ruined and—what are you up to now, lass?" Dane asked, his brows drawn tight as she suddenly swept

305

into her rooms.

Tess immediately went to an ugly brown satchel and pulled out her yellow duffle. Dane had put it in there to be less conspicuous. She jammed her hand deep into the bag, slipping her fingers beneath the vinyl-covered cardboard that supported the bottom. She tore free the packet taped beneath, then returned to the sitting room. Standing before Dane, she pried up two brass tines, then opened the paper envelope. Men craned their necks to look as she leaned over the table and tilted the pouch.

Across the hastily drawn map spilled a fortune in colored marquis-cut diamonds.

"Is that enough?"

Some men cursed, others whistled quietly, yet all moved closer, gaping from the stones to her and back.

"Mother of God!" Dane whispered, picking up a gem the size of his thumbnail. "How did you come by such a treasure?"

The officers waited with breath held as she swung her gaze to Dane. Tess braced herself, straightening her spine and lifting her chin.

"I stole it."

"What?" everyone shouted. Dane fell into a chair.

"I wasn't after those." She gestured to the stones. "I broke into this building—"

"You were a thief?" Dane bellowed, appalled.

"No! Well, yes—for one night," Tess knew this was coming and struggled with how to put it so they could understand. "Sloane was about to give some damaging, ah, material on my friend Penny to the newspapers. Pen asked me to get it back." Tess shrugged. "It was hers anyway. Hell, Sloane even told me where to find the packet! I should have seen that coming because along with the incriminating stuff," she tossed a thumb at the gems, "was that little surprise."

Dane stood abruptly and paced a few steps. "A bloody thief!" He stopped and glared at her. "God's teeth, this is what you've been hiding from me?"

She planted her hands on her hips. "Look, Blackwell, Sloane put those diamonds in there hoping I'd get killed for them! And I wouldn't even be here, except they saw me leaving. Pen and I traded places and I took her cru—ah, passage on the *Nassau Queen*."

Dane looked at the diamonds. *I wouldn't be here,* repeated in his head.

"Are you saying you wouldn't do the same if a friend needed you?" she asked, inclining her head sharply toward O'Keefe.

Eyes shifted to see how he'd answer.

"The lass has you there, my friend," Ramsey said quietly.

Dane's shoulders slumped, and he rubbed the back of his neck, his gaze moving between Tess and the gems.

"Are you offering those stones?"

"Sure. Why not? I can be the bait to—"

"Never." Dane shook his head slowly.

"But I could get inside, then help you."

" 'Tis preposterous to even consider the—"

"You said he likes jewels—"

"Tess—!" His voice grew steadily louder.

"—And I can be as helpless as he wants."

"Damn you, woman!" He took a step, itching to shake her. "I will not hand you over to the whoreson, and that is the end of it!" They stared, green ice battling with silver fire, and Tess knew he wouldn't relent.

"Okay, fine. You lost your chance to get this guy where it hurts." Tess leaned over the table and scooped up the gems, pouring them into the packet. "Me no help, you no diamonds." She marched across the room, opened the door to the hall, and walked out. Dane, Ramsey, and the officers stared at the open door, then Dane bolted like a pistol shot.

"Come back here, woman!"

"Go to hell, Blackwell."

He flew down the stairs, Ram, Gaelan, and Aaron not far behind. Several pairs of eyes followed her as she ran through the common room and out the door before he could stop her. He shoved aside chairs and people, quickening his step.

"Sweet Christ. You cannot expect me to endanger your life, too!"

He was several paces behind her, yet she didn't stop. "But you'd gamble with yours regardless of the hazards."

" 'Tis different. I'm a man." He overtook the division between them, and just as he reached her, she lifted her skirts and took off.

"Try again, Blackwell. That doesn't wash."

People paused to stare at the handsome couple arguing in the streets.

"Come with me to the inn before I'm forced to carry you back. Now, Tess," he demanded. " 'Tis not safe!"

"Safe!" She stopped abruptly, and he nearly slammed into her. "You're the one so hellbent on revenge, you can't see what will happen to the rest of us if you're killed. Go ahead! Do it!" she shouted. "Let this bastard waste your butt. If you don't give a crap

308

about your life, than why the hell should I?" She turned and ducked down a side street. "I'm used to being alone," she muttered under her breath.

He heard and followed. " 'Tis why you've hidden from me today. Because I have threatened this little cocoon you've made for yourself." His inescapable conclusion made Tess slow her steps.

"I care for you, Dane. Maybe too much." Her throat swelled.

He met her stride. "Care? 'Tis a weak word, lass. I care if my breeches are clean."

She halted, facing him. "What do you want from me?"

He spread his arms out. "Have I demanded a thing?" His gaze locked with hers, and Tess knew he wouldn't come right out and say it.

"What if I get sent back into my time?" She choked on her torment.

" 'Twill not happen." His words were sharp with pain as she gave voice to his fears.

"It might, and we couldn't stop it!" Her eyes misted, her heart beating out her panic.

"I will," he challenged, covering the space that separated them. "With the last drop of my blood." Swiftly he caught her about the waist, gathering her close. "Your century gave you up, Tess, tossed you into my arms, and I mean to keep you." His mouth crashed down onto hers, his lips hard and slanting as he mashed her to his body. I'm losing her, he thought, and deepened his assault. Flames licked where their bodies touched, searing their blood. A heady steam rose around the pair as he devoured her lips, begging what he dared not ask of her: a promise to stay with him, to live in his time.

"Let me help you, Dane," she whispered breathlessly against his mouth, and he shook his head. "Dammit! Don't you know how much you mean to me?" she cried, squeezing his biceps. "Don't you realize by now I'd do anything for you!"

His fingers dove into her hair, tilting her head back. "Anything, Tess?"

"Yes," she insisted, tears glistening.

"Then marry me."

Tess stared into eyes pale as sea foam, turbulent, and knew she had to make her decision now or lose it all. Her time or his.

"Aye," she breathed on a sigh.

Dane stole it, kissing her until he felt her legs buckle, then abruptly spun her about so she could see they stood in a churchyard and that a man in brown robes was coming toward them.

She looked back over her shoulder, eyes wide. "N-n-now?" she sputtered.

Dane didn't give her the chance to ponder overlong on the matter, and with a hand at the small of her back, gently nudged her toward the friar.

"Get Duncan quickly," Ramsey ordered from somewhere off to the side. "He won't want to miss this!"

Chapter Twenty-five

Tess's thoughts spun chaotically as Dane spoke to the old friar. Married? Now? This minute? She gulped, turning a pleading look to where Ramsey was leaning against the crumbling stone gate, but the man was no help, folding his arms over his chest and chuckling quietly as if he were laughing at some joke only he was aware of. She returned her attention to the ancient priest. Bobbing his head with approval, the friar waved a hand toward his chapel, sandaled feet shuffling as he led the way.

"Haven't you ever heard of an engagement?" Tess whispered out of the side of her mouth.

Dane smiled, prodding her along. "I have you this close to an altar, love, and will not give way to chance."

" 'Fraid I'd turn tail, huh?"

"Aye."

"Gee. You could have said no."

His expression grew serious as he ducked beneath the archway and pulled her into the coolness of the church. "I would always have the truth spoken 'atween us, Tess."

She smiled up at him. "Yeah, me too." Her hand felt tiny in his warm grasp. "But you could at least give me a chance to change." Hunter green was not the color she imagined as a wedding dress.

Boldly he appraised the slim body encased in satin as they walked up the aisle. "You look most enchanting, m'lady." Aye, vibrant, rosy, fresh from a good row, he thought with a stirring in his loins.

"Dane! We're in a church," she reminded, cheeks reddening. "Seriously. I'm all sandy, salty—"

"And scared?" he questioned with a sympathetic smile.

She met his gaze. "Who wouldn't be?"

Before the altar, Dane gathered her against him, his expression tender-sweet, and Tess was caught breathless as he spoke. " 'Tis my promise I give you this day, Tess, to see you safe and happy, round with our children and old with theirs. You've naught to fear of my time, little one. I will not let it harm you."

Tess blinked, and a tear spilled, her gaze searching his face. Pinch me, I'm dreaming, she thought. He really wants to marry me! Not just for some archaically chivalrous belief that he's doing justice to my soiled honor or for the chance to take me to bed again. He *really* wants to marry me! Tess let that sink home for a full thirty seconds. God, how did she get this lucky? To have a new life with a trusting man like Dane. Handsome, unpredictable, gallant, tender Dane. Men like him were a dying breed in her time, and Tess wanted and loved all of him.

Dane thought the world had ceased revolving when she did no more than stare at him. His heart sat like a stone in his chest, heavy and dead as he brushed a soft kiss to her lips and whispered, "Please, my love, marry me."

Her throat tightened, hearing the quiver in his voice. The request was filled with a tense desperation, a sudden fear she never dreamed he'd share with her, with anyone. He was giving her the chance to run.

"Yeah, pirate, I will," she breathed against his lips, slipping her hand into her skirt pocket and removing the packet. Images suddenly flashed in her head; the figurehead, the perfect-fitting clothes, his teasing, and his touching. Dane absolutely furious with her. Dane unconscious, still as granite. Dane carrying her to his bed. The dolphin, the black wall. *I was meant to be here. I love this man too much to believe otherwise.* She leaned closer, their breath a warm flutter between them.

Someone called out his name, and Dane groaned when she denied him the taste of her. *I shan't survive much longer,* he thought, shifting uncomfortably, Tess's teasing grin doing considerable damage to his barely checked desires. They turned to see Duncan skid to a stop at the end of the pews, Dane's coat slung over his arm. Behind him, sailors bumped and collided when they realized what was about to take place. Quickly the old mariner strode forward, his smile so smug and pleased it would have to be chiseled off, Tess decided, as Dane slipped into the dark green jacket.

"Are we ready now?" the friar beamed, delighted to perform a ceremony that was not over a mutilated body about to be put in the ground.

"Aye," she answered eagerly, moving close and discreetly slipping the packet of diamonds into Dane's coat pocket.

Their eyes never wavered as Dane and Tess spoke vows to love, honor, and cherish. Yet Tess interrupted the ceremony once to have the word *obey* omitted. The friar looked appalled at the request and even more astonished when Dane's shoulders shook with silent laughter as he nodded agreement.

"He'll bloody well regret that," Ram whispered and received a sharp poke in his sore ribs from Duncan.

They sealed the marriage with a kiss brimming with silken joy, the observers growing silent with the love they witnessed joined before God. The cheer that followed shook the wood beams of the old stone church as Tess was torn from Dane's embrace and handed from man to man. Burly arms wrapped around her, nearly crushing delicate ribs as sailors congratulated the captain's bride. Bruised and dizzy, Tess suddenly found herself before Ramsey.

With a chuckle nothing short of lecherous, the *Triton* captain swept her into his arms and claimed her mouth. Dane observed the kiss with raised brows; that Ram seemed to be giving his wife a goodly portion of his mastery did not rouse the groom's anger, for Tess was limp as a rag in the man's embrace. Ramsey pulled back, staring at her with a perplexed look on his face.

"Tess, ah, I—I?"

"Don't sweat it, O'Keefe," she said, smoothly moving out of his arms. "Your day will come."

Tess turned to Dane, a mischievous smile floating across her lips as he tucked her hand in the crook of his arm.

"You delight in teasing the poor sot, don't you?" Dane whispered as they trailed the friar to sign the marriage certificate.

"No, but bursting his bubble was a nice start."

They laughed quietly as the old priest scribbled in a massive book, then turned a slip of the parchment around for their signatures.

"Your birth date and name," Dane told her.

"What do I write?" she asked, quill poised. "I mean, I was born—" she leaned close and lowered her voice to scarcely a whisper—"in 1964."

Dane held her gaze. "Pen that, Tess. I will have this legal and binding."

"Our kids will thank you for that," she shot back, and he stared at her for a moment, then grinned hugely and pressed a quick, hard kiss to her lips. Tess did as he asked, then watched as he scrolled his signature, dark and bold, sprinkled sand on the ink, blew, then folded the document and tucked it in his pocket. A little cry escaped her as he bent slightly, slipped his arm beneath her knees, then straightened, holding her high against his chest.

"Dane?" He strode out of the church to the applause of his crew. "Put me down," she protested softly when he continued out of the yard.

"I have restrained myself long enough, love." He lengthened his stride.

She grinned, looping her arms around his neck. "This is that rutting business you mentioned earlier, right?"

He made a pained sound. "God, aye."

People stopped and gawked, blinking to be certain this was the same couple that had been screeching at each other moments before.

"Where are you going? The inn is that way," she said, pointing back over his shoulder.

He gave her a wicked smile. "You wish the entire inn to hear your cries of pleasure?" he murmured huskily, watching her skin flush beneath his warm regard. Thank God the house was ready.

"My, aren't we confident." She nuzzled at his neck. God, he smelled great.

"I shall try my utmost to please my bride."

"Give you sixty years to get it right," she challenged.

"My pleasure, love." He stepped over a low stone wall and paused, his body stirring to her little pecks. "Tess?"

"Hmm?" Her tongue slid around his ear, and she felt his soft shudder.

"Do — ah — do — ah," he swallowed — "do you wish to see where we'll spend our wedding night?"

"Uh-ah." Her hand wiggled inside his jacket. "Later." He strode up the steps and kicked open the door. "You know, Blackwell, you break far too many doors for a man your age." Her fingers moved into his hair, and she turned his head, her lips molding over his as he carried her across the threshold. He eased her to her feet, letting her slide down the length of him as he reached behind and shut the door. The click of the lock echoed in the silent house. He leaned back.

"Lights," he managed to say.

"Don't need 'em."

Another pained sound as he slipped from her grasp. She giggled when he stumbled in the darkened house, cursing softly, yet remained where she was. The spark of flint caught her eye before the room filled with a warm glow. It was spacious, done in pale gray and deep blue, but she wasn't interested in the decor, her attention immediately focusing on the staircase. She moved toward it and was already on the first steps when he came to her.

"Hungry?"

"Yup." She hitched up her skirts in each hand, then grabbed the fabric of his coat, pulling him, the green gown a satin envelope around them.

"I could seek out a bit of cheese and bread—" She shook her head slowly, backing up the stairs. "Some wine, perhaps?" He advanced.

"Not food I want."

He grinned, lopsided and sexy. "What does the lady desire?" His voice was husky, deep, sending a hot thrill over her body.

"As if you didn't know. I've been trying to get you into bed for a week." They stood on the landing. "Now you have no excuse."

"I could not in all good conscience destroy your reputation."

"Chivalry is not dead," she murmured, leaning into him and shoving the coat from his shoulders. She opened the door, pulling him inside, assuming this was a bedroom. It was, thank God. She flung the coat aside, then started on his shirt, slipping free the buttons, working her way down. His hands rested on her waist, tightening the closer she came to his waistband.

"Tess, ah—Tess?"

"Yeah?" She yanked the shirt from his breeches, spreading the cloth wide.

"I believe 'tis the groom's opportunity to initiate—" Her lips found the skin at his throat, teeth nibbling softly, and Dane forced himself to muster his thoughts. Gently he grasped her hands, drawing them down to her sides. Moonlight spilled across the car-

317

peted floor in a sharp slice of silver, the expression on his face making Tess go still.

"I would savor this night, my love." Dane cupped her face between callused palms, pressing his mouth to hers. His kiss was unhurried, a tender worship, and Tess's heartbeat slowed, the heat moving gradually over her body like a cloak of warmed honey. His fingers slid into her hair, and with a gentle pressure he pulled her flush against him, and she felt the strong steady beat of his heart vibrate through her.

The snugness of her bodice eased and Tess scarcely noticed as the fabric slipped from her body, her attention centered on the lips tasting her own. She gave herself over to him, letting him do as he pleased. And he did.

His mouth moved down the length of her throat as he pushed the heavy skirts down over her hips to pile on the floor. He caressed the skin bared to his touch, leisurely arousing her, warm fingers playing over her taut belly covered in thin green batiste. He knelt, his hands molding the length of her legs before he propped a dainty foot on his thigh and made slow work with the delicious chore of removing her slippers and stockings.

"Dane," Tess breathed, grasping his shoulder as his lips trailed up the inside of her thigh while he slowly drew the stocking down.

"Aye, love?" He tossed the garment aside.

"I don't think I can last much longer."

He stood slowly, his gaze savoring the sight of her veiled in dark green. "You will, my witch — all night."

His eyes spoke the promise of torture she'd receive for teasing him these days before he bent her back over

318

his arm, his lips closing over a nipple covered with thin batiste, outlining the taut peak with his tongue until the fabric was damp and clinging. Her lips parted with a sigh of pleasure, her hair grazing the floor, and Dane realized several advantages to marrying a gymnast. Suddenly he slipped his arm behind her knees, lifting her from the floor, and carrying her toward the bed, gently placing her on the fluffy down. Tess rose up on her knees at the edge, brushing back the white netting that draped in a misty web from the canopy, her gaze dancing over his wide tanned chest as he stripped off the shirt. His boots thunked to the floor, and he lifted his gaze, his fingers hovering at the band of his pants.

Tess wet her lips, the anticipation of seeing him completely naked making her thighs burn. "Hurry, Blackwell, now," she said, and Dane swallowed thickly as she crossed her arms in front of her and grasped the hem of the chemise, drawing it slowly up over her head. His hungry gaze shot to the scrap of black fabric between her thighs as the chemise fluttered noiselessly to the floor.

Sweet Christ! Never had he seen anything more erotic than that scanty bit of nothing.

Tess couldn't help but notice that reaction. "You like, huh?"

His gaze moved upward from the mere threads caught high on her hips, beyond the tight muscled stomach, over her breasts, firm and round, the nipples taut and damp, peeking through the curtain of silky black tresses, to her oval face. The essence of femininity, he thought, blood rushing to his loins. Sultry, alluring. His.

"Aye, very much, love," he finally managed, flipping the buttons to his breeches and peeling the snug fabric down.

"You know, for a man who's complained about restraints," she said, absorbing the naked sight of him, "which you imposed on yourself, I might add—" Every inch of him was lean and hard, rippling as he kicked the trousers aside—"you certainly take your sweet time."

Her last words were squeezed off as his arm shot out to bring her hard against him. "You try me, woman," he growled.

"That's the idea," she replied, resting a hand possessively on his hip, his manhood stiff and thick between them. Small palms stroked the ropey muscles of his back, the tightness of his ribs, the subtle curve of his taut buttocks as Dane mashed her to him, her breasts scorching the skin of his chest. His mouth devoured hers, the storm unleashing as he hooked a thumb beneath the thin strap, yanking the panties down. His wild eagerness caused the delicate silk to rip.

"So much for savoring the moment," she giggled against his lips, then kissed him ravenously.

Pure energy, he thought, flinging the remnant aside, the suggestion of being inside her just too much, and he bent a knee to the mattress, tumbling her to her back. His lips, hot and wet, seared over her pale skin, sampling the rosy crest of her breast, then drawing it into the hot suck of his mouth.

A fire gathered there, spreading rapidly outward to her limbs, and beyond thought, Tess could do no more than moan as he divided his attention between the lush mounds until they were moist and sensitive.

His hand was equally occupied, sliding down her

320

body to cover the dark juncture between her thighs, and she opened for him. Gently he parted the dewy folds, catching her gaze as he slipped a finger inside, then withdrew slowly. Her lids fluttered, her low purr of delight was ambrosia to him as he teased her, watching her bite her lip, then release the shiver into the night. He traced an intricate design over her heated flesh, and Tess burned, her pulse racing as he introduced another finger, coaxing forth a flood that dampened his hand.

"Dane, please," she begged, urging him atop her and failing.

He shook his head slowly, enjoying her wiggling, her pained pleas. "Nay, my heart, I want more of you — much more."

"Greedy pirate," she gasped, twisting on the sheets as he manipulated her passions to a luxurious frenzy. His movements spoke of a man who knew women, knew where to touch, how to bring the greatest pleasure. Tess didn't mind, knowing she would forever reap the benefits of his torrid past. Unable to let him have all the fun, Tess grasped a handful of his hair, pulling him to meet her lips while her free hand wedged between them, searching, her small fingers wrapping around his manhood. He growled lowly, hot and solid in her palm, his large body quaking against her as she stroked him. The sensation thrilled her.

"Tess, love, cease, I will be of no use," he murmured, drawing her hand away.

"Wanna bet?" she panted, a supple limb gliding over his haunches, her hand caressing his stomach and chest as he shifted. Dane nibbled a blistering path over her flat belly, the gentle curve of her hip, drowning in the scent, the taste of her. She shuddered, the fragile whisper sounding loud in the room as his wide shoulders nudged her legs further apart. His warm breath fanned the dampened mound between her thighs.

She reached. "Dane! No! I-I never—!" His lips brushed the ebony curls and Tess fell back with a defeated sigh, the fire surging with amazing accuracy. His hands on her inner thighs, Dane spread her, leaving her bare and glistening to his bold attentions, and Tess dug her head into the pillows, pliant and weak beneath his mouth and tongue. Her breath came in quick, shallow pants. She trembled violently, her world pitching crazily at the unfamiliar caress as his tongue slickly circled the core of her desire. She was nearly in tears when he rose up, bracing his hands at her sides, hovering above her.

His smile was wicked as she clawed at his shoulders, pulling, moaning deeply when his weight settled in the cradle of her thighs. His manhood pressed against her opening as he laced his fingers with hers, holding her gaze. Dane pushed, filling her softness, and her feline murmur of satisfaction was enough to destroy his slim thread of control. Her skin closed immediately around him, sucking him farther inside, and Dane knew nothing could be more glorious than Tess. She was beautiful, an enchanting temptress, weaving an exotic spell around him. My witch, he thought, my spirited Sea Witch.

Dane moved. The breath quivered on her lips, tumbling into his mouth as he pumped a slow, gentle cadence. Tess's tongue licked at his lips, outlining the chiseled curve, tasting herself there, yet her gaze never wavered. His eyes fairly glowed green fire with his need, his features sharp and taut. His bound hair slid over his shoulder, black ribbons grazing her cheek. She felt the blood pulsing through his arousal and into her. He was rock hard and throbbing, and every cell of her body tingled with excitement as he loved her.

Her smooth pale skin contrasted sharply against his own, a new pearl against rich polished oak. The breeze, steaming and salty, fingered the sheer netting that shrouded the lovers. Time ceased to mean anything. They were mates of one world. Theirs.

Her nerves sizzled, muscled legs wrapping deliciously around his waist, holding him snugly within her moist depths. Dane thought he'd pass out from the exquisite torture of being inside her. It would never be enough. He wanted more. And strove to forge them together, clutching her tightly and driving into her, whispering her name, his strong body quaking with the coming explosion. She clung to him, greeting his savage thrusts, thirstily taking his mouth. Skin rubbed skin. Slick and hot and greedy. Her nails dug into his back. Muscles bunched. Breaths mingled. Her body clenched and pulsated around him. Then she arched, crying out as the inferno ruptured inside her, bursting in rolling swells of incredible ecstasy. Dane plunged wildly, a low guttural groan ruffling her hair as he spilled himself deep inside her. And she took it all: his seed, his heart, his love.

More than raw passion held them on the pulsing crest for the briefest moment, shivering with the power of their release. Dane kissed his wife, the touch reverent as they floated to earth on gentle waves, the rippling currents ebbing to a quiet, contented bliss that softly buffeted the lovers with tender hope.

Chapter Twenty-six

"That was fun. Let's do it again."

Dane chuckled tiredly. "The woman is trying to send me to an early grave," he murmured into the crook of her neck.

Her foot slid luxuriously down the length of his leg. "What better way to go?" She was slack beneath him and loving it.

He lifted his head, brushing a damp lock from her cheek, his gaze following his fingertips. "You're an incredible woman, Tess," he whispered.

After that, *he* was calling *her* incredible? Her hands gently rubbed his slick back. "Magnificent in bed as he is on the floor. Gee. What another plus."

His grin bore a touch of masculine arrogance. "That you've naught to compare with is certainly to my advantage."

She nipped playfully at his chest. "Now don't go getting a swelled head, Blackwell," she murmured dryly. Her hands moved lower, fondling his tight buttocks.

" 'Tis well I do not, love, yet if you continue

touching me like that," he moaned when feminine muscles squeezed him more fully inside her. "Ahh — there are other parts of me I fear shall swell quite rapidly for your pleasures."

Tess laughed, husky-soft and mischievous. "My, such an accommodating man I married."

Dane saw the startled flash in her eyes. "What ails you, Tess?" he asked with a frown, feeling her grow tense beneath him. Dane shifted his weight, lying on his side, and curling close around her.

"Jesus, Dane." She rubbed her forehead. "I'm not wife material." Her whispered words sounded almost panicked. "I don't know the first thing about being one in this century. I can't cook without electricity. I lived in a world with machines and packaged food and —"

"Tess," he interrupted calmly. "You will not lift a finger if that is your desire. The servants will see to such matters."

"You have servants!" she wailed. "Oh, that's just great! I can't get used to Duncan puttering around me, let alone an entire staff." She paused, eyeing him cautiously. "Just exactly *how* rich are you?"

His lips twitched; she looked a bit insulted at the thought. "You will want for naught, love."

"Careful, Dane, that's a loaded question to any woman."

"Spend me into the poor house, my little witch," he murmured, bending to sample the lush morsels displayed for him. "I freely admit I did not wed you for the domestic tranquility you would bring to our marriage." His mouth opened.

"Then why did you marry me?" The words tumbled from her lips in a frightened rush, her body growing still as glass beside him, and Dane paused on his way to his target. He settled back a bit, his gaze searching her features. And he saw her heart laid open for him, braced and ready to take the plunge of cutting words. Ahh, love, he thought, what a brave and fragile creature you are.

"Because, Tess," his knuckles fanned across her cheek, "I'm mad with love for you."

Her eyes widened a fraction, and he heard her sharp intake of breath.

"You're not just saying that 'cause I made an honest captain out of you," she managed in a small voice. "Are you, Dane?"

Tender humor lit his features. "Oh, nay, my sweet, nay."

Hot tears pricked her eyes, pewter soft and glossy. "I—I didn't think any man could." Her lowered lip quivered, and she bit it to hold back the flood, squeezing her eyes shut. The crystal droplets trickled down her cheeks. Her voice broke as she whispered, "I love you, too."

Dane's heart slammed against the wall of his chest, ceased pumping, he swore, for an entire beat, then thundered wildly. His vision blurred, and he swiftly gathered her close, raining kisses over her face and throat. She cried, the sound ripping him in two.

"Ahh, God." He pressed her head to his chest. "Do not weep, Tess, I beg of you. I cannot bear it."

"Oh, shut up, it's a woman thing. You wouldn't

understand."

"If you insist."

"Do you have a choice?"

He grinned above her, loving it when her curves yielded against him. "I think mayhaps I've loved you since you boldly confessed to searching my rooms," he said after a moment.

"Cabin," she corrected with a sniffle, draping a leg over his thigh. "That was so long ago. Why didn't you tell me sooner?"

His hand moved to the curve of her buttocks, filling with the plump mound. "I did not want you to believe I was saying the words merely to keep you here."

She gave him a shove. "Lame excuse, Blackwell. It's not like I've got a rip in time handy." Then she leaned back, baring her bosom to his hungry gaze. He leered suggestively, lowering his head.

She pushed at his shoulder. "You know, I don't even know where you live—or do you just ride the seas for the American cause?"

God, he loved the way she talked. "My family purchased land in the Florida Territory. 'Tis just begun to yield sugar cane and fruit from trees I'd imported from the tropics," he said, then sought the skin denied.

She held him back again. "Those wouldn't be oranges, by any chance?"

He groaned, his lips hovering over her taut nipple. "Why do I sense you already know that?" He met her gaze and saw laughter dancing there. "Speak what is on your mind, witch."

"Florida is noted for its oranges in my time, Dane, along with its beaches, seafood, and resorts." Her pitch rose as his lips closed over the rosy crest, taking it fully into his mouth.

Briefly Dane wondered what might become of his plantation but was more interested in making love to his wife again. If she'd cease this prattling.

"Wh-what's the name of this place?"

Her hand, soft as a kitten's paw, burned over the skin of his chest. "Last I was there, 'Coral Keys' graced the gates."

She stilled, lifting her head from the pillow. "But—that's where I lived! Good grief! Do the citizens have you to thank for it?"

He gave a small shrug, his lips and tongue worrying the plump underside of her breast, a hand massaging her buttocks. " 'Tis but three families within the lands surrounding my home," he murmured against her skin. "The city is half a day's ride."

"Well, ah—you'll be pleased to know Coral Keys doesn't sta—ohh, jeez—!" His fingers found her, warm and wet, and Tess couldn't speak as he thrust into her.

Dane refrained from asking if she knew of his family's heritage, his descendants. Nay, their descendants. Would the future change now that Tess was here in his century and married to him? Sweet Jesus, it was too confusing to ponder overlong on the theory, especially knowing she was ready for him. Their time was now, and it made him even more determined to get back what was rightfully his. The plantation would not survive long without him. And he would not survive without Tess.

He suddenly found himself shoved onto his back with a force he wouldn't have believed her capable of. She was like a prowling cat, feline grace and that black hair draping her back as she slithered on top of him.

Her lithe body was like glowing embers searing his skin, woman-hot and musky, nearly painful it felt so good. Her fingers slid into his hair, holding him captive, and Dane's head reeled when her lips feasted on his own. Briefly she caught his lower lip between her teeth, nibbling, sipping, then brushed her tongue across his teeth, savagely outlining the inside of his lips, before thrusting deep inside his mouth. Dane thought he'd come apart at the seams with the wild thrill of her. He was stone rigid and burning to the point of agony when she spread her thighs over him, and he tried to muster the strength to move his arms. He never got the chance.

She sat up, straddling his hips, her raven tresses an untamed swirl about her. A devilish grin coasted across her lips as her fingers wrapped around his arousal, slowly stroking him until he thought he'd explode in her hand. His muscles went rigid with excitement, the blood pulsing in his groin as his hands molded up her thighs to cup her buttocks and bring her closer to his heat.

"Come to me, Tess. Quickly."

"I love you, pirate," she whispered, holding his gaze as she guided him smoothly inside her. "Let me show you."

She did, the ride white-hot and primitive. Moments later Dane arched, his hoarse growl of rapture scorching the walls of the house.

Thundering hooves vibrated against the deserted shore, water fountaining out behind in a cool salty mist as the gray roan raced across the ocean's hem, kicking up clumps of sand and broken shells in its wake. Feminine laughter tumbled over the crush of waves, the pure sound ringing down the barren coast. The rider's clothing clung to her, thin and damp from the spray, molded to her body like a second skin, outlining supple curves, firm breasts taut with cold. Snugly behind her sat a bare-chested man, dark breeches covering him from waist to knee, his hands familiarly around her slender waist. A full moon hovered in the onyx sky, splashing the couple with gentle strokes of silver.

The mount veered sharply toward the tree line, and upon reaching the seclusion of the private lagoon, they slid from the steed's back, coming together in a heady embrace, their silhouettes blending into one beneath the shroud of palms. Liquid crystal flowed effortlessly down the jagged rocks, spilling into the tidal pool with a soothing trickle. The tiny realm captured the lovers, yet abandoned them to their desires, the elements.

A solitary figure stood motionless, watching the lovers with dispassionate eyes from his perch on the rise above. A thin smile twisted the observer's lips as the man peeled off his breeches, then drew the thin nightrail up over her head, tossing it carelessly aside before he drew her into the waters with him. The stranger watched *her*. Her body was sleek and muscled, a perfect sculpture in alabaster, he decided as she vanished beneath the water. He observed the lovers' frolic, his lips on her skin, her breasts, his hands stroking her most delicate places. His ears caught the soft husky murmurs of their lust. Abruptly the man lifted her onto the rocky edge, spread her thighs and entered her swiftly, the pounding rhythm of his body increasing until her cry of delight filtered up to where the stranger stood on the incline.

Bored with the view, Phillip turned away. He'd seen the like far too often since last eve, having observed the pair in their sexual play from across the avenue. The spyglass was truly a handy instrument, he thought as he swung onto the saddle of his horse and began his cautious descent. The tolling of the church bells had sent the curious to the chapel and the less honorable to Phillip. Little coin had left his purse to discover who had wed. His only adversary was here. On his island. Phillip even owned the house Blackwell and his bride occupied. Phillip owned everyone. And what a lark, he thought with a throbbing in his loins, for Dane's bride to be so lovely and young.

"You are a bloody fool, Blackwell," he whispered. "You have placed your only weakness at my feet."

Phillip hovered on the fringes of darkness, watching the pair inside the stable. Dane wasted his time currying the beast while that lovely bit of flesh stood patiently near the doors. Phillip moved silently closer, wanting a better look at the woman, the soft light and her transparent nightrail giving him a display of her shapely assets. His gaze honed in on the darkness between her thighs, and his groin tightened sharply. His fingers itched to have her beneath him, any way he desired. And to have Dane know of it in glorious detail. Mayhaps even watch, Phillip considered, then quickly stepped back when she abruptly faced the doors. Unknowingly she moved toward him, her step cautious, her head turning left and right, searching. She lifted the gown, walking off to the right. He smiled when Dane catapulted himself out the doors seconds later, looking very much the panicked husband, calling out to her. So—Blackwell, your weakness has a name. Tess.

The sun spilled its soft radiance into the chamber as Dane loosened the ties to the transparent netting, allowing it to shroud his sleeping wife in a feathery cocoon. His gaze slowly drifted over her still features, smooth and flawless, to the cloud of black contrasting against the creaminess of her slim, bare back, to the sheet tucked haphazardly around her hips and that sweetly rounded bottom. The most passionate creature he'd ever know. Or will know, he thought with a tired grin. He was exhausted, spent like an old pipe, losing count of the times they'd made love since vows were spoken. The lusty witch, he thought, then reluctantly turned away, donning his shirt, then slipping into his boots. He'd worked up a healthy appetite, now ravenous for something more than his bride, and after stealing one last look at her, he quietly left the room.

He rapidly descended the staircase, frowning when he heard noises from below, and quickened his pace. His nostrils caught the aroma of sausage, and he followed the delicious scent, his mouth watering. When he entered the kitchen, he discovered Higa-san shuffling back and forth between the counter and table, ladling porridge into a bowl, then forking sizzling fat brown sausages onto a plate.

The ancient man glanced up and, with an elegant gesture, directed Dane to the chair. He poured steaming Brazilian coffee into a china cup, then pushed it toward the captain. Dane didn't waste a moment and seated himself, snapping out a napkin and grabbing up the utensils. Tess would be appalled at this breakfast, he thought, slicing pork, then shoving the greasy chunk into his mouth, yet it was far better than the meager finds he had managed on their "midniqht grazing," referring as she had to their foraging through the cupboards last eve. He closed his eyes, savoring the flavor with a moan, then devoted his attention to the meal. He was on his third helping when the back door burst open and Duncan barreled inside, his arms laden with sticks of wood.

"Afternoon, sir," he beamed, then looked past

him, his smile faltering a bit. "The lady, sir, she is not with you?"

"Sleeping, old man, and let her be for a space."

Duncan chuckled, dropping the wood into a bin. "Tired the lass out, did you?" he teased good-naturedly, dusting his hands on the seat of his breeches.

Dane grunted a noncommittal response, knowing nary a soul would give him peace for staying abed with his bride for more than a day before showing himself. 'Twould shock the bloody lot of them, he decided, if they knew 'twas she who had exhausted him.

Soon after, word went out that the captain wanted his officers assembled and crewmen accounted for. Unnoticed, Higa-san shuffled in and out with buckets and trays, and as the day progressed, the house gradually filled with men, most holding their heads in their hands, shushing anyone that spoke above a whisper.

"And the location of Captain O'Keefe?" Dane queried, hovering over a sketch of the warehouse as he covered a yawn.

When his question received no response, he glanced up. Men exchanged cautious looks between themselves, their reluctance to offer an answer evident. Dane tossed the graphite on the table, relaxing into his chair. Only his eyes shifted to the *Triton*'s first mate.

"Been holed up in his cabin, sir, since you wed Lady Ren—ah—Mistress Blackwell." The red-haired officer said it as if he was betraying his captain.

Dane's expression didn't change. Was Ram's heart still bleeding for Tess? he wondered, then quickly cast aside the notion. Ramsey O'Keefe's loyalties with the gentler sex shifted more frequently than the currents of the sea.

"Did not one of you loggerheads bother to see if the man was alive?"

"Aye, Capt'n. Dumped 'im in 'is rack meself," the coxswain answered, his mammoth arms blocking Dane's view as he leaned across the table and snatched a sweet pastry from the platter. "Proved himself a buck of the first 'ead 'afore he winked out tho'," the sailor chuckled as he examined the confection, deciding where to bite first.

Dane groaned. "I suppose I should consider myself fortunate he failed to start another row," he muttered into his coffee.

The room went instantly silent.

Dane cursed viciously, slowly setting down the fragile porcelain, grinding his teeth. "Damn! 'Tis vital we not bring attention to ourselves. Get me O'Keefe. NOW!" he roared. Men scattered. "And those involved in the brawl are held by the code, confined to the ship and docked a week's pay! Blast!"

His temper had not cooled when the sound of horse hooves thundered outside the house over an hour later. Officers filed inside, expressionless when they saw the look on the captain's face. Dane remained in his chair, toying with the cup handle as Ramsey entered, a huge package wrapped in white cloth firmly in his hands. Grinning from ear to ear,

Ram carefully set the flat parcel aside, then dropped into a chair, slapping Dane on the shoulder.

"Ahh, Blackwell, you've the look of a man well-loved."

Dane turned his head slowly, his expression carved in stone as he said, " 'Twould take a century to be loved enough by Tess."

"Where is the lass? Don't tell me you've exhausted h—"

"Enough, Ram," Dane gnashed. The man's debauchery would cost them their lives. "My wife's state of wellness is none of your affair."

"Someone mention me?"

Heads swiveled around at the feminine voice, mates leaping to their feet.

"Good afternoon, gentlemen," she responded to the greetings, yet her eyes focused on her husband. Her smile was for him alone as she swept into the massive kitchen, her command to sit down dropping sailors like obedient puppies onto their seats.

Dane felt a goodly measure of pride as Tess strolled toward him. She took his breath away and, if he calculated correctly, that of every man in the room. Her skin glowed from her bath; her hair, a mass of smooth onyx, was caught simply off her neck by a thin ribbon. Burgundy satin and heavy lace rustled as she walked, the enticing sound competing with the pounding of his heart.

Dane held out his arm, and she flew to him, kissing him firmly on the mouth, uncaring of the spectators. Her fragrance, of spice and wildflowers, filled his head, her nearness alone easing the rage that boiled in him.

"I love you," she whispered, yet all heard.

"And I you, my sweet," he replied freely, tucking her close to his side.

Tess turned to the group, zeroing in on the man at the opposite side of the table. "Ramsey O'Keefe! Well, I thought I'd find you sprawled on the floor by now." She glanced at Dane. "Your voice carries quite well," she pointed out.

Dane bent his head close. "I apologize, love. Did I wake you?" he whispered into her ear.

Her hand rested on his chest, smoothing the fabric. "No, I missed you lying beside me," she murmured just as softly, and Dane groaned, his grip at her waist tightening.

Unaware of the exchange, Ramsey shifted around the table edge. "Good day to you, lass." He grasped her hand, lightly placing a kiss to the back. "Marriage becomes you." He enjoyed the gentle flush of her cheeks.

"I definitely agree," she said, glancing up at Dane. The smoldering look that passed between the couple made men squirm in their seats. "So—what do you have to say for yourself, O'Keefe? This time?" she stressed.

Ram laced his fingers behind his back, looking at the floor. "I fear I've no defense, lass."

"Forget it, Ram. The little-boy act doesn't cut it. Fess up."

Ram grinned, adoring her honest retorts. "If you must know, I've a wedding gift—for Dane." Ramsey

337

braced the package on the chair, carefully removing the strings.

"If you believe this will soften my anger, O'Keefe—"

She dug her elbow into Dane's side. "Be nice. It's our first wedding gift. And I'll soften your anger," she promised out of the side of her mouth, her gaze on the present.

Ramsey drew the cloth away.

Tess sucked in her breath and stumbled back against Dane, an icy chill snapping down her spine.

Propped on the rustic chair before her was the sole reason she was in this century.

Chapter Twenty-seven

The portrait. The same painting she saw in the Rothmere Building, Tess realized, the night she stole the diamonds. And the woman in green was her!

"Ahh, Ramsey. 'Tis beautiful," Dane said, unaware of her reaction. "The likeness is amazing." Men shuffled, craning their necks for a better look.

As if in a trance, Tess stepped closer, extending a hand.

"Nay, Tess," Ramsey said, gently blocking her touch. " 'Tis still wet."

Her arm fell slowly to her side, her eyes scanning the portrait. She'd forgotten all about it.

" 'Tis a first, I believe, gentlemen," Ramsey laughingly addressed the group. "The lass is utterly speechless."

No response from Tess.

Dane and Ram exchanged puzzled looks.

"Tess?"

Dane's hand touched her shoulder, and she flinched violently, whirling about. She looked like a startled animal, gray eyes round, blank, staring straight through him. Then slowly she focused, her features softening as she was, it seemed, drawn back into the room with him.

Dane glanced briefly past her to the roomful of men, then said, "What ails you, love?" and gently pulled her from earshot.

"I've seen that painting before, Dane." She gripped his biceps. "In my time. The night I stole the diamonds."

Dane's skin prickled with cold, his features pulling taut. His gaze shot to the painting as if trying to see beyond the heavy oils, then to Tess and back again to the canvas. His eyes went sharp and narrow; Tess could see his mind clicking the facts into place. His smile nearly lit the room when he returned his gaze to her.

"Did I not say you were destined to be here?" he whispered, slipping his arms about her and pressing her soft curves to his body.

"That sounds suspiciously like an 'I told you so.'" A black brow rose slowly, his clear pale eyes daring her to contradict him. God, he was male arrogance supreme. And she decided it was best to ignore it. "You know, I was just as shocked then." She rubbed the fabric covering his arms, wondering how a gift from Ramsey to Dane ended up in the hands of a jackass like Phalon Rothmere. *"That"* she nodded to the painting—"is the only reason I was seen and forced to run."

"To me." His smile broadened.

She sighed with mock tiredness. "Have it your way, Blackwell."

"Be most assured, *Blackwell,* I usually do." He kissed her, a hard press of his mouth and tongue,

340

swift and full of possession, then looked over the top of her head. "Thank you, Ram," he said sincerely. " 'Tis a gift I will cherish."

"My pleasure." Ram bowed slightly to his friend.

Tess turned in Dane's arms, leaning back against her husband. "Thanks, Ramsey." She examined the painting. The image had a sensual quality, soft and mysterious, her gown molded to her by the breeze, the ocean's mist surrounding her bare feet. "Aside from being truly flattered, you'll never know how much this—" Her gaze dropped to the signature. *"You* painted this?" she burst incredulously.

"I am offended, Tess," he said, straightening his waistcoat and lifting his chin with an injured air. "One would assume by your tone you believe all my talents lie in—"

"Your breeches," she finished with a cocky grin. Masculine laughter filled the kitchen.

"Ahh, the sharp tongue of a wife," Ram chuckled, settling his rear against the table ledge and folding his arms. " 'Tis most fortunate 'tis you who must suffer the barbs, Dane, and not I." His smile was sad, a touch envious, and no matter what he spoke, Ram's eyes mirrored his emotions. Dane recognized the hollow ache, for he'd seen it in his own reflection these past years.

The danger and adventure were losing their appeal, the constant defense to the death robbing a man of his more tender feelings. Ram thirsted for something closer to the heart and was fain to forgo his rakehell existence to discover women—beyond the pleasures of his bed. After five and thirty years,

341

that the secret to capture this still escaped Ramsey's grasp was eating him alive. Dane looked to the canvas. The man had released his heart in the work; it showed in the tender strokes of the brush. Dane had been ready to love when Tess swept into his life, and now 'twas Ramsey's turn. He need only find a lass willing to endure that lusty arrogance. Or, Dane thought with a half smile, gently set it in its place.

" 'Twas bloody near brimming, Dane, every friggin' crate bearing the markings of French, Spanish, English, and American imports. Christ, even the Portuguese have been attacked!"

"Calm down, Ram, we'll get him." Tess patted his shoulder, then leaned over to pour him some more rum. "There's no use in getting your garters in a twist over things you can't change." He made a face at her theory. "Yet."

Dane followed the gentle sway of her hips as she moved toward the kitchen to check on something she called a "pizza." She was certain they'd all love it, yet swore each officer to secrecy. Dane understood 'twas not a family secret, but that Tess had no desire to change history. All Dane knew was that the aroma wafting from the kitchen was heavenly.

"Chow's on," she called out as she entered the parlor, Higa-san and Duncan trailing behind her, each carrying a platter. She set the trays on the table, then arranged napkins and flatware. The officers stared at the red mess on bread dough, cautiously glancing at Dane. It looked repulsive, Dane had to admit, but would not dream of insulting her.

342

Her flour-dusted appearance spoke the difficulty she'd undergone to prepare the—the—pie?

"Ohh, Jeez, you big babies," she said when no one made a move. She snatched up a slice and slid it onto a plate. Then, to Dane's horror, she picked it up with her fingers—something she never did—and chomped into it. Her eyes closed, and she smiled, cheeks bulging. "You don't know what you're missing," she said around the pizza, then chewed. Dane followed suit. His brows shot high into his forehead at the first sample.

"I thought you said you could not cook?" he reminded her after swallowing the first bite.

"I said without electricity," she whispered behind a napkin. "I lived alone, Dane, for over nine years. I had to learn for myself."

Tess served up another slice, then held the plate out to Ramsey. The dare was clear.

He groaned, settling into a chair and obediently taking a bite. His eyes widened, his tongue snaking out to catch the sauce.

" 'Tis utterly sinful, lass," he mumbled.

"Well, you ought to know all about that," she returned tartly, and he winked at her.

Gaelan moved forward, the remaining men following their captain, assuming if he were still standing, 'twas fine enough.

Tess nodded to the fountaining praise as men devoured slice after slice. She'd worked hard all afternoon, peeling tomatoes for sauce, begging Higa-san for spices, slicing vegetables, pounding the hell out of dough, and even conceding to adding sausage to the pizzas. Duncan insisted it needed meat. It was the cheese she had to substitute, but whatever kind it was, did the job. It snapped and dripped like mozzarella, though the taste was a bit sharper.

Plates in hand, Dane and Ramsey moved to the low table before the sofa, examining the map. "We can set charges here, and here," Ramsey's finger left a stain. "The office is here." Another stain and he licked his fingertip, then blindly reached for another slice. Tess slapped his hand, then, having gained his attention, gestured for his plate. He looked like a little boy asking for another cookie.

"Are we to blow it up, sir, all of it?" Gaelan was clearly astonished.

"I see no other choice. We are not to let the goods be sold for profit. Nor traded for weapons."

"I can't believe you have to waste all those supplies. Just think of the people it would help," Tess said, handing Ramsey the pizza.

Dane glanced up, his gaze slipping over her from head to toe. "I sympathize with you, love. But 'tis all or naught. We cannot take on so much cargo. Escape would be far too risky if we are below the water line. The *Witch* is fast, but not if her pursuers are riding high."

"There's got to be a way." Tess settled her hip on the arm of the couch, leaning down to look at the map. "Look, station men forward and port." She pointed to the front and side doors. "One man cracks the locks, lets the others in from inside, and have a bucket brigade to carts outside." She pointed out the route, then leaned back, her hand braced

344

on the sofa back. "It's on the docks and the *Triton* is already there or the *Witch* could easily slither up to the pier. High tide's at two bells; that should be enough time. Load what you can afford as ballast, then torch the place."

She was learning, Dane thought, smiling at her use of nautical terms. "I cannot involve anyone else beyond Ram."

"Aye, and I nearly had to bludgeon the sot to be included."

"This mission was for all of them, Dane. The creep who killed your sister is *your* problem." A rumble of agreement rounded the parlor, and Dane shot Tess a look of annoyance. "Don't look at me like that. It's not like you don't have enough trained men, and I'd bet the farm they'll be there whether you order it or not."

Ram grinned. "Your wife is right, Dane."

"I know, blast it all!"

Tess slipped onto his lap. "The plan's not perfect, but —"

"Do you propose to destroy it with my men inside?"

She shoved at his chest. "Be nice to me. I sleep with you," she threatened, and the room burst with deep chuckles. "You can set off a charge from outside." Dane frowned, shifting her from his lap, clearly interested in what she had to offer. "Roll a keg or two of gunpowder in, then toss in a Molotov cocktail."

"What the ruddy hell is that?" Ramsey asked.

"It's a bottle filled with something ignitable, like

345

lamp oil or a high proof of liquor, and a rag stuck in the neck, just enough to soak up a little of the liquid. That stuff—"she pointed to the bottle of black rum—"ought to do the trick. You light it, toss it in, and when the bottle breaks—kaboom."

"And it will ignite the gunpowder," Dane finished, relaxing back into the sofa and pulling her with him.

"Or catch anything on fire. You can place the remaining crates near the gunpowder, set off the crate, and wait for them to catch the powder that way, too. It's difficult to time, of course, but we can do the job without much noise. Or you can set a fuse. Kegs inside, long line of thin rope to the outside, but you risk the chance of the fuse burning out on its own."

Dane rubbed his chin thoughtfully, then glanced to his side. "This just came to you?"

"No." She pinched him. "I've been thinking about it since I first saw the floor plan."

He looked down at the woman nestled close to his side. "I believe mayhaps we would have won the war years earlier if you were on our side, love."

"I want to go."

"You cannot."

"Give me one solid reason?"

Dane's lips tightened. "Because I do not want you there."

"Not good enough, Blackwell." She folded her arms over her breasts, which served only to force the abundant flesh nearly free from captivity. Dane averted his gaze. She'd no idea of the sensual picture she presented.

"Tess, love."

"Don't you dare use that with me now, pirate. I'm going!" She started to take off her gown. Dane glanced up, momentarily entranced by the sight of her shimming out of the dress and the bare leg she exposed.

"You know I can help. I can bust the locks."

"Your expertise as a thief is not required," he nearly snarled, priming his weapons, then sending a shot home.

"Sarcasm doesn't become you, Dane." She marched over to the dresser, pulling her black cotton Lycra suit from the drawer.

He grabbed it, tossing it aside. "Nay! You are my wife, Tess, and I order you to stay here!"

Her head turned slowly, her eyes piercing and sharp. "Excuse me?"

"I forbid you to leave this room."

"You forbid, *you* forbid," she repeated softly, the storm brewing. "Listen up, Blackwell. I won't be treated like some possession! Ordered? Hah!" She thumped his chest. "You've got a rude awakening coming, buddy, if you think you can talk to me like that! I am my own boss. No one, *no one,* tells me what to do! Just because we're married doesn't give you the right to take over my life whenever you damn well please." God, she was glorious in her rage, Dane thought as she yanked on his shirt, pulling him down to meet her face. "If you want one of those milquetoast wives who wait around for a man to tell them what to do and where to go, give the right response, stand at the door with pipe and slippers, you, Captain Blackwell, married the wrong woman."

Dane knew exactly what kind of woman he married. Just as he knew he couldn't win this argument now. He was pressed for time. "I cannot complete this mission if I am constantly worried for your safety."

"And what the hell am I supposed to do? Twiddle my thumbs?"

"You could wait for me."

The idea was not high on her list.

"I could go along, too."

"God's teeth. Will you never give in on this?"

"Will you?"

"Ughhh! Blast you, woman!" he raged at the ceiling, then stormed to the door, jackboots thumping. He paused, his back to her, his hand on the latch. "I love you, Tess. More than my own life."

His shoulders slumped when she did not respond. He opened the door and ordered the guards to allow no one to pass, then glanced back over his shoulder. The raw pain in her eyes ripped him apart. But he had to do this for her own good and his. He quietly stepped out.

Through the red haze of anger, Tess reached for the black bodysuit.

Chapter Twenty-eight

Hanging on the outside of the sill, Tess looked once more toward the door. She knew Sikes stood on the other side, his burly form blocking her path. She'd done everything just short of sexual favors to get past. Sweet talk didn't work on the Marines this time. Damn you, Dane! She wouldn't have to resort to this if he'd listened to reason. She'd been in on everything since the beginning and wasn't about to be excluded now, whether he liked it or not. Hell, they'd still be sitting in the living room wondering how to get out of this mess if not for her!

She glanced back over her shoulder, then pushed off, twisting sharply, her arms outstretched to catch the tree limb. She met the mark and instantly tightened her muscles, trying hard not to sway. The branch groaned, leaves rustled, and she released, dropping to the ground and crouching into the shadows. The guard posted at the corner of the house twisted at the soft sound, peering in her direction. Crap, she thought, holding her breath as he started walking. He moved closer, and she tried not to burp or something as vile and give her position away. But he walked right past. She rose slowly, grabbing a handful of soft earth as she straightened, smearing it on her face, then wiping her hands on the seat of her tattered breeches. She scanned the area, then took off in a run toward the docks, lock picks jammed down the tight lycra sleeve concealed beneath her husband's shirt, bare feet padding silently against the deserted road.

Continental Marines with their musket barrels pointed in all directions guarded the street like a pinwheel of firepower as carts rolled slowly away from Whittingham's warehouse and down the pier. Cloth had been wrapped around the wheels to muffle any noise, goose grease soothing any squeaks. Armed men were posted at strategic spots, ready to give the signal if the others were heard or if anyone should approach. Laughter and boisterous song from a nearby tavern drifted on the humid breeze. Waves gently sloshed against the stone embankment, a calming familiar sound to nerves yanked tight as rigging.

Dane hefted a crate onto his back, his stride slow and cautious. Sweat trickled down his temples, muscles straining to hand over the wooden box as quietly as possible.

"Careful, Dane, your bride will be in a fit if you injure something essential." Ramsey grinned, white teeth flashing in the dark.

"My bride is in a fit now," he muttered softly. And no doubt ready to claw my eyes from my skull,

Dane thought, the look on her face repeating in his mind with annoying clarity. He would make it up to her, of course, if she chose to speak with him again. "Where have you been for the past hour?" Dane asked suspiciously, his hands on his hips. Ram's expression was mischievous, as usual. "Forget the inquiry," Dane waved before he could answer. "I do not believe I wish to know." He then went for another box.

The last of the crates for ballast were loaded onto the *Triton* when Gaelan signaled for the kegs of gunpowder. It took two men to carry in each of the four squat barrels. The ignitable dust was un-corked—Dane chose to do this himself—and he poured small piles on the remaining crates, then left the opened kegs near the largest and most costly containers of spirits and silks and spices. Ramsey blocked his path as he went for the crate of Tess's "cocktails."

"You have a wife to think of now."

"I've no intention of dying this night, Ram." He moved him bodily aside and lifted the box of rag-stuffed bottles. "And I believe, as senior officer, I have that choice."

"Aye-aye, sir." Ram saluted, his smile not reaching his eyes, displeased that Dane would not allow him to do this small service. "A bloody waste of good rum," Ram grumbled, looking at the dark bottles.

"How a man of your caliber can stomach the vile brew is still a mystery." He shook his head ruefully, moving toward the doors. "I swear 'tis sieved through filthy smallclothes."

Ram tightened his lips in an effort not to laugh out loud. He knew Dane preferred the smoother drinks to the harsh black rum rationed to the men.

"Make certain the way is clear," Dane ordered. Ram strode off to see that the men had departed and were well from sight, then drew a black gelding just inside the warehouse doors. Dane handed over the box before he mounted the beast, then reached for the cocktails, carefully placing them in the saddlebags braced across his lap.

"Be gone with you," he told Ramsey, holding the last one in his hand. Ramsey's shoulders drooped, and he opened his mouth to plead his case once more. Dane's eyes narrowed. " 'Tis an order, O'Keefe."

Ram nodded, reluctantly walking through the doors, then mounting his own steed and moving down the pier. He looked back once. Dane had the reins caught between his teeth, the horse stomping and prancing as he struck flint.

She was lost. Tess was sure of it. She'd been to the docks before, and nothing around her looked familiar. Having to stay in the shadows wasn't much help, and she hadn't made it very far. At least she didn't think she had. She kept moving toward the sound of water. Already she'd passed a couple of taverns and recognized several of the crew. Can't ask directions, she thought, thankful that most who'd seen her simply disregarded her as a boy.

She stopped at a darkened intersection, settling her rear on a hitching rail and considering her situation. Awfully noisy for one A.M., she thought, laughter, a baby's hungry cry, and the slow clop of hooves melting with the cooing of the island birds.

It took a full minute before Tess realized she'd gone in a complete circle. A couple of blocks away, above the low roofs of small homes, she could see the distinct arched windows of the house, and beyond that, the inn. Damn, Renfrew, your sense of direction is the pits! Dane was probably finished by now, she decided, pushing away from the rail. She hadn't taken more than two steps when a rustling sound reached her ears. She turned, her heart picking up its pace as she strained to discover what was making the noise. Man or beast? Her imagination taking flight, she half-expected Jason to suddenly appear brandishing a bloody hatchet. A second later the friar materialized from the tree line, and Tess sighed heavily, sagging against the post.

"Mistress Blackwell?" He peered closer. "Is that you, my child?"

She fanned herself. "Ah, yes, it's me, Father Jacob."

"What on earth are you doing out this late?" He scanned the area. "Alone?"

Tess straightened. His gaze was roaming up and down her clothing, halting and squinting at the black Lycra she knew he could see at her throat. "Why are you disguised as a boy, lass?"

"Um, well, I, ah, was, ah." Oh, Jeez, she couldn't lie to a priest! "I was looking for Dane," she blurted in a rush. "And thought I'd draw less attention dressed like this." She plucked at the trousers, having never felt quite so awkward about wearing pants before this moment.

He smiled gently at her flushed face. "Then we must get you to him, lass. 'Tis not safe for such a delicate creature as you to be out unescorted." He walked with a determined step toward her, offering his arm. The lass had sneaked out, he deduced, knowing well her new husband would never have allowed such a liberty freely. The man's short steps had barely covered the space between them when the thunder of hooves came from all directions.

The priest moved swiftly to her aide, pulling her along. She let out a sharp cry, stumbling when a horse barreled into their path. Father Jacob yanked her protectively behind him but a second horse skidded to a stop in back of her, its rider chuckling nastily, the animal's breath snorting hotly on her neck. She sidestepped, trying desperately not to get tromped on, when a carriage, black and massive, careened around the bend to block their escape, chains and wood screaming as it came to a grinding halt. The friar muttered something in Latin. The small gold-trimmed door burst open.

"Join me, mistress," a silky masculine voice commanded.

"In your dreams, buddy! Come on, Father." She started to move between the horses, but the riders tightened the circle about them. Then she heard an unmistakable *click*. She whirled toward the carriage to see a pistol barrel emerge from the darkened interior, ringed fingers closed around the weapon.

"Get in."

"Do not, lass."

"I won't, Father," she assured, then said, "Look,

mac, you've obviously got the wrong person. I don't know who you are, and I'm definitely not going anywhere—"

He tsked softly. "You force my hand, lady. Kill the friar."

The casually spoken words made Tess's heart freeze mid-beat. A rider swiftly tossed a rope around Father Jacob's torso, yanking it tight, pulling him from Tess's side. A gun barrel was suddenly pressed firmly to his temple.

"Please—don't hurt him!" she begged, moving toward the conveyance. "I'll go, you damned coward! I'll go!"

"For the love of God, mistress, nay!" Father Jacob screamed, wildly struggling with his bonds. "Do not go! Run, RUN!"

"I shall caution you not to insult me further, madame." Tess gulped thickly at yet another threat. "And be quick about it." The jeweled hand waved the gun impatiently, giving her a view of a lace cuff and blood red brocade. She stepped onto the landing, ducking slightly.

"Nay!" the priest cried hoarsely, struggling to get to her.

The weapon fired, blasting near the back of her head, making her ears ring, and singeing her braided hair. She twisted sharply, waving frantically at the white smoke as the friar dropped to the ground with a thud, blood gushing from what was left of his head and pooling on the dirt. Her legs trembled, her stomach rolled violently, and for a split second Tess couldn't move a muscle.

"You bastard!" Tess screamed, lurching at the

killer. She clawed and scratched at his face. "What the hell did you do that for?" Her nails raked his cheek, yet he made no move to stop her. "I agreed, for Christ's sake!" His blood wet her fingertips, giving her little satisfaction.

"Witnesses, my lovely," he said, and Tess froze. His tone was smooth, liquid, far too controlled for what he'd just done.

A roaring blast ripped into the night, the earth shuddering with the force. The man grabbed her arm, yanking her into the carriage and slamming her against the far wall at his feet. Above her head he brushed back a short red curtain with the nose of the gun. Explosions erupted in erratic repetition. The blaze of yellow flames radiated against the ebony sky, the brilliant glow lighting his face for an instant. His fingers tightened on her arm. It was his only response. Citizens raced from their homes. He let the curtain drop back into place, slowly looking in her direction, his face expressionless. I'm a dead woman, she thought, struggling in his grasp, trying to peel off his fingers, her strong feet kicking viciously. He grunted once at her assault, then quite calmly backhanded her, the pistol butt smashing against the side of her head. Pain detonated in her skull, her surroundings narrowing rapidly. His shadowed silhouette swam in her line of vision, blond waves framing sharp, handsome features, then he smiled—shark-cold, a slow baring of white teeth as his gaze rested on the blood she could feel trickling down the side of her face. Then unconsciousness took her past the agony as she slumped onto the carriage floor.

* * *

Wood smoldered, then burst, flames waving like
wisps of orange silk. Gunpowder sizzled and
smoked, the sulfur trails burning rapidly toward the
kegs. Dane touched the flint to the cloth and threw
the last bottle into the warehouse, then reined
around sharply and kneed the beast. The frightened
charger bolted out the open doors seconds before
the first explosion ruptured. Debris burst from the
building, shattered wood shooting like flaming bul-
lets and dropping into his path. He skillfully maneuvered the horse over the wreckage, hastening his
pace. Dane never saw the hunk of burning timber
fall from the sky, yet felt the pain when it impacted
with his body, knocking him from his mount.

Whittingham jolted awake at the loud crash. He
leapt from his bed, and, as fast as his chubby legs
would take him and raced to the window, brushing
back the drape. His eyes widened at the sight. All
he could see was the vibrant glow of flames against
the night. His warehouses!

"Bloody hell! Blood friggin' hell!"

He snatched up his breeches, jamming his foot
into the legs and hitching them over his nightshirt.
He grabbed the pistol kept loaded on the commode,
shoving the barrel into his waistband as he took up
more powder and shot, then thundered out of his
room. He'd kill Phillip. He had his coin, and it
would be just like the bastard to destroy *his* stores.
The ledgers, he panicked, I must retrieve the

damned proof. Nigel nearly fell down the stairs in his haste and stumbled against the door, pausing to catch his breath and bellow for the servants to bring the carriage round. He opened the front door and ran out, nightcap askew, sweating profusely as he tripped and fell down the stone steps.

"How good of you to join us, Whittingham." Nigel lifted his gaze upward from the booted toes poised before his face. His vision climbed higher, up the long body, pausing at the gun barrel pointed at his nose. His eyes shot to its owner, and the young blond man smiled. "You weren't by chance going for these, were you, sir?" he asked with a grin, waving his ledgers triumphantly.

Nigel groaned, and the man's smile fell, his expression turning cold and hard. "By order of the President, George Washington, I charge you with treason on the high seas against the United States of America. Is that clear, sir?"

Nigel struggled to his feet, spitting dirt and pebbles at the young man's boots.

"Who are you, and what gives you the right to—"

"This gives me the right, sir." Gaelan Thorpe produced documents to back his claim, then neatly stuffed them in his coat pocket, ordering his men to shackle the fat little Tory.

Sitting on a milking stool, Dane leaned his head back against the doorframe of the stable, his breath hissing through his teeth as Duncan applied a salve to his arm.

"She should be tendin' this," Duncan muttered

tightly as he wrapped the bandage.

Dane glanced to his side. "I doubt her care would be as tender this night, my friend."

" 'Twould serve you right, Dane."

Dane looked at the old mariner with a bit of surprise. "You seriously believe I should have taken her along?"

Duncan considered the question for a moment. "Aye, the lady is not like any other female, Dane. She's a true mate and can pull her own."

"She is my wife. Cannot even you understand that I dare not risk her being harmed?" Duncan chuckled despite the sharp tug he gave the ends of the cloth, and Dane winced, shoving off his hands. "Sweet Mercy, old man! Mayhaps suffering her anger would bring me less agony." Dane flexed his scorched arm.

"I see through your eyes, Dane," Duncan said, climbing to his feet and looking down at the young captain. "My Meggie was like your bride, full of vinegar and spice, ready to fight the British face-to-face with her pots and kettles if I'd but allowed it. But she fought in other ways—smuggling information—" Duncan looked away, his eyes misting, the pain of his loss stabbing through his wide chest." After ten years the mere mention of her name still brought him to his knees. "I could not stop her in doing what she wanted—nay, *needed* to do, lad. 'Twas a wee bit like trying to stop mornin' from comin'. Yer Tess, God bless her, has Meggie's heart." His smile was tender as he looked back at Dane. "You've lived a dangerous life, lad. Now is not the time to coddle the woman for *your* own peace of mind. 'Twill destroy yer love. Me 'n' Meggie never had the opportunity to make peace before she was—" Duncan swallowed thickly, his Adam's apple bobbing.

Dane came to his feet, giving the old man's shoulder a gentle squeeze.

"I hear you, Duncan. I swear, I do."

Duncan turned his back to Dane. "Go on wit' ye, ye young whip." He waved. "She'll be havin' me hide if she knows 'twas me that kept you from her arms."

Dane pushed away from the wall and strode quickly toward the kitchen door, eager to make amends with Tess. He smelled of smoke and spilled rum and considered washing and changing before going to her, but the ache to hold her needed appeasing. He took the crooked steps two at a time, thrusting open the door. There was a collective sigh from the men scattered about the kitchen, and their soft thanks to the Lord warmed Dane's heart.

They raised their tankards. "A successful plan, sir."

"To Mistress Blackwell," Aaron bellowed, "and her finely brewed—what were they, Gaelan?"

"Molotov cocktails, I believe, Mr. Finch."

"She is not here?" Dane asked, scanning the room.

"Nay, sir. She has not shown herself."

Several expressions showed their concern about this. Dane grabbed a tankard held out for him and washed the burn of smoke from his throat, then thrust the pewter at Aaron as he strode from the kitchen. He climbed the stairs, gesturing in dismissal to the guards.

"She ceased asking to be let out hours ago, sir," Sikes offered. "Bless her heart, she tried well, tho'."

Dane nodded curtly, feeling even more rotten at how he'd treated her. Locking her away? God's teeth, what was he thinking! He waited until the guards were down the stairs before he turned the key and pushed open the door. His gaze darted to the bed. It was mussed, the depression in the pillow telling him she had been there. He frowned, stepping inside and calling her name. His eyes lit on the open window, then to the spot where he'd tossed the black garment, and Dane instantly knew the depth of her hurt. Tess was no longer in the house.

Chapter Twenty-nine

Dane moved swiftly around the room, searching her trunks, trying to discover what else she had worn and mayhaps taken with her for protection. Ahh, Tess, what have I done? His shoulders drooped when he ascertained the leather pouch of tools was all she had with her. Leaning his forehead against the bedpost, he cursed his insensitivity and her recklessness, truly understanding how deeply she'd wanted to be with him: enough to risk her life to escape. Escape! He rubbed the back of his neck. Jailing his own wife. Sweet Christ, what mind was he in when he did that?

Duncan was right; his coddling would destroy what they had. He stiffened, looking toward the window. Where in God's name was she now? he thought with a strike of fear. Surely she'd heard the explosion? Time had well passed for her to return. Was she staying away to see that he suffered? I do, my love, I do, he thought, his heart brimming with guilt. Fool! 'Tis my fault. I should have realized the

362

woman would never sit idly and take orders. From anyone.

"Sir?"

Dane didn't move. "You should have counseled me sooner, Duncan. I am too late. She has fled."

Duncan's expression fell. "There is someone here to see you, lad."

"Send them away or tend the matter yourself." He waved. "I've a wife to find." Dane went to his trunks, retrieving pistol and sword. He primed the weapons and checked the honed edge of the blade. Duncan remained silent, still standing at the door.

"Please, sir, come with me, now."

Dane looked up at the pleading tone, his features pulling tight. Duncan appeared ready to cry, he thought, his heartbeat escalating. Dane dropped the weapons into the trunk and ran out of the room, leaping down the stairs, his boots thundering on wood floors. He froze in the center of the parlor, his gaze on the wretched-looking man standing at the door, a thin packet in his gnarled hands.

"You be Capt'n Blackwell?" he asked, shuffling from foot to foot.

Dane nodded curtly, his eyes pale jade and narrow.

"This be fer you." The messenger held out the package. Terror crept up Dane's back, settling heavily on his shoulders as he reached. He turned the parcel over in his hand. There were no markings. Only his eyes shifted to the man. "Who gave this to you?"

The man shrugged, glancing away. Dane withdrew a small blade from his boot and slit the ties, peeling back the layers of parchment.

His bellow of rage ricocheted throughout the house, penetrating the rafters, making the men in the building shiver at its power. Gaelan's eyes went wide at the agonized sound, and he quickly set his mug on the table and raced from the kitchen, officers fast on his heels. He halted just inside the parlor. Dane was on his knees in the center of the room, his head thrown back, a paper crumpled tightly in his hand. Gaelan's sight flitted to the filthy man standing near the door, attempting to flee past the burly Sikes.

The captain slowly came to his feet, then with a harsh growl, he lunged.

"Who gave this to you?! Who?!" Dane shouted, hauling the man up off the floor by his shirt front. "Spill his name before I tear it from your bloody throat!" He shook him so hard the man's teeth clicked.

"Ah-ah bloke in red, I swear! Paid me ten shilling to give it te ye. Here—take the coin." He tried frantically to reach his pockets, seeing his death in those green eyes. Dane slammed the man against the nearest wall, sending a powerful fist into his ribs. The air left his lungs in a sharp grunt, and there was the unmistakable crack of bone.

"Jesus! 'Tis only a messenger!" Gaelan was there, using all his strength to keep the captain's fist from bludgeoning the man to death. "For God's sake, Aaron! Help me! He's mad!" It took no fewer than four men to hold him back.

"Release him, sir," Gaelan pleaded. "He is naught but a courier."

Dane's breath came fast and hard, his eyes green frost with rage as they knifed the henchman. A muscle ticked violently in his jaw. He shrugged his men off like an old coat, then stepped back, letting the small visitor drop to the floor with a hard *thunk*. Staring at nothing, he slowly raised his trembling hand, unfurling long fingers from around the parchment. Gaelan took it, spreading it open. A familiar odor of gunpowder rose up to meet him.

In the center of the crumpled paper was a swirling lock of black hair, one end thick with coagulated blood. Through the crimson stain smeared on the paper, three words could be seen.

Dane loves Tess.

"Oh Phillip, what have you done?" Elizabeth pulled the dressing gown tightly about her, her eyes on the still body sprawled across the bed.

"Go to your rooms, Lizzie. 'Tis naught of your concern." Phillip removed a blade sheathed at his waist, hovering over the woman.

"Phillip! Nay!"

He spared her an impatient glance, then cut the woman's clothing from neck to waist, an angry red line blooming in the wake of the blade.

"What on earth—?" he spoke to himself, fingering the black covering, then pulling at it. His eyes widened the merest fraction when it gave beneath his touch. He released it as if burned, then rent the fabric to her thigh. Both peered closer at the bright scrap of fabric covering the essentials, then Elizabeth stepped back.

" 'Tis her, is it not?" He didn't answer, his hands smoothing over the woman's body. Elizabeth's anger flared. "Is it not?"

"I would do the honors of introduction, but as you can see—" Phillip stripped off his waistcoat and bent one knee to the mattress.

"He will surely kill you now," she said in a panicked rush.

There was a smugness in her tone he didn't care for, and he swiftly left the bed, moving toward her.

She retreated. "I apologize. I didn't mean that."

"Are you trying to anger me, my pet?"

"Oh, nay, Phillip. I swear."

He advanced, catching her about the waist. "You know what happens when you anger me, Lizzie."

She swallowed thickly, immediately understanding the look in his eyes. "Oh, please, not again. I did not mean it, Phillip," she begged. "But Dane—" He shoved her back onto the bed, then grasped the neck of her nightrail, tearing it from her shoulders. Elizabeth trembled, knowing it was not she that had brought this urge but something more than the capture of Dane's bride. She banished the horrifying thoughts before they could form and let the pain overwhelm her as he bit into her tender nipple. He shoved the night clothes up about her hips and wedged himself between her thighs. He didn't bother to remove his clothes, simply opened a few buttons of his breeches. He took her violently, his eyes never wavering from the unconscious woman lying beside them as he quickly climaxed.

"For Chrissake! Can't you do that elsewhere?" Tess moaned, avoiding a look at what was transpiring beside her.

"Leave us," he said to Elizabeth, withdrawing from her and fastening his breeches. Elizabeth knew not to disobey, moving quickly off the bed and racing from the room.

The pounding in her skull told Tess to ignore the odor of sex and go back to the painless black void. She felt for the tender spot, her fingers coming away with dried bits of blood. Her memory instantly flashed to the friar, his lifeless body bleeding on the dirt. Bile rose in her throat, and she rolled off the bed and onto the floor, blindly reaching for the chamber pot and retching violently, managing to aim, and vomiting until nothing else came up. He made no comment, and she slumped back against the side of the bed.

Oh, Father Jacob! I'm so sorry, Tess screamed silently. Tears dripped off her chin. The friar was dead because he happened to be in the wrong place at the wrong time. The old man was dead because of her. No! *He* was responsible. And she'd make the son of a bitch pay with his balls.

She started to stand, then fell back onto the floor when she discovered her clothing shredded. Jesus! What a pervert!

"What were you doing?" she sneered, not looking at him. "Checking to see if I was really a woman?"

"Of that I am quite certain, my dear."

Tess cringed at the implication, clutching the ruined clothing about her. Oh God! Did he rape her while she was unconscious? She fought the new rush of tears. No. Now, don't panic, she told herself, examining her body and discovering she still had the lock picks tucked in her sleeve. She didn't feel as if she'd been sexually assaulted, and somehow Tess was certain he hadn't gone that far. But he would, she realized. He killed for the hell of it.

"Do get off the floor, Mistress Blackwell. 'Tis so unbecoming of a lady."

The air rushed into her lungs as she twisted sharply, glaring over the mattress to see him reclined on a settee, casually popping bits of food into his mouth. He brushed crumbs from his brocade waistcoat, lace frothing from his wrists, gems sparkling in the oil light. Beneath the expensive clothes and jewels, he was pond scum. Squarely she met those eyes, ice blue and empty, and he paused in his eating. Tess wasn't stupid. This was the man Dane sought—Desiree's killer. I understand the hatred now, she thought, wanting to see the bastard die a slow and agonizing death. She grabbed the bedcovers, yanking them off the bed and pulling the thick satin about her shoulders. Dane's probably frantic by now, she thought guiltily, and likely taking it out on the men. Knowing how idiotic it was to leave the house was minor now. She had to figure out how to deal with this murderer. God. A murderer!

"Welcome to my home, Mistress Blackwell." He made a sweeping gesture to the lavish pink and

368

white bedchamber.

"Can't say I'm pleased to be here," Tess snorted, climbing to her feet. With measured steps she crossed the elegant room to examine the wound in the mirror. She could see him in the reflection. He looked like a vampire, his skin milky white, making his lips appear blood red. He hadn't moved, and she could feel his pale eyes raking down the back of her spine as she took up the pitcher and poured water into a bowl. Her fingers shook as they brushed the hairs clipped short near the purple bruise. It didn't surprise her. She rinsed her mouth, then soaked a cloth, dabbing at the sticky cut.

"Jeez." She winced at the sting. "You sure packed a wallop in that punch, ah—?"

"Phillip," he supplied, leaving the settee and shifting around the low table. "Phillip Rothmere."

Tess spun around. Rothmere, Was it possible this man was Phalon and Sloane's ancestor? What a trip! He moved closer. Though slender and willowy, Phillip measured no more than four or five inches taller than she, yet she'd already felt the strength in those thin, elegant hands. Killing hands. He advanced. She sidestepped. "What do you want from me?"

Phillip smiled to himself. She was a graceful creature, he admitted silently, as she moved like a queen across the carpeted floor in tattered rags and bedcovers. He would enjoy squelching her hopes. "Why, everything, my dear."

Tess darted, and he swiftly covered the distance, his hands catching her shoulders. He felt her tremble beneath his touch. It aroused him, the smell of fear. His gaze briefly skimmed her features, flawless but for the bruise. He bent close. She flinched, jerking her head back, small hands shoving at his chest. With surprising speed, he shackled her wrists at the base of her spine. She wrestled to be free, and he tightened his grip, pulling her up until she was forced to stand on her toes. His tongue slithered out to lick at her wound. She made a soft panicked sound.

"I apologize, mistress. My temper, you see."

A silver spark flamed in her eyes. The bastard thought *that* would take care of it? "Take your filthy paws off me," she ordered softly.

His smile was quick, not reaching his eyes. "Your life is mine now, Mistress Blackwell." He pulled her flush against him, dragging the coverlet away. "Your body is mine." She struggled as his hand moved roughly over her bared breasts, twisting her nipple, his body warming to her battle. "The sooner you understand this—"his smile widened a fraction—"the healthier."

Tess felt his arousal press against her. It was a target she couldn't ignore and brought her knee up hard to meet his groin. He barely flinched, mashing her tighter, his grip on her hands cutting off any circulation. Pain shot up her arms to her shoulders. His eyes watered, his lips curling in a snarl that instantly calmed to a pleased smile.

He's not used to anyone fighting back, she realized, but he enjoys it. Takes real brains to antagonize a killer, Renfrew, she railed at herself,

370

recognizing the huge mistake she'd just made. Her childhood on the streets had taught her well about creatures like Phillip. His type preyed on one's fears, enjoyed playing the dictator, the struggle of his helpless victims, their screams and cries arousing him. Well. He'd got her once, but it was the last time. Dane would come for her, *that* Tess was certain of, yet in the meantime, she had to find out all she could about this slime ball in order to help Dane when he arrived.

"Since you've mangled my only clothes," Tess said, her terror of him masked as deeply as she could bury it, "I suggest you provide me with more."

"Phillip! What are you doing?" Tess's gaze shifted over his shoulder to the woman entering the room. She was blond and beautiful, her gown a rich blue and heavily adorned with gold. Pear-shaped sapphires glistened around her neck, and Tess didn't mistake the venom those dark eyes directed at her.

"The lady desires fresh garments, Lizzie. Provide them." He didn't take his eyes off Tess.

"But, Phillip, she's far too thin," Lizzie said in a snide tone. "Naught of mine will fit the—"

He didn't look at Elizabeth. "Are you questioning me again, my pet?" His voice was pleasant, yet somehow threatening. Lizzie cringed and looked away. She's afraid of him, too, Tess thought. What a combination!

"Nay, of course not, Phillip." She and her haughtiness were gone, departing in a crisp rustle of fabric.

371

He released Tess, turning sharply and striding to the door. "Dress and come join me for breakfast."

"No, thanks. Lost my appetite."

He paused, twisting to look her. "Do not force me to come and retrieve you, Mistress Blackwell. I assure you it will be most unpleasant." He briefly bared his teeth, sharp and white, his eyes fathomless, offering nothing but a solid promise of pain and torture. "That is to say, unpleasant for you." He was gone, and Tess reached for the commode, trembling uncontrollably. She didn't know how long she could take this. Hurry, Dane, she prayed, gazing out the window into the darkness. Oh, please, hurry!

Dane sat in the chair, his body tense and tightly coiled as Gaelan shoved Whittingham into the room. His gaze shifted, skewering the fat man. "I want a detailed plan of Rothmere's house."

"Surely you are mad, sir!" Nigel bristled, straightening the cuff of his nightshirt. "He would kill me."

Dane stood abruptly, the chair scraping back. "*I* will kill you if you do not!"

Nigel staggered as the man lunged at him like an enraged panther, his muscles rippling as he lifted Nigel up to meet his face.

"You will draw a map," his tone was glacial, his eyes narrow, predatory. "And if I find a crevice or a corner out of place, be assured this world is not large enough for you to escape me. Is that clear?" Nigel nodded meekly, the thought of bargaining

with this man quickly tossed aside. Though his appearance spoke of a man living on the edge of his emotions, it was those eyes, burning with hatred, pale frost green, displaying a desperate need for revenge, that sent Nigel to quake in his slippers. He needs a kill, he thought. And 'twill not be me.

"You cannot get to him. 'Tis impenetrable unless he allows you entrance."

"Nothing is that safe." Dane released the man with a snarl of disgust.

" 'Tis so." Nigel straightened his clothing. "Over forty guards, a moat, the walls. 'Tis why he selected the location."

Dane shoved Nigel into a chair and pushed parchment and graphite in front of him. "Draw as if your life should depend on it." The look Dane dealt the man said that it did.

I at least will be prepared, Dane thought, raking a hand through his hair, then rubbing the back of his neck. It was tearing him apart to know Tess was in Phillip's hands. His stomach twisted, clenching in a tight knot. His worst nightmare. Phillip had the upper hand. And if I were not so driven with revenge, he railed silently, Tess would be safe. Sweet Christ! After finding the priest—he wasn't certain she was even alive. Nay! He immediately banished the agonizing thought. Phillip enjoyed the taunt, the torture Dane was suffering, knowing the twisted bastard had possession of his most cherished love.

I must get to her and soon. She is intelligent and resourceful, he reminded himself, trying to regain control of his emotions, and she is exceptionally strong for a woman. He'd no doubt she was already attempting to regain her freedom, taking advantage of what lay at her fingertips. But Phillip was mad, and madness brewed ungodly power. Dane had to get inside the white fortress and, it seemed now, he must be invited.

wrong for a woman. He'd no doubt she was already attorning to it in her own wicked ... to ... advance

Chapter Thirty

"Allow me the honor of introductions."

Phillip's voice jerked Tess's attention away from the veranda doors. The couple walked beneath the archway with an almost comical flourish. "Don't bother. You're Phil, I'm Tess, and she's Elizabeth Cabrea."

Lizzie's eyes widened, and she glanced quickly at Phillip.

Bennett's log had revealed the gruesome details about Desiree's murder, and Tess supposed the man had intended to blackmail Phillip, but now she needed to put that knowledge to good use. And Tess knew her target. The weakest link.

She moved slowly around the room, casually examining the knick-knacks. "What did you do, Lizzie, hold Desiree down for him?"

Elizabeth paled. "Nay!"

Tess spared her a glance. "You enticed her to come with you that day, didn't you, Lizzie?" she asked, fighting to keep anger from her voice. "Kinda like leading a lamb to slaughter, wasn't it?"

Elizabeth dropped into a chair. "Phillip, make her stop."

"Cease, Lizzie," he warned. "She knows naught."

"Suit yourself, Phil." Tess shrugged, observing his reaction, turning a Dalton piece over in her hands. He was frowning, and she knew it was because of her clipped speech. "You betrayed all women, Elizabeth. You delivered that innocent girl into his hands, and for what? Money? What was your cut?" Tess's gaze bounced off the deep blue stones draped around her neck. "Those sapphires? You got cheated, big time," Tess said disgustedly replacing the porcelain. Out of the corner of her eye she saw Lizzie's shoulders droop a bit more. "My husband will be pleased to know you're here, too." Tess lifted a silver creamer from a service, then put it down when she saw her reflection, the bruise on her cheek an ugly purple. No wonder it hurt so bad.

Servants paraded into the dining hall, each bearing a tray laden with food. Her stomach protested at the sight. Jeez, it was four in the damned morning!

"Blackwell cannot rescue you, my dear," Phillip said with a ring of smugness. "This dwelling is impenetrable."

"Yeah, right," she scoffed, running a finger over the polished sideboard. "For Dane?" Let them stew, she thought.

"Sit down, Mistress Blackwell," he commanded, taking his seat.

At the mention of her name, a slender dark-haired man clad in black paused in his serving, his

376

wary eyes darting to Tess, then Phillip. She caught it, Rothmere didn't, too busy with filling his plate. Was the butler an ally? The staff had refused to utter a word when she tried to question them earlier. Jeez. Were they prisoners, too? Tess wondered if she could trust one of them to get a message to Dane as she dropped into a chair, staring at the platters. I can't eat this stuff, she thought, uncertain if the food was poisoned, which was probably silly since Phillip and Elizabeth were digging in like there was no tomorrow. There wasn't, for them, she thought confidently, scooting eggs onto her plate.

Phillip wanted her husband, and she was nothing but a lure he had to keep alive until Dane arrived. God, what a morbid thought! But what if she could find something better, she pondered, glancing out the open doors. Guards shifted back and forth like Dobermans sniffing prey.

"I suggest you banish all thoughts of escape, Mistress Blackwell," Phillip said, and Tess glared at the skinny bastard.

"Never say die, Phil."

His brows drew together thoughtfully, unable to recognize her accent. "Might I ask where you hail from?"

"The twentieth century. How about you?" Score one for the good guys, she thought when Phillip choked on his tea.

He cleared his throat. "It will do you no good to fabricate tales, mistress." Then he shoved a large portion of sausage into his mouth.

"Tales, huh? I know this might come as a shock,

but I don't lie." He gave her a condescending look. "You've got it all figured out, don't you? Dane will storm this—this crumbling pile of rocks, and you'll have a chance, right?" Another annoyed look. "Guess again, chump. He didn't travel this far to do something so predictable. Regardless of his loyalty to me, he'll get *you*, Phil." Tess looked pointedly at Elizabeth. "You, too, Lizzie. Was it your suggestion that Phillip slit Desiree's wrists and allow her to bleed to death in that potting shack?"

Tess hit a nerve, at least in Elizabeth. The color drained from her features while Phillip absently toyed with a dinner knife, looking at her more strangely than usual.

"I suppose cutting out her tongue so she couldn't talk was your idea, eh, Phil?" Tess took a sip of juice.

"Oh, Lord, Phillip—!"

"Shut—up—Lizzie." She obediently paid close attention to her meal.

"Was that before or after you let those men have at her?"

He didn't respond to her latest dig, but simply wiped his lips and tossed the napkin aside, then leaned back in the chair. Without a command a servant was instantly at his side, removing his plate.

"I would restrain that flip tongue, mistress."

Tess shrugged. "Call me reckless. How long have you been stuck here, Phil? A year? Two? Don't you want it over? Or are you two planning to spend the rest of your lives hiding like cowards?"

"I am well-pleased with my home, my life. I see

no reason to change it."

"Come on, Phil, give me a break! Your warehouses are in ashes. Whittingham has probably been arrested by now, spilling his guts to save his own skin. And you can't tell me you didn't expect Dane to come after you!"

His eyes narrowed a fraction, and Tess sought to twist the knife a little.

"Nah." She relaxed in the chair. "You didn't think he'd find you at all. You led him here, you know, with Bennett, the attacks on the ships. Might as well have left a trail of bread crumbs."

She was far too clever for a female, Phillip thought, the reminder of his mistakes gouging at his composure.

"What's the connection between you two, anyway, besides that you killed his sister and stole his family's fortune?"

Phillip stood abruptly. " 'Twas my fortune! Mine!"

Now we're getting somewhere, she thought. "How so? It was in *his* home, in the possession of *his* father."

"Grayson Blackwell stole from my father! His partner! And the whoreson kept all when my father was killed!"

"Isn't that how it goes, though? Remaining holdings to the surviving partner?"

"Nay, it belonged to me!"

She shook her head. "I don't think so, guy. It should have gone to your mother, or did you just evolve from swamp slime?"

Another nerve, she thought when he reddened and clenched his fists. Tess went for the jugular. "What happened to your mommy, Phil?"

Elizabeth nearly fainted, slumping in the chair and fanning herself. "Mistress Blackwell," she whispered, daring a glance at Phillip. "I beg you not to pursue this subject."

Tess didn't give a crap what she wanted. "Weren't your parents married?" Tess was a bastard, and it didn't mean squat to her, in her time, but here—

Phillip was still, unbelievably rigid, then like the smoothing of fabric, he relaxed and settled into his chair, crossing his legs.

"Aye, they were wed." Tess marveled at the sudden change. "But Father left her for another woman." Beneath the table Phillip took Elizabeth's hand. "Since his marriage to my mother was arranged, he claimed to have never loved her, and the focus of his devotion turned to his—convenient," he said with disgust, "and their spawn." Tess heard an odd sound, a soft snap, and Elizabeth screamed once, sharp and loud. Tess looked from one to the other. Elizabeth was battling tears, and Phillip grew calmer by the second. "Mother perished from a broken heart and, well, his whore—" His smile was a slow one, filled with a sadistic satisfaction. "I daresay she met with a most unfortunate accident."

Elizabeth looked away, her quickening breath heard from across the table. Phillip just kept staring, empty, cold. It was better than a confession.

"The child?" Tess ventured softly.

"Well-tended, I assure you."

Elizabeth's once pale skin flamed red, and she fumbled under the table, tears spilling from bleak eyes. Phillip rested his elbows on the linen-covered surface as she twisted away and fled the room. He linked his ringed fingers, appearing neither to notice nor care about her departure as he addressed Tess.

"One would believe you would already be privy to this information, Mistress Blackwell. Or are there secrets in your new marriage?"

Tess ignored that. "I gather you know my husband as something other than simply the brother of your victim?"

"Aye." He sipped his tea, the jibe bouncing off his thick hide. "We were educated together. At Eton."

Tess regarded her lap. Eton? Eton? Then it dawned on her and she looked up, her features pulling taut.

"Ahh, I see you have heard of the school," he murmured. "The finest birching academy England has to offer a young pup."

"And the strictest." They beat students, Tess recalled, and inflicted horrible punishments for minor infractions. "How could your father send you there?"

"Grayson did, both of us." He leaned forward a bit, seeing no reason not to relay the tale since she wasn't leaving — at least not alive. "After my father's demise, Grayson provided me with an education and the barest essential but kept what was rightfully mine for his heir."

"Sounds to me like you were treated well. He could have done nothing." With a son like Dane, Tess decided, Grayson probably provided more than Phillip chose to recognize. "And you honestly don't know what went on between Grayson and your father?"

A muscle ticked beneath his eye. "I do. And need I remind you that I have sufficiently taken what Grayson prized most?"

"Desiree," Tess answered, looking away.

"Nay, his company," he said as if she should know better, and Tess shot him a contemptuous glare. He smiled thinly, coming to his feet. "The girl was merely a way to get closer to Grayson." He waved airily. "You must understand that the man had not known me since I was but a youth, with nary a notion of who I actually was," he said as he moved to the sideboard and lifted a small silver box, flipping the lid and dipping two thin fingers inside. " 'Twas remarkable, really. So easily duped." He brought the pinch to his nose and sniffed, depositing snuff into each nostril. "And Elizabeth—" he withdrew a handkerchief, watching her as he blotted at his nose, his wide lace cuff fluttering. "She was Dane's lover and had been in the Blackwell household a'fore." He shrugged elegantly clad shoulders. " 'Twas simple enough," he said, enjoying the slight loss of color in her face.

Dane and Elizabeth? Tess couldn't picture it. "Doesn't it bother you she slept with your enemy?"

"Nay. Of course not." He flicked a lace-ruffled wrist, strolling around to her side of the table. "I sent her to his bed."

"Gee. What a prince," she mumbled, scrambling to her feet and backing away.

"Phillip! How on earth could you tell her such a thing?" They glanced to the door, and Tess immediately noticed Elizabeth's hand wrapped in a scrap of silk that matched her blue gown, one finger bound to a twig.

"Leave us, Lizzie." He sauntered closer as Elizabeth started to do as she was told. Tess's words halted her.

"You whored for him." Her voice dripped with outrage as she stepped back. "How could you let him treat you like that?" She gestured to her wounded hand. "Like *that!* What the hell's he got on you?"

Elizabeth's round-eyed stare shifted from Tess to Phillip, who wasn't paying her any mind. "You could not possibly comprehend the matter," she said.

"Try me, sister," Tess snapped, her hands on her hips. "After today I've heard it all."

" 'Tis none of your affair." Elizabeth bowed her head, cradling her throbbing hand but not before Tess recognized the glazed look in her eyes. She's taken something, and Tess wondered what drugs were available in this time.

Phillip stared at Dane's woman. Her disgrace will be a sweet victory. And to have Dane witness it would be—sheer ecstasy. His body heated to the thought, ingraining the image in his mind. Aye, 'twould be fitting to steal *that* from Dane also. He stepped closer.

Tess retreated until she found herself up against a warm body. She jolted, nearly leaping into Phillip's arms, but caught herself and glanced over her shoulder. A smelly man with a hideous scar across his throat blocked her retreat. Then his hands closed heavily around her arms. Phillip advanced. Tess swallowed, her panic rising as she looked to Elizabeth. The blonde stood motionless, a peculiar smile curving her lips. She made no move to stop him.

Dane shifted for a more stable balance on the tree limb, then sighted down the spyglass, mentally comparing the white fortress with the sketch Whittingham had made. This was his third occasion to be perched like a bird as he searched for a sign. Tess would do *something* if she could. If she was alive. Insects buzzed around him, birds squawked, yet he allowed nothing to destroy his concentration.

No guards outside the wall. Bloody arrogant of you, Phillip. Torches blazed near the entrances and beside each window, illuminating the white structure like a pagan offering to the gods. His lips curved slightly, knowing the fires left anything beyond their glow in complete darkness. Another advantage.

With the scope to his eye, he scanned the towers, not doubting for a moment that Phillip would ensconce her in the most difficult to reach section of his private prison. His gaze swept the house again; then he paused, squinting harder, focusing through the glass on the farthest window. His smile was slow, his relief immeasurable. She was alive. Ahh, God bless you, my love! Then he had another look to be certain he wasn't imagining it. Dane almost laughed. 'Twas so like Tess to leave her panties dangling from the stone sill in sweet invitation.

Phillip saw the fear in those lovely eyes before she managed to cover it. "I have offered you much this morning, my dear. What will you provide in return?" He pressed against her, his cold fingertips drifting over the bosom her burgundy dress exposed.

Tess shivered with revulsion, turning her face away. "Like you said, Phil, you offered. I didn't push." Jeez, he had bad breath, too.

"But I know naught of you."

"Let's keep it that way, huh? Adds a little mystery."

He actually chuckled, the sound low and sinister, making her skin crawl. She couldn't draw a decent breath, sandwiched between them, and Tess thought she'd do something stupid like pass out. He was a cold-blooded killer, and she played a dangerous game.

"Back off, Rothmere," she warned, gathering the courage to look him in the eye.

"You haven't the choice, my dear." His cold, clammy fingers slipped inside the loose bodice, and Tess felt she'd vomit any second. Would serve him right, she decided, swallowing repeatedly. He bent his head, the grip on her arms tightening when she tried to twist away. I can't let him, she thought, afraid she wouldn't survive anything dealt by Phillip. Tess's hand slipped cautiously into her pocket, fingers wrapping around the lock picks. It was little defense, but all she had.

His long fingers roughly clenched her jaw, his foul-smelling lips hovering close. Tess sent her elbow into the guard's gut, then swiftly brought the pick upward, aiming for Phillip's eye, but only managing to stab at his cheek. The thin metal hooked in his skin and she yanked, raking it across his flesh. He howled, jerking back and covering his cheek. He glared between her and the pool of blood in his palm, then drew his arm back to strike. He swung and instantly Tess dropped to the floor. The guard took the intended blow, staggering back with an agonized scream as Phillip's rings sliced open his face from forehead to jaw.

Tess scrambled to her feet, but Phillip was quick, grabbing her by the arms and dragging her up to meet his face. Blood poured from his cheek in thick pulsing waves, running down his throat, staining his lace jabot and coat.

"I will enjoy every scream," he told her in a icy voice.

"You're just pissed off 'cause I outsmarted your ass."

His thin blond brow rose, sending a shiver of terror racing through her. "Are you claiming to be a worthy adversary, my dear?"

God save me, Tess thought, he was completely

composed, showing no sign of pain. Christ, he needed about twenty stitches!

"What? The lady has no witty retort?" He ran his hand down her arm to her wrist, gripping tightly. Tess fought with everything she had as he yanked her along, managing to keep him from leaving the room entirely. He called for aid, yet surprisingly none came.

"A man approaches, sir," a guard called from behind Tess. Phillips narrowed gaze moved toward the veranda doors. "The signal?"

"Sent, sir." The messenger's eyes drifted to Tess.

"And?" he demanded impatiently.

" 'Tis Lord Whittingham, sir."

Phillip frowned, glancing at Tess. "Bring him to me." He unexpectedly released her, and she banged into a chair. "We will continue this another time, be assured, my dear." He drew out a neatly pressed handkerchief, snapped it open, then held it to his cheek. It reddened instantly.

He walked away without a backward glance, heels tapping.

Tess slithered to the floor, breathless with receding fear. So, there was a signal, huh?

A pair of polished shoes appeared in her line of vision. She lifted her gaze to see the butler, his hand offered in assistance.

Chapter Thirty-one

White stucco bleached as old bones was visible in the darkness. Windows glowing with candlelight gave the aura of fire inside a skull picked clean. Lavish flower beds draped red around the house like a torn peasant skirt, a bleeding slope to the high wall, black iron spikes protruding from its wide flat surface, resembling scepters of Lucifer.

Thick chains grated in their metal guides, the scrape vibrating in the night. Wood creaked and hinges whined as the drawbridge was let down slowly, giving safe passage over shifting water. The rhythmic sound of waves crashing from beyond the residence could be heard over the command to enter.

On the ground a few feet away, Dane lay flat on his stomach, his body clad in black from head to toe, his face smeared with soot. He blended into the darkness like a stalking panther, only his pale green eyes glowing with a feral determination.

Nigel Whittingham tossed the torch into the moat. It hissed and sizzled as he walked slowly, his heavy trod thumping on the bridge. Dane crawled quickly across the damp earth, digging with his elbows to propel himself to the water's edge, the smoke from the extinguished torch shielding his body when he met open ground. He slid down the bank, his hands making purchase on the rough wood, legs dangling over the black water. Dane maneuvered only a foot or two, hands shifting side by side along the drawbridge almost in time with Whittingham's steps. Almost. The instant the Englishman's foot met the path to the house, the bridge jerked on its ride back up. Dane held on, muscles straining, but the rise was swift. Vertical over the water, he reached out to grab a spike just as the wood fitted into its stone frame. The old iron crumbled in his hand and he groped for security on another, swinging a leg out to catch anything that might keep him from falling into the moat. His booted toes dug into the ancient mortar, fragments tumbling into the water with soft plops as he quickly adjusted his grip, then gradually moved away from the torchlight, inch by painstaking inch. Patience, he told himself, nocturnal sounds muffling the scrapes of his boots.

When he determined he was well enough away from the entrance, he pulled himself up until his eyes cleared the edge. Whittingham passed beside a bubbling fountain in the center of the courtyard, then vanished from his line of vision, moving beyond, Dane knew, into the house. Close to his hiding place, three guards slowly paced, and he counted at least ten farther up on the slope, walking a measured path through the gardens. Dane watched. The pattern was the same, their manner bored and haphazard. The trio nearest to him smoked pipes, each taking a turn as lookout. Not toward the wall, he realized, but for movement from the house.

* * *

Phillip strode into the study, scarcely sparing the man a glance, pressing the cloth to his face. Whittingham rushed toward him but stopped short when he saw the bloody handkerchief.

"Dear God, man, what happened?"

Phillip dropped into a leather chair. "It gives me a bit of character, don't you think?" He turned his head so Nigel could admire the wound.

The Englishman turned green, his expression sour. "For the love of God, man, have someone sew you up. Damned wretched, that."

Phillip replaced the cloth. "The damages, Nigh?"

"Gone, all of it. Blown to hell."

Another payment, Blackwell, Phillip thought with a tired sigh.

"But that is not why I've come." Phillip looked up, waiting for the man to deliver his news. "Captain Blackwell wants in."

"Naturally."

"You will not allow him entrance?"

Phillip merely raised a brow.

"Bloody hell, man! He has my daughter!"

Not one muscle in Phillip's expression changed.

Whittingham clenched his teeth. "Then he said to give you this." He removed a pouch from beneath his waistcoat and tossed it to him. With a bored manner Phillip dropped the bloody cloth and opened the sack, dumping the contents into his palm. A diamond the size of his thumbnail glistened against his smooth white skin.

Nigel had never seen this side of the man as Phillip

held the gem up to the light, the diamond's facets catching the glow and splashing it on the walls in filtered blues, pinks, and lavenders. Phillip was entranced, nearly hypnotized by the stone, his eyes flaming with strange greedy pleasure.

"Well, the Blackwells are rather impatient to part with still more of their fortune." Phillip swallowed, his tongue feeling thick.

Nigel eyed him cautiously. The man made no move to staunch the flow of blood. "He said there is more."

Phillip smiled thinly. "I can only wonder how much his precious bride is worth."

Gaelan turned his back from the house, struck flint and checked his timepiece. Three more minutes, sir, and we're coming in, he thought, wishing the captain had allowed at least one other to join him. He turned back toward the structure, lifting the spyglass to his eye. Dane was like a predatory animal, hunting, hungry, as he slipped over the wall and moved behind unsuspecting guards, then disappeared into a clump of flowers. Gaelan held his breath when one of the guards turned his head in Dane's direction, peering curiously toward the flowers. The first mate lowered the glass, drawing his sleeve across his sweaty brow, then whispered to the man beside him. "Prepare to board, Mr. Finch."

Dane's powerful legs carried him swiftly to the side of the house. He paused in the dark, stepping back and glancing briefly around him before he removed the rope secured to his belt. The wind whipped at his shirt. He had only a moment to get to Tess before his men boarded. The guards began to move in his direction. Bloody hell! Why did they choose now to become devoted to duty? He made a swift wide circle over his head, the rope whining through the air, its sound blending with the wind. He snapped his wrist, and the iron grappling hook caught on the roof ledge. He jerked it once, then positioned his hands to climb. Thickly muscled arms lifted his body off the ground. One hand moved to overtake the rope when he heard the distinct click of pistol hammer, a second before he felt the cold barrel at the base of his skull.

"Make your choice, mister."

Dane silenced a curse, his shoulders tense as he slowly released the rope.

Beyond the wall, planks taken from the hull of Phillip's ship were positioned vertically on the bank. At the signal, the wood slots simultaneously lowered until their ends met the wall's edge to bridge the moat. Feet familiar with the roll of the sea covered the dangerous distance as if born to the task. Pistols and muskets were drawn and primed, a deadly assortment of swords and knives winking in the moonlight as Continental Marines assaulted the stone prison to fight for their captain and his lady.

"What do you want?"

The dark-haired man extended his hand farther.

"Merely to help you from the floor, madame. I assure you."

Tess sent him a nasty look. "I've heard that before, thank you very much." She climbed to her feet on her own power, not ready to trust anyone in this house.

"I am not your foe, Mistress Blackwell." His smile was gentle, wrinkling the corners of his young eyes.

She frowned. "Do I know you?"

He eyed her into silence, then glanced meaningfully beyond her. Tess twisted to see Elizabeth staring at her mangled hand, oblivious to her surroundings.

"Elizabeth," she called softly.

No response. She looks catatonic, Tess thought.

"Look, Jeeves, I want out. If you want to join me, fine, but—"

"He will not allow you to leave, Mistress Blackwell," Elizabeth muttered, her tone resolute.

"I don't give a cra—"

A sharp blast drowned out her words, gunfire ringing through the massive house. Tess whirled about. White smoke drifted from the study. Phillip appeared, shoving a pistol into the band of his breeches along with its mate, that horrifyingly calm smile playing across his lips. He walked down the corridor, his step uneven as he blotted at blood splatters on his clothing and face.

"You see," Elizabeth whispered into the sudden quiet. "No one leaves Phillip."

"Your husband is prepared to bargain for your life, mistress." He held the diamond up for her to see, then dropped it into his pocket.

Tess pushed the butler aside when he tried to shield her. No one else would die for her, she vowed, stumbling back as Phillip advanced on her.

"The gems, my dear."

Tess overturned a chair to block his path. "I-I don't know anything about—"

He shoved aside the furniture, moving forward. " 'Tis a shame you are such a terrible liar, madame." His hand darted out to grab her arm and haul her against his side. His skin was pasty white, and he licked his lips repeatedly. "I've no patience for lies this night, Mistress Blackwell." He raised the gun and, with the barrel, stroked his mutilated cheek, the blood congealed and thick. " 'Tis a small matter of a debt to be settled a'tween us."

Tess saw her death in those ice-blue eyes. Diamonds or no diamonds, he wanted her blood.

From all directions came gunshots, screams of pain and victory crowding the air. Phillip hissed, his lips twisting cruelly before he bellowed for his guards, dragging Tess along with him as he raced to the veranda doors. Nearly a hundred men advanced, dispatching his sentries like farmers chopping cane. Overturned torches ignited swiftly, burning dry palm grass.

Two guards suddenly burst through the pantry doors, dragging a lifeless man by his arms. Tess's heart clenched, immediately recognizing her husband.

"Found 'im climbin' to the roof, sir." They dumped their prisoner at Phillip's feet.

"Oh, God!" Tess cried, tearing away from Phillip and sliding to her knees beside Dane. She checked his pulse. Thank God!

Phillip chuckled, the sound hollow as an empty well, making her skin prickle as Tess struggled to roll

Dane over onto his back. His handsome face was marred with scrapes and his clothing was torn, but other than that, she couldn't find any injury that would render him unconscious.

Behind her Phillip snatched a crystal water pitcher from the sideboard and moved to stand over Dane. "Well, Captain Blackwell," he said silkily, emptying it in his face. "How convenient of you to join us."

Dane's hand instantly shot out, latching onto Phillip's ankle and jerking hard, tumbling the man to the floor as he came upright. Phillip grunted, the pitcher shattered, and his gun slipped from his grip, spinning across the polished floor. A guard lunged at Dane, and the captain twisted around on one knee, his silver blade whizzing through the air and sinking into the man's chest. The guard fell, dead before he hit the floor. Dane turned; Phillip was climbing to his feet. The second guard raised his pistol.

"Nooo!" Tess screamed; Dane was unarmed!

Dane shoved her back and dove for the man's legs. At the impact, the gun went off. A peal of agony burned around them before the guard's back hit the parqueted floor. Then a second shot fired. For a breathless moment the house was silent. White smoke hovered around the butler, a flintlock in his hand.

Tess scrambled across the floor to where Dane lay sprawled on the guard's legs. "If you're hurt, Blackwell, I swear, I'll kill you!" Her hands rubbed over his body, searching for the wound as he sat back on his haunches.

" 'Tis good to know such things, love," he offered, shaking his head to clear it.

"Captain!" the butler shouted. Too late. The air

abruptly left Tess's lungs when an arm clamped around her waist, yanking her off the floor and away from her husband. In one smooth motion, Dane leapt to his feet.

Phillip shoved the gun barrel tightly beneath Tess's chin. "Another move, old boy, and your bride will simply lose her head." A grin, despite the blood gushing from a wound in his thigh. He'd taken the stray ball.

Dane skewered the man with his pale eyes, his body coiled tight with reined fury. " 'Tis hopeless, Rothmere. This fortress is mine." To prove the point, Dane gestured to the entrances. Thorpe, Finch, and Cambert stood there, each flanked by more than a dozen armed Marines.

"Yet your wife is mine, Blackwell."

"I would kill her myself," he scoffed. "And I guarantee you will not survive to know of it." Pistol hammers clicked almost in unison. "We shall see this debt settled — regardless."

Phillip's bland expression faltered a bit: bloody cocksure bastard. "I owe you nothing!"

"But 'tis not so, Phillip." Elizabeth stared at a gilded box resting on the table. "I told you he would —"

"Do not interfere, Lizzie!" He blinked, trying to focus on Dane.

"But you always say that, Phillip. 'Do not question me, Lizzie.' 'You've angered me, Lizzie.' 'You shall suffer for that, Lizzie.' " Her fingertips caressed the edges of the box. " 'Tis really growing rather tiresome, you know."

Dane's scowl darkened at her senseless prattling, but he didn't take his eyes off Phillip as the man slowly dragged the barrel down Tess's exposed throat.

"What will you pay for this pretty face, Blackwell? More diamonds?"

Powerless to help his wife, Dane smashed down the violence churning inside him and dipped his fingers into his pocket, then tossed a packet on the table; diamonds slipped out, scattering across the polished surface.

"You are your father's son, Phillip. Will you gamble everything for the speed of a ball?"

"Oh, look, Phillip, diamonds!"

Phillip's eyes widened a fraction, and his head turned slightly toward the sparkling gems.

Tess felt rather than saw her chance and brought her fist down on his wounded leg, twisting away. Phillip howled even as he reached again for his captive.

Dane lunged at him like a savage animal, knocking the gun from his hand, his powerful square fists singing into the man's thin body. Bone cracked beneath each solid punch. Skin split, blood splattering the walls. Dane never gave him a chance, his fist connecting beneath the man's chin. The crushing blow shifted Phillip's jaw and lifted him off the floor, sending him back against the wall. Even as his legs buckled, he scrambled wildly for his gun. Boiling with unsuppressed fury, Dane grabbed him by the throat, strong fingers squeezing. Frantically Phillip clawed at his hands, his skin turning purple, blue eyes bulging in their sockets.

"Dane! No!" Tess screamed. He didn't cease. Gurgles spilled from Phillip's lips, then foaming blood. Tess latched on to Dane's arm, yanking. "Don't do it! Please!" Dane immediately released his hold, his powerful arms wrapping around his wife as Phillip slumped to the floor, coughing red mist.

"*Naayy!* Kill him!" Elizabeth shrieked, wide panicked eyes shifting from Dane to Phillip. "Kill him now!"

Phillip wheezed and choked.

When no one made to oblige her, Elizabeth quickly scooped up the fallen pistol and leveled it at Phillip. "Your bastard seed shall never know such madness!"

She fired.

Dane turned Tess's face into the bend of his shoulder as blood fountained from Phillip's throat. She clung to her husband. "Oh, God. Take me away from here. Please," she whispered into his shirt, and he immediately lifted her in his arms, quickly stepping over dead men as he carried her toward the corridor.

Elizabeth sank to her knees on the floor. "See what happens when you anger me, Phillip."

Dane halted at that, twisting to see her tenderly stroking Phillip's hand. "Dear Lord, he's made her as crazy as he," Tess sympathized, and Dane started to turn away when Elizabeth called his name, not taking her eyes from the pale lifeless hand.

" 'Tis yours." She waved toward the gilded box resting on the table.

Dane's eyes shifted from the box to his wife. Slowly, he set Tess to her feet. He didn't have to say it; Tess knew his family's fortune lay in that small chest.

"I'll wait here," she told him.

"The fire, sir," Gaelan said urgently. " 'Tis spreading!" Smoke circled their legs as the first mate gestured with his pistol for the crewmen to vacate quickly. "I shall retrieve it, Capt'n," he assured with a quirky smile when Dane went for the chest.

Dane nodded once, then ushered Tess to where the butler stood in the hallway, motioning to them. He pressed a hand to a wood panel and it sprang open. "To the ship, sir." With a bow he gestured toward the stone tunnel.

Tess eyed Dane, inclining her head to the butler.

"You know Jeeves here?"

Dane smiled at her saucy look. "He is Ramsey's boatswain, love. Jamie Wilcox. Though I was unaware, Ram had stationed men inside."

Tess playfully socked Jamie in the chest. "You coulda told me."

Jamie rubbed the tender spot. "A fine thanks," he mumbled, then grinned, following them into the damp narrow passage.

Chapter Thirty-two

"I can walk, you know."

Dane ignored her, his legs carrying them swiftly toward the cabin, his crew grinning at their captain's haste. He hadn't said a word since they'd left the island and had refused to allow her from his side even as the long boat took them to the *Sea Witch*. His expression was tight with a frown, and Tess could see a muscle clenching in his jaw.

He strode into the cabin and kicked the door shut behind him, releasing her legs and letting her slide down the length of him. The thought of that whoreson's hands on his wife made him crazy, and the coolly stored anger and fear for her life released itself. His mouth was suddenly on hers, savage and hot, before her feet touched ground. Her arms wound around his neck, and she clung to him, answering the power, reveling in the swift burn that raced through her body. His thigh pushed between hers, his hands, warm and large, rubbed the length of her, molding her breasts, stroking her slender waist, sliding down to cup her buttocks and drag her across the surface of his leg. She whimpered against his lips, the intensity of his touch leaving her trembling and breathless. She'd never seen him like this. So impatient, so desperate! She pulled her mouth away, but he didn't cease, devouring the skin at her throat, then moving lower.

"Dane." Her breath came in urgent gasps. The gown peeled away from her shoulders.

"Do not deny me, Tess." His voice was rough. "I beg you." He lifted her so he had perfect access to her breasts. "Ahh, God, I *need* to banish his touch from your memory."

Tess melted, wrapping her legs around his waist as he carried her backward to the bed, tumbling her to the feather mattress. His ravenous mouth never left hers as he tore at the constricting garments. He immediately covered her with his long body, entering her swiftly, deeply, cupping her buttocks to bring her closer to his heat. He moved, loving her wildly, hungry with tender greed. Together they clung, reaching the summit with a hoarse cry, descending slowly, the aftershocks still rippling through them as she whispered, "I love you, pirate," in a watery voice.

His arms tightened about her as if to bring her into himself. He squeezed his eyes shut, placing a kiss to her damp shoulder, not wanting her to see the fear he could no longer hide.

Dane settled back against the bowsprit, pulling his wife firmly against the length of him.

"I should blister your lovely bottom for sneaking

out," he said, even as he rubbed the mentioned posterior.

"Dane! The crew."

He grinned wickedly, the wind tossing black curls. "They've orders to venture no farther than midship."

"In that case—" She wiggled between his thighs, nibbling the bronze skin at his throat.

He groaned as her hands molded over his chest, small fingers slipping beneath the fabric of his shirt. "Are you trying to gain my forgiveness?"

Her smile was impish. "Is it working?"

"Ahh, love. Aye."

"Duncan asked me to deliver this."

Tess and Dane pulled slowly apart at the sound of Ramsey's voice. He held out a folded paper, its edges brown with age. She glanced at Ram, her eyes questioning its existence as she accepted it.

"He said it fell out of the diamond pouch when he was tidying the cabin."

Ramsey's lips twitched, and Tess flushed, remembering the sensual debris of clothing she and Dane left scattered around the spacious cabin. She wore breeches and Dane's shirt now, and Ramsey's roving eyes told her he liked what he saw. But his easy manner didn't last long, fading quickly to an inner turmoil that she could see beyond his weak smile. The *Witch* was attempting to catch up with the *Triton,* and Tess wished they'd hurry. Maybe he would be his old self when he was on his ship again? Ramsey was acting strange, quiet and almost sulking. No teasing, no carefree chitchat. It was like he'd lost his favorite toy. Or woman. Tess grinned to herself: likely the latter.

She focused her attention on the envelope. How come I never noticed this before? she wondered, turning it over in her hands. Breaking the wax seal that had obviously been replaced several times, she unfolded the crackling paper, reading quickly.

Mistress Tess Blackwell,
'Tis my wish that you understand the past, mayhaps to know the future and prevent the death I have witnessed.

It was from Elizabeth! Tess looked up, squinting. The island was a speck on the horizon, the smoke merely a tiny gray flag against clear skies. Tess hoped she'd escaped, then quickly amended the thought. She had to have; the Rothmere clan lived in the twentieth century, and she recalled the mention of Phillip's bastard. Tess continued reading.

Shall I begin with Phillip's mother, Wilhelmina? A rather common woman, really, who believed power came with money and gems. Devlin provided well for them both, yet she desired more. Like Phillip, 'twas never enough. She was wrong, you know. Phillip had wealth, other than what he'd stolen from Grayson, yet never had power, merely greedy servants. I am not so addlepated to let it drive me to take my own life as Wilhelmina had. *I* will make the name Rothmere mean something again. Oh, dear, I really am getting ahead of myself, aren't I? Devlin and my mama were

403

lovers. I am the product of that union.

I am a Rothmere.

Tess blinked. Elizabeth? His half sister? Oh, Jesus! The baby! She glanced over the remaining words: details of his sexual abuse of her, the torture, allowing men to—she couldn't read any more.

"Tess?"

Dane's puzzled gaze shifted from the letter to her.

Tess took a deep cleansing breath before she said, "It's from Elizabeth. When she wrote it, I don't know. She tells everything, about the diamonds, what Phillip did, everything." She held it out for him, but he didn't even read it, folding the letter and tucking it in her pocket.

" 'Tis over, my sweet. History."

She smiled widely. "Well, we know how that can change."

"Aye, thank God." He placed a soft kiss to her lips. "I love you, Tess."

"Me you too," she sighed against his mouth. "Wanna go back to the cabin?"

"Bloody newlyweds," Ramsey snorted, his forearms braced on the port rail. He glanced to the side to glare at the pair, then straightened abruptly, his attention riveted somewhere beyond them. "Sweet Mother of God! What the ruddy hell is that?" he demanded.

Tess twisted around. "Jesus H—no!"

"Capt'n, 'tis the bloody wall again!" a crewman bellowed, fear sharp in his voice.

The black wall shifted, undulating, tentacles of mist following them across the sea.

Dane grabbed Tess about the waist, mashing her to his side. "Prepare to come about!" he shouted. Crewmen scurried, frantic to adjust sail and spar.

Ramsey's gaze slid to Tess. Her fingertips were turning white from their grip on Dane's arm, her eyes wide, stark with horror. He'd never seen her so terrified. And Dane, Ramsey thought, the man was bloody desperate, shouting orders, yet refusing to release his wife.

"Why do you fear this apparition, lass?" Ram asked, climbing onto the bowsprit for a better view. He frowned back over his shoulder, unaffected by the wild commotion on the *Witch*. "You know what this be?"

She looked uncertainly up at her husband. "Tell him, love," Dane urged, his ears tuned to the creak of the rigging as it shifted to bring the frigate away from the wall.

"It's a doorway, Ramsey. To the future." His brows rose a fraction. "I don't know exactly to where—but that," she glared at the curtain, "is a rip in time."

Ramsey's gaze snapped between the wall, Tess, and Dane, an eagerness lighting his features even as he considered she must be jesting. The future? Then Dane briefly met his skeptical gaze and nodded curtly, and in those pale green eyes, Ramsey glimpsed the man's tortured fears.

" 'Tis coming for us, Capt'n!" a seaman screamed.

"Port hard to lee!" Dane shouted. "Now!" He yanked Tess from the path of scrambling sailors and swinging gaff sail.

" 'Tis followin'!" the boatswain bleated.

Tess moaned, feeling the pull, the nausea, the heaviness of her limbs. "Oh, jeez! Dane! It wants me back! I can't—please! Not now!" She clung to her husband, fighting the violent tug that seemed to come from the marrow of her bones. No, she prayed, I'm happy now. "Don't let it take me, Dane, please." Tears wet her cheeks.

"Never, love." Dane crushed her to him, twining rope around his free arm and praying it would keep them together. "If you depart, I shall be with you."

Ramsey stared at the black curtain that reached up to infinity. The future? His head jerked around, and he studied Tess hard, trying to read beyond that horrified expression. He knew the moment he met her she was different, so spirited and intelligent, damned resourceful. Even compared to a man. His brain pounded with all he could remember since. Her speech, her manners, her views, her ability to decipher code, plan strategy: the list was endless. He returned his gaze to the wall. Was it possible? To step into another time?

He looked back again at Tess, the sharp motion making his head feel light, drugged. Then an odd sensation gripped him, a sudden piercing of flesh, sinew, and muscle, sand-rough fingers clamping like a vice onto his bones, tugging.

'Tis an invitation, Ram thought, hugging the ropes. Nay, a demand.

"Your journey was long to find your heart mate, Tess," Ramsey said, his face bloodless with the clawing nausea. "Mayhaps I must take the same to discover if such exists for me."

406

Tess's eyes widened as he gave them a jaunty salute. "Ramsey! Noooo!" she screamed as he dove into the water.

The instant Ramsey surfaced, his powerful arms knifed through the ocean toward the ebony curtain.

"Raamseeey!" Her cry ended in a dry shriek, her throat gone raw.

Ram ignored her.

"Damn you, O'Keefe! Come back!" Dane shouted over the railing.

"Do something! We have to stop him!" she pleaded to Dane, her fingers twisted in the fabric of his shirt. "He won't survive!"

Dane ordered a line tossed to him and a long boat lowered.

The sea suddenly became wild, waves cresting high, smashing against the hull, pitching the frigate like a cork buoy bobbing against the swells.

Ramsey swam.

Frightened, her body still feeling the wrenching energy, Tess stumbled away from the rail, pulling Dane with her. "Dane, please!"

He grasped her shoulders, forcing her to see beyond her panic. "He's too far, Tess. And look at him, he *wants* to go." She did look.

Near the curtain, Ramsey turned and raised an arm to wave, his smile broad, excited. Suddenly the tendrils of mist wrapped around his chest, lifting him out of the water and pulling him into the blackness. Then he and the wall vanished, and once again the sea calmed, the waters a pure aqua blue.

Ramsey O'Keefe was gone.

In the stunned silence of the crew, she turned into

Dane's embrace and cried, "Oh God, he doesn't realize—he won't survive."

"You did." He gently rubbed her back, his gaze riveted to where he'd last seen his closest friend. Blood of God, if he had not laid witness to it, he would never have imagined such a sight!

She sniffled, raising her head. "But I went *back* in time! It's possible he went forward!" No one would ever know where he'd end up exactly.

"Do not underestimate Ramsey, my love," he said calmly. "He's resourceful. And mayhaps—?"

"He'll find love? His heart mate?" It peeved her Dane wasn't more upset.

He brushed a wisp of hair from her cheek, tucking it behind her ear. "I've come to believe anything in our universe is possible."

She smiled weakly; her presence was proof of that.

Shudders trembled through her as she laid her cheek against his chest, studying the calm, blue ocean. Yeah, he'd wanted to go, no doubt about that. Tess couldn't fault him; he was the adventurous sort, anyway. Oh, Ramsey, she thought with a secret smile, are you in for one hell of a surprise!

Dane tightened his embrace, then gave a nod of deep respect to the sea. Tess was his—forever. The chance that she'd be taken from him was gone, thanks to the *Triton*'s master.

Epilogue

A Few Months Later

Grayson Blackwell smiled at the woman sleeping in his son's arms as the carriage rolled down the long drive to Coral Keys.

"I still cannot believe she convinced me to free all the slaves."

Dane's head turned from the view out the carriage window, and he smiled at his father. "They stayed on, did they not?"

"But the cost—"

"We can well afford to pay them, and 'tis only reaso—"

Grayson put up a hand. "Spare me, son," he said with a grin. "She has won already."

"She does have a way of getting what she wants." Dane plucked a drooping curl from her cheek. "In truth, Father, I never dreamed I could be this happy," he admitted, placing a kiss on the top of her head.

"Nor I." The lass filled the emptiness in his heart,

Grayson thought, where it had been so brutally gouged. "Have I told you how much I admire your choice of a bride, Dane?"

"Thanks, Papa," Tess said, sitting upright.

Dane grinned. "You little sneak."

"Playing possum has its merits."

Grayson threw back his head and laughed, and Dane's smile widened. Everyone felt Tess's zest for living, and it showed even in his father. Gone was the stooped, disheartened gentleman; in his place was the strapping man Dane had known as a youth. Tess had done that. She'd taught him not to feel guilt over Desiree's death and bullied him into taking charge of a life lost because of Phillip.

"Ahh, home at last," Tess said, bounding out of the carriage the second it stopped.

Grayson glanced at his son and shook his head. " 'Tis a wonder you are not drained of all energy attempting to keep up with that woman," he said, alighting from the carriage.

Dane followed, smiling wickedly. 'Twas energy well spent.

Feminine laughter tumbled into the foyer as Tess swept the velvet cape from her shoulders and tossed it to the waiting servant. Dane leaned against the doorframe, watching as she whirled around the room with an imaginary partner.

"Oh, Dane. This has got to be the most exciting week of my life. Imagine, the honor of dancing and dining with the President!"

" 'Twas he that should feel honored, my love. I fear George will never be as he was after meeting you."

She faced him. "I can't believe you call him George!"

"Bah!" Grayson snorted. "He is simply a man, my dear."

Tess grinned, coming over to them. She knew exactly what Dane would look like in thirty years; he was the image of his father, though a bit taller and less gray. She never had the heart to tell Dane that the Rothmeres would someday own this house; the pain was too new. But she was working on a plan, one that would take two hundred years to put it back in the hands of a Blackwell.

"Just because you don't agree with some of his policies, Papa, doesn't mean they don't have potential."

Dane covered a chuckle.

"What were the two of you discussing so intensely that evening?" Grayson wanted to know.

"Land battle strategy."

Grayson's eyes widened. "Surely he did not listen—!"

"And why wouldn't he?" Her hands were on her hips, lips pressed tightly, and Dane knew that stance too well.

"I think I shall graciously retire now," Grayson said, chagrined, backing toward the stairs.

"A wise choice, Father."

Tess's features softened, and she caught Grayson's arm, walking up the staircase with him. She glanced back over her shoulder to Dane, and he nodded, his lips twitching.

"I don't need tucking in bed, young lady," he gruffed.

"Humor me. I don't have a father, except you." His lips curved. "And I want to make sure you're comfortable and happy."

"Then you'd do well to see that room filled." He gestured to the nursery.

"It will certainly be my pleasure to try."

He chuckled. Saucy wench, he thought, kissing her cheek, then disappearing into his bedchamber. "Only one brandy tonight, Grayson," he heard as he shut the door.

Dane dropped into a stuffed chair, prying off his shoes and wiggling his toes. He was deliriously happy and feeling more fit than ever, the latter attributed to his wife's insistence that he dine on foods not swimming in cholesterol or cooked to death, as she chose to put it. Her two hundred years of knowledge certainly was an advantage.

He sipped his brandy, watching the amber liquid swirl and coat the glass. She had conceded to more than anyone could imagine to be his wife. And Dane's heart swelled with love every time he thought of her sacrifice, thanking God every day she'd sailed into his century.

"Hey, pirate."

He looked up, his eyes widening as she sauntered across the room, slipping her arms out of her gown. He swallowed, his gaze absorbing her graceful moves as she revealed her slim, muscled body to his hungry eyes. His manhood reacted with amazing swiftness.

"The door?" he managed.

"Locked."

"And Father?"

"Asleep."

She paused before him, and Dane could do no more than stare as she shoved the midnight blue gown and petticoats down over her hips, then stepped out, kicking them aside. She loosened her hair, shaking out the inky mass before hooking her thumbs beneath the tiny ribbons at her hips and slowly tugging the panties down. She flung the silk scrap onto the pile, then took the drink from him, setting it aside as she climbed onto his lap. Suspended from a thin gold chain around her throat was a single marquis diamond. It was all she wore.

"Your father wants grandchildren. Think we can accommodate him?"

"Here?" His hands moved up the curve of her bare buttocks. "In the parlor?"

"Yup." Her breasts swayed as she freed the buttons to his breeches with agonizing slowness. "Too many people to wake up upstairs, you know." Her mouth hovered close to his. "The bed creaks, and with you and that great hip action—"

"God's teeth, Tess," he breathed, "you never cease to shock me."

"Yeah, pirate, and you love it."

He crushed her to him, staring deep into eyes soft as smoke. "Ohh, aye, my witch, that I do." He claimed her mouth as she claimed his body. The voyage of the *Sea Witch* was over, harbored tenderly in his loving arms. She was home—just in time.

About the Author

"Romance is everywhere. I'm surrounded by real-life heros and heroines with incredible tales of adventure, separation, and enduring love," says Amy J. Fetzer, in regards to her globe-trotting life with her Marine husband. "How could I not write about it?"

At the sale of *My Timeswept Heart,* a 1992 Golden Heart finalist, Amy J. Fetzer lived in Okinawa, Japan, with her husband, Robert, and their sons, Nickolas and Zackary. She encourages readers to write to her, through Zebra Books of course, because she never knows where she'll be living next.